CUR
8/11

Edgar

D0430344

"I love THE KILLING SONG, in which the best sister act in crime fiction, known as P. J. Parrish, has crafted one of the best criminals ever. Their serial killer is as brilliant as he is ruthless, but he makes a critical mistake when he murders the baby sister of reporter Matt Owens. Heartbroken and driven, Matt tracks the villain from Miami's South Beach to the catacombs of Paris, in a story so riveting you won't be able to stop turning the pages."

—Lisa Scottoline, *New York Times* bestselling author of *Save Me*

THE LITTLE DEATH

"Louis Kincaid is the detective I would want on the case if it was someone I knew on the slab. *The Little Death* is P. J. Parrish's best work yet!"

—Michael Connelly

"Sex, murder, and money, all set in the insanity that is Palm Beach society."

—Brad Meltzer

"Louis Kincaid and P. J. Parrish get better with every book."

—*Orlando Sentinel* (FL)

The Killing Song is also available as an eBook

Also by P. J. Parrish

*The Little Death**
*South of Hell**
*A Thousand Bones**
An Unquiet Grave
A Killing Rain
Island of Bones
Thicker Than Water
Paint It Black
Dead of Winter
Dark of the Moon

*Available from POCKET BOOKS

P. J. PARRISH

THE KILLING SONG

Pocket Books

New York   London   Toronto   Sydney

Pocket Books
A Division of Simon & Schuster, Inc.
1230 Avenue of the Americas
New York, NY 10020

This book is a work of fiction. Names, characters, places, and incidents either are products of the author's imagination or are used fictitiously. Any resemblance to actual events or locales or persons, living or dead, is entirely coincidental.

First Pocket Books paperback edition August 2011

POCKET and colophon are registered trademarks of Simon & Schuster, Inc.

For information about special discounts for bulk purchases, please contact Simon & Schuster Special Sales at 1-866-506-1949 or business@simonandschuster.com.

The Simon & Schuster Speakers Bureau can bring authors to your live event. For more information or to book an event, contact the Simon & Schuster Speakers Bureau at 1-866-248-3049 or visit our website at www.simonspeakers.com.

Cover photo by Paolo Gadler/stock.xchng

Manufactured in the United States of America

10   9   8   7   6   5   4   3   2   1

ISBN 978-1-4391-8936-8
ISBN 978-1-4391-8938-2 (ebook)

ACKNOWLEDGMENTS

Dear readers,

Most of you know by now that there are two of us. But we doubt you know how many stand behind us and beside us to make our books possible. Here are just a few:

Love to Daniel, who several years ago, in the Paris café Le Rostand, serenaded me with the lyrics to the Stones' song "Too Much Blood," drawing appalled looks from the matron sitting next to us but inspiring this story nonetheless.

Love to our agent Maria Carvainis for talking us off the ledges.

Special thanks to rock music aficionados Jim Fusilli and Cameron Cohick for plumbing the dark corners of their souls for morbid lyrics (I owe you a Burberry scarf, Roon); to Phillip and Davis Ward for the ephemera about Duke U and the modern newsroom; to Barbara Hijek, news researcher of the *South Florida Sun-Sentinel*; to Andy the computer geek; to Dr. Doug Lyle for his medical and forensic advice. And finally, to our French friend Cecile Gauert, who patiently corrected our French. *Nous vous disons un grand merci.*

To all our supporters at Pocket Books, a huge thanks. Many writers complain of copy editors bleeding all over their pages, but this book was improved greatly by Aja Pollack, who caught many errors and kept our tangled time line straight. Special mention must go, finally, to our talented editor Abby Zidle, who let us get our way but let us get away with nothing.

And lastly, we must thank our sister-in-law and cellist Ginger Gordon for answering our questions. To all the other cellists who helped us: We will honor your request to remain anonymous because, as one of you plaintively told us, "Cellists really are the nicest people in the orchestra."

He couldn't take his eyes off her.

The last rays of the setting sun slanted through the stained glass window over her head, bathing her in a rainbow. He knew it was a just a trick of light, that the ancient glassmakers added copper oxide to make the green, cobalt to make the blue, and real gold to make the red. He knew all of this. But still, she was beautiful.

His mother was there in his memories suddenly. He was watching her sitting before her mirror, remembering the way the lamplight turned her white skin gold. And he could remember what she said as she painted her lips. *Every woman, for just one moment in her life, should be able to be the most beautiful woman in the room.*

He stared at the girl. The sun had set and the glow had faded. Her moment was gone.

He looked away, focusing on the music before him. Vivaldi, *The Four Seasons.* He didn't need to read it. He knew every note by heart. He had played it a thousand times, so much that any pleasure he had ever taken in it had long ago died. As he played, he watched the faces of the audience. Tourists, mostly, and easily amused.

A pause in the music. They had finally come to the last movement, "Winter." Fifteen more minutes and he was free.

His eyes flicked to the violinist, then, on cue, he drew his bow across the strings in short little bursts, the notes sounding like the cold chattering of teeth. There was little for him to do now, just keep a steady background beat, so he let his mind wander, let his eyes wander.

Back to the girl. She was in the front row and though it was dim now, he could still see her clearly. She was staring right at him, her mouth moving rhythmically, as if she were trying to sing along. It took him a few seconds to realize that she was chewing gum. A surge of disgust moved through him. Why did all the American girls chew gum? Didn't they know it made them look like cows?

He looked away. He hated it when people weren't polite.

"So where are you taking me?"

He looked down at the girl. She laced her arm through his and snuggled closer. Her nose was red. The musicians had been warmed by the small space heaters at their feet, but there had been no such comforts for the audience in Sainte-Chapelle. And now they were scattering into the cold night, bound for their four-star hotels or the nearest bistros.

"Are you hungry?" he asked.

She shrugged. "I grabbed a sandwich before the concert. I'm not used to eating as late as people do here."

"Then a drink?"

She smiled. "Never too late for that."

He disentangled himself from her grasp and hoisted up his case. They started walking toward the bridge. As they crossed over to the Left Bank, a tour boat approached, its garish flood-lights trained on the Seine's stone embankments, seeking out lovers in the shadows for the tourists' titillation. But it was too cold for anyone to be out tonight. The lights found only rats scurrying into their holes.

In a café on boulevard Saint-Michel, he steered her to a corner table. He carefully positioned the large black case out of the aisle. She pulled off her gloves and glanced around. "I guess they don't have real booze here," she said.

"Excuse me?"

She sighed. "It's just that I've been here for two weeks and I am dying for a decent martini."

"You should have said something. We could have gone to Le Fumoir."

She shrugged. "That's okay. It's just that I don't really like wine all that much, you know? And it's so cold and I can't seem to get warm. No one told me Paris was going to be freezing."

"It's January," he said.

"Yeah, well, maybe I should have waited. April in Paris and all that stuff, right?"

He smiled, then caught the waiter's eye. When the man came over, he ordered for both of them. When the waiter returned with the drinks, the girl stared down at hers.

"What's this?"

"*Vin chaud.* Hot wine. Try it."

She set aside the cinnamon stick and took a sip. She smiled. "Good."

"They add spices to it. I'm glad you like it."

For the next half hour, he just listened. She loved to talk— about her job as a computer-something; about her six-toed cat, Toby; about her boyfriend who had emptied their bank account and run off, which is why she had decided on impulse to come to Paris; about her dream to be a tennis pro at the Houston country club where her parents kept her on their membership so she'd meet a quality man and get her life in order.

"They never forgave me for divorcing Dean and not popping out four blond babies," she said. This came after the third *vin chaud*.

He suspected she wanted him to ask her more about Dean, but he was tired of listening to her. He was even getting tired of looking at her, realizing now that whatever he had seen in her face before was gone. When he had spotted her this afternoon in the Tuileries, he had been immediately attracted to her. He had impulsively introduced himself and then invited her to be his guest at the concert.

But now, as he looked at her in the harsh light of the café, he realized she wasn't beautiful at all. True, she was blond and blue-eyed, but whenever she opened her mouth she became plain. He looked away, out the window at the people hurrying through the cold.

"So, how old are you?"

Her voice drew him back. "Does it matter?" he asked.

"I guess not." She finished the *vin chaud* and picked up the cinnamon stick. "I kind of like older guys. Especially when they look like you. Dean was blond. But I always had a thing for the tall, dark and handsome ones." Her eyes lingered on his, then drifted toward the black case propped in the corner.

"You've got quite a big instrument there," she said with a smile.

He didn't answer.

"Is it heavy?"

"You get used to it," he said.

She was sucking on the cinnamon stick. For a long time she just stared at him, then she said, "Take me home."

He felt relieved. "Where are you staying?"

"No, I mean to your place."

When he hesitated, she countered with a smile. "I mean, why the hell not? It's my last night in Paris, right?" she said.

He knew that if he waited too long to answer, she would be insulted. A part of him didn't care. A part of him wanted to put her in a taxi and be rid of her. But the other part, that part of him that slept just below his consciousness, was coming alive. He could feel it, a dull humming sound in his brain that soon would echo in a vibration in his groin. He could repress it. He had before.

He stared at the girl. *But why?*

He would not take her to his apartment on Île Saint-Louis, even though it was just across the bridge. He would take her to the other place. It was, after all, what she deserved.

She was talkative on the long ride. But as the car descended the steep hill behind Sacré-Coeur and slid into the darkness, she grew silent.

He saw her staring at the empty streets and crumbling buildings awaiting demolition, at the slashes of graffiti on the metal shutters of the Senegalese restaurant. And at the Arab men in skullcaps who sat hunched in white plastic chairs, their dark faces lit by the green fluorescent lights of the cafeteria. They were in a neighborhood called La Goutte d'Or, far from the cafés of the Left Bank, far from any notion of what the tourists believed the city to be. Goutte d'Or. *Drop of gold.* Centuries ago, the name referred to the wine grown in the local vineyards. Now it was slang for the yellow heroin sold in bars and the back rooms of luggage stores.

He parked the car. The girl didn't move, so he got out and opened her door. She was staring at the battered steel door with the number forty-four above it.

"You live here?" she asked.

"It's cheap," he said.

He retrieved his black case from the backseat and held out his free hand. She hesitated, then slipped her hand in his.

He hit the switch just inside the entrance door, illuminating a sagging staircase and peeling walls. He motioned and she started up ahead of him. At the fifth floor, he set the case down to get his key. The lights went out and she gasped.

For a long moment, he didn't move. He could hear her breathing hard next to him. In the close darkness, he could smell her, smell everything about her, the slightly sour wine on her breath, the vanilla shampoo she had used that morning, and the musky smell of her sweating body beneath the damp wool of her coat.

"Don't worry," he said. "It's just the hall light. It's on a timer."

He unlocked the door and led her inside. He set the case aside and watched her face as she took in the details of the room. A sagging futon, a metal bookcase holding a CD player and discs, an archway leading to a kitchen and an open door revealing the edge of a toilet.

"What's that smell?" she asked.

"What smell?"

"Like . . . somebody's been cooking meat or something."

"Oh, there's a butcher shop downstairs," he said, unwinding his scarf and taking off his coat. "Would you like a drink?"

"Yes . . . no. I mean, no, if it's wine. And no water either. The water tastes weird here. You got any grass?"

"No, I'm afraid not." On his way to the kitchen, he closed the door to the bathroom. He uncorked a bottle and poured himself a glass of Bordeaux. He took a drink and pulled off his tie, watching her as she walked slowly around the room. She leaned in to peer at the titles of the CDs, then moved toward an alcove behind the shelf.

"Hey, you have two of them," she said as she reached into the alcove.

He was next to her in two quick strides, grabbing her arm. "Don't touch it!"

She gave a small cry and wrenched her hand free. "Why not?"

"The grease from your hands," he said. "It's bad for the strings."

She took a few steps away, rubbing her wrist. "Well, you touch it when you play. What's the difference?"

He took a breath and carefully removed the cello from its dark corner. "I touch only the neck."

She was still frowning, like she was trying to decide something now. But he was the one who had decided. She didn't know this, of course. She was oblivious, not even smart enough to read this in his face. She just looked at him, like a dumb animal. Finally, she nodded toward the black case across the room, the one he had brought in from the car.

"So, why do you have two of them?"

"That one is for others," he said. "This one is for me."

And for her.

She was staring hard at him now. Then she shrugged off her coat and tossed it on the floor. She plopped down on the futon and looked up at him with a smile.

"Play something for me," she said.

He stared at her, the cello resting against his chest. For the briefest moment, he considered it. He had never tried it that way before and the idea was intriguing. Would it feel different than the others? But why? She wasn't worth it. It would be like playing for a deaf person.

"No," he said.

"Why not?" she said.

"I don't feel like it." He carefully put the cello back in its corner. When he turned back, she had scooted down on the futon, and now she lay propped up on her elbows.

"So, how do you say it in French?"

"Say what?"

"How do you say, 'Let's fuck'?"

He was silent, staring at her breasts, clearly outlined beneath her blouse.

"Tell me," she said. "I bet it sounds really nice in French."

He turned away, picking up his wineglass and taking a drink.

"Come on, how do you say it?"

He shut his eyes.

She was laughing. "God, what's the matter? You're all red. Am I embarrassing you? Okay, you don't have to say it. All you have to do is just do it. Just fuck me, okay? And make it—"

He threw the glass toward the futon. It shattered against the wall, spraying her white blouse red. She gave a yelp and her eyes widened as he came toward her. But even as he straddled her hips, her fingers were working on the buttons of his shirt and her mouth was opening eagerly to accept his.

But he didn't kiss her. He didn't take off her blouse or touch her breasts. He didn't even look at her face as he wrenched her skirt up over her hips, pulled the tights down her legs and wedged his knees between her thighs. At first, the roughness aroused her and she was panting as she helped him out of his clothes. She gave a half-laugh, half-cry when he entered her and she wrapped her arms around his back, pulling him deeper inside her. But the more he pushed against her, the harder he tried, the softer he became.

She pushed against his chest. "Hey, hey," she said hoarsely. "Stop, okay? If you can't . . . hey, it's—"

He slapped her and she let out a sharp cry. He sensed the change in her, felt her body retreating under him. He could almost smell the fear coming off her skin. But that didn't stop him. He kept pushing against her, ignoring her cries, waiting, waiting for the blessed release. But it did not come. It never did. Not this way.

He felt a sudden searing pain and fell back panting, holding his neck. He was so stunned that it took him several seconds to realize what had happened. She had scratched him. And now she was inching back toward the wall, away from him.

He looked at his bloody fingers, then at the girl. She was staring at him as she pulled her skirt down.

"Look," she said, "maybe you should just take me back to my hotel, okay?"

"No," he said.

Her expression hardened. "Great. First you can't even get off and now you won't give me a fucking ride." She stood and pulled up her tights. "So much for the French being great lovers."

She kept talking, but he didn't hear her. He turned and went to the cello case. He unlatched it and reached into the small pouch on the inside of the lid. He took his time as he decided which one to use. The Larsen D? No, she wasn't worth it. The Jargar A was too thin and he had never been able to count on it. The Spirocore C had a nice sharp attack.

Finally, he made his choice and closed the case. When he turned to face her, she was standing with her back to him, buttoning her blouse. He moved quickly, quietly. She didn't have time to turn, to react. He looped the steel string around her neck and gave a hard tug.

Her hands came up clawing. Her scream died into a gurgle. He pulled harder, bringing her back against his chest. He pulled on the string once, twice, enjoying her fear. He was careful not to pull the string too tight because he wanted this to last. And he knew just how much pressure was needed to hold her, to make her black out. But he also knew how to keep her alive. He closed his eyes, burying his face in her vanilla hair.

Then he gave the string a sharp jerk. The steel cut into her neck and she gave a violent quiver. Blood sprayed the wall above the futon. Finally, she went limp. He caught her beneath the arms before she fell and held her against his chest.

He scooped the body up in his arms and carried it to the bathroom. He put the body in the old bathtub and took a step back to look at it. For a second—just one second—he saw Hélène. But this one wasn't beautiful like Hélène.

And this one wasn't worth keeping.

He went back out, shutting the door. The spray of blood on the wall over the futon made him stop.

Damn it!

He had cut the carotid artery, and it had left a mess to clean. No matter. It would have to wait. Her blood was still warm on his hands and the hotness in his groin was building. He had to hurry now. If he didn't, the moment would be gone.

The room was cold on his naked body, but he was sweating in anticipation. He went to the corner and carefully pulled out the other cello, the beautiful one, the Goffriller Rosette. More than three hundred years old. So many great hands had caressed it. But no one else would ever play it now. No one else would ever hear it now. Except him.

He picked up his bow, took the cello to a chair and sat down. Setting the cello between his bare thighs, he rested it back against his chest. He cradled the cello's neck on his shoulder, the C-string tuning peg touching his ear. He paused, holding the bow over the strings, watching the blood drip from his neck down onto the burnished maple. He closed his eyes, imagining the molecules of his blood being absorbed into the cello's body.

The bow came down slowly across the strings. The first notes of Elgar's cello concerto filled the small dark room.

The ache in his groin was building and as he played, eyes closed, he could feel himself hardening again. His breathing deepened. The sweat poured from his brow. He swayed, pulling the bow, thrusting.

He was lost in the music and the burn of anticipation. Then, suddenly, there it was. What he had been waiting for. One note. A vibration that began in his fingertips and raced down through his body to his groin. As the wolf note sounded, the release came. He cried out as his body convulsed.

The bow dropped from his hand to the floor. He sat there, head down, gasping, holding the cello in his embrace.

I couldn't take my eyes off her.

Maybe it was because I hadn't seen her in two years, and in that time she had passed through the looking glass that separates girls from women. Whatever it was, Mandy was beautiful, and I couldn't stop staring.

She was dancing with some dickhead in a Dolphins jersey. Not just a fan jersey, but one of those "authentic" NFL versions that lets the wearer pretend he's a stud running back. He had even paid to have his name put on the back—DARIUS. That the guy actually looked like a football player pissed me off. That he had ten fewer years than me and twenty more pounds of hard muscle made me stay in my chair.

That, and the knowledge that Mandy would kill me if I butted in.

I sat there, sipping my Dewar's and crunching the ice, my eyes never leaving her and the faux pro. She had been dancing with him for the last half hour. Finally, she stood on her tiptoes, gave the guy a kiss on the cheek and snaked her way through the crowd and back to the table.

"Was that necessary?" I asked as she slid into the chair.

"What?" Her face was glistening with sweat and her eyes were shining.

"The kiss thing."

She laughed but even in the dim bar light I could see the blush creep into her cheeks. "He was nice," she said. She took a sip of her wine spritzer. "He's a Miami Dolphin."

"Oh, yeah? What position?"

"Running back."

"He told you that?"

She nodded, her eyes searching the crowd for him again. She spotted him sitting at a table and waved. He waved back.

"Mandy, he's not a Dolphin," I said.

She looked at me. "How do you know?"

"First, I know the whole roster and there's no running back named Darius. Second, no player would be caught dead in a jersey off the field. They all wear Coogi sweaters."

She stared at me for a moment. "Why do you always do this?"

"Do what?"

"Ruin things."

I looked away, on the pretense of trying to signal the waitress. The music was loud and throbbing, some kind of rap thing that I didn't get and never would. It felt like someone was taking a jackhammer to my head.

Suddenly I felt her hand cover mine and I looked back at her.

"Bear, it's my last night here. Let's just have some fun tonight, okay?" she said.

Maybe it was the way she said it. Or the fact that I hadn't heard her use my nickname in such a long time. Maybe it was the fact that seeing her dancing with that young handsome guy made me feel every one of the twelve years between us. Maybe it was the fact that I had never quite accepted that my little sister wasn't little anymore.

I managed a smile. "I'm sorry."

She leaned over and kissed me on the cheek. I caught a whiff of Shalimar. I had sent her the perfume for her birthday last month, just like I had given her a bottle every birthday since she turned sixteen. Shalimar and Juicy Fruit gum. That was my little sister's scent. Except tonight there was a new under note there—a muskier, more womanly scent that mixed with the wine spritzer.

Her eyes searched the crowd and she bobbed her head to the music. The Dewar's was gone so I crunched more ice. I studied her face, lit by the pink glow of the bar's neon. Her long straight blond hair was alive in the breeze, her nose was sunburned, her blue eyes dancing.

The music stopped for a second. "So," I said. "Tell me at least that you're having a good time."

She grinned. "The best. Thanks for talking Daddy into letting me come."

I gave a half smile and waved to the waitress, holding up my empty glass. The music started up again.

"You won't tell Daddy, will you?" Mandy yelled over the din.

"Tell him what?"

"That I danced with a black guy."

I stared at her. "That guy was black?"

It took her a couple seconds to realize I was kidding. But then she laughed so hard she knocked over her wineglass.

"No more for you," I said.

"Aw, come on, Bear."

"Nope. You're cut off. I can't stand a woman who can't hold her liquor."

The waitress brought my fresh Dewar's and mopped up

the spilled wine. Mandy had gone back to watching the dancers again, swaying to the music like it was the soundtrack of her life. Which it was, of course. I suddenly felt so much older than thirty-three. And I was just as suddenly fifteen, thrust back to my room in Raleigh, Nirvana pulsating on the CD player, Dad pounding on my locked door. I looked at Mandy, wondering what her life was like in that house now. I had escaped, fleeing the hothouse of North Carolina for the fresh air of Miami. But she had never been farther from home than Atlanta.

That was why I had finally broken down and called home last month. That was why I had asked my parents if Mandy could come and visit me. A birthday gift, I had called it. But I hoped it would be an emancipation. I wanted her to know there was a wide, wonderful, awful world beyond the small one she knew.

My cell chirped. I pulled it out and looked at the number. I grimaced and set it down on the table.

"Girlfriend?" Mandy asked with a smile.

"My editor," I said.

"Do you even have a girlfriend?" Her smile was playful.

"Dozens."

"You're such a liar, Bear."

"So, how was graduation?" I asked, to change the subject.

She shrugged. "Depressing."

"Why?"

"No one can find a job," she said. "Not one of my friends has a bite."

Mandy had majored in business. I took a sip of scotch, thinking about how it had been when I had left Duke. I had abandoned my plan to go to med school and spent a year bumming around the Far East. When I finally came home, I landed a sports job at a newspaper in Fort Lauderdale. I had felt like my life was just beginning. Mandy sounded like hers was stillborn.

"I'm thinking of going back and getting a teaching degree," Mandy said. "Elementary school."

"The pay is shit," I said.

Her smile turned rueful. "That's what Daddy said."

"What does Mom say?"

"She thinks I should get a job at Saks and wait until things get better. Or stay in school and go for my MBA."

I shook my head slowly. "And live at home, right?"

She was quiet for a moment, toying with the stem of her wineglass. "I'm not like you, Bear," she said softly.

"What do you mean?"

"I like being home. And I can't just go off to some place I don't know. I'm not brave like you."

I laughed. I couldn't help it. But I regretted it when I saw her hurt look. "*Brave* is not a word anyone would apply to me," I said.

We fell into a silence. Mandy filled the void by looking around the bar. I filled it by taking two long draws on the Dewar's. I put the glass down to see Mandy staring at me.

"That's your third," she said.

"I know."

"You know I can't drive a stick, Bear."

It was an innocent enough remark, referring as it was to my vintage Corvette. But it was also an admonition that I didn't need another drink. I would have been irritated—I had heard about my drinking from friends—but there was a touch of sadness in her face. And I knew she was remembering the same thing I was remembering. That hot June night when she was nine and I showed up at her friend Trudy's house to drive her home. I had been partying hard at the Kappa Alpha house after graduation. She knew I was drunk but trusted me anyway. I drove the Opel into a tree on the way home. I broke my collarbone, arm and three ribs, and spent a year in traction. Mandy was luckier. She hit the windshield and ended up with only a scar over her left eye.

I couldn't see the scar in the bar light. The plastic surgeon was one of the best, a colleague of Dad's at Duke Raleigh Hospital. Mandy never brought the accident up, never once reminded me of it. My parents . . . well, that was something else entirely.

"Come on, let's get going," I said, rising.

"But it's early!" she said.

"Wrong. It's going on two. And your flight is at ten thirty."

"Okay, but I need some more pictures first."

She grabbed her big gold feedbag of a purse off the bar stool and I waited patiently while she rummaged through its dark depths. She finally pulled out her phone, a sleek Day-Glo pink thing that made my cell look like something from the last century.

She jumped off the stool and came over to my side, pressing her cheek against mine and holding out her phone at arm's length.

"Cheese!" she said.

She snapped several photos, then tossed her phone into her purse. "Give me yours now," she yelled over the music.

"My what?"

"Your phone. I'll take some for you."

"Just send me the ones you took."

"Do you even know how to download pictures?"

"Sure."

She shook her head, took my phone and snapped off a couple quick shots of our heads together.

She handed me the cell and kissed my forehead. "Now you have me with you forever," she said.

I stared at a photo of us on my cell. "You cut off the top of my head," I said.

"Oh shoot, let me try again."

"I like this one. I need a haircut anyway."

Mandy laughed. I downed another quick swig of scotch and rose. Mandy slipped her purse over her shoulder. "I have to hit the john first."

I watched her disappear into the crowd and leaned back in the chair, glad to have the extra moments to finish my drink. It was a typical October Miami night—hot, sticky, but with a brisk wind thanks to the tropical storm hovering over Nassau. The hurricane-watch party at the big pool bar at the Clevelander was just starting to kick into second gear. This wasn't my scene, but I had brought Mandy here because she had wanted to dance and I knew she would get a kick out of it.

I smiled, remembering her face as she watched the South Beach crowd. The glossy, brown-skinned, navel-pierced girl in the leopard bra and thong. The emaciated guy with an albino boa constrictor wrapped around his tattooed chest. The white-haired man in the perfect seersucker suit gallantly shepherding his purple-wigged wife into a Bentley. I had watched Mandy watching the circus parade, watched her devouring it all, and my heart ached. I wanted everything in the world for her.

I signaled the waitress and paid the bill in cash so we could make a quick getaway. I glanced at my watch and looked toward the restroom doors by the bar. I spotted Mandy but she was back on the dance floor, gyrating with Darius again. She saw me and waved. I gestured to my watch. She held up a finger and mouthed the words "One more dance, Bear."

I shook my head, smiled and took another drink of scotch. I looked out toward the ocean and watched lightning zigzag silently over the black sky.

When I looked back, Mandy was gone. So was the Dolphins guy. The band had ended its set and the sudden quiet quickly filled with laughter, then the softer pulse of recorded music.

I scanned the crowd, crunching more ice, waiting for her to emerge. I watched the door beyond the bar, but she wasn't in the constant parade of women coming and going. Finally, I got up and went to the restroom. There was a long line waiting to get in. I stood there for a moment, feeling stupid. Finally, I asked a woman going in to check and see if there was a blond girl in a turquoise blouse inside.

The woman took forever to return. "Your date's not in there," she said.

"Thanks," I muttered.

I pushed my way back to the dance floor. I wove through the sweating crowd, looking for a swatch of blue. I was also looking for a white Dolphins jersey. No sign of either Mandy or that Darius guy.

A hard pit was forming in my gut.

I went back to the table. It had already been taken over by two couples. I swung back to the dance floor, scrutinizing every face, even as my gut told me that she wasn't there. I tried to remember exactly where Darius had been sitting with his friends, but none of the faces registered in my memory.

"Damn it, Mandy," I whispered.

Colors and sounds swirled around me as I tried to think. Maybe she was waiting outside?

I hurried out to the street. I looked up and down the river of people flowing on the sidewalk, searching for her blond hair. Nothing.

I did a quick tour of the nearby shops and bars, thinking she had wandered off to find another souvenir. But I didn't spot her. I looked across the slow-moving cars on Ocean Drive toward the beach, then jogged across. There were plenty of people on the beach, kids mostly. But no Mandy. I hurried back to the street.

The cell was still in my hand and I punched in her number. My eyes scoured the crowd as I listened to the rings. It went to voice mail.

"Mandy," I barked. "Where the hell are you? I'm outside the Clevelander." I hung up.

A car crawled by, blaring out rap. Music spilled from a nearby dance club. A woman shrieked with laughter. I checked my cell to make sure it wasn't on mute. I stared at it, willing it to ring.

I dialed again. Again it went right to voice mail.

The cold nub that had formed in my gut was growing. I was never one to trust vague feelings. I was a reporter and trained to believe only what I could see, what I could prove.

But the feeling rising up and putting a choke hold on my heart now was real.

Mandy was gone.

3

The cop just looked at me through the open window of the cruiser, his jaw working a wad of gum.

"Look," I said slowly, trying to be calm. "I know my sister. She wouldn't just leave. Can't you guys—"

"Back away from the car," the cop said.

I took a step back and held up my hands.

The guy took his time getting out, then he motioned me back to him. I had spent the last half hour searching for Mandy and finally had waved down the Miami Beach PD squad car as it rolled slowly down Ocean Boulevard. The cop was on the short side and I knew from experience not to mess with the short ones.

"She isn't answering her cell," I said for the fourth time.

He was staring at me now, at my sweating face. "You been drinking pretty hard?" he asked.

"What?"

"How much have you had, buddy?"

"I don't—two, three drinks. Look, I need some help here. She's been gone almost forty minutes."

"Did you check the john?"

"Yes, I went back to the bar and, yes, I checked everywhere." I wiped a hand over my face. "Look, man, she's not from here. She's not—"

The cruiser's radio crackled and the cop turned back to listen. I heard his partner in the car respond, something about a fight on the beach.

When the cop turned back to me, I yanked out my wallet and held up my press card. His eyes narrowed as he looked at it.

"So?" he said.

"Give me a break here. I spent five years covering Miami-Dade PD," I said.

The cop was working the gum harder.

"My name is Matt Owens. Call over to the station. They'll vouch for me. Ask for Detective Brinkley."

The cop heaved a sigh and turned to the open window of the cruiser. I listened to him talking to his partner but my eyes were scanning the crowd.

"Hey, buddy," the cop said.

In the glare of the neon I could see something pass over his eyes, and I knew he had a daughter.

"You got a picture?" he asked.

"Picture?" It wasn't registering. Nothing was at this point.

"Yeah, a picture of your sister. If you got one, I'll keep it with me the rest of my shift and keep an eye open."

"I don't have—" I stopped and stared down at the cell phone in my hand. I punched a button, hoping it was the right one. Our faces flashed onto the small screen, the last of the pictures she had snapped of us at the Clevelander. I wasn't happy with the cop's offer but I knew it was all I was going to get from him.

"You got a cell phone or a computer that accepts pictures?" I asked.

"Yeah." He read me off the number and seconds later, his phone's display lit up.

"Pretty girl," he said.

"Yes, yes, she is." I wiped a hand over my face. "You gonna look for the guy?"

"Black, wearing white Dolphins jersey with the name Darius on the back. We got it."

I nodded numbly. "And my number. You have it there. Please . . . please give me a call if you find her. Anytime tonight. My name is Matt—"

"Matt Owens. I got that, too."

The cop walked back to his cruiser and I started down the sidewalk, my phone still in my hand as I scrolled through my contacts. Nora Brinkley had been my off-the-record source for many of the stories I broke in my early days on the police beat. The crumbs she slipped me about investigations provided me the respect of my editor and enough awards to fill my bathroom wall. The Pulitzer finalist certificate that came later— that one I kept framed over my desk. In return, Nora got three years of sleeping with me and an engagement ring that she returned in a coffee can filled with used kitty litter.

I pressed the button to dial Nora and, as it rang, continued to scan the streets for Mandy. It was past three now, and the night creatures were out in droves.

Nora's sleepy, smoky voice hit my ear. "Hello?"

I spoke loudly to be heard. "Nora? It's Matt."

"Matt?" she asked. Then, for a dig, "Matt who?"

"Come on, Nora. It's me. Please don't hang up. I need you."

"The only thing you ever really needed from me was two aspirins for your hangover."

I shut my eyes for a moment, then took a breath. "My little sister's missing," I said.

"Amanda? Missing from where? North Carolina?" Nora's tone changed immediately, softened with concern. I heard the click of a lighter. I knew she had grabbed a cigarette from the pack she kept hidden in her nightstand.

"No, from South Beach," I said. "She just disappeared off the dance floor about an hour ago."

"Where were you?"

"In a club," I said. "Look, I really need some help here. Maybe you could get your guys looking for her?"

"They're not my guys, Matt," Nora said. "And I don't have the power to ask a shift of officers to look for an adult woman who's only been missing sixty minutes."

"She's not a woman. She's still a girl and she doesn't understand what kind of place this is!"

"Calm down."

I knew she was right but I couldn't slow the pounding of my heart. The faces on the street were beginning to blur, like I was on some kind of cheap high.

"Where are you?" Nora asked.

I looked around. "Eighth Street."

"Go to the News Café and grab a coffee. No booze. Keep calling her and stay there," Nora said. "I can get there in a half hour."

I knew that Nora was rolling out of her bed at this hour only because somewhere, deep down inside her, no matter how many insults she threw my way, no matter how many dirty looks I got when I walked in the Miami-Dade PD homicide room, I knew she still loved me. And I knew that like I had done so many times before, I was using her.

But standing here on this street with my heart hammering and my eyes burning with tears, I didn't care.

*   *   *

I was at the curb when Nora's red RAV4 pulled up. I had ignored her warning and downed another scotch at the café. It was the only way I could keep from jumping out of my skin. Alcohol had always been my decompressant of choice. Hours of amping up on caffeine and bad food during the day meant I usually needed something to bring me down at night. But it was getting harder and harder to keep the cycle going. And the last scotch hadn't made a dent.

Nora eyed me as I got in. "You shaved your beard off."

"What? Oh, yeah. About a year ago." I had been doing another scan of the crowd and just now turned to see Nora. Right after Nora and I split up, I pressed my boss for a new assignment; it was just too hard to hang around the cop shop and pretend nothing had happened. I got promoted to the *Miami Times*'s investigative team, so I hadn't seen Nora in more than a year now. Her hair was longer, her eyes more wary. Still a head-turner without trying.

"I like you better without it," she said as she put the car in gear.

We drove slowly north on Ocean Boulevard, me leaning out the window to scan the sidewalk. It was a slow-moving stream of people wedged between the banks of hotels and a levee of tables curbside. There were some guys on ladders putting up hurricane shutters. The knot of fear in my gut was slowly dissolving into despair. There was no way I was going to find Mandy in this crowd.

Nora started peppering me with questions. She asked me again about what we had done that night, where exactly we had gone, where exactly Mandy had been when I last saw her, who she was dancing with. I knew Nora was just trying to calm me down, but her quiet cop monotone was just making it harder.

"How long was this last dance?"

I swung to face Nora. "I told you. No more than a few minutes. She waved to me, signaling she just wanted one more dance."

I saw a flash of doubt in her face before she looked back at the street. Nora had met Mandy once, when I had taken her home to meet my family right after we got engaged. It hadn't gone too well, that dinner at the Savoy. Nora had soldiered on through the tension and Mandy had played her usual role of peacemaker. So Nora knew what Mandy meant to me. Mandy was the one who loved me.

It started to rain. The neon became a blur of pink and green. Nora switched on the wipers. But there was no sign of Mandy or anyone in a Dolphins jersey.

"I think we better head back to the station," she said.

There was no one in the homicide squad room when we walked in. I had no idea what time it was and glanced around for a clock. All I saw were bulletin boards, crime-stopper posters and the big rain-streaked windows dotted with the dull orange lights of the freeway. Nothing had changed since I had been in here more than a year ago. My eyes went to the far wall where the massive white dry-erase board hung. It was where the detectives listed all the recent homicide cases. Names, case numbers, disposition—black marker for closed, red for open.

"Missing Persons is going to have my ass tomorrow," Nora said. "They're already insecure down there and don't like us infringing on their territory."

"I know," I said. "I appreciate everything you're doing. What do you need from me?"

"I've already called in her number so we can track her by her GPS, but I'll need a photo, too. Email me that one on your phone so I can print it and make some copies. And you need to fill out this form."

I slid into a chair and started on the form. It was a simple query: missing person's name, age, physical description, clothing. All that was easy and I rushed through it until I got to the line that read: EMERGENCY CONTACT/NEXT OF KIN.

Jesus. That would be my father, Martin L. Owens.

My eyes drifted to the phone on Nora's desk. *No,* I told myself. *Not yet.* Mandy's plane didn't leave until ten thirty and there was still time to find her. I put myself down as next of kin and moved on down the form. I paused again at the section that asked what personal effects the missing person might have with her.

I listed: cell phone, silver earrings, silver ring and . . . what else? That big gold purse. But other than her cell and treasured iPod, I didn't have a clue what was in it.

The radio on Nora's desk suddenly came alive. I looked up, straining to hear something about Mandy, but it was an armed robbery in Liberty City. I went back to my form, angry that someone else was wasting the cops' time when I wanted them looking for Mandy.

"Finished," I said, looking up.

Nora pushed another sheet of paper to me. "Give me a full written description of her dance partner."

That didn't take long. I wrote down his age, weight, height and the name on the shirt and looked up.

Nora was on her cell phone, her back to me. She wore dark jeans and a lightweight black jacket with MDPD stenciled on the back. Her hair was wet and slightly wavy from the rain.

I'd always liked it like that, liked how she looked right after she got out of the shower. But I was certain now that I had never told her that.

She snapped her cell closed and turned to me. Her eyes had a thin swirl of alarm just under the deep brown surface.

For a second, all I could think about was that big white board with the black and red lettering on it.

"Matt," she said. "The techs have located Amanda's phone."

I jumped to my feet. "Her phone? Where?"

"On the beach."

"What about Mandy? Is she there? Is she okay?"

"All we know is that the phone is there. Someone just turned it on, which triggered the GPS signal. I've got some Miami Beach uniforms headed that way to secure it. I don't know what we're going to find, so I should probably leave you here—"

"No fucking—"

"But I won't," she said, cutting me off. "Let's go."

I had been to hundreds of crime scenes as a police reporter, interviewed dozens of witnesses and seen my share of dead bodies, although not many close up. When I got a phone call, there had never been a time that I didn't hop in my car and peel out, filled with the twisted hope that the murder I was heading to would be sensational enough to make the front page.

But now, I couldn't even take a step.

Nora took my hand. "I'll be with you, Matt."

4

We arrived at the beach just before dawn.

Sometime during the last couple of hours, the tropical storm had morphed into a category-one hurricane and was moving our way. The sky was roiling with gray clouds that lent a putrid green tint to the ocean. Surging whitecaps pounded the shoreline while seagulls danced in the air, looking for something to scavenge in the seaweed and garbage that rimmed the shore.

The light was thin, the rising sun a white blur behind a silvery veil of rain. In the distance, silhouetted by the bleak backdrop, the faded pink band shell rose like a giant sea crab in the sand.

My throat felt tight and my brain was spinning in panic. Nora had told me three times that the beach cops had found nothing out here except Mandy's phone, but I was afraid she wasn't telling me the truth, thinking I couldn't handle it. Or maybe I was afraid the Miami Beach cops had lied to her. Or maybe I was just afraid.

I realized with a start that Mandy and I had been on this exact spot yesterday. She went shopping for souvenir T-shirts in the stores along A1A, and afterward we'd wandered across the road to this same band shell. Some old guys were playing Glenn Miller shit.

"We were just here yesterday," I said.

"Excuse me?" Nora said. "You and Amanda?"

"Yeah. We stopped and listened to the band."

"I'll need to know more about that later," she said. "In fact, I'll need to know everywhere you've been with her, but right now, let's go talk to the cops."

As we walked against a wet wind toward the band shell, two uniformed cops turned to us. One of them was from Miami-Dade PD, the other from the Beach PD. Nora seemed to know the one from her department and they exchanged greetings as we neared. My focus was on a third man hunkered near the steps to the stage. Whiskers, bleary eyes, filthy gray hair and tattered dirty clothes. A homeless man.

My brain kicked hard with questions: *Did this man hurt Mandy? Did he see something?* But then I noticed one of the cops had Mandy's pink cell phone in a plastic bag and I forced myself to listen to what he was telling Nora.

"We started the trace three hours ago, like you asked, Detective, but we got nothing," he said. "The phone was off, including the GPS signal, until about forty minutes ago, when suddenly the sucker came alive. We were able to zero in on it within minutes."

"Is this the man who found it?" Nora asked.

He pulled the homeless man forward. "Tell the detective how you found the phone."

The man wiped his nose with his sleeve. "I found it over there," he said, pointing to the band shell. "Right in the middle of the stage."

"What were you doing up there?"

"Looking for a place outta the wind to sleep things off, you know?"

"You see anyone around here before you crawled up there?"

"Well, just before light, there was a couple of kids down there aways," he said, pointing south along the water. "I think they were . . . well, you know, having a little private fun, if you get my meaning."

I couldn't keep my mouth shut. "What did the girl look like?"

The homeless man recoiled from me like I had raised my fist. "Hell, buddy, I don't know. It was far away."

"Yeah, but don't tell me you didn't creep a little closer to watch," I said.

"Matt, knock it off," Nora said. She turned back to the man. "Did you watch the couple?"

The man shrugged. "Maybe for a few minutes," he said. "What's the harm? They come out here to do that shit, they don't seem to care about nothing, why should I?"

"What did the girl look like?" Nora asked.

"I dunno."

"Think."

"She was like Mexican or Cuban," the man said. "Lots of thick black hair."

Nora looked to the cop. "You run a check on this guy?"

"Yeah, he's clean. And I got his ID and prints, too, figuring you'll need them down the road if we find the girl dead."

I felt a clutch in my chest but forced myself to stay quiet. And again it hit me how often I had heard that kind of talk and never thought twice about the indifferent tone.

"If you don't mind," Nora said to the other cop, "can we run this guy in on a disorderly so we don't lose him if we do need him again?"

"Not a problem, Detective."

The Miami Beach cop took the homeless man toward his cruiser. I was glad they were detaining him but still worried about what else of Mandy's might be out here on the beach. Where was her purse? It was easy to notice, a big gold thing. Had her abductor taken that, too, and left it nearby? And what if *she* was out here somewhere, unconscious?

"Nora," I said. "I'm going to walk down the beach and start looking—"

"No, you're not," Nora said. "I have two cruisers on their way here. They'll search the beach with metal detectors and in another couple hours there'll be enough tourists and locals out here to do the job for us. You know how people are when there's a storm coming. We'll put out some bulletins asking them to turn in anything they find."

"Yeah, like tourists will do that."

Nora stared at me, annoyed. "It's all we can do, Matt. I can't leave officers out here all day based on what little we have. Especially not with a storm coming."

"I know," I said. "But I can't just stand here."

Nora drew a notebook from her pocket. "Then start telling me where you and Amanda have been over the last week. Other than this place."

I stared dumbly at her. But then I realized what she was trying to do. If Mandy had been abducted by someone, there was a chance he had been stalking her. The thought made me sick to my stomach as I conjured up an image of some creep following us, watching Mandy, waiting.

"Matt?"

Nora's calm voice brought me back. "Okay," I said. "Let me think." I was looking around the deserted beach, my mind trying hard to retrieve the last couple of days.

"She flew in Saturday, four days ago," I said. "We stayed in that night, ordered pizza, because she was fighting off a cold."

"You still living in that place in the Grove?" Nora asked.

I nodded. "I took her to the Dolphins-Bills game Sunday. It was a four o'clock game. We came right home after because she was still a little tired."

Nora prodded when I didn't go on. "What did you do Monday?"

"She wanted to go shopping, so we had brunch in the Grove and then we went to Lincoln Road. We walked around a lot. There was this little shop where they sell old designer stuff and she went in there."

"The Fly Boutique?"

"Yeah, that's it. She bought a Pucci scarf. She said she was going to wear it as a belt. That's Mandy, you know? She's like that, has a way of taking stuff and putting her special twist on it. Wait, I just remembered. She was wearing the scarf tonight and I—"

"I got that already, at the station. Where else did you go?"

"Yeah, okay," I whispered. My head hurt and I couldn't seem to remember anything, like the last four days had vanished. "We went to Books and Books. I wanted to get the new Pete Dexter. I was going to buy her a paperback to read on the plane going home. She told me she had downloaded a Jeffery Deaver book to her phone to read."

"What else, Matt?"

"We had lunch there at the café, outside. Stone crabs. She had never had stone crabs before."

Nora was quiet. I felt a small surge of anger building inside me, resentment that Nora was making me relive all this. But

I knew she was just doing her job. I drew in a deep breath and pulled up the next day from my memory.

"The next morning we went to the beach," I said. "Rented a cabana and we just laid around reading. That night it was rainy, so we went to the Fontainebleau."

"Why?"

I shook my head. "I don't know. It's so fucking Florida. She loved it. She wanted to have a cosmo because that's what the women in *Sex and the City* drank. After that, she walked down the staircase to nowhere. She made me take her picture."

I pulled out my phone but didn't have the energy to punch up the photograph.

"Anywhere else?" Nora asked.

I hesitated. "I took her to Mac's."

Nora's eyes swung to me. We had both been to Mac's Club Deuce on Fourteenth Street many times. It was a classic dive bar that attracted drunks, cops and drag queens. I had taken Mandy there because I knew it was the kind of place she needed to see and never would in Raleigh.

"Did you ever notice anyone?" Nora asked finally.

I felt a sudden wave of fatigue rush over me and I shook my head slowly.

"Matt?"

"No," I said softly. "I didn't notice anyone."

Nora let the quiet grow. It had stopped raining and she used the moment to cup her hands and light a cigarette. I knew she never lit up unless she was nervous. "What about yesterday?" she asked finally.

"We came back over here to the beach. We went up to the old boardwalk by Twenty-first Street and just walked. That's how we ended up here."

The name came to me, totally unexpected.

"Reginald and the Retros. The song was 'Moonglow.'"

Nora heard the catch in my voice and looked over at me. "Matt?"

"These old couples were dancing and having a great time. I was singing along and Mandy was laughing. God, she was laughing. She was laughing and telling me I was an old soul at heart."

I ran a hand over my face and turned away, facing the surging green waves. The sting of salt air hit my face and I started to wonder about the hurricane. How could we look for Mandy in a hurricane?

"What about after you left here?" Nora asked gently.

"I wanted to show her the art deco stuff, you know, the old hotels. We had dinner at the Essex and then went to the Clevelander so she could dance." I paused, spent. "That's all," I said.

Nora's cell phone rang, the same ringtone she'd had when we were together. The Beatles' "Let It Be."

She tossed the cigarette to the sand. "I need to take this," she said. "Maybe you should think about calling your family. Wasn't Amanda scheduled to fly home this morning?"

Nora walked away from me before I could answer her. I checked my watch, surprised to see it was already seven thirty A.M. At the moment, I couldn't remember the exact time Mandy's flight departed, but strangely, I did remember that she was due to land in Raleigh at twelve thirty. And I knew my father would be waiting there, in his black Cadillac Escalade, to pick her up.

"Matt."

There was an edge in Nora's voice that made me spin back to her. The wind was blowing her hair in windmills and her nylon jacket flapped against her body. The look on her face dissolved what remained of my strength. I put out a hand to steady myself but found nothing but air.

"We've found a body, Matt," Nora said. "We think it's Amanda."

5

It was raining hard by the time we got there. I saw the lights first, a blur of strobing red and blue that made my eyes hurt. Then, with each pass of the wipers, the details emerged. An old hotel, its limestone façade gray with age, its windows covered with plywood. It had taken us no more than ten minutes to get here from the band shell, so I knew we were still somewhere in the art deco district.

Nora slowed the RAV to a crawl as she peered for a place to pull in among the squad cars. The car was still moving when I yanked on the door handle.

"Matt!" she yelled.

But I was already halfway to the hotel steps. A big cop in a black slicker grabbed me by the shoulders and tossed me back. I went sprawling into a bush and sprang back on my feet. Before I could catch my breath, Nora was at my side, one hand pressed on my chest, the other holding out her badge.

"It's all right!" she said to the cop. "I got him."

I didn't hear what else she said to him. I was staring at the open door beyond the yellow crime tape. I couldn't see anything but a blur of bodies inside. A hand on my sleeve made me jerk around. Nora was there, her hair hanging wet in her face, her badge on a chain around her neck now.

"You can't go in there," she said.

"Bullshit! I have to—"

"Matt, stop! You've got to stay calm here."

My chest ached. It hurt to take a breath. I looked at the hotel, then back at Nora. "Is it her?"

Nora wiped a hand over her face. "I don't know. The uniform said that it's a young blond woman."

"She was wearing a blue blouse, a turquoise thing that—"

"The body is nude," Nora said.

I shut my eyes. "I have to get in there," I said.

"They'll never let you in if they think it's your sister." She was quiet for a moment, then I felt her hand on my arm. "Stay here," she said.

I watched her go back to the cop, talking to him, pointing my way. Then she waved me forward. "I told him you're with the *Times*. He wants to see your press ID," she said.

I fumbled for my wallet and held out the card. The cop gave it a glance, then waved us past the tape. "Stay behind me and don't touch a thing," Nora said as we went up the steps.

"I know the drill," I said.

She shot me a look, then went inside. I trailed behind her, not making eye contact, trying hard to conjure up a mask of indifference. As we climbed a trash-strewn staircase, I could feel a change come over my body, like my temperature was dropping a few degrees and my heartbeat was slowing. Details registered now with startling clarity—the glare of graffiti, black streaks of mildew on the old flocked wallpaper, a smell of must and sea salt, the smudge of brown rust on my palm as I lifted it off the iron stair railing. I had moved into that blessed out-of-body state that had always served me so well. I had become a reporter.

The feeling stayed with me as we climbed to the third floor.

More uniforms and black slickers. I followed Nora down a dim hallway with light sconces hanging from wires. The smell of dirt and decay was heavy here. I felt the soft press of bodies decades dead, and weirdly, an echo of music, like what those old men had been playing at the band shell.

Nora had stopped at a wide entranceway. The two French doors had been taken off their hinges and were propped against the peeling walls. The entrance was guarded by another cop. It was a big room, filled with gray light. The wind was stronger here, the smells stronger here. I stood five feet behind, unable to move.

"Matt?"

Nora was in front of me. She had a white net over her hair and she was pulling on a pair of latex gloves. "You have to stay here," she said. "I can tell if it's Mandy."

The reporter in me was gone. I wasn't sure what was left.

I nodded. Nora gave my arm a squeeze and I watched her walk into the room wearing paper shoe covers. I closed my eyes in an effort to relieve the sandpaper feel on my lids and leaned against the wall. I could hear the roar of the storm intensifying, feel the cool swirl of wind on my face. Then something awful happened. I tried to pray. I had never prayed before, not even all those times my mother had dragged me to church. I had watched her, watched the pastor, watched the faces of everyone else, and wondered what they were praying for.

I tried to remember the words, any words. But there was nothing there.

"Please," I whispered. "Please."

Wind. Just wind. I opened my eyes and looked toward the doors.

Beyond the cop, I could see bodies moving. More black slickers, uniforms. No sign of Nora. I moved closer. Between the movements of legs, I caught a glimpse of something pale on the floor. But I couldn't see what it was, and suddenly I had to.

A thudding sound drew my eye to the hallway. Three more slickered cops coming forward and two guys in sports coats. The cop standing guard at the open door was distracted checking IDs and it was just enough of an opening for me to slip behind him.

My brain was working enough for me to know I had to be careful or I would get thrown out. I couldn't bring myself to look to the center, so I focused on the room. It was large and circular, with a raised stage at one end. I heard a tinkling sound and looked up. A chandelier, webbed with dust, most of its crystal strands broken, swayed in the wind.

To the east were big windows with broken glass panes framed by faded blue drapes that were moving like ocean waves. I forced myself to look down. The floor was old terrazzo, a pattern of stars. It might have been blue but it was caked with litter, debris and dust. I crept around the edges of the black slickers, circling, circling, moving closer to that pale thing that was the center of attention in the middle of the floor. I spotted Nora kneeling down and saw something on her face close to relief. For the first time, I had hope that it wasn't Mandy there on that dusty floor.

Then, suddenly, the circle opened for a second.

I let out a long hard breath.

Flashes of images like quick camera clicks. White flesh. Blond hair. Arms and legs spread wide, her body positioned carefully so her head and each limb matched the star pattern in the middle of the terrazzo floor. And a dark hole in the middle of her chest.

"Oh," I said.

Faces turned to me.

"Oh, oh, oh no . . ."

Nora was suddenly there, blocking my view. I tried to push her aside so I could see more, see if Mandy would get up and move. But Nora was stronger than me. She had my arms and was pushing me back, the white net thing on her hair falling off as I flailed against her. I hit the wall with a jolt. My legs gave way but Nora held me up.

"We're going to walk, Matt," she said. "We're going to walk out of here, okay?"

I was weeping.

"Come on," she said quietly.

I made it down the stairs to the second floor and then had to jerk away from Nora. I retched and everything came up onto the dirty floor. I put out a hand on the wall to steady myself as my stomach went through spasms of dry heaves. Finally it stopped. Nora's hand was cool on my neck. I wiped my face and looked around at the faces of cops standing in the hallway.

"Get him out of here, Brinkley," someone said.

I half fell, half staggered down the next flight of stairs, my momentum stopped only by a man sitting on the bottom step. I glanced at him as I pushed by, catching a glimpse of yellow hard hat and plaid shirt. His eyes locked on mine as I passed. His face was streaked with tears.

I stumbled to the door and rested my head against the frame. I felt Nora come up behind me. I turned and looked back at the man sitting on the stairs.

"Is he the one who found her?" I asked.

Nora looked back at the man. "Yes. He got here at seven thirty to open the site. They're renovating this place."

"Can I talk to him?"

"No. Not now."

I looked out at the pouring rain. A white van pulled in between two cop cars. Two guys carrying cases got out and trudged up the stairs. The trailing one paused to take one last drag on his cigarette and tossed it to the gutter before going in. Their slow pace irritated me. I closed my eyes. Through the haze of my pain I heard words, the stutter of men's voices, and then a low chuckle. Football. They were talking about a fucking football game. I turned to the two uniforms.

"Don't," Nora said sharply.

I turned away, back toward the open door and the rain. I don't know how long I stood there like that, just staring out into the gray sheets. It could have been minutes, it could have been hours. Then I felt Nora touch my arm.

A short woman with dark curly hair stood next to her. Pantsuit the color of the rain, white blouse, gold badge dangling. She had to look up to meet my eyes but I felt as if she was looking down. Nora gave a nod toward her.

"This is Detective Janet Molina. She's in charge of your sister's case."

"I'm sorry for your loss," the woman said.

I gave a tight nod. I tried to think of something to say but nothing was coming. Whatever adrenaline had kept me going in the last couple hours was now gone. My bones ached from the effort of standing.

"You're her only next of kin?"

I blinked hard, trying to focus. Kin?

"No," I said. "No, I'm not."

"Excuse me?"

"My mother and father . . . I mean, Mandy has, we have . . ." I wiped a hand over my eyes. I looked at Detective Molina's bland face and then at Nora's stricken one, then held up a hand. "I have to . . . would you excuse me for a moment?"

"Matt?"

I ignored Nora and moved away. I walked down a dark hall and found a corner. A desk, with cobwebbed cubbyholes and old keys still dangling from their hooks. I slipped behind the desk and into the shadows. I pulled the cell from my pocket. My hands shook as I dialed the number. He picked up on the third ring.

"Dad? It's Matt."

6

There were bodies everywhere. Slumped on chairs, lying on the floor, crammed in every corner. And the noise. Babies crying, voices braying in a babble of languages, all amplified by fatigue and nerves spun tight to the breaking point.

He stood perfectly still, a tall figure in the middle of the chaos, and tried to figure out his next move. He looked up again at the board that announced the departures, but nothing had changed in the last two hours. And a glance up at the big-screen TV, tuned to CNN, confirmed what the ticket agent had already told him: Hurricane Jackie, now swollen to a category three, had stalled just west of Nassau. Everything on the board at Miami International read DELAYED or CANCELED.

A trickle of sweat made its way slowly down his spine. He hadn't slept in two days and he knew he needed to stay sharp. He hoisted his case and Vuitton duffel and headed off in search of the men's room. Inside the stall, he opened his leather ditty bag. He popped a vial and gulped down a large oblong pill, the second one he had taken in the last three hours. He hesitated, then shook out a third round white tablet.

The two Provigils would keep him alert for at least forty hours. The third tablet, the GHB, well, he would keep it ready in his pocket until he was on the plane and could give in to the deep drugged sleep he so desperately craved.

Outside at the sink, he splashed water on his face, straightened his tie and picked up his duffel and case. He went back to his gate and patiently took his place in the long line of surly passengers. As usual, he hadn't eaten much, so by the time he got to the counter, the Provigil had kicked in.

The fog had lifted. He was in control again.

The young woman behind the counter barely looked up at him as she stabbed at the buttons of her computer. Her hair had come loose from its ponytail and her lipstick had long ago vanished. Her Air France name tag, hanging on her limp blouse, read CLAIRE.

"It's bad, isn't it?" he said.

She gave a snort and brushed her hair back.

"So what are my chances of getting to Paris by tomorrow?" he asked.

"You've heard of snowballs in hell?" she muttered.

He ground his teeth but kept his smile. "There's nothing you can do? Maybe see if there's another airline that—"

"Look," she said, staring at him with tired eyes. "All flights going east are on hold because of the storm."

"I have to get out of Miami," he said.

She shook her head, still punching buttons.

"Claire," he said.

She looked up.

"I must get out of here," he said softly. "Now."

Her pupils were moving like tiny black pinballs, and he knew that people had been screaming at her all day, pushing their ugly faces across the counter, breathing their Cinnabon-and-stale-coffee breath in her face, making her feel small and angry and ugly.

"Je suis désolé que tout le monde ait été si méchant avec vous aujourd'hui."

"What?"

"Oh, I assumed you spoke French," he said with a smile. "You look French."

She brushed her hair back. "No, I'm not French."

"Then that was rude of me. I said that I am sorry that everyone has been so mean to you today."

Her smile almost touched him.

"It goes with the job, I guess," she said. Her eyes held his for a moment then drifted over his shoulder. "What's that?" she asked, nodding.

He put a hand on the black case. "It's a cello."

"Wow. You're a musician?"

He nodded, smiling. The Provigils were giving him a sudden rush of energy. He had an image of taking Claire up to the Marriott and bruising those thin colorless lips back to life.

"I have a concert tomorrow in Paris," he said. "A very important concert. Can you help me?"

She hesitated, then held out a hand. "Let me see your ticket and passport."

He handed them over. She punched some buttons, frowning. The man in line behind him was pressing close, his body odor coming off him in waves.

"I can get you to Dallas," Claire said, looking up. "There's a flight to Charles de Gaulle from there at six thirty."

"Dallas?" he said.

"The only flights out are going west because of the hurricane."

He nodded. "Then I will go to Dallas."

She hesitated. "I only have first class."

"That is fine," he said with a smile. "Do you have two seats available?"

"Two?"

He nodded to the cello case.

"Oh," she said softly. She punched more buttons, then looked up. "Yes, but it will be an additional eight thousand dollars onto your current fare."

"It is worth it," he said.

The setting sun was a red streak outside the window. He reached across the cello, strapped into the window seat, and pulled down the shade. Reclining his seat slowly back, he closed his eyes. The Provigils were still humming in his blood. He needed to silence them.

He opened his eyes and watched the stewardess as she unclasped her seat belt and started moving in the galley. He caught her eye and motioned her toward him.

"What wines do you have?" he asked.

"If you'll give me a few minutes, sir, I can—"

"No, I need a glass of wine now. What do you have? A Bordeaux preferably."

She glanced toward the galley. "I'll check, sir."

"Never mind. Just bring me a glass of whatever is back there."

He closed his eyes again. His veins were jumping, as if there were a current running through them. He needed to come down.

The woman came back with a glass of red wine. He waited until she was gone before he took the pill from his pocket. Washing it down with the wine, he closed his eyes and waited.

He let his mind drift. Back to Miami. Back to the blond girl in blue. He wondered what it felt like for her, if it had felt different for her than it did for him. Of course it had. He had been taking the GHB for years, using it to summon sleep when it was nowhere near. But she, well, he was certain she had never taken anything stronger than the white wine she had been drinking that night. So when he had taken her in his arms on the crowded dance floor, eased her away from the black man and plunged the needle into her arm, the effect had been immediate. She had become pliant, disoriented. That was the beauty of liquid gamma hydroxybutyrate. The victim looked only as if she were drunk.

The black man? Well, it had been easy enough to convince him that the girl was his sister and that she needed to sit the next one out.

He hadn't really planned this one. It had been an impulse. But that afternoon on the beach, when he had spotted her at the band shell, he knew he had to have her. There had been no one for the last nine months, not since that horrible girl he had invited to his concert last January. The urge was coming more often now. And the girl in Miami had been so very lovely and so very blond.

He had followed her, watching her and the man carefully. He was very protective. But that had only made things more intriguing. How was he going to get her away from him?

He took a sip of the red wine.

Last night, he had followed them to the restaurant and then to the dance club. He had sat at the bar, watching her, waiting. He knew that when the black man asked her to dance that third time, he would have his chance.

The stewardess came by and refilled his wineglass. The alcohol was mixing nicely with the drugs.

Again he wondered what it had felt like for her. The GHB granted him rest. For her?

He smiled. Rest of a sort, he presumed.

She had been alive, of course, when he took her to the old hotel. Alive enough to be warm but dead enough to do nothing to stop him. It was dark and the rain had swept the streets clear of people, so no one was there to see him carry her from the alley up into the old hotel. He had found the place beforehand, drawn to the decrepit ballroom by its neglected beauty. And there, under the shattered chandelier and upon the dusty terrazzo star, he had killed her. After, as her body was growing cold, he had gone back downstairs to the rental car. He brought the cello up the stairs. He sat on a broken chair and played the Kodály sonata. The wolf came when summoned, the notes carried away with the rising wind.

He arrived in Paris to a cold pearl-gray morning. The taxi driver had balked at the sight of the cello case, but a quick twenty-euro note to his palm kept him quiet. Then, the address—a grand apartment on the east end of Île Saint-Louis near the old Rothschild compound—brought a raised eyebrow from the driver, who now anticipated a very good tip.

The maid had readied the apartment for his arrival. A bouquet of white roses, a neatly folded copy of *Le Monde*, fresh grapefruit juice in the refrigerator and a brioche from Hédi's, its butter bleeding through the wrapping paper.

He dropped his duffel in the center of the floor and stowed the cello in the hall closet. He hit the button on the espresso machine as he passed through to the bedroom. He stripped quickly and showered. The GHB he had taken on the plane had left him lethargic but he knew sleep was still impossible.

He was sitting at the table in his robe, staring down at the fast-moving green Seine, when the door buzzed. He shut his eyes. It buzzed again and again. He knew it was her and that she would not give up.

At the intercom, he hit the button to open the door downstairs. He heard the grind of the elevator and left the front door open before going back to his place at the table. He was reading an article about the global warming summit when she came in.

"Laurent?"

"Here," he called out.

She came in, a jangle of bracelets and strong perfume. He resisted the urge to pull away as she planted a kiss on his cheek.

"You shaved," she said. "Nice."

"There's coffee," he said, gesturing toward the kitchen.

"None for me. My kidneys are floating." She sat down across from him. He turned the newspaper to the sports page.

She was quiet and he could feel her eyes on him but he didn't look up.

"So," she said. "How was Miami?"

"Hot. Exhausting."

She reached over and ran a hand through his thick black hair. "You've let your hair get too long."

He pulled away and she smiled. "But I guess that is what the women like now, right?"

She shrugged out of her coat and draped it on the chair. "You look tired. Did you manage to have any fun while you were there?"

"Fun?"

"I suspect not," she said with a smile. "No ancient cathedrals or ruins in Miami for you to prowl, right?"

"They have some lovely old art deco hotels."

But she wasn't listening. She was digging in her briefcase and finally produced what she was looking for. She slapped the faxes on the table. "The reviews were brilliant," she said.

"Put them in your scrapbook."

She sat back in the chair. He could feel the hard stare of her dark eyes but didn't look up. "Why do you have to be such an asshole?" she said.

He was silent, sipping his espresso. "You know I don't read the reviews, Maud."

"Then I will read them to you." She pulled out her reading glasses and squinted. "'His playing rises from the innermost recesses of his soul.' That was the *Miami Times*. 'He recalls a young Rostropovich.' And here is the *Palm Beach Post*. 'With the Rachmaninoff, he demonstrated himself to be an artist of great promise—'" She looked at him over the glasses. "I thought you hated the Rachmaninoff."

He didn't answer. Maud set the fax sheet down with a sigh and took off her glasses. "You're not my only client, you know."

He rose suddenly. "No, but I am your best."

He went to the kitchen to refill his coffee. When he came back, she was sitting there, hand under chin, staring out at the river. He sat down across from her.

"I'm sorry," he said.

She didn't look at him.

"I am not sleeping," he said. "I am not myself."

She finally looked over at him. "What are you taking?"

He shrugged. Maud pulled over his espresso and took a drink. He turned the fax sheet around and read it. "'An artist of great promise,'" he said wryly. "I'm thirty-six years old."

"Vous avez commencé tard dans la vie."

He hated it when she tried to speak French. Her Manchester accent made it sound especially ugly. "I know I started late," he said.

Maud was quiet. They had had this argument before. He wanted her to book him into better concerts, more prestigious venues. She kept telling him he had to be patient. He was tired of being patient.

"I think this is a good time to talk about what's coming up," Maud said. She dug into her briefcase again and pulled out her BlackBerry. He watched her in irritation. He hated all the little technical things everyone was using now. He kept track of all his appointments in a bound book from the Corto Moltedo boutique in the Palais Royal. The only reason he had a cell phone was because Maud had insisted. She had also bought him a small notebook computer so he could get email. He hated getting the emails from her; it was like being on a leash. But once he discovered he could use the notebook to download music or even watch videos of performances, he didn't mind it so much.

On the plane from Dallas, he had spent an hour watching a grainy black-and-white video from 1954 of Casals playing the Bach Suite No. 1. Just the man and his cello alone in the stark shadows of an ancient Catalan monastery.

"They want you to teach a master class at the Forum de Vioncello in Madrid," Maud said.

He looked up. "I don't teach."

"Laurent—"

"It's useless. They are all idiots. No, tell them no."

She scrolled through the BlackBerry. He watched her, drumming his long fingers on the table.

"That is all you have?" he asked finally. "I need things to do."

"The season is ending, Laurent." She paused. "Well, there is that invitation from I Solisti Veniti in Padua. Three concerts. But you told me you didn't want to travel after Miami."

He was staring out the window at the trees. The leaves were losing their gold color. Winter was coming, and with it would come the closed-in feeling he always got this time of year. The sky turned the color of pewter and he could almost feel its weight. And now, in the last few years, it had become even worse, this claustrophobia, as if everything were tightening around him, choking off his air. That girl last January, the one he had garroted in a rage—that was the first time he had lost control. She had been a mistake; it had been a mess.

It hit him in that instant. That was why he had killed the girl in Miami. It had been a signal. It was his instincts telling him he needed to get back in control. And perhaps he needed to find new grounds again. Too much blood had been spilled in Paris. It was too close to home. He had to go somewhere else.

Italy.

"Tell them yes," he said.

Maud looked up from her BlackBerry and smiled. "I'll email them today."

"And Spain," he said.

She stared at him. "What?"

"I want to go to Spain as well."

"But you said you won't teach," Maud said.

He looked out the window at the green water of the Seine. "I need a change of scenery."

As I watched him walk toward me, I was struck for the first time with an image of myself thirty years into the future. While it was obvious from the day she was born that Mandy was the beneficiary of my mother's fair beauty, I seemed to be a slowly emerging replica of Dr. Martin Lowell Owens.

At sixty-three years old, he was a large man with unruly white hair and a ruddy face that most people read as good health. I knew, though, that it came from his love of fine brandy and the stress of being the South's most renowned cardiac surgeon.

Anxious to be where he needed to be, Dad was walking a few feet ahead of my mother, Ginny. She was clutching a Chanel bag and looking like a woman stranded in a war-torn country. I knew my father loved her deeply, but I couldn't believe that at this moment he was not right by her side, supporting her as they took this long walk down the crowded Miami airport concourse.

I remembered a time when I was thirteen and I had struck out at the Little League championships to end the game, causing my team to lose. On the way back to the car, I wanted his arm, but he rushed on ahead. Every Saturday, he made time to see my games, but he was always in a hurry afterward, always busy running off to repair someone else's heart.

My father stopped in front of me, taking note of my disheveled appearance but saying nothing. He turned briefly to bring my mother up to his side, then looked back at my face. His expression was a mixture of grief and shock. And I thought I could also see a faint, underlying current of blame. Somehow that didn't surprise me.

My mother leaned against my father as if all of her strength had been left back in North Carolina. Her honey-colored upswept hair was perfectly styled, as it had been for the last twenty years. She had managed a coat of lipstick but nothing else about her was as I remembered. It was as if she had died a small death in the space of one day. I gave her a long hug, then faced my father.

"We should get our bags," Dad said. "I'm sure there are many things to take care of."

"There isn't anywhere you need to be at the moment, Dad," I said.

He looked beyond me, across the crowded terminal. Gray light from the high windows caught him full in the face, bringing into vivid focus every wrinkle, whisker and eyelash. Tears filmed his red-rimmed eyes. I had never seen my father cry and I didn't want to now.

"I've reserved a room for you at the Bayfront Hotel, in Coconut Grove," I said. "It's not far from my place. I can take you there now and you can settle in, get some dinner."

"Good," he said. "Good."

Dad reached back to take Mom's arm and, with his briefcase clutched in his other hand, stepped around me and started toward the baggage claim area.

The lower concourse was worse than upstairs. People were everywhere, delayed by the hurricane. I stared at the slowly circling carousel and finally closed my eyes to calm my pounding headache.

"Matt, how long will this take?" my mother asked.

I looked down at her. "A while, Mom. Do you want to sit down?"

Mom looked around but if there was an available bench, I was sure she couldn't see it. She was only five-three.

"Come on, I'll find you somewhere," I said.

"She's fine where she is," Dad said.

I stared at my father, stunned at his tone. But just as I opened my mouth to argue, I realized that his wanting to keep Mom here wasn't about her faint condition. He didn't trust me not to lose her, too, in what he once called "this hellhole of a place" I'd chosen as my home.

We were on 836, a few miles from the airport, and stuck behind an eighteen-wheeler. I couldn't fit everyone in my Corvette, so Nora had lent me her RAV.

"How bad is this hurricane going to get?" Dad asked.

"It's turning northeast," I said. "This should be the worst of it."

Dad watched the road for a minute, then cleared his throat. "So, tell me again what happened last night," he said.

I gathered patience. I had already spent hours at the Miami Beach PD retelling the story to the Latina detective whose name I couldn't remember at the moment. Nothing I had given Nora was worth anything to the new detective, it seemed. She needed her own version. Now my father did, too.

"We were at a club. She was on the dance floor for one

more dance before we left. When the song ended, I couldn't find her."

"And this was what time?"

I tried not to hesitate. "Almost two A.M."

"Were you drinking?"

I glanced at my mother in the rearview mirror. She was watching me, also wanting an answer. Suddenly I was in my crashed Opel again, blood trickling into my eyes, Mandy's whimpering in my ears.

"Yes," I said. "We both had a few. It was a nightclub. People drink in nightclubs. But Mandy wasn't drunk."

Dad ignored my edgy tone. "Have the police questioned the boy she was dancing with?"

"He was the first person I went looking for," I said, "but he disappeared, too. The cops have a description of him and a partial name. They'll find him."

"What did he look like?"

I knew my father was not a bigot, but I wasn't sure at this moment how he would react to the idea that Mandy's last dance partner had been a black man in a sports jersey. My father had many black colleagues, but he was still a descendent of a Confederate general and lived in an all-white gated community.

He'd hear it from the police later, but for now, I gave him only a general description and reminded him that there was a widespread search for the man even as we drove.

"I want to see her," Dad said.

I was so stunned I nearly lost control of the wheel. "What?"

"I want to see my daughter," Dad said again. "Take me to the morgue."

"I already officially identified her, Dad," I said. "There's no reason for you to go down there."

"I need to see my daughter."

"Why? Don't you believe me that she's dead?"

In the sudden quiet that followed, everything seemed to close in on me—the moist, warm air of the car, the steady thud of the wipers, the pummeling of the rain. I kept my eyes straight ahead, staring at the watery glow of red taillights.

The image of Mandy lying on that dirty ballroom floor came back to me. I had no idea how she looked now, if they had cleaned her up, wiped away the blood, combed her hair. But I had this sickening vision of her on a steel table, covered with a paper sheet, her skin pasty, her lips blue.

"I want to see my daughter," Dad said again. "I'm asking you to make that happen, son."

I pulled my cell phone from my pocket and dialed Nora.

It wasn't called the morgue anymore. In fact, it didn't even look like one. The Joseph H. Davis Center for Forensic Pathology was a huge modern building, set at 1 Bob Hope Road and guarded by a bronze cannon salvaged from a Spanish galleon that sank off Miami four hundred years ago. Inside, there was nothing to hint at the grisly work that took place all day and often into the night. With its air-freshener smell, Florida landscapes, mauve sofas and plush palms, it looked like a four-star hotel.

"Are we meeting the medical examiner?" Dad asked.

"No," I said. "We'll be seeing one of the assistants."

I sat my mother down on a sofa and went to the desk. When I told the receptionist that Detective Brinkley had called on behalf of the Owens family, her face softened with sympathy.

She made a phone call and we waited in the deserted lobby. Dad stood near the door, reading the morgue's mission statement. Mom's eyes were vacant and dull, her hands gripping her purse.

"Mr. Owens?"

I turned to greet the man coming through the double doors but my father had already stepped forward to extend a hand. The ME's assistant was a small black man with a cap of gray hair.

"You don't have a police officer with you?" he asked.

"No," Dad said.

"Then I must advise you, sir, that a person's visit to a deceased loved one can—"

"I'm a surgeon, sir," Dad said. "I assure you, I don't need anyone to hold my hand. Please take me to Amanda Owens."

The assistant looked at me, and I gave him a small nod. If I couldn't talk Dad out of this, this man wasn't going to be able to.

"I'll stay here with Mom," I said.

I watched them until the doors closed behind them, then went and sat down next to my mother on the sofa. She had her wallet open to a picture. It was of Mandy in front of our home, wearing a hot-pink shirt and white shorts. Her smile projected the sheer joy of being sixteen and beautiful. It reminded me how she had looked those last moments on the dance floor. *One more dance, Bear.*

"I can't take my eyes off her," Mom whispered.

I wrapped my arm around my mother's shoulders. She felt small and fragile and I pulled her closer, finally finding the courage to say the words that had been on my lips for hours.

"I'm so sorry," I whispered.

Mom touched my cheek. "Oh, no, Matty," she whispered. "You mustn't blame yourself."

"But if only—"

"Hush, Matty," Mom said. "Amanda wouldn't want you to do this. She loved you so much."

I lowered my head against my mother's shoulder, but I didn't cry. My mom was gripping my hand like I was the only thing standing between her and the abyss of loss. And I realized that I was now her only child.

"Mr. Owens."

The assistant was waving me back into the hallway. I excused myself from my mother and followed the man down the long hallway.

The man stopped at an open doorway. "There," he said softly. "I thought you might want to comfort your father."

When I looked inside the room, I felt a small tearing in my chest. Mandy was lying on a table, her body draped with a white sheet. Her head was propped on a metal brace, creating a sharp, perfect profile and a cascade of damp blond hair. Her skin wasn't pasty white but a soft pink, her lips an odd shade of raspberry.

I didn't see my father right away, then his head came into view just over Mandy's shoulder. I realized he was sitting on a stool on the other side of the table. His cheeks were streaked with tears, his lips moving in what I assumed was prayer. And although his eyes were open, I sensed he hadn't seen me come in.

I walked around the table to him and waited for him to acknowledge me, but he didn't. He was intent on Mandy, smoothing her hair from her forehead, his whisperings now audible.

It wasn't a prayer. He was talking to her about the day she was born. I knew because I had heard the same story many times from my mother. How her arrival had interrupted the Tar Heels–Blue Devils game. The frantic drive to University Hospital in a rare southern snowstorm. The short labor of thirty minutes, because, as my mother had always said, her "little girl was anxious to get living."

His story finished, Dad lowered his head to the table and started to cry.

"Bunny," he whispered. "My little Bunny."

I bent down, wrapped my arms around my father's broad shoulders and closed my eyes. When I opened them, I found myself staring at Mandy's face and, for the first time, felt no need to turn away. I wanted to burn every detail of her into my memory.

8

The office was almost deserted when I got there. I had been working from home most of the last two years, so I had forgotten how quiet things could be at eight in the morning.

After the scene in the morgue yesterday, after depositing my parents in their hotel, I had gone home and gotten as close to drunk as I could on the half bottle of scotch I had stashed at my place. When the scotch didn't work, I added a Vicodin left over from an old touch football injury, and I finally drifted off listening to Elvis Costello's *Goodbye Cruel World*.

When I woke up sometime after five, I was curled in the oversize La-Z-Boy, the Bose earphones still on my head and dark shapeless dreams in my brain.

Now I was at the office. Because there was nowhere else to go.

There were a couple guys tucked in their cubicles but they were working Starbucks lattes instead of the phones. It occurred to me, around the edges of my consciousness, that it wasn't just the early hour that accounted for the emptiness of the newsroom.

The paper had been going through spasms of downsizing for the last five years as circulation and ad revenue shrank. Even though I seldom came into the office these days, I knew how bad it was. I got the emails inviting me to the pink-slip parties.

The lucky ones got buyouts, but the latest had just been axed. In the ten years I had been here, the editorial staff had gone from three hundred to one fifty. Bureaus had been closed, editions abandoned, deadlines compromised.

I had survived, so far. I was one of three reporters left on the I-team, but investigative journalism cost time, money and patience. I knew that when the next round of cuts came down from the twelfth floor, my name might be on the list.

I think that was part of the reason I didn't come into the office anymore. It was hard to watch something you love die the death of a million little cuts.

The receptionist looked up as I flashed my ID badge.

"You want a paper?"

Through the fuzz of my brain, I realized she was holding a copy of that morning's *Times*. I went back to get it, thanking her. The paper was warm, with that mossy melted-plastic smell I loved.

I made my way past the business department and through what used to be the arts and entertainment sections. My cubicle was its usual messy nest. Towers of yellowed newspapers. A dead plant with a deflated balloon that someone had sent me for my birthday six months ago. A calendar still stuck on February. A crusted Dunkin' Donuts travel mug that I had given up for lost.

I threw the mug and plant in the trash and sat down. The computer monitor was coated with dust. I used a sleeve to wipe it clean and powered it up.

After logging in, I just sat there, staring at the computer. I had no idea what I was doing there, but it was better than staring at the walls of my cottage or going to the hotel to watch my mother turn into a ghost.

As I swiveled slowly away from the screen, my eyes fell on the copy of the *Times*. The story was there at the bottom of the front page, along with a small color photograph of Mandy. She was smiling. It took me a moment to realize it was the photo I had given to the cop back on the beach.

At least they had cropped me out.

The story was written by Jeannie Laughlin, a young woman who had been brought in from the community news office to take over my old cop beat. Jeannie had called me last night.

I'm sorry, Matt, but I have to ask you—

You need a quote, right, Jeannie?

What I really need is to talk to your parents. I called their home in Raleigh but—

Leave them alone, Jeannie.

Matt, come on, you know that Darcy wants—

Don't go near my parents. I'll give you a fucking quote, but you don't go anywhere near my mom and dad, you understand?

The call had made me remember something I had wanted to forget. It was my first week on the cop beat. I had to call the parents of a fifteen-year-old girl who had fallen off a horse at camp and broken her neck. My job was to get a quote. But no one had told them yet that their kid had died. I had gotten there first.

A part of me understood that this wasn't Jeannie's fault. She had fought hard to make it to the mainsheet. But I also knew exactly how this whole thing had gone down.

Sometime after Mandy's body was found, a computer feed had come into the office from the Miami Beach police. By nine A.M. Jeannie had fed the first details onto the *Miami Times* web page. There hadn't been much but it didn't matter. The battle for readers was now on the Internet, not the streets. What mattered was who got it posted the fastest. The *Times* was competing against bloggers and titty galleries. It was all about clicks now, not journalism or taste or decency.

Mandy's body probably hadn't even made it to the medical examiner's office before that smiling picture of her made it to the web. I hadn't watched any TV, but I was pretty sure that by the noon news, they had jumped on board. A pretty young blond tourist murdered on South Beach was juicy stuff.

I picked up the paper and started to read.

An unnamed source in the Miami Beach PD had revealed that Mandy was stabbed with "an ice pick–like instrument" and that cops were searching for a "person of interest."

There was a paragraph that identified me as the victim's brother and as a *Times* employee, but Jeannie hadn't used my quote. To be honest, I couldn't remember what I had given her.

The more I read, the tighter the knot in my stomach grew. Jeannie had managed to contact a few of Mandy's college friends. The quotes broke my heart. I tossed the paper aside.

I turned back to the computer. The cursor was blinking slowly, like a heartbeat on a medical screen. I watched it for a long time, then positioned my fingers on the keys. I started to type.

BY MATT OWENS

I didn't understand her grief then, that mother whose toddler had disappeared from the playground and was found dead in a drainage ditch four days later. I covered the story but I never understood her pain when she told me, "I only looked away for a moment."

"What the hell are you doing?"

I spun around. Darcy Tuchman was standing behind me. I hit SAVE and CLOSE and the screen went blank.

Darcy parked a big hip on the edge of my desk and stared down at me over her glasses.

"Too late. I saw it," she said. "I'll repeat the question. What the hell are you doing?"

"I have to write this, Darcy."

"Well, you can write it but I'm not going to print it."

I massaged my neck and closed my eyes. When I felt her hand on my shoulder, I looked up.

"My office," she said.

It took every bit of my waning strength to lift myself out of the chair and follow her through the newsroom. Darcy's office took up some prime east-side real estate, with big windows that offered a commanding view of Biscayne Bay. Hurricane Jackie was now a depression heading to the Carolinas and the sun had come out in full force, making my eyes hurt.

Darcy pointed to the sofa and I sank down into it. She headed toward her desk, and I watched her as she rifled through some papers. She was sixty-something, silver haired. She was the one who, ten years ago, had seen something in my sports writing and asked me to come work cops for the *Times*. She was the only person in the newsroom I trusted to edit my stuff.

She took off her glasses, letting them dangle by the purple beaded cord around her neck.

"I'm sorry about your sister, Matt."

I slumped back against the cushions, nodding. "Thanks."

"How are you holding up?"

I kept my eyes trained on the windows.

"Never mind," Darcy said. "Stupid question."

I couldn't bring myself to look at her.

"Matt," she said softly. "I don't think you should be here right now."

It took me a few moments to work up the guts to face her. "Where should I go, Darce?" I said.

"Home."

I shook my head slowly.

"You can't work this story, Matt," she said.

"Why not?"

"Do I have to tell you this?"

When I didn't reply, she came out from behind her desk and sat down next to me on the sofa.

"First, it isn't your story, it's Jeannie's," she said. "And second, you're too close to it."

"I can write a good first-person feature."

"This isn't therapy." She must have felt me draw away because she let out a long sigh. "Sorry, that was low."

Her phone rang but she ignored it.

"You're forcing me to be a bitch here, Matt, but I don't care," she said. "I want you to take two weeks off."

My eyes shot up to her. "You're ordering me out of here?"

"If I have to suspend you, I will. For your own good."

I leaned forward and put my head in my hands. I could smell ink on my hands, hear a phone ringing.

Darcy's hand was on the back of my neck, cool and gentle. Finally, I felt her get up off the sofa but I didn't move. A moment later, the lights in the office went out. When I looked up, Darcy was standing by the door.

"Stay here for a while. Get some rest," she said. She left, closing the door behind her.

I sat there for a moment, then slowly unwound my body onto the sofa. I closed my eyes, and when sleep finally whispered in my ear, it came in the voice of Elvis Costello.

I was a fine idea at the time.

Now I'm a brilliant mistake.

9

Later that day, I finally worked up the courage to go to the hotel to see my parents. The first hour was spent sitting around their room, then another two hours at the hotel restaurant, where we picked at our salads and sipped water. My mother rambled on about the funeral arrangements back in Raleigh and my father complained about how the ME was dragging his feet on the autopsy.

But worse were the moments of silence, when the air grew thick with grief and blame, so palpable I felt like I was suffocating.

I finally extricated myself by feigning a migraine, something I'd had as a teenager but hadn't experienced since arriving in Miami. I hit the liquor store on the way home for a fresh bottle of scotch.

I spent the rest of the day curled in the La-Z-Boy, the TV tuned to the Home Shopping Network with the sound off to be sure I wouldn't get any news.

It was past ten when I heard a knock at my door. The emails of condolences from coworkers had flowed in, but tonight I had made a decision not to answer computer, phone or door. Then I heard Nora's voice.

"It's me, Matt. Open up."

I moved on stiff legs to the door, taking my scotch with me.

Thirty-eight hours had passed since Mandy's body had been found and Nora looked as if she'd worked every minute of it. Limp jeans, smudged mascara and dull hair. She held a thin manila folder and a small paper bag.

"You're drunk," she said.

"I'm medicated."

She came in and took the glass from my hand. I didn't protest, slumping back down into the La-Z-Boy. I saw Nora staring at it. I knew she was remembering the day she had given it to me for my twenty-ninth birthday.

I was remembering a lot of things about us in that moment. Good things. Like squeezing into the La-Z-Boy together to watch the Dolphins. Like making love with such ferocity that I could barely walk after. Like the routine we had every time I was coming home from assignment. I always called from the airport and asked if she would pick me up. And she always answered, "I'll be there."

Then, after one too many betrayals, one too many times when I backed away from the intimacy, she had answered my airport call with, "I can't be there for you anymore, Matt."

Nora looked down at me, then drained the glass in one long gulp. The sudden fire of straight scotch flushed her face with color. Even exhausted and irritated, she was still beautiful.

I had to look away.

"I'm on thin ice here," she said. "I only have this information because I know people at the Miami Beach PD. It's not my case. It belongs to Detective Molina."

"I know."

"I have her permission to share some things with you but I won't be able to answer many questions about where the investigation is at."

I nodded, my eyes going to the file in Nora's hand.

She opened it and handed me stapled papers. My premed classes had given me just enough knowledge to understand most of the medical jargon, and I had seen other autopsy reports from my days on the cop beat. But my mouth went dry as I read one detail: The only wound was a small round hole just under the sternum, where something long and narrow had been thrust in and upward to puncture Mandy's heart.

I cleared my throat and looked up at Nora. "Jeannie's story in the *Times* said it was an ice pick."

"An ice pick or something like it," Nora said, sitting down across from me.

I looked back at the report. The illustration of the human body had been marked with two other circles. One was around the figure's pubic area, along with the words "SEVERE TRAUMA TO VULVA AND VAGINAL AREA."

Horrible images exploded in my brain but I forced myself to stay detached and professional. "She was raped?"

"Yes, but he left no semen," Nora said.

"He used a condom?"

"We don't think so," Nora said. "It looks like he ejaculated outside of her body. They found semen on the floor near her body."

"So you have DNA from him?"

"Yes, but he's not in the system."

I was disappointed that there was no instant match, but having the DNA was something. When they did find a suspect, the match would make a conviction a slam dunk. And the bastard would fry.

I refocused on the autopsy report, studying the other small circle. It was drawn on the figure's left arm and labeled as a needle mark. I knew Mandy had never done an illegal drug in her life.

"Do they know what she was injected with?" I asked.

"Gamma hydroxybutyrate."

"The date-rape drug?"

"Yes, we did a rush tox screen. Based on your statement and the injection point, the ME thinks she was stuck with a needle on the dance floor."

"But wouldn't the effects of injected GHB be almost instantaneous? Wouldn't she have passed out right there in the bar?"

"Not necessarily," Nora said. "It's possible she was given just enough to make her drowsy. In that case, she would've appeared drunk and could have easily been led away."

God, why hadn't I watched her more closely?

"Any leads on the Dolphins man?" I asked.

"Not yet," Nora said. "Officers canvassed the clubs last night with the sketch you gave us, but so far, nothing."

I stared at the faceless drawing for a few more seconds, then handed the report back to Nora. I knew enough about GHB to know that Mandy was probably out of it by the time the bastard raped her and may not have felt much. Maybe she hadn't felt much fear, either. And hopefully, she never saw the ice pick in her killer's hand.

I could not imagine sharing any of this information with my father, even though I knew he would find out eventually. If not from the medical examiner, then from some jerk with a microphone who would ask him how he felt about his daughter getting stabbed with an ice pick.

"Does Jeannie Laughlin have the autopsy report yet?" I asked.

"I don't know what's been released," Nora said. "But my

guess is they'll release the rape, the fact she was posed naked and, of course, the sketch of the black man."

"Do you have any crime scene photos with you?" I asked.

"Some, but none of Amanda," she said. "I didn't think you'd want to see her that way again."

I nodded slowly. "Can I see what you have?"

Nora pulled out a short stack of eight-by-tens and held them out to me. They were exceptionally sharp and vivid in color, picking up the blue and green of the terrazzo floor, a faded mural of a beach scene on one wall, the glint of the old chandelier. One photo, which caught the shades of the rainy morning sky through the dusty windows, looked grotesquely beautiful.

I continued to sift through the photos, stopping at a shot that included a partial photo of Mandy's head and another that captured her pink toenails. But for the most part, there was nothing to see in the pictures but fast-food trash, crumbling plaster, broken glass, loose screws, bent nails and torn plastic sheeting.

"I have one other thing for you," Nora said. "As you know, we haven't found her purse or her clothing but we found this near her body."

Nora was holding Mandy's pink iPod and I just stared at it. Somehow, for a split second, seeing it brought Mandy back into the room for me, back to life. Then, like a punch to my chest, her spirit was gone.

"We think it might have fallen from her purse or her killer dropped it in his rush to get out," Nora said. "Detective Molina said it's been processed and that I could return it you. If this were my case, no way would I release a personal effect like this so soon, but it's not my case. So, this is yours, if you want it."

Of course I wanted it. I took it in my hand as if it was the most precious thing on earth, and at that moment, it was. It was still covered in black fingerprint dust and I rubbed it on my sleeve to clean it. It didn't help.

"I need to go," Nora said. She stood and held out a hand for the photos.

I gathered them up as I rose. "I'm keeping them."

Nora's eyes snapped with annoyance. "Those are the property of the department," she said. "The last thing I need is for them to fall into the hands of a reporter who's lost his objectivity."

I wondered if she knew that Darcy had ordered me to take time off. "That's a cheap shot, Nora, even for you. What, you think I'm no better than some asshole blogger?"

"Give me my photos."

"No."

"I can get fired if I let you have those."

I considered that. If the district attorney was going to come after me, I'd take my chances. But I wasn't going to cause Nora any more grief. Before she could say anything else, I went to my office and locked the door. I slapped the first picture on the scanner glass and hit PRINT.

"I know what you're doing, damn it!" Nora called from the hall.

She pounded on the door for almost a minute, then gave up. When I had copied all the photos, I hid them in my desk drawer and took the originals back to Nora. She was standing by the front door, arms crossed, eyes so dark with anger they brimmed with tears. I felt like shit but I didn't care.

"I won't tell anyone where I got them," I said.

She snatched the pictures from my hand and left my cottage. I stayed at the open door until I heard her start her car. I knew she could have arrested me and as I went back inside, I wondered why she hadn't.

I poured myself another scotch and sat down with Mandy's iPod. When I touched the dial, the screen lit up, showing the main menu.

I took a long drink of scotch, my thumb light on the iPod dial as I called up the playlist. I just wanted to see something that had been part of my sister's life, because I'd always felt that music was part of us all. It was something people discovered a preference for early on, like finding the right beat to complement their inner rhythms. For me, it had started with the punk rockers of the eighties, bands like The Clash and the Sex Pistols. They had led me backward to Zappa, the Velvet Underground and the Stones.

Mandy's music was as foreign to me as Irish sea chanties. As I scrolled through the songs by the likes of Shakira, Ke$ha and Lady Gaga, I was struck with a strange pang of sadness, different from the profound grief I had been feeling.

It took me a second to understand what it was. It wasn't just the loss of my sister. It was the loss of things she would never know. Like seeing Venice with someone she loved. Holding her squirming newborn. Finding her place in the world.

I wiped my eyes and started to turn the iPod off so I could finish my drink and go to bed. But a final impulse had taken hold of me.

I twirled the dial to see the last song that had been played. It was sick, this need to know the last song she had heard. But I couldn't help it.

The display came up.

"Too Much Blood" by the Rolling Stones.

I stared at it for a second, started to turn the iPod off, then stopped. It didn't make sense. My sister hated old rock. She had told me a hundred times in the car to turn it off, and just this past week she had rifled through my CDs and made fun of my "old fart music." I wasn't sure she could even name any of the Stones.

I wasn't familiar with "Too Much Blood," but suddenly I needed to hear this song that was older than Mandy was. I grabbed my headphones and stepped out onto the patio.

Seconds later, I was listening to Mick Jagger. For a few stanzas it didn't sound much different than most of their other stuff, Jagger shout-singing against a ragged beat. But then suddenly he wasn't singing about dancing and making love anymore.

A girlfriend in Paris . . . cut off her head . . . took her bones to the Bois de Boulogne.

I shut my eyes, feeling sick. But I had to hear it all. Jagger finally wrapped up the song with a repugnant refrain.

Too much blood.

I ripped off the headphones and stood there, the night air cool against my wet face.

10

Byte Me was an electronics store on South Dixie Highway, tucked between a pawnshop and discount shoe store.

I discovered the store when my old Dell laptop crashed and took three weeks' worth of work with it. A tech named Andy had managed to salvage my notes from the infected hard drive and save my investigative piece. I had been back to the store several times since, once to have Andy talk me into buying a new Mac and at least five times after that whenever I needed help learning to use the thing. He was the best geek I knew.

Now I was hoping he was smart enough to figure out how the Rolling Stones song had gotten onto Mandy's iPod.

Andy was behind the counter, bent over the guts of a PC. On the shelf above his head was a television playing a Three Stooges movie with the sound off.

He heard the bell on the door and looked up at me. He wore magnifying goggles and his hair was gelled up in the shape of a fan and sprayed with a rainbow of colors.

"Heya, Matt," he said, pulling off his goggles. Then his face sobered. "I read about your sister online, man. I'm sorry, really sorry. That's just so, so sad, man."

"Yeah, thanks."

I pulled out the iPod and laid it on the counter. "Can you

get into the hard drive of this thing and tell me anything about the downloaded songs?"

"Most guys couldn't, but I can," he said. "What do you need to know?"

"I'm not sure," I said. "Can you just print me out a report or something that tells me where the songs came from and when they were downloaded?"

"I can try."

Andy picked up the iPod and started toward the rear of the store. Then he turned back. "What's all this black stuff?"

"Fingerprint dust."

"Oh wow. This belong to your sister?"

"Yeah."

He gave me a tight nod, then disappeared behind a beaded curtain. I stood at the counter, watching the Stooges for a moment. Then I pulled a folder from my pocket.

It was a Delta ticket to Raleigh for tomorrow morning. My father had given it to me at lunch an hour ago. The fact that he had bought it for me pissed me off. I had planned on going home, of course. But Dad buying me a ticket seemed his way of making damn sure I was.

I looked at the departure time. It was ten thirty, the same flight Mandy would have taken home. Then with a stab to my heart I realized she would be on the flight with us.

I stuffed the ticket back in my pocket. Looking for something to think about besides the funeral, I studied the gadgets in the display case—MP3 players, iPods, iPads, Kindles, CD players, refurbished iPhones, paper-thin battery chargers, BlackBerrys and other shiny things that jumped to life with the touch of a finger or the sound of a human voice.

"Here we are," Andy said.

He came back to the counter with the iPod and a sheet of paper. It was a printout of the file structure on the iPod's hard drive. It listed every song Mandy had downloaded in the last year. The last song was "Too Much Blood."

Date downloaded: October 21, 5:22.

I stared at it. October 21 was two days ago, the day Mandy disappeared.

"Is this time A.M. or P.M.?" I asked Andy.

"It's listed in military time, so that makes it 5:22 in the morning."

At five in the morning, Mandy was already in the hands of her killer.

"This has to be wrong, Andy," I said.

"I suppose the internal clock could've been screwed up at the time," Andy said. "But that would be pretty weird, since it's accurate now. Someone would've had to mess with it before downloading that song, then reset it after. That would take an expert tech. Plus, why would anyone want to disguise the time they downloaded something?"

I showed the printout to Andy, pointing to the Stones song. "Is there any other way this could be wrong?"

"Not that I can tell."

Five twenty-two in the morning. Mandy was unconscious or dead. The only person who could have downloaded this song was her killer.

I looked again at the printout. "This doesn't tell me where the song came from," I said.

"You mean like an iTunes account name?" Andy asked.

"Yes."

"There's no way to tell from the download who owns the original music account," Andy said. "All I can tell you is this iPod was connected to a computer at 5:22 A.M. and the song was added."

I was thinking that if the killer transferred the song while in that ballroom, there might be a traceable wireless connection. "What about an IP address?" I asked.

"I doubt it," Andy said. "Plus, you got to understand, Matt, you don't need to be on the Internet to download a song from a computer to an iPod. That song could have been on the source computer for weeks or years."

"You're sure about all this?" I asked.

"Well, maybe there's an expert who could tell you more, but I can't. The iPod is a great little gadget but limited in its internal intelligence."

I rubbed my eyes and sighed. Andy looked disappointed that he hadn't been more of a help.

"Whoever downloaded this song killed my sister," I said. "I can't believe with all this technology there's no way to trace him."

Andy nodded in sympathy. "Even if we could trace a music account, if your guy is illegally ripping music, you'll never find him. He might as well be invisible."

I picked up the iPod. If I turned it over to Nora or Detective Molina, they would have access to the techs in the FBI, who might able to expose more data. But if Andy was right, no amount of fancy technology was going to lead anyone to Mandy's killer.

I was quiet, looking now at the ugly black smudges on the pink iPod. "Do you have anything that will clean this?" I asked Andy.

Andy quickly produced several iKlear towelettes. I carefully cleaned the black fingerprint dust from the iPod. I knew I'd have to tell Nora what I had learned. But right now, I wasn't going to let go of the only piece of Mandy I had left.

11

The scent of gardenias filled the room, so thick I could taste the sweetness on my tongue. Someone had mentioned to someone else that Mandy loved gardenias, so that's what people had sent. I had no idea if Mandy liked gardenias or not, but I did know her favorite flower was the white rose.

It had been her favorite since she was seven years old and saw Princess Diana's funeral on TV. I had gotten a letter from her when I was at college telling me that when she died she wanted white roses around her, too. I remembered this too late to stave off the onslaught of gardenias, but when I ordered my arrangement, I made sure it was white roses, a blanket of them to cover her casket.

I took a sip of my water and looked around the visitation room.

There was organ music coming from somewhere. It was vaguely familiar, but I had long ago forgotten most of the hymns I'd learned as a child. What I could remember were the walks home from church, Mandy in her ruffled baby dresses, me in my clip-on ties. Mom and Dad would stroll ahead and I would drag Mandy along next to me. Sometimes, she would tire and whine and Dad would ask me to carry her. I complained, but secretly I didn't mind. Mandy liked being on my shoulders. She said it made her feel big. I never told anyone it made me feel big, too.

I looked around at the visitors. Many of my parents' friends were here, and I had suffered through the receiving line, shaking the hands of men who still commented on how much I'd grown.

But it was the students I had been watching. There were probably thirty of them, a few showing up in jeans and casual shirts, unconcerned about etiquette or how they looked. They just wanted to say good-bye to a friend. I watched them as they filed by the casket, not ashamed to cry, not afraid to make a small joke or tell a funny story about Mandy. I admired them for that.

But I also pitied them. They were so naïve, so ignorant of what the world was really like. And how quickly, if you looked away for just a moment, things could change.

I needed some air. I stepped outside into a perfect North Carolina autumn day. Green grass, cobalt sky and flame-colored leaves that floated through the air like clouds of bright butterflies.

"Excuse me, are you Mandy's brother?"

The man was probably twenty, with broad shoulders and sandy hair.

"I'm Roger," he said. "Roger Washburn."

His gray eyes dulled with disappointment that I didn't know who he was.

"Roger Washburn," he said again. "I was Mandy's boyfriend."

I forced a smile. Mandy had never mentioned this kid but I wasn't going to tell him that.

"Yeah, sorry," I said. "Nice to meet you."

"She talked a lot about you," Roger said. "She really admired you."

I had difficulty finding my voice. "Thank you."

Roger fell silent, hands stuffed in his trousers. His suit was stylish and fit him well, and I figured he came from a little money. But I didn't think he was a serious prospect for Mandy. Had he been, she would have told me when she was in Miami. He probably saw her as most young men did, charming, pretty, with an energy that pulled others into her orbit. And if you were lucky enough to be noticed, she had a way of making you feel as if you were the most important person in her life, even when in reality, you were just another handsome face in a crowd.

"We'd only been seeing each other for a few weeks," Roger said. "But I think I was falling in love with her."

"Did you tell her?" I asked.

He shook his head. "I wasn't brave enough."

I couldn't resist. "Next time, when you feel it, say it. Don't wait until it's too late."

"Yes, sir."

Roger moved away from me and I saw my mother standing near a row of white cape jasmines. She was wearing a straight black dress with a high neck and long sleeves, her blond hair tucked under a pillbox hat with a net half veil. She was speaking with a woman I recognized as a colleague of Dad's.

When I walked over to her, Mom politely excused herself, took my hand and led me away. We walked across the lawn, leaves crunching under our feet, the warm breeze fluttering my mother's veil. Her hand felt small in mine, but her grip was tight. She smelled like powdered sugar and I realized that she had always smelled like that.

"This is a beautiful place," she said. "The grounds are lovely. Maybe we should've had the service down in the gardens. I heard they offer that."

"It'll be fine inside," I said.

Mom pulled me toward a stone bench near a fountain. I assumed she was tired, so I sat her down. She patted the bench and looked up at me.

"Sit with me, Matty."

For a few minutes, we were quiet.

"How are you holding up?" she asked finally.

"I'm okay," I said.

"You haven't had a drink since you've been home," she said.

I told her I had cut back, and for once it was the truth. I hadn't had a drop of booze since arriving in Raleigh two days ago, not even when I was alone. Maybe it was because I was afraid that if I drank, I would crumble. Or maybe I had more respect for my home, and my folks, than I realized. I wanted to believe it was the second reason.

"You know, you never sent that copy of your Pulitzer certificate you promised me," she said.

I was quiet, embarrassed that I couldn't even remember talking to her about it. It was the conversation with my father, when he dismissed my story—an investigative piece on pharmaceutical companies secretly paying doctors to use their patients as guinea pigs—that I could clearly remember.

"I'll send it to you when I get home, Mom," I said. "I promise."

She turned her attention to the funeral home. More people were arriving for the service. She didn't seem interested in going over to greet anyone.

"So, how is your novel coming along?" Mom asked. "The one about the young boy?"

Something else I had forgotten I shared with her. Two hundred pages that sat in my drawer, stalled at chapter thirty-three by writer's block. Or booze. Or something.

"I'm still working on it," I said. "I'll finish it one day."

"Don't wait too long," Mom said. "I'd like to read it before I pass on, you know."

I squeezed my mother's hand. I couldn't stand the thought of losing anyone else right then.

"So, when you go home, will you be working on Mandy's case with your friends at the police department?" Mom asked.

I thought about the iPod and the fact I still hadn't told Nora about it. "I don't know," I said.

"What about Nora, that police officer you were involved with?" Mom asked. "Wouldn't she help you?"

"We don't talk much anymore," I said.

Mom nodded. "I was sad when you told me you had broken the engagement."

"If I told you I broke it, I must've lied out of embarrassment," I said. "She ended it."

Mom was quiet for a moment. "I liked Nora. I always had the feeling she was good for you, Matt. I even . . ."

Her voice trailed off.

"Even what, Mom?"

"I had even hoped you would have children. I'd like to have grandkids someday."

I felt kicked in the gut, though I knew Mom didn't mean it that way. With Mandy gone, so was the dream of the towheaded grandbabies Mom had planned to let run amok through the big house.

The sun was dipping below the trees and I knew it must be near six. I had my short eulogy tucked in my jacket pocket. When Mom had asked me to deliver it, I had been afraid I wouldn't be able to get through it. But that autopilot feeling that had come over me back in Miami was still with me, and I was confident I wouldn't break down.

For two days now, the feeling had kept me going. Kept me going through long hours at the funeral home helping with Mandy's arrangements, the longer hours spent at home, mindlessly thanking people for coming, saying hello to people on the phone I didn't remember, stuffing yet another casserole into the refrigerator.

In a strange reversal of roles, I had become the strong one. And my father . . .

He performed the requisite role of grieving host. But afterward, when there were no more hands to shake, when the shadows in the huge house grew long, he shrank into a man I didn't recognize. He stood for long periods of time staring out at the dark yard or sitting alone in Mandy's bedroom. He ate only when my mother reminded him to. He spoke only when necessary. When he walked, I could hear the soft rattle of pill vials in his pants pockets.

"I'm worried about Dad," I said softly.

"I know," Mom said. "But he will be fine. It will take some time, but he will be fine."

Something in her voice made me turn to look at her. She had lifted her veil and for the first time today, I noticed how good she looked. I was about to ask her how she was doing when I saw the small silver cross around her neck. I remembered she had spent more than two hours at her church last night, finding peace and acceptance in the unfathomable. I knew that, in time, she would be okay. And that Dad would be okay because of her.

Mom laced her fingers through mine. We were quiet for a long time before she spoke. "When is your flight home?" she asked.

"Saturday."

"Maybe you should go home sooner."

The remark surprised me and for a moment I wondered if she was trying to push me away. But her fingers had tightened around mine as she had said it.

"Dad expects me to stay longer," I said.

"I'll talk to him," Mom said. "I think you need to be at home, with your friends."

"I don't know."

Mom brought my hand to her cheek and held it there for a moment. That powdery scent was everywhere, bringing a flood of memories and a grip to my heart.

"There's nothing you can do here, Matty," she said.

I couldn't bring myself to look at her. I had never felt really grounded in my life, but at that moment, even with my mother at my side, my father near, my childhood embracing me, I felt unbearably alone. Like the whole world was distant, absent, all but dead.

I heard someone calling to us. It was the minister, waving us toward the open doors of the funeral home.

It was time to say good-bye to my sister.

At seven on Thursday morning, I kissed Mom good-bye in the kitchen, embraced Dad in his study and caught a cab to the airport. By eleven, I was stuck in the Atlanta airport on my layover, delayed by a thunderstorm. I sat on the floor in a corner, playing solitaire on my laptop while I chewed on a rubbery ham and egg sandwich.

I was relieved to be out of the well of misery in Raleigh but I still couldn't get my parents out of my head. I realized how my perceptions of them had changed over the last few days and I wondered if any child ever really knew their parents until they were given the chance to view them through something other than a child's narrow lens.

I had, and what I saw surprised me. My father was not a miracle worker, nor the tyrant I had sometimes thought him. He was only a man, as easily wounded as any other. And my mother, whom I often pitied for playing the role of the suffering, self-sacrificing wife, was resolute, calm and loving. It would be her strength that would help my father find his.

A glance up at the departure board told me that my flight to Miami was still delayed. I considered closing the laptop and listening to some music but the only thing I had with me was Mandy's iPod.

I don't know why I had brought it with me to Raleigh. But its presence was like a weight around my neck that was growing heavier with each day.

Too much blood.

Why was that damn song on the iPod? And what did it mean? I stared at the solitaire cards on my computer for a moment, then brought up a new screen. I went to the *Miami Times* website and scrolled for fresh news about the investigation into Mandy's murder, but there was nothing. I closed the site.

I was about to power down when an icon on my desktop caught my eye. I clicked on the LexisNexis icon, then typed in my user name and password. Within seconds, I was staring at the welcome screen for one of the most powerful search engines in the world.

My brain whirring, I typed in "HEADLINE serial killer ice pick."

That netted me fifty or so pages. The search had to be narrowed, so I added to the path "Rolling Stones music clues."

Now things were getting interesting. My screen was full of articles on murders with musical angles, along with an article about cults that had appeared in *Rolling Stone* magazine. I skipped that one and started scanning the others. A thirty-six-year-old woman bludgeoned in Oregon with an electric guitar. A coed raped, dismembered and dropped in a Dumpster behind a Michigan music store.

I skimmed a dozen more articles, then tried to narrow the search again, adding "rape masturbation." That got me mainly erotica and porn articles.

I laid my head back against the wall and tried to think of what else would get me closer to a crime resembling Mandy's.

The song—the damn song. I added "Too Much Blood."

That netted me nothing but general articles about the Rolling Stones and the song. I tried to remember the lyrics and a line about the Texas chain saw massacre came to my head. But I knew that would get hundreds of articles on the movies. So I tried "Texas" instead. Nothing stood out except the fact that a lot of women seemed to get murdered in that state.

Then I remembered another line from the song.

He had a girlfriend in Paris.

I changed the search code so I would get datelines and lead paragraphs, then typed in "murder rape Paris."

I found myself staring at an article in the *International Herald Tribune*, dateline Paris. A twenty-five-year-old American woman was murdered and left in a place called Le Moulin de Longchamp in the Bois de Boulogne.

Bois de Boulogne . . .

The same place mentioned in the song.

The story was short, offering only minimal information. The victim was Tricia Downey, from Houston, Texas, and she was in Paris alone on vacation. She had been found nude and had been raped. The only thing found at the scene was a cassette tape. The police had no suspects.

If there was a follow-up story, I couldn't find it. I paged back to the original article and read it again, hoping I would find a tidbit of information I had missed. But there was nothing.

Except now I noticed the date on the article. This woman had been killed last January.

I looked again to the departure monitor. My flight status still read DELAYED but six lines down I saw a Delta flight going to Paris.

The idea was crazy, the connection razor-thin. I didn't know the city, couldn't speak the language. How was I going to convince the French police that a murder in Miami could be related to a homicide that had happened in Paris nine months earlier? I didn't even know anyone in France.

Cameron Cohick.

We had worked together at the Fort Lauderdale paper when I was doing sports. He had left abruptly to follow his girlfriend who was going to Paris, and I had left to work at the *Miami Times* soon after. I remembered hearing later that he had ended up working for the *Herald Tribune*. But that had been almost ten years ago, and the *Herald Tribune* had offices all over Europe. Chances were he wasn't even in Paris anymore.

There's nothing you can do here, Matty.

Mom was right. There was nothing I could do there. But maybe there was something I could do in Paris.

I closed my laptop and stuffed it in the case. I paused. Passport. I needed my damn passport.

I ripped open the Velcro tab on the front and rummaged through the old papers. I pulled out the sliver of blue cardboard with the gold seal. Since being named to the *Times*'s investigative team, I had learned to keep the passport and a packed duffel ready to go on a moment's notice.

With budget cuts, I hadn't had a reason to use the passport for the last five years. Out of carelessness or disgust, I had abandoned it to the laptop case.

I opened the passport and let out a sigh of relief. It expired in less than three weeks.

A glance up at the departures board told me that the flight to Paris, with a connection through JFK, left in ninety minutes. I gathered up my bags and broke into a run.

12

When I exited the doors of Charles de Gaulle airport just after six in the morning, the cold took my breath away. I had gone home to Raleigh with only my sports coat, a couple shirts, one tie and underwear. When I left, it had been seventy degrees.

In Paris, it was maybe forty and had started to rain. I turned up the collar of my sports coat, hoisted up my laptop bag and duffel and went in search of a taxi.

Back in Atlanta, I had managed to get off a call to the *Herald Tribune* office before my flight left. It had been after seven P.M. in Paris, but I convinced a woman at the *Herald Tribune* that I needed to get an important message to Cameron Cohick. I wasn't sure the guy would even remember me. But when I had powered up my phone on arrival in Paris, I was relieved to see a text message from him.

MEET U @ CAFÉ LE SELECT
99 BLVD DU MONTPARNASSE

The cabdriver took the piece of paper on which I had written the address, grunted, and we sped off. I sank back in the seat and closed my eyes. I had gotten the last seat on the Delta flight connecting through JFK—a middle seat in coach in front of a cranky four-year-old—and despite the fact I was a white-knuckle flier, I had resisted the urge to drink. I hadn't even taken an Ambien. Now I was beyond exhaustion.

It was a full-blown rainstorm by the time the taxi stopped. I sat up, eyed the pink neon script spelling out "Le Select" and thrust some dollars at the cabbie. He responded with an angry rush of French but finally took the money. I ran through the cold rain to the café.

I paused inside to get a grip on my duffel. A fat gray tabby cat sprawled on the bar stared at me. Except for a couple drinking coffee in a corner and a waiter stacking glasses, the place was deserted. Ten years had passed since Cameron and I had last seen each other and I was looking for a beefy guy with long blond hair and glasses. The image frozen in my brain had him dressed in jeans and a Bob Marley T-shirt, slouching into the newsroom to file his rock concert review. When the wafer-thin man in a tan raincoat and Burberry scarf came forward, hand extended, it didn't register.

"Hey, Matt."

I blinked the grit from my eyes. "Cam?"

"It's me, man." His big smile creased his face, like one of those drama masks. "Lots of water under the bridge."

Our handshake migrated to a back pat. "I didn't recognize you without the glasses," I said, pulling back.

"Contacts. Good of you not to mention the thirty missing pounds."

"You look great, Cam."

"Wish I could return the compliment."

I laughed. I laughed because it all came back to me in that moment, that ease I had always felt around Cameron. Ours hadn't been a friendship, really—I'd never given it enough of a chance for that. It had been a bonding born of our mutual love of classic rock and roll. We had gone to a few concerts together, shared some beers, but then Cameron quit abruptly to follow a woman to France.

"You still with . . ." I couldn't retrieve her name.

"Suzanne? That flamed out fast. But I'll always have Paris." He smiled and picked up my duffel. "Come on, let's get you some breakfast and you can tell me more about that extremely weird email you sent."

We took a table out on the glassed-in terrace. Large heaters drove the chill from my bones and a good omelet, washed down with espresso, brought me back to the world of the living.

Cameron toyed with an unlit black cigarette while I talked. In the email I had fired off, I had told him only that I was investigating a possible link between a Miami murder and one here in Paris. I hadn't had the stomach to tell him about Mandy. But now it all just poured out, from those first awful minutes of panic to the moment I had seen her body on the ballroom floor.

He listened carefully, not saying a word, until I finally sat back in the chair, spent. Cameron waited until the waiter had brought me a fresh espresso before he spoke.

"I'm sorry, Matt. Truly I am," he said. "Sorry for the crack about how you look."

I held up a hand and looked out the window. The rain had let up some and the street had filled with people.

"I looked up that old murder in our archives," Cameron said, drawing my attention back. "There wasn't much more than what you already know. But I found more stuff in *Le Monde*."

He pulled a paper from his trench coat and gave it to me. I looked at it and handed it back. "I can't read French."

"Oh, sorry." Cameron took it back and scanned it quickly. "Her name was Tricia Downey. She was twenty-five and was here on vacation from Houston. She wasn't reported missing for about a week, until her parents contacted the police here. She was supposed to have been home in time for a family birthday party and when she didn't show up, someone figured out she had never returned from Paris. They eventually found her under Jeanne Dupont in the morgue here."

"Jeanne Dupont?"

"Oh, sorry. That's what they call Jane Doe here."

"There's a picture of her, right?"

Cameron nodded and handed it back. The article was printed off a computer and was blurry. The small black-and-white photograph showed a pretty woman with large eyes.

"What about where she was found?" I asked. "That Bois de something place."

"The Bois de Boulogne. It's a park in the western part of the city."

"Like in the Stones song, 'Too Much Blood,'" I said.

"'Too Much Blood'?" Cameron said, then there was a look of comprehension, and I knew he was trying to remember the lyrics.

"Do you know anything about where she was buried exactly?" I asked.

"She wasn't. She was found in an old windmill."

"A windmill?"

He nodded. "The Moulin de Longchamp. It's out by the racetrack. Paris was filled with windmills once."

I took one more look at the photograph, then folded the paper and put it in my breast pocket. My mind was humming, but despite the caffeine, I knew my body would shut down soon. I glanced at my watch and realized it was still on Miami time.

"What time is it?" I asked Cameron.

"Near nine." He tossed some euros in the saucer. I was about to protest when I remembered I hadn't changed my money yet. "Listen, my place is right around the corner," Cameron said. "Why don't you come over and crash for a while and then we can figure out where to go from here."

"Can we go to the windmill first?" I asked.

"Now?"

I nodded. "I don't know why, but I need to see it."

He studied me for a moment and I wondered what he was thinking. We had known each other only for a short while a long time ago, and I suspect he wondered what Mandy's murder had done to my mind. Hell, I was beginning to wonder the same thing.

He rose and stuffed his cigarettes in his raincoat. "Come on, my car's right outside."

As we drove through the rainy streets, I tried not to think about Mandy. I tried to concentrate on what was streaming by my window. The graceful gray façades of the old buildings, the grasping branches of the bare trees that lined the streets, the odd juxtaposition of a filigreed church against a streamlined boutique. When the black spire of the Eiffel Tower appeared suddenly through the slow sweep of the wipers, I leaned forward to stare. I felt an odd tug of sadness as the thought took slow shape in my brain that it wasn't right to see such a place when your heart was broken.

Cameron kept up a low-key recital of his life in Paris. I was grateful for the chatter. He had been hired onto the *Herald Tribune* after his breakup, working the copy desk. He didn't miss writing, he told me. He didn't even miss covering music.

"Radiohead's *OK Computer* was the last great rock album for me," he said. "After that it's all beeps and blats and white noise."

I mumbled something about the new stuff having no reference to the past. We crossed another boulevard and entered the park. Cameron explained that the Bois covered more than two thousand acres, more than twice the size of Central Park. Over the years since Louis XIV had set the land aside, it had been home to bandits, prostitutes, mansions and occupying armies. It housed lakes, zoos, museums, a world-class horse track, bike paths, carousels where children played and shadowy paths where gay men gathered.

And one windmill.

We parked the car and walked through the drizzle. In the distance, I could see the clubhouse and the white rails of the racetrack. The squat windmill appeared through the lace of the autumn trees like a ghostly vision. It was perched on a hill surrounded by a small moat, its gray stones girded by brown vines, its top capped by a metal cone with a spire. Four huge wooden vanes stood out against the gray sky like monstrous arms.

I stopped and stared. Cameron came up behind me. "It's been here since the thirteen hundreds," he said. "It was part of an abbey but then the king kicked the nuns out and turned it into a water pump or something."

"Can we go in?" I asked.

Cameron shook his head. "Not open to the public."

"Then how did the murderer get in?"

"Good question."

We crossed a bridge and passed a gabled caretaker's cottage. A rocky path led up to the windmill's base and a heavy wooden door with a big padlock. I let out a breath and looked back at the racetrack. A lone horse and his rider stood out against the dark green of the turf. But there was no sign of Cameron.

Voices . . . in French, one of them sounding pissed off. A few seconds later, Cameron came around the path, a short fat man in a green windbreaker following.

"He's a caretaker," Cameron said. "I talked him into letting us in."

"How?"

"You can pay me back later when you get your money changed."

The man unlocked the door and pulled it open. I stepped inside the windmill. It was cold and damp, the stone floor dotted with puddles. The only light came from the small slotted windows far above. Whatever mechanical works had been here centuries ago had been taken out. There was nothing to see now but a soaring empty space intersected with heavy wood beams. My eye was drawn to a round gray stone in the middle of the floor. It was about five feet across with a hole in the middle.

Cameron came up to my side. "What do you think this was for?" I asked.

"A millstone of some kind?" He sniffed and wound his scarf around his neck.

The round stone reminded me of some kind of primitive altar. "Was she nude?" I said.

"What?"

"The girl who was found here. Do you know if she was nude?"

"Yes, she was."

I pointed to the stone. "Was she lying here?"

"I don't know."

I pulled the paper from my jacket and looked at the date: 16 Janvier 2010. Her body had probably been well preserved by the cold.

I heard a flapping noise and looked up. Two pigeons were perched far above on the beams. I watched a feather float down, following it as it drifted against the stone walls.

The *circular* stone walls. Suddenly I was back in that ballroom in Miami Beach. That circular ballroom.

It was a coincidence. But it was a damn weird one.

"We have to get the tape," I said.

"What tape?" Cameron said.

"The *Herald Tribune* story said there was a cassette tape found with the body."

Cameron nodded. "I forgot about that."

"We have to find out what kind of music was on it."

"Matt, have you considered that it might not be music?" Cameron asked. "It could be anything."

It took a moment for my brain to digest that, because in my desperation to connect this to Mandy's death, I had just assumed the tape would be of music. But then I remembered something Nora had told me about investigations. It's all a puzzle, she had said, and you can't see the whole picture at first. All you can do is gather the pieces and see how they fit.

"I have to find out what was on the tape, Cameron," I said.

"Matt, we just can't waltz into the police station and demand to see a piece of evidence," Cameron said.

"Just get me to the right guy," I said.

13

On the drive to the police station, Cameron tried to tell me how French law enforcement worked. He explained that Paris, being the capital, was a jurisdictional jigsaw puzzle. The city was divided into twenty districts called arrondissements, arranged in a clockwise spiral like a snail. Each district had its own name, mayor and character.

And its own police department.

I knew this was Cameron's polite way of trying to tell me my *Miami Times* ID wasn't going to unlock doors here. I knew, too, that cops were basically the same everywhere, that they didn't like reporters or outsiders. And here, if the cliché was true, they didn't like Americans.

But I was convinced I could get someone to listen to me.

"We're here," Cameron said as he jerked his rumbling Citroën to a stop. "Remember, be polite. Everything starts with 'please.' Just tack *'s'il vous plaît'* in front of everything."

I squinted up at the police station. I'd expected something Gothic looking, maybe with gargoyles over the doors. Instead I was staring at a very ordinary glass entrance in a two-story gray building. It could have been a hair salon in one of those street malls back in Hialeah had it not been for the French flags hanging from a railing.

Inside, the lobby was full of tired hookers, homeless men, and slender dark-haired people dressed in black and smoking cigarettes as they waited their turn at the desk. Except for the flow of French, it could have been any precinct back home.

The desk was manned by a weary-looking man of some rank, given the numerous patches and two white hash marks on his sleeves. Cameron grabbed my sleeve and pulled me up to the desk.

The cop's gaze shifted to my face and, in a quick sweep of my wrinkled sports coat and red-rimmed eyes, probably assessed me as another tourist who had been pickpocketed. Surprisingly, he found a smile and—bless him—a familiar language.

"How may I help you gentlemen?" he asked.

Cameron flashed his press card and introduced us. He started to explain our reason for being here but I stepped in front of him. I didn't want Cameron to leave anything out and I thought that maybe if the cop heard the story from me—the grieving, jet-lagged brother—I'd garner some immediate sympathy. The officer gave my press badge a cursory glance, listened quietly for a few seconds, then interrupted me.

"Your name again?" he asked.

"Matt Owens."

"And the deceased was your sister, Monsieur Owens?"

"Yes, sir."

"My sincere condolences." He picked up a pen. "And she was killed here in Paris?"

I realized he had heard nothing I said. "No, Miami Beach."

"Miami Beach, USA?"

"Yes, but—"

"You are aware, Monsieur Owens, that you are in France?"

"Of course I am," I said.

"I am afraid you will need to see an inspector," the cop said. "May I schedule—"

I was suddenly pushed out of the way by a cop dragging a man in tattered clothing. I stepped back to get away from the guy's wino smell. Cameron wiggled into my space at the desk, chattering half in French, half in English, but I could tell from the look in the officer's eyes that his patience was wearing thin. I thought about elbowing my way back and making a scene just to get some attention but then realized I would probably be arrested. Cameron was right. Cops were the same everywhere. Insular, imperious and stubborn.

I was about to turn away but then I noticed a woman standing behind the counter. It was hard to miss her. She was maybe six feet tall, dark skinned, with a halo of long dark curls. She wore a white blouse and black slacks, but there was a badge hanging around her neck. Her eyes were pinned on Cameron, and it seemed to me that she was listening intently to his appeal. For a moment, I had hope that this woman—who I was sure was of some rank—would intervene and we would be on our way to solving Mandy's murder.

But then she walked away into a back room, where she was swallowed up by a cloud of blue uniforms and smoke.

I suppose she had heard more than she needed to. I tried to imagine how Nora and Detective Molina would react if I pitched the same theory to them, that Mandy had been murdered by a globetrotting Rolling Stones fanatic who had left his previous victim in a Paris windmill.

"Cameron," I said. "Let's go."

"But I'm making some progress with him."

"Let's go."

I left the police station and walked out into a cold drizzle. As I waited for Cameron, I pulled up the collar of my sports coat with shaking hands.

Cameron emerged from the station and spotted me hunkered by the car. He unwound his Burberry scarf and held it out. "Take this."

When I hesitated, he added, "I buy them off the street for three euros."

I took the scarf and wound it around my neck.

Inside the car, I slumped against the seat. The cold and my exhaustion suddenly collided, and I felt myself sinking into the hell that had been life for the last eight days.

Losing Mandy. Finding Mandy's body. The long hours spent sitting across from my father, staring into his red-rimmed eyes. The constant hold on my mother's hand. The blur of faces at my office in Miami. The blur of faces in North Carolina. Too little sleep. Too much booze. Too much pain.

I was no cop. I was starting to think I wasn't even a very good investigative reporter.

"Maybe I should just go home," I said.

"Matt, you've come a long way to give up so soon," Cameron said.

For the first time since I stood over Mandy's body, my eyes burned with hot tears—not a sudden rush of emotion I could blink away but a deep, painful swell that choked off my air. I hadn't broken down yet and, God, I didn't want to break down here, not in this little car in the middle of a foreign city, sitting with a man I barely knew anymore. I constricted every muscle in my body to hold myself together. I kept my body clenched until that autopilot feeling kicked back on.

"Listen," Cameron said. "Why don't you come stay with me for a few days and think things out? If nothing else, you need the rest. I have a nice lumpy sofa."

Slumped against the seat, I dropped my head in his direction. "Do you have any scotch?"

"No, but I have some excellent cognac," Cameron said.

"That'll do," I said.

14

A slash of red across the restaurant caught his eye. A bright red scarf. And long flowing hair the color of wheat.

She was sitting by the window, reading a book, her right index finger looped through the handle of her coffee cup. She raised the cup to her mouth and blew softly into it. Her lips were very full. He liked the way they pursed when she blew on the coffee.

He watched her for the next hour. Watched her playing with the plastic snow globe she had picked up in the souvenir shop. Watched her finish her peach tart, tuck her Fodor's in her purse and wind the red scarf around her slender white neck. In the crowded elevator traveling down from the restaurant in the Eiffel Tower, he stood behind her, closing his eyes as he breathed in the grassy scent of her hair.

When they reached the lawn of the Champ de Mars, she paused. She had her guidebook in hand and was looking around, as if lost. He was tempted to speak to her, but something told him to hold back. She started off down one of the streets leading away from the park. He followed.

He hadn't planned this. It was too soon, and he hadn't even felt the urge.

But there was something different about this one, something so very special. Yes, she was blond. Yes, she was beautiful.

But it was more than that. If her hair were in a braid it would almost be as if—

She was gone!

He had lost sight of her amid the bustle of rue Saint-Dominique. He froze, his eyes scanning the crowd.

Then, suddenly, he spotted the red scarf. And there she was, maybe twenty meters ahead. He hurried to catch up. When she turned toward the river, he suddenly knew with certainty where she was going.

He stayed three people behind her at the ticket booth at the Musée d'Orsay. The huge main-floor gallery—the museum was once a train station with a soaring glass roof—spilled out before him. The red scarf made it easy for him to follow her as she made her way swiftly through the crowd, like a silvery fish through water.

He followed her up a staircase, but then she surprised him by veering away from the salon with the Monets and Renoirs, slipping into a small side room.

The darkness of the room caught him off guard. He had been in the museum before but never in this little corner. He supposed the lights were so low to protect the fragile pastels housed behind the glass. After the brightness of the main gallery, this felt as close and dark as a cave. It was lovely.

There were only a few people in the room. He spotted her looking at something behind the glass. He went to her side.

He allowed himself a few moments to take in the pastels, the muted colors glowing softly in the low light, the rounded forms of the dancers, the perfect sweet whiteness of their skin.

He looked at the girl in the red scarf. There were tears in her eyes.

"Are you all right?" he asked.

His voice startled her. She looked at him, wiped her eyes and looked away. In the dim light he saw a redness creep into her cheeks.

"Yes, yes," she said. "It's silly, so silly."

"What is?" he asked.

Her eyes were still bright with tears as she looked back at him. "I didn't think they would be this beautiful."

"You haven't seen a Degas before?"

"Just in books."

"It is never the same, is it?"

She shook her head. "I saw a picture in an art book when I was thirteen." She nodded toward one of the pastels behind the glass. "I think it was that one. I wanted to be a ballerina. I took classes until I was eighteen."

"But you grew too tall," he said softly.

Her eyes went to him. "How did you know that?"

"I am a musician. I've worked with dancers."

She was studying his face. "Do you play for the Paris Opera Ballet?"

He nodded. It wasn't a lie. In his student days, he had played in several orchestras but he had hated it.

"I'd love to see the opera house," she said.

"You can buy tickets. *Don Carlo* is playing there now."

"No, I mean really see it, the insides."

"They have tours, I believe."

Her eyes sparkled. "Do they let you go underground? The place where Erik took Christine?"

He was confused, but then he understood. "Like in *Phantom of the Opera*," he said.

"I've seen it four times," she said, smiling. "Once on Broadway, three times when it came to Orlando."

It was hard for him to cover his disappointment that her frame of reference was a modern musical. But she was so very pretty, her skin as luminous as that of a Degas dancer.

"Come with me," he said.

"Where?"

"I'll take you to the opera house."

He led her out of the room and down the wide marble staircase to the main floor. It was warm and he offered to carry her coat along with his own. When she took it off, he was pleased to see that she still had the elegant body of a ballerina.

In the architecture gallery, he stopped and pointed, and when she saw it, her hand went to her mouth.

When she turned to him she was smiling broadly. "I thought you meant the real opera house."

He smiled back. "This is the best I can do."

She went toward the exhibit, a five-foot-tall scale model of the old opera house. It showed the building cut in half, all its interior rooms exposed, like an ornate old dollhouse, everything from the huge stage to the tiniest dressing room. And there, below it all, were the arched stone passageways of the house's catacombs, where the doomed phantom had taken his beloved hostage.

"It's beautiful," she said. "Thank you."

"It is my pleasure. I like showing off my city's small secrets."

She was smiling. "You didn't tell me your name, you know."

"Laurent."

"Casey," she said, extending a hand.

He took it gently.

It was very warm in the gallery. He could feel a dampness on the back of his shirt. He became aware that she still had not pulled her hand from his.

Was it the way her skin felt, so cool against his own hot flesh? Was it the sharp cut of her collarbones above the softness of her blue sweater? The way she walked? The way her hair smelled?

No, he knew exactly what it was. She wasn't like any of the others. She was different. She was just like Hélène.

She finally pulled her hand from his. She was staring at his chest.

"What a beautiful necklace," she said.

At first he didn't know what she was talking about. But then he realized his shirt had pulled open, exposing the necklace that he always wore.

"Is it old?" she asked.

"Yes, very old."

"May I?" She reached out and touched the medallion. He hadn't been expecting it. It made him feel off balance. He held his breath.

"I love antique jewelry," she said. She let the medallion fall.

"It was a gift from my mother," he said.

She smiled. A smile so lovely and so very familiar, like a half-forgotten song from another time in his life. It came to him in a flash, an impulse so strong he couldn't stop it. The words were out before he could stop them.

"Would you like to have it?" he asked.

She took a step back. "What?"

"I insist. It is certainly a better souvenir than a snow globe."

Her eyes clouded for a moment.

He covered his gaffe with a quick smile, not wanting her to know he had been watching her before. "It should be worn by a beautiful woman." He quickly pulled it up over his head and held it out to her. "I want you to have it."

She hesitated, then took the necklace.

"You should put it on now," he said.

She smiled and slipped it over her head. The medallion hung perfectly between her collarbones. For a long time he could only stare at her. She seemed to be growing softer, a blur of blue eyes and blond hair. And then, suddenly, she took shape again, and Hélène was there instead.

"Do you like *Les Misérables*?" he asked.

She was fingering the medallion and looked up at him. "*Les Miz*?"

"Yes, that's what I meant."

"I've seen it twice."

"Would you like to see where Jean Valjean hid from Javert?"

"Another model?"

"No, the real place this time."

Another lovely smile. "It sounds like an adventure."

"It will be," he said.

Rain was threatening again. It had barely let up since he returned from Miami. But the woman at his side seemed undeterred by the weather. She was talking about seeing *Les Miz*, and yes, she assured him, she had read the book, too, but not in French. She said she cried when Fantine died and Jean kissed her cold hand.

She told him her name was Casey Hoffmann and she was

in Paris for only two days, that she and her friend Paula Ridley had saved their money for years to come to Europe. With their Eurail passes, they had been to Munich, Zurich and Lucerne. But two days ago, in Strasbourg, Paula had gotten food poisoning and had been forced to spend her first night in Paris at the American Hospital in Neuilly. Now she was confined to bed at their hotel.

It was the Hotel Albion, she said. Very clean and cheap but the room was so small she could stand in the middle and almost touch both walls, she said with a smile. Did he know it?

He told her he did, and that it was a nice place. He was having trouble concentrating. He couldn't stop staring at her face.

"I felt guilty going out today," she told him. "But Paula insisted that I try to enjoy myself."

"And are you?" he asked.

"I am now," she said with a smile.

When they got to the kiosk in the Place de la Résistance at the river, he bought two tickets. The woman stared at the sign—VISITE DES ÉGOUTS DE PARIS—but it was obvious she didn't know what it said. She balked when she saw the heavy metal door propped open over a narrow staircase leading down into the earth.

"What is this?" she asked.

"The sewers," he said.

"What?" She started to laugh.

His smile was patient. Even though he had planned none of this, he was confident he could make this work out. He knew he had to be careful with this one, that the usual easy charm, nice dinner with wine, would not be enough. There was a depth and grace to this one. This one was worth the effort. This one would be different. This one, in the end, would not disappoint him. He just had to be patient this time.

"It's very interesting, I promise," he said, pointing to the sewer entrance. "There's a very good museum. Very few tourists know about it."

She peered into the hole, then looked back at him with a wry smile, as if she understood that his last words had been some strange test of her sophistication.

"Okay, let's go," she said.

The smell was not as bad as he remembered it. But he had not been down here in a long time, and never in this part that had been sanitized and organized for the tourists.

The old tunnels had been rigged with bright lights but there was nothing that could be done to dispel the dank feeling. He followed her as she moved slowly along, reading the exhibit signs, translating the French for her and explaining how the sewers had changed over the centuries. They walked along the metal catwalks, over small swift-running rivers, under huge pipes and cables.

Finally, when she turned to face him, she was holding the red scarf over her face.

"I'm sorry about the smell," he said.

She let the scarf fall. "'Here among the sewer rats, a breath from hell, you get accustomed to the smell.'"

He stared at her.

"It's from *Les Miz*." She laughed, and it echoed through the tunnels.

He was dumbstruck. Then he laughed in delight. He took her arm. "Come on, I want to show you something."

They headed down a side tunnel, a narrower one from the main one with the exhibits. At a barricade, he ducked under.

She hesitated, then followed. He saw one of the blue enamel signs on the wall that told him they were now under avenue Bosquet, but it had been so long that he wasn't sure where to go. The tunnel narrowed, the lights grew farther apart. A right turn? No, it was left. Yes, there it was.

A metal gate. He was certain she couldn't read the print on the rusted red sign above it: LES RISQUES SONT NOMBREUX ET PEUVENT ÊTRE MORTELS. But the one word above it was clear: DANGER.

"I don't think we should be here," she said.

"It's all right," he said. "Besides, this is the old part, from the eighteen hundreds. It's quite beautiful. I know you will appreciate it."

The gate opened easily. Which meant, he knew, that workers were probably in the area. He would have to be careful.

They entered a low-arching tunnel of stone. He had to stoop slightly as he walked slowly behind her, and the sound of running water grew stronger the farther they went. They emerged into an intersection of three high tunnels with arched openings and the roar of water.

He took a moment to savor the beauty of the old place. To his eye, it looked like the apse of an old rural church, a place where sinners came to be absolved and saints were buried underfoot.

He looked to the woman and wondered if she saw it as he did. But then her expression gave away her thoughts, and he saw it all through her eyes. The floor was wet and slick. The stone walls glistened in the sickly green glow of the overhead light. Water was pouring out of two viaducts low on the walls and down into a three-foot-wide trench in the floor. A rat struggled to find footing on its edge, then gave up and floated away.

He had to get her back.

"I shouldn't have brought you here," he said. "I should have understood you are far too delicate for this."

"I'm not delicate," she said. There it was, that smile again. God, she was so very lovely.

"Would you have dinner with me tonight?" he asked.

Her expression changed. The smile lingered, but there was caution in her eyes now. He could see it, even in the dim light.

"There is this restaurant, Le Coupe-Chou," he said. "It is very special to me and—"

Her smile faded some. "You've been very sweet, but I don't think—"

"Hélène, please, you have to—"

She took a step back, the smile gone. "My name is Casey," she said.

Casey? He stared at her. God, what was wrong with him? Of course she wasn't Hélène.

"I think we should go," she said.

He felt a slow burn of anger. At himself for being so wrong about her. But also at her for not giving him more of a chance.

"Please," he said. "Have dinner with me."

She took another step away from him. "I think I better go back to the hotel," she said. "I really have to check on my friend." She glanced around. "Take me back, please."

He didn't move. Didn't say a thing.

She was staring at him. Then she started past him, but he grabbed her arm.

"Hey," she said.

"I have to have it back now," he said.

"What?"

"My necklace," he said, raising his voice above the roar of the water. "If you are not going to be with me, then you must give it back."

She jerked away. Her fingers went to her neck but her eyes didn't leave his.

He could see it in her face that she was thinking now that she had made a mistake. She was thinking about how stupid she was to trust a strange man in a strange country. And then, there it was, that question that always came to them.

Why?

There was a ripple of fear in her eyes now, and he knew she was thinking of escape. But to where? She couldn't get past him on this narrow walkway, and she didn't know where these tunnels went, not like he did.

She pulled herself up to her full height. "Let me go," she said loudly.

He shook his head. "I can't."

The fear in her eyes had turned to panic. But she was trying very hard to hide it, and he felt a genuine respect for her strength. She would have been so perfect. She would have been so—

She pivoted quickly and was running away, toward one of the tunnels.

He started after her, down the slick walkway. He didn't hurry because he knew she would soon get lost. But when he caught up to her, what then? His anger was building, not just because she had rejected him. Not even because she had disappointed him. No, it was because she was forcing him to do something he really hadn't wanted to do, hadn't really planned to do.

As he followed her, he reached in his coat pocket. He always kept one there, even though he had never had to resort to it before. But she had left him no choice. His fingers found the cello string and he clenched it in his fist.

He found her in a cul de sac, standing on a small metal bridge, the water raging beneath her feet. There was no light back here, just the barest reflection from the main tunnel. But he could make out the red scarf and the white oval of her face.

He started toward her.

Her scream—earsplitting and shrill—froze him in his tracks. It went on and on, an animal noise riding on the roar of the water. When he realized she wasn't going to stop screaming, he jerked the string taut between his fists and came toward her.

Her hand came up just as the wire string came down. If she had been shorter, if she had been weaker, if he hadn't miscalculated her will to live, the wire would have hit its mark.

But the side of her palm took the first cut of the wire, and she pushed against him.

He stumbled on the slippery stone and struggled to regain his balance. She was backed against the wall, holding her bloody hand. All the images of Hélène were gone now, dissolved by his rage.

"*Salope!*" he hissed.

He ran at her, fist raised to strike her. Again she tried to push him away, but this time he was able to grab her arm. He gave it a hard twist backward and she cried out in pain. She started to go limp.

Too late he realized she was faking. Then he felt a searing jolt of pain as her knee came up into his groin.

He gasped and doubled over, trying to pull in a breath. He reached out for her and she spun away.

He looked up to see her flailing arms, her white face. Then she tumbled backward into the trench.

As he rushed to the railing, the only thing he saw was the trail of red scarf being sucked into the rushing gray water. The only thing he could think about was the necklace around her throat.

15

I dreamed I was on a cruise ship and we were hit broadside by a tidal wave, like in *The Poseidon Adventure*. I fell five stories into icy water and then couldn't get to the surface because there were too many bodies blocking my way.

Cameron's face was above me when I jerked awake.

"Get dressed," he said.

"What? What time—"

"After ten. You've been asleep for twelve hours."

I swung my legs over the edge of the sofa, disoriented in the gloomy light of Cameron's apartment. It took my brain a moment to realize it was ten in the morning, not evening.

"Matt, come on, get dressed," Cameron said, coming back into the room and thrusting a coffee cup at me.

"Why?" I wrapped my hands around the warm cup.

"They're pulling a body from the river. It's a young woman."

I was awake instantly. I grabbed my clothes off the chair and made a quick stop in the bathroom. Cameron was waiting at the open front door with one of his raincoats. I shrugged into it as we raced down the stairs and out into the cold.

"How did you find out about this?" I asked in the car.

"I was coming home from work and Athena called me. She's a reporter at the *Trib* and saw the police alert come in.

She's, well, she's my fiancée. I told her about you." He felt my stare and glanced over. "Not everything. Just enough."

I let it go. The traffic was heavy and I braced my hand against the dash as Cameron sliced the Citroën through the congestion. Ten minutes later, we turned left onto a broad street running along the Seine. I caught a glimpse of Notre Dame's gray hulk across the river but everything else was a blur.

Then I saw the familiar strobe of blue lights.

Traffic was stopped. Cameron drove the Citroën up onto a curb, slapped a PRESSE sign on the dash, and we jumped out. A crowd had gathered on a low bridge. For a second, I expected to see the blue-caped gendarmes, like in some corny movie, but the cops holding back the crowd looked like they could have been from Miami's SWAT team.

Cameron got by the rope line by flashing his press ID and I stayed close behind. As we tried to descend some stairs to a walkway on the river level, he was stopped. He was arguing with two cops who I assumed were detectives. The taller of the two was a woman in black leather with wild curly dark hair. I realized she was the same cop I had seen in the police station yesterday.

Our eyes met and through a feathery rain, we stared at each other for three or four long seconds. Then she turned her attention back to the river. I took advantage of the chaos and slipped down the stairs so I could get a better look. I found myself by the river's edge, behind drooping yellow tape and a young officer in a rain slicker.

I touched his shoulder. *"S'il vous plait,"* I said.

It must have been my bad accent that betrayed me but I was grateful the officer answered me in English.

"Yes, sir?"

"Could you tell me what happened here?"

"A woman is in the river."

More confident now that I would not be thrown out of the area, I took a longer look around. Two police boats were nestled against one of the bridge's low-slung arches and I could make out a black dot in the swift-moving green river. Two divers. They were swimming around a gray form that looked like it was caught on something just below water level. The divers were trying to put ropes around the form but the current kept moving them away.

"Do they know what happened to her?" I asked.

"It is probably a suicide."

I looked back at him. "Suicide?"

He let out a long breath. "There are thirty-seven bridges on the Seine," he said. "People here jump off them all the time, women mostly."

I was staring at a spot of red in the green water. It was a scarf around the woman's neck. She was fully clothed.

"*Merci*," I said to the officer.

As I turned away, disappointment came over me like a damp blanket. It was quickly followed by disgust at myself for hoping that this woman's death had been a murder. In my desperation to make some sense of Mandy's death, I was willing to grab hold of anything, be it a couple lines from a song or a stranger's suicide.

I turned away from the river. I spotted Cameron coming up the steps and went to him.

"It's a suicide," he said.

"I know," I said.

"I'm sorry, Matt," Cameron said. "I shouldn't have gotten you all riled up."

I looked up toward the black skeleton of the Eiffel Tower.

"It's okay," I said. "Let's go."

He had a good view from his place in the crowd atop the Pont Neuf. Luck had been with him during his trip to Miami and it was with him still. He was lucky he had been watching the morning news when the story of a woman being pulled from the Seine came on. He was lucky he was even awake, since his night had been spent in fits and turns, his mind resistant even to the GHB.

He had known immediately that the woman in the river had to be the same one who had fallen into the sewers. He knew what happened after heavy rains, that the sewers overflowed into the river, washing garbage, dead rats and bodies—yes, bodies—into the Seine. But he had come here to make sure it was her.

It was crowded on the bridge, and he was having a hard time getting close enough to see anything. There were divers in the water, men in black suits and yellow gloves, trying to extricate the woman's body from what looked like a wire around one of the bridge's pillars.

He spotted something red. It was her scarf, floating like a bloody slick on the green water. The yellow gloves moved about her body like feeding fish. But everything else was too far away for him to make out.

Did she still wear his necklace or was it lying in the bottom of the sewers?

Laurent moved down the bridge, pushing his way to the railing. His eyes began to burn, not from the wind but from the pain of loss.

The divers had freed the woman! Now they were moving her along the surface of the water on her stomach.

His mind screamed at their incompetence: *Turn her over! Turn her over so I can see her neck!*

He had to get closer, but there were too many officers, too many barriers. They weren't letting anyone down to the walkway below. He spotted a man with a camera, one of those fancy ones with a long lens like a telescope. He was Indian, the woman with him dressed in a green sari with a red bindi on her forehead.

"Excuse me," Laurent said, hoping they spoke English. "May I look through your lens?"

The man lowered the camera and stared at Laurent. Laurent pointed to the camera lens, then gestured toward his eyes. The woman said something to her husband in Hindi and the man reluctantly offered his camera to Laurent.

The camera gave him a clear view of the divers and the woman. They were moving her like she was a raft they were returning to shallower water. She was still facedown.

Turn her over!

The divers neared the bank and other men standing on the walkway reached down to grab the woman's arms. As they lifted her up, she lost her other shoe.

The Indian man touched his arm, but Laurent roughly shrugged him off, ignoring the chatter of Hindi.

Now . . . yes! They flipped her onto an orange board. Her head dropped in his direction, her hair covering her face like wet straw, her arms dangling to her sides. One of the men in yellow gloves lifted her arms to secure them and—yes!—moved the red scarf so they could fasten a strap across her chest.

There it was!

Lying on her chest like a gold coin.

He shoved the camera back at the Indian man and moved swiftly down the bridge, pushing people from his path, always keeping one eye on the woman as they carried her toward a waiting van.

The stone steps leading down to the walkway were cordoned off. Two policemen stood at the yellow tape. Laurent stopped, suddenly realizing he could call no attention to himself. He knew he had nothing to fear, and it was likely that the police would believe this was just another suicide.

But there were other bodies to consider. Bodies that had been discovered and were clearly homicides. Other bodies that still lay just under the surface of the city.

Control yourself.

Laurent watched as the woman was transferred to a black body bag. Watched as she—and the necklace—disappeared. He felt the sting of tears. He had not cried in years, twenty years maybe.

He wiped his face. He had to think clearly now. Think about getting the necklace back. But how?

He watched the van pull away, his mind replaying everything the girl had told him. Something about a friend. Yes, a girlfriend, she had been traveling with a girlfriend. Eventually she would realize her friend was missing and she would go to the police. And eventually, she would be the one who would get the dead woman's personal effects.

What was her name? He closed his eyes, concentrating. Paulette? No . . . Paula.

He remembered now that she had food poisoning and had been confined to their hotel. Damn . . . what was the name of the place?

Then it came to him. The Hotel Albion.

He had to be in Spain in less than a week. He would tell Maud to cancel the Spanish engagement if he had to.

He heard a whispering in his ear and spun. But no one was there, the crowd had left and he was alone on the bridge.

Yet he could hear her, clearly, as if she were right next to him, telling him, just as she always had, that everything was going to be all right.

L'espoir est le rêve d'une âme éveillée, Laurent. That is what his mother had always told him, *Hope is the dream of a soul awake.*

He would get the necklace back for her.

16

Yesterday, after we had left the bridge, I told Cameron I would be going back to Miami as soon as I could rebook my flight. He took the rest of the day off, insisting on showing me around the city. It was cold but at least it had stopped raining, so we just walked.

I wasn't used to walking. Miami was a car town, and even in the Grove, where I lived, people would drive three blocks to a restaurant rather than hoof it. Truth was, for all its tropical allure and gleaming buildings on Brickell Avenue, Miami just wasn't a city that made a human being feel welcome walking on the street.

Paris was different, I discovered. And as we walked—for miles with no particular route or destination—I found myself unclenching my muscles for the first time in a week. We sat on benches, poked around in a store that sold antique maps, had a beer in a Vietnamese café. We walked through Pigalle, where the hookers hunched in doorways like molting birds.

We took the funicular up to Sacré-Coeur and looked down over the city spread below. My heart still ached, because I knew Mandy would have loved to have seen Paris, and I still hadn't been able to shed a tear for my sister. But at least I didn't feel like something was devouring me from within.

We ended the day eating Greek food in some dive by the river, then went next door to a jazz club, where I smoked a couple of Cameron's foul cigarettes, pissed in a urinal next to a guy dressed like a woman and drank too much really bad shit that the waitress had promised me was American scotch.

Now it was the morning after and I was standing in Cameron's phone-booth-sized john staring at the shelf looking for aspirin. Finally, I gave up and went back to the kitchen. I tried to make coffee with the press but it came out filled with grounds. I poured a cup anyway and took it back to the sofa.

Cameron had left me a copy of that morning's *Herald Tribune*. I thumbed through it, stopping on page four at the headline WOMAN PULLED FROM SEINE.

I was surprised to find out she was an American. Her name was Casey Hoffmann and she was a tourist from Orlando, Florida. When she didn't return to her hotel by evening, her friend Paula Ridley had contacted the police. Despite what the cop had told me about it being a suicide, there was no mention of it in the article.

But I knew from my own experience that there would be no official ruling on the cause of death until a medical examiner had confirmed it.

I leafed through the rest of the paper—the first paper I had looked at since leaving Miami—but all it did was make me want to get home and bury myself in work. It was the only thing that ever helped. Every time something had gone wrong in my life, I had relied on work to distract me. Right after Nora left, I threw myself into the pharmaceutical investigation that had won all the awards. For six frenzied months I was fine. But when it was finished, the hole in my heart was still there. A Pulitzer certificate made a lousy patch.

I tossed the paper aside. I picked up my coffee and began to wander around the apartment.

Cameron had warned me it was "a dump," that he didn't make much at the *Tribune* and had no ambitions to carry the journalistic lance into battle anymore. The place was tiny, just a living area with a kitchenette, one bedroom and the john. But it had two great things going for it: heavy wood beams that crisscrossed the ceiling and a beautiful stone wall that Cameron said was a surviving part of the city's twelfth-century barricades against invaders.

The place had another thing going for it. Everywhere you looked, it told stories, interesting stories, about the man who lived within.

Sometime last night, a couple of drinks in at the jazz club, Cameron had leaned close and said he had something important to tell me. Amazingly, I could still remember it.

If you stand with one foot in the past and the other foot in the future, Matt, all you'll do is piss on the present.

Last night, it hadn't registered. But now, as I wandered around Cameron's place, it did.

I looked at the shelves of CDs and antique books, at the Japanese prints on the walls and the butts of black cigarettes lying in an antique Limoges saucer. I looked at the bottle of Moët champagne in his fridge and the butter that was so good I ate it with a spoon. And I stared for a long time at the framed picture that I found on the bedside table of Cameron with his arms around Athena. I took all of it in and I felt a stab of envy.

I was scheduled to go home in two days. What awaited me back there? An empty cottage with a stained La-Z-Boy, where my packed duffel sat by the door and the only thing of value

I had taken the trouble to hang up was that damned Pulitzer certificate. One of my feet was mired in the past of a dying profession. My other foot was forever pointing toward the future, which I always assumed would be better than anything I had tried to create in the moment.

Mandy . . . I had talked big to her, telling her to live her life large. But I had lived my own life so very small.

And Nora?

I was saved from thinking about that by a knock on the door. It surprised me because I knew the only way into Cameron's building was by the keypad down at the street door. I opened the door a crack. It was a woman with dark intense eyes.

"Yes?"

"Matt Owens?"

"Yeah, that's me."

The crack filled up with an ID badge of some kind. I saw a photo and a couple words that registered: *Prefecture de Police*.

"May I come in?"

"How did you get—?"

"The concierge let me up. May I come in, please?"

I stepped aside and she came in. She gave my robe a quick look and the room even less notice before those eyes, as dark as the grounds in the coffee press, came back to me.

"I am Inspector Eve Bellamont," she said.

She was every inch as tall as me, maybe taller with that corona of dark curls. Standing there in my ugly robe and black socks—she wore jeans and a black leather jacket—I felt a ripple of intimidation.

"I understand you have been asking about an old murder case here," she said.

I suddenly realized this was the same woman I had seen at the bridge yesterday, and the day before at the police station. It seemed pretty odd that we kept crossing paths. And it was more than odd that she had bothered to track me down.

"Yes," I said. "I was asking about the woman found in the windmill."

"I was told that your sister was murdered," she said. "I'm sorry." There was the barest hint of compassion in her eyes.

"Thanks," I muttered.

"I was also told that you think it has some connection to the case here."

I decided not to say anything. It was an old reporter trick. People hated silence; if you waited them out, they would always fill it. But this woman just stared at me calmly.

"You have come a long way to ask about this," she said finally.

"Only four thousand miles, give or take a couple," I said. I realized I was still holding the coffee cup. "You want some coffee?" I asked.

She shook her head.

"Probably smart," I said. I went to the kitchenette and poured the coffee in the sink. When I turned back, Eve Bellamont was looking around the apartment, but her eyes quickly came back to me.

"Why do you think your sister's murder has anything to do with my case?"

Her case? Well, that was interesting at least. And it suggested that the windmill case was still open. I saw something in her eyes and I wondered if she had meant to drop that nugget.

She was determined this time not to say another word. We were playing some little game here, and it was obviously my serve.

"My sister had an iPod," I said. "There was a song on it, an old Rolling Stones song. The song is about a serial killer in Paris who buried his victim in the Bois de Boulogne."

She was quiet, waiting for me to go on.

"It was not the kind of song my sister liked," I said. "I think it was put there by her killer."

Eve Bellamont still said nothing, so I pressed on.

"I read that a tape was found with the woman in the wind-mill," I said. "What was on it?"

"Monsieur Owens," she said, "I cannot tell you the details of an ongoing investigation."

"Well, then, maybe you can tell me what you're doing here?"

She hesitated. "I have an open case and you are asking questions about it. You were also at the bridge yesterday. I do not think you were just there out of curiosity."

"I thought maybe it could be related to my sister's murder," I said.

"It was a suicide," she said.

"Are you sure?"

"We have many suicides here."

"So I'm told."

From down below came the ring of a school bell and then the screams and laughter of children as they poured into the courtyard.

"According to the paper, the woman was American, from Orlando, Florida," I said. "Do you get a lot of American tour-ists jumping off your bridges here?"

Eve Bellamont said nothing.

"Sure seems like a long way to go to kill yourself," I said.

"She had just broken off an engagement," she said.

"Who told you this?"

Her dark eyes snapped. "We talked to her best friend. She said that they had taken their trip together so Mademoiselle Hoffmann could forget about her fiancé."

I was thinking of Nora and how, when I broke off our engagement, she had sent the ring back in a can of kitty litter. I knew all women were different. But I still wasn't buying the idea that a woman would come thousands of miles to kill herself over a busted relationship.

"This Paula person," I said, "she told you her friend was upset about the broken engagement?"

"Yes, that is what she told us. I know you think it might be strange for an American woman to commit suicide in a foreign country, but believe me, it does happen."

I was quiet. Any hope I had harbored that this woman might be willing to listen to me about Mandy was fading.

"May I ask how long you are staying in Paris?" Eve Bellamont said.

The question surprised me. "I'm scheduled to go home the day after tomorrow," I said.

She gave a small nod. "Again, my condolences for the loss of your sister." She started for the door.

"Wait," I said.

I went to my computer bag and dug out one of my business cards. I held it out to her.

She took it, read it and looked up. "You are a reporter?"

I nodded. "If you find something, anything, that might connect the woman in the windmill to my sister's murder, I would appreciate hearing from you."

The dark eyes held mine for a moment, then she tucked the card in the pocket of her leather jacket. I followed her to the door and closed it behind her. I went back to the table and picked up the newspaper. I read the story about Casey Hoffmann again. I didn't care what the cops here believed, it just didn't feel right that this woman would come all this way to kill herself. And most suicides were desperately lonely endeavors, not something done with your best friend in tow.

It was crazy. It was just another symptom of my desperation. But I suddenly knew what I had to do.

I had to talk to Paula Ridley.

17

I waited for Paula in the lobby of the Hotel Albion, a nice two-star hotel that seemed to draw a lot of American and Japanese tourists. Cameron had been able to get the info on where Paula Ridley was staying, but I was on my own once I got there. I showed my press ID to the desk clerk and persuaded him to call Paula Ridley's room and tell her a reporter wanted to talk to her about her friend Casey. I felt bad about the deception but I had confidence I could make her feel better once we were face-to-face.

I didn't have a clue what Paula looked like, but as I saw a woman in a purple sweater and black pants emerge from the elevator, I was sure it was her. She was short and plump with kinky brown hair and big round eyes. The kind of girl who was just heavy enough to be told too often, "Oh, but you have such a pretty face."

It was a pretty face. But it was etched with something I recognized all too well—the stunned look of grief.

She scanned the lobby, and I waved to her. When Paula extended her hand to me, it was ice-cold.

"Hello," she said nervously. "Are you the reporter?"

I nodded. "My name is Matt Owens and I'd like to talk to you about your friend Casey. Are you up for that?"

"Oh, you're American?"

When I nodded again, the relief on her face was painful to see.

"It's been so hard," she said. "I'm all alone here and the police have been really mean. It's like they don't care about Americans."

"I'm sure it's not that they don't care," I said. "They're just trying to be professional."

"I suppose," Paula said.

Her skin had a gray pallor and I remembered suddenly she had had a bad case of food poisoning. I asked her if she wanted to sit down and when she nodded, I led her to chairs by the window.

"I heard you were ill," I said. "Are you feeling any better?"

She nodded. "The people at the hospital were very nice. But it's hard to be so far away from home, to be alone, you know?"

Paula's eyes drifted around the lobby before settling back on me. "So what are you going to say about Casey?"

How did I explain things to this poor woman? I had to lie, at least initially, and hope that later she would forgive me.

"Well, I'm not sure yet," I said. "But I want to get things straight. It's important that I get it right, don't you think?"

Paula nodded woodenly.

I wondered how direct I could be without pushing her too hard. "I heard that the police think your friend was depressed over a broken engagement," I said. "I was just wondering if that was true."

She sighed. "She was at first. But then one day she surprised me and said she had some money saved up for her honeymoon. She said she wanted to use it to take a vacation instead, and she asked me if I wanted to go with her. I had some money saved and I'd never been anywhere, so I was excited to go."

"You and Casey were good friends?" I asked.

"Best friends, since fourth grade," Paula said. "We work together at Disney World. You ever been there?"

I shook my head.

She managed a small smile. "I'm just a hostess at Pinocchio Village Haus. But Casey, she was a Polynesian dancer in the Spirit of Aloha dinner show."

Her smile faded. "The trip seemed to make Casey really happy because she had always had this dream to travel, you know?" She paused. "I told all this to that woman detective. I also told her that Casey would never . . ."

Her voice trailed off as her eyes welled with tears.

"So you don't believe Casey committed suicide," I said gently.

"God, no," Paula said. "She's Catholic."

I gave a nod of sympathy.

"But it's not just that," Paula said. "It's that, well, Casey was a real strong person, and she really loved life, you know? I mean, like I said, she was sad after Jack broke things off. But she told me she was ready to move on with her life."

Tears were falling down Paula's face. She looked away, as if ashamed.

"How long have you been in Paris?" I asked.

"What?" Paula had trouble coming back to me.

"How long have you been here?" I repeated. I was thinking that if someone had followed Casey, as I believed someone had stalked Mandy, knowing where Paula and Casey had been would be important.

"Two days," Paula said. "But I was sick and in the hospital the whole first day. Yesterday, I was in bed here all day."

"So Casey went out alone?" I asked.

Paula nodded. "I didn't want her to waste her time in Paris looking after me. I told her to go out and have fun."

She pulled a Kleenex from her pocket and blew her nose before she went on. "I slept straight through, so I didn't even realize she hadn't come back to the hotel until really late," she said. "Her bed hadn't been touched. I mean, we joked about her finding some handsome foreign guy to make Jack jealous, but I knew she would never really do that."

When she lowered the tissue, her face was swollen. "I got worried and called the police. They came here and showed me a picture and asked me if it was Casey and I . . . I ''"

She broke down again. I waited until she had composed herself.

"Can I ask you a few more questions?" I asked gently.

Paula nodded.

"Did Casey tell you where she was going that day?"

Paula shook her head. "But she had this travel journal and she had been writing stuff in it during our whole trip. It's probably still in her purse."

"Do you have it?" I asked.

She shook her head again. "The police still have it. They told me I have to go pick up her things." Her eyes found mine. "I know I have to do it, but I don't want to, you know? It's all been so hard. I had to be the one to call her parents. It was awful. Her mom just cried and cried. You can't imagine what this has been like."

I wanted to tell Paula that I knew exactly what it was like, but I kept quiet.

Paula was crying again. I touched her hand.

"Do you want to go get a cup of coffee?" I asked gently.

She looked up at me and gave a small smile. "That's nice of you, but I have to go pick up Casey's things. They said I also have to bring her some clothes to wear home." Her eyes were beseeching. "What do I take? They said it didn't matter, since she'd be in a casket and no one would see her until she got to a funeral home in Orlando. But I can't just take Casey any old thing, can I?"

I had no idea what to say.

"Casey was so picky about her clothes," Paula said. "She loved red. She bought this beautiful red scarf in Munich and—"

"I'm sure whatever you take will be fine," I said, interrupting her.

Paula nodded and slumped in the chair, her eyes vacant. "So, do you have enough?" she asked me softly.

"Enough what?"

"For the story you're writing."

I hesitated, then decided that Paula deserved the truth. "Paula, I'm not writing a story," I said. "I'm a reporter, but that's not why I wanted to talk to you."

Her eyes clouded. I leaned closer.

"My sister was murdered in Miami Beach," I said softly. "This is going to sound crazy and I can't explain it all right now, but I think she was murdered by someone who is here now, in Paris. When I heard about Casey, I thought maybe her death might be connected. So I had to talk to you."

Paula paled. "You think Casey was murdered?"

I put up a hand, wanting her to lower her voice. "I don't know," I said. "But after what you told me about Casey, I have to look into it further. Would it be okay if I contacted you again, if I need to?"

Paula was staring at me. I couldn't imagine what was going through her head as she tried to digest what I had just told her. And for a second, I almost regretted drawing her into my half-baked theory. I held out my business card and a pen.

Paula took them and wrote down her home phone number and address in Orlando.

"Can I ask you to do something for me?" she asked.

"Of course."

"Would you come with me? I mean, to give them Casey's clothes? I have to go to some institute or something. The man at the desk gave me directions on how to get there, but I'm afraid I'll get lost or something."

She was all alone in this city, and I knew what it was like to be in a foreign country and have everyone turn a deaf ear to what you were trying to say.

"Yes, I'll come with you," I said.

She gave me a weak smile as she rose. "Give me a few minutes, okay?"

She started toward the elevator, then looked back. "I'm sorry, you don't have anywhere you need to be, do you, Mr. Owens?"

"I'm exactly where I need to be," I said.

The institute turned out to be the Institut Médico-Légal, Paris's medical examiner's office and morgue all rolled into one big redbrick building in the twelfth arrondissement, something I wouldn't have known except for the taxi driver pointing it out as we drove there.

We were in a part of Paris I suspected few tourists ever saw. It resembled an industrial riverfront in any American city, although slightly cleaner. The institute sat on the Seine, strapped there by a railway line. In sharp contrast to the modern buildings around it, it looked like a nineteenth-century asylum, complete with an ornate iron gate.

Inside, Paula and I were greeted by a woman who spoke

English. When Paula gave her Casey's name, she made a phone call and asked us to wait.

A door opened and a man in a white lab coat motioned for us to follow him. I put my hand on Paula's back and we went down a hall that again made me think of some turn-of-the-century madhouse. Every door was closed and the signs over them were all in French. I had discovered that French signs were fairly easy to translate given the Spanish I had picked up in Miami, but now I didn't pay much attention. I was worried about Paula and hoped she wouldn't break down.

The man led us into what I assumed was a viewing room for families of the deceased. The blinds on the window were closed. Paula turned to me, clutching Casey's folded clothes to her chest.

In the taxi, I'd seen that she had chosen a red sweater and black skirt but now I could see a ruffle of white lace sticking out from the folds of the skirt and knew Paula had also brought Casey a bra and panties.

The door opened again and a different man came in, introducing himself as Monsieur Gravois.

"May I offer my condolences to the both of you," he said, taking Paula's hand.

She mumbled a thank-you, then looked to me. I introduced myself as a friend of Paula's and mentioned the clothes. He took them gently from Paula, using extra care to keep them folded, preventing the lingerie from falling.

"These are quite lovely," he said. "You selected with care, I can see."

Paula started to cry. Gravois handed her a handkerchief and looked to me. "Would you like to see the deceased at this time?" he asked.

Paula shook her head. I debated the question, then decided I couldn't put Paula through it. I knew if I needed a picture of Casey Hoffmann, Cameron could get me one.

"Can Miss Ridley get a copy of the autopsy report?" I asked.

"It is not ready," Gravois said. "And I'm sorry, autopsy reports can only be released to the family. I believe we have their address, yes?"

Paula nodded.

"Did you bring her travel arrangements?"

Paula dug into her purse and produced an itinerary and airline ticket. I thought about Casey's family having to make these heartbreaking arrangements from Orlando and I suddenly realized that both Mandy and Casey had been away from home when they died.

Gravois said he'd be right back. He returned with a large plastic bag and a clipboard. In the plastic bag, I could see the red scarf right away, folded atop what looked like a gray coat and other clothes. There was also a small manila envelope.

"Her purse?" I asked.

"Not recovered, monsieur."

Paula looked at me. "Should we go now?"

"Mademoiselle Ridley," Gravois said, "if you would be so kind as to look at the effects and make sure everything is in order, we would appreciate it. There is a release you will have to sign."

Paula set the plastic bag on the table and took out the clothing. She picked up the manila envelope. I put a hand on her shoulder as she laid each item on the table.

Seven euro coins. A gold ring with a green stone. A necklace with a small gold medallion. And three wrinkled ticket stubs, like the kind given at tourist attractions.

Tears fell silently down Paula's face as she stared at the items on the table.

I picked up the stubs. If my stalking theory was right, these were my bread crumbs.

"Can you tell me where these are from?" I asked, holding them out to Gravois.

He pointed to the largest. "That is from the Eiffel Tower, of course."

"And this?"

"The Musée d'Orsay."

"Excuse me?"

"It is a museum not too far from the tower."

"And this one?" I asked, showing him the third.

Gravois grimaced. "That is from Le Musée des Égouts."

I stared at him.

"The sewers," he said.

I noticed the word "*musée*" on the stub. "The sewers are a museum?" I asked.

"*Oui*, it is a museum that is open to tourists but not many people venture down there. It is not well known in the guide-books."

I glanced at Paula. "Does that sound like somewhere Casey would go?"

Paula was fingering the gold necklace and needed a moment to catch up on the conversation. "A sewer?" she said. "God no, Casey didn't like dirty things."

I was suddenly eager to get back to Cameron and ask him about the sewers. Or, if we were able to get out of here quickly enough, I could go there before they closed.

"May I keep these tickets?" I asked Paula.

She nodded numbly.

Gravois again offered his condolences, said something about contacting him if we needed any help and left.

As he walked away, Paula watched him anxiously. Then her head swung back to me.

"What's wrong?" I asked.

She was still holding the necklace. "I didn't want to say anything while that guy was here," she said. "But this is not Casey's."

She held out the necklace and I took it. It was an odd design, a gold medallion about the size of a quarter and made of two pieces, stuck together like two watch batteries. Something was engraved in script on one side of it but it was in French and too tiny to see clearly.

"Are you sure she didn't buy it that day?" I asked.

Paula shook her head. "We were getting low on money and she was watching every cent."

I tried to hand the necklace to her but she pushed it back to me. "You keep it," she said. "If Casey was murdered, maybe this is important. That's why I didn't say anything to that French guy. I was afraid he would keep it."

"It might be valuable," I said.

"Maybe to someone," Paula said. "But not to me."

I dropped the necklace into my coat pocket with the ticket stubs. I helped Paula put the clothing back in the plastic bag. When we were finished, Paula leaned back against the wall. She looked exhausted.

"You okay?" I asked.

She nodded. "Thank you," she said softly. "I couldn't have done this alone."

I put a hand on her arm. "No one should have to."

From his window table in the café, Laurent had a clear view of the Institut Médico-Légal across the street. He had been sitting here for the last hour, waiting for Paula Ridley to emerge.

Back at the Hotel Albion, he had told the clerk he was a representative from the embassy, there to assist Mademoiselle Ridley in transporting her deceased friend's remains back to the States. But the clerk told him that Mademoiselle Ridley had just left to go to the institute.

He knew immediately what that meant. Within the hour, she would be in possession of the blond woman's belongings. And that meant she would have the necklace.

Laurent finished his coffee, his eyes on the brick building. He had no idea what the woman looked like, but when the short plump brunette emerged from the entrance, he knew it was her. She was dressed like an American in a shapeless blue raincoat over a bright purple sweater and black slacks.

Laurent rose, tossed some euros on the saucer and started toward the door. He froze, staring out the window.

Who was that man with her?

They were standing close and now the man was putting his arm around her. A boyfriend? No, impossible.

He had to get closer. He left the café and crossed the street to stand with the people at the bus stop. He could see the man clearly now.

Sandy brown hair, tanned. Something oddly familiar about him.

A tightness gripped Laurent's chest.

It was the man from Miami Beach, the one who had been with the blond girl. What was he doing here in Paris? What was he doing with the Ridley woman?

Laurent took a deep breath, trying to think. There was no reason to believe the American man had seen him at the Miami club. No one had ever seen him before. So how—?

The song on the iPod.

Laurent smiled. He had worked so hard on his musical puzzles, matching each girl and location to the perfect song, as if he were leaving a trail of clues like the villain in one of those old Inspector Maigret novels. No one had been intelligent enough to even see there was a puzzle, let alone decipher it. But the American had figured it out. Impressive, yes, but it wasn't anything to worry about.

The American was looking up and down the street. Laurent realized he was probably searching for a taxi and didn't know you could not hail one off the street, that you had to go to a taxi stand.

The American said something to the Ridley woman and pointed. He took her by the arm and they started down the street. Laurent saw they were heading toward the metro stop in the plaza.

He watched them disappear underground and followed.

*   *   *

When Paula Ridley and the man got off the train at the Bastille station, Laurent trailed behind. After a few moments of confusion, they found their way to their connecting train. He knew where they were headed—to the huge hub station Châtelet. He knew that once they got there, he would have no chance to get her alone.

He boarded the car behind them, keeping them in his sight. When they got out into the teeming rush-hour crowd of Châtelet, he followed.

The man—he had heard her call him Matt—was looking around, as if lost. Laurent stood nearby, watching them and trying to stay calm. He hated the metro when it was like this, hated the stinking press of the crowd and the cacophony of trains and voices. To make things worse, a man was playing a violin, a case open at his feet holding money.

The screech of the violin rose to meet the screech of an arriving train. Laurent shut his eyes against the pain.

When he opened them, he saw the man lead Paula Ridley to a large metro map on the wall. The man was pointing to the color-coded metro lines and trying to explain to the stupid woman which train they had to take to get back to her hotel.

"The green line," she said, repeating it like a schoolgirl. "You're sure?"

"I'm sure," the man said. "Take the green line in the direction of Port de la Chapelle. I have to catch the purple line that goes to the Left Bank."

He wasn't going to go back with her to the hotel.

The American man had his hands on her shoulders. "You're sure you don't need me to go with you?"

"No," she said. "You've done enough already. I'll be fine."

He glanced at his watch. "Okay, if you get lost, just ask someone for help."

She smiled, said something, then gave him a peck on the cheek. Finally, the man was gone, sprinting up the stairs. Paula Ridley was alone.

Her face was blank as she stared at the signs, then she turned back to the metro map. Laurent watched as she put a finger on the worn dot of the Châtelet station and traced the green line running out from it.

He realized in that second that she was looking at the wrong green line. The darker green one that would have taken her to her hotel did not even connect here. She was looking at a light green line, one that designated an express train that would take her miles out of her way.

He stepped forward.

"Excuse me, mademoiselle," he said. "Do you by chance need some assistance?"

Paula turned, her face flushed, clutching the plastic bag that held his necklace to her chest. "I think I'm okay," she said. "I just need to find my stop."

"And where might that be?"

Her blush deepened, like a rash. "I'm just going back to my hotel. I need to catch the green line to . . . Notre Dame de something. Like the cathedral, Matt said."

"If you're looking to go to the cathedral, you're heading in the wrong direction."

"I don't mean the church," she said. "I mean the street named that."

Homely and *ignorant,* he thought.

"May I ask your name?" he said.

"Paula Ridley."

"Mademoiselle Ridley," Laurent said.

She seemed pleased to hear her name spoken with a French accent. He almost had her.

"If you would allow me, I am going in the same direction and can escort you to the proper train," Laurent said. "You'll be at your destination in ten minutes."

Her eyes filled with a thin veil of suspicion. Apparently, at some point in her vapid life, someone had taught her not to go off with strangers. He had to make himself less threatening.

"I know how confusing this can be," he said with a smile as he gestured toward the metro map. "I get lost down here myself sometimes."

She was chewing on her lip.

He gave her a nod. "I am sorry to have bothered you. Have a good evening, mademoiselle."

He started away.

"Wait!"

He turned back.

"If you can just get me to the green line, I think I can make it from there," Paula Ridley said.

He walked her up the staircase and down another, through one echoing tile tunnel and down another, weaving in and out of the peddlers and kiosks of the small underground village that was Châtelet. Finally, they arrived on a less crowded platform. No shops or peddlers here. Just a handful of people preoccupied with getting home from work. And one saxophone player bleating in the corner.

He steered her to another metro map. "Here we are," he said, pointing. "The green line."

He could tell by her empty expression she could read none of the signs, not even the one that told her the train he was about to put her on was an RER train to the suburb of Seine-Saint-Denis.

No one went there unless they lived there or beyond, or were going to the football stadium. It was home to more than a million of Paris's immigrants, honeycombed in housing projects. The neighborhoods were still scarred by the burned hulks of buildings from the riots several years ago.

The train was coming.

"Get off the first time it stops," Laurent said. "You'll be right at your hotel entrance."

"Thank you for helping me," she said.

"Enjoy your stay in Paris," he said with a smile.

The train squealed to a stop. Doors bumped open and people pushed toward the car. He urged her forward so firmly she nearly tripped and had to catch herself on a pole. It would have been an ideal time to snatch the plastic bag and run. But someone stepped in front of him and Paula was swallowed up by bodies.

He gave her a quick wave, then hurried away. Just before the doors closed, he slid into another car.

The train started. He watched her through the connecting doors, watched her eyes as she stared at the sullen young black men and at the women in head scarves. He watched her stare out at the black tunnel rushing by, watched her as she wondered why the train was not stopping anywhere like all the others had.

It was a long ride to the Saint-Denis stop. He knew what awaited her if she tried to go upstairs. Nightfall and the shadows of a neighborhood where no one lingered on the streets after sunset.

But if he was lucky—and he always was—she wouldn't get that far.

Finally, the train jerked to a stop. The doors banged open. Paula Ridley jumped to her feet and ran so quickly from the train, he laughed.

He exited his car and stayed behind a post while Paula stood on the platform and looked around. Her eyes moved over the graffiti on the concrete walls, the trash that blew in small cyclones as the train rumbled away. Finally, her eyes settled on the station sign that read not NOTRE DAME-DE-LORETTE but STADE DE FRANCE SAINT-DENIS.

The six or seven people who had disembarked the train had already hurried up the stairs, and there was no one left on the dark platform. No one would be coming either, Laurent knew. The next train was ten minutes away.

Paula started to cry.

He reached deep in his pocket for his weapon and stepped out from behind the post. Her back was to him and he moved silently and quickly, extending the telescoping tool. As he stepped up behind her, he took aim at the middle of her back, knowing she carried the package over her heart.

She heard him and spun. His thrust came down toward her chest, the point of the weapon catching on the hard package. It punctured the plastic, then got caught on something inside.

"Stop it!" Paula screamed. "Help me! Help me!"

He wrenched his weapon free and stabbed at her arms and shoulders while he pulled viciously at the package.

"Give it to me!"

Still, she clung to it even as her hands grew red and slick with blood. His face was wet from the spatter and the weapon kept getting caught in her coat.

Thoughts ricocheted in his brain.

The necklace.

His hands. If he got cut, he couldn't play.

The stupid woman who had floated away from him in the sewers. And his own stupidity for wanting her.

The woman suddenly fell to her knees and the package slipped from her hands. Blood poured from a wound in her neck and he knew she would be dead within minutes.

He grabbed the package and used the sharp point to rip it open. Clothes spilled out—a red scarf, a coat, a skirt and sweater, one shoe, and finally an envelope. He snatched it up and tore it open with such fury that some coins and a ring popped out and bounced down the platform.

There was no necklace!

He shook the clothes, tossing them aside, until finally there was nothing left in front of him but damp concrete.

He spun on his knee and grabbed the woman by her coat, yanking it open. He tore at her sweater, exposing her neck. But she wasn't wearing the necklace.

"Where is it?" he screamed, shaking her. "Where is it? Where is my necklace?"

The American man, the one she had called Matt.

"Did you give it to him? The necklace! Did you give the necklace to him?"

Voices echoing in the stairwell.

Laurent stood up, hands dripping with blood as his eyes raked the platform one last time for his necklace.

With a furious cry, he grabbed Paula's arms and threw her off the platform to the tracks below. Breathless, he gathered up the clothing and plastic bag and heaved it all into the darkness of the tunnel. He collapsed the telescoping tool as he moved quickly away from the blood smears.

He leaned against a post, trying to calm his thundering heart. His hands were stained red, and when he licked his lips, he could taste the woman's blood. And his trench coat . . . it was streaked with blood and torn at the shoulder.

How was he going to get back to the center of the city looking like this? Why had this been such a mess? What was happening to him?

Voices! Far down the platform. People . . . they were coming closer.

The blood. There was too much blood. What was he going to do about all the blood?

Three young men approached, laughing and shoving at each other. Laurent froze as he realized one of them was covered in blood.

Then the others came into focus, one with a face painted like a zebra, the third wearing a pink stovepipe hat.

The bloody one saw Laurent and stopped cold. Then he smiled, revealing plastic vampire teeth.

"Quel costume, mon mec! Formidable!" he said.

The trio staggered away, screaming with laughter.

Laurent closed his eyes and let out a breath.

Halloween. It was fucking Halloween.

Tonight, the streets would be crowded with the idiots who had adopted the stupid American celebration. Tonight, the streets would be filled with drunks covered in fake gore. Tonight, he could walk down the avenue de Champs-Élysées covered in Paula Ridley's blood and no one would notice.

Laurent laughed at his stroke of luck.

Tonight, he would be invisible.

19

The kettle whistled, drawing me to the stove. I carefully measured the coffee into the press, poured the water in and took the press back to the table by the window.

While I waited for the coffee to steep, I stared at the items spread out before me. The gold necklace, the Delta ticket for my flight home tomorrow and the stubs that had been in Casey Hoffmann's coat.

I picked up the stub from the sewers. It was cold in the apartment, but I could feel the slow creep of sweat as I thought about what had happened yesterday.

It had been rude of me to leave Paula at the Châtelet station, but the truth was, I wanted to get out of the metro. I had problems being in closed-up places, especially underground ones. I sometimes think that was one reason I moved to Miami. There was something about all that blue sky, water and flat land that let me breathe easier.

By the time I got to the sewers, I had convinced myself I could handle it. But when I looked down at the narrow metal staircase, my heart began to race.

I forced myself to go down into the gloom. As I moved slowly along the slick walkways, staring down into the fast-moving gray waters, I tried not to think about the fact I was underground and tried to concentrate on the questions surrounding Casey Hoffmann. Why would a woman like her have come to a dismal place like this? And why had no one seen her disappear?

But then, suddenly, all thoughts of Casey vanished. I felt my heart kick into high gear. I had broken out in a cold sweat and the gray walls seemed to be closing down around me. The nausea hit me like a punch to the gut, and I closed my eyes against the sting of bile in my throat. That is when it all came back to me, in a swirling rush of smells and feelings.

I was ten years old.

Summer camp, away from home for the first time. Late night, stealing away from the tents with Joey and Hank, running through the cool dark woods. Nervous laughter as our flashlight beams picked up the boarded-up entrance of the abandoned emerald mine. The echoes of our footsteps, the drip of water, as we made our way through the dank caverns. Then . . . Hank's taunting dare to crawl into the hole because that was where the emeralds would be found and I was the smallest.

The scrape of the rock on my knees, the pounding of my heart as I crept along in the dark. The groan of old boards over my head and then . . . the loud snap as they broke, and the blanket of dirt that smothered me.

They told me later that I was in there for five hours before they dug me out. I remember nothing of the whole thing except the terror of total blackness and silence. My only other memory was of my mother's crying and her arms crushing me to her when they brought me out.

The smell of coffee brought me back to the apartment.

I realized I was still holding the ticket stub from the sewers. I tossed it in with the cigarette butts on the Limoges saucer.

Cameron emerged from the bedroom, tucking his shirt into his pants. He glanced down at my airline ticket.

"So what's the verdict?" he asked. "Are you going home tomorrow?"

I picked up the gold necklace. "I don't know."

He studied me for a moment. "I only have to go into the office for a couple hours today because of the holiday," he said. "Want to meet later for lunch?"

I nodded, engrossed in trying to decipher the engraving on the medallion. I held it out to Cameron. "Can you tell what this says?"

He squinted at the necklace. "*Deux coeurs*. Two hearts. *Très romantique*. Is this yours?"

I shook my head. "I don't know who it belongs to."

After Cameron left, the apartment walls seemed to close in around me, so I went for a walk. Most of the shops were closed and I remembered that Cameron had mentioned it was a holiday. The only thing that was open on his street was the florist, who seemed to be doing a very brisk business.

The day was cold but the blue sky was so bright it made my eyes water. I wandered into Luxembourg Gardens and sat on a bench watching some old men playing a bowling game in the dirt. The sharp clack of the metal balls made my head hurt.

I felt tired and defeated. Maybe it was my panic attack in the sewers or being with Paula in that godforsaken redbrick death place yesterday. Maybe it was just the fact that everything seemed to be made of mist here. Cops who had questions but no answers, like some bad existential play. And somewhere, maybe, a phantom who had taken my sister from me.

My thoughts kept circling back to Nora. I decided that to-morrow, when I got back to Miami, I would give her Mandy's iPod and let her do her job. My trip here had been nothing but a quixotic quest.

I decided to go back and wait for Cameron. As I turned the corner onto his street, I stopped. The woman inspector with the curly hair was standing outside Cameron's door.

She turned and saw me coming.

"Inspector Bellman," I said.

"Bellamont," she said.

I nodded and wound Cameron's scarf tighter around my neck. "What brings you here?"

"I need to talk to you."

"About what?"

She looked around the street. "Can we go inside?"

"What, now all of a sudden you want—"

"Casey Hoffmann's friend was stabbed yesterday," she said.

I stared at her.

"She was attacked in a metro station."

"Attacked? Is she all right?"

Eve Bellamont shook her head slowly. "She is still alive. But she has not been able to tell us anything."

The words were registering now. "Metro station? But I was with her, I left her—"

"I know. That is the only thing she said."

A couple brushed by us on the narrow sidewalk.

"Please, can we go upstairs?" Eve Bellamont said.

It took me three tries to punch in the right code to open the door. Eve followed me up the winding staircase and into the apartment. In her black jeans, leather jacket and huge hair, she seemed to fill the small place. I gestured to the sofa and she took a seat.

I shrugged out of my coat and went to the table. The coffee press, the ticket stubs and the necklace were still where I had left them. I swept the necklace into my jeans pocket and turned to face Eve Bellamont.

"Why did you go to see Paula Ridley yesterday?" she asked.

"Because I don't believe Casey Hoffmann committed suicide and I wanted to find out more about her," I said, sitting down at the table.

"How did you find Mademoiselle Ridley?"

I didn't like Eve Bellamont's accusing tone and I wasn't about to put Cameron in a tough spot with the cops, so I told her I was a good reporter and that finding information about people was what a good reporter did.

"Don't play games, Monsieur Owens," Eve Bellamont said. "It does not appear that Mademoiselle Ridley is going to live."

I was stunned into silence. The only thing that was registering in my brain was Paula's face when she pulled back after giving me that kiss on the cheek. She had trusted me and I had left her there alone.

The inspector was saying something but I didn't hear it. It was only when she said my name sharply that I drifted back.

"I asked you a question," she said.

"I . . . I'm sorry. What was it?"

"Why did you go to the institute with her?"

"She was upset. She asked me to."

"Where exactly did you leave Mademoiselle Ridley?"

"At the Châtelet station," I said. "I showed her which line to take to get to her hotel."

Eve Bellamont just stared at me with those dark eyes. I realized with a start that I was possibly a suspect.

"How did this happen?" I asked. "The station was very crowded, why didn't anyone—"

"She got on the wrong train. She was on an express RER that goes to the *banlieue* Seine-Saint-Denis. It is not a place a tourist should be."

My mouth was dry. "I want to know exactly what happened to Paula," I said.

Eve Bellamont considered me for a moment, then sat forward and leaned her elbows on her knees. "As I said, Mademoiselle Ridley told us only that she had been with you. About the attack itself, we know only what the three men who found her told us. She was lying on the tracks unconscious. She had been stabbed repeatedly. She lost a lot of blood."

"Why?" I asked softly.

Eve Bellamont just stared at me. "Why what?"

"Why do you think someone wanted to kill Paula?"

"It could have been a mugging—"

I shook my head.

"But I don't believe it was," she said. "Her purse was still there, and the attack was too violent. Whoever did this wanted something."

Eve Bellamont picked up a small leather binder and took out a paper. "This is a list of Casey Hoffmann's personal effects. We know Mademoiselle Ridley picked them up at the institute. We found everything except a necklace. So we assume her attacker took it." Her eyes locked on mine. "Do you know anything that might help us?"

The necklace was still in my pocket. It occurred to me that I knew something Eve Bellamont didn't, that the necklace did not belong to Casey. I couldn't prove it, but I also believed that Casey's death—and now this attack on Paula—had something to do with Mandy's death. I knew, too, that if I just handed this necklace over to Eve Bellamont, she would make no effort to connect any of this to Mandy.

But there was one big problem. I was the last person seen with Paula Ridley. And I had the necklace that they assumed her attacker had stolen. If Paula died, there would be no one to speak for my innocence.

"Monsieur Owens?"

I forced myself to stay calm as I looked at Eve Bellamont. "No," I said. "I don't know anything."

For a long time, the room was quiet. Then, finally, Eve Bellamont slapped her binder closed and stood up.

"When are you going home?" she asked.

"Tomorrow."

"I think you should make arrangements to stay longer."

"Why? Am I a suspect?"

"Until I know more, yes."

Something inside me snapped. I stood up. "Look, it's not me. It's him. And it's not just Paula. It's Paula and Casey and that woman in the windmill. And it's my sister, goddamn it."

Eve Bellamont stared at me.

I began to pace in a tight circle. "Casey Hoffmann did not kill herself," I said. "Paula wasn't mugged and I know there is something that connects my sister to all of this. I know it!"

"Monsieur Owens . . ."

I stopped. "What was she stabbed with?"

"Who?"

"Paula! What the hell did he use?"

"Why do you ask that?"

"Just tell me!"

"We think it was an ice pick."

I sank back down in the chair and shut my eyes. I didn't feel vindication. I felt only sickened.

"Monsieur Owens. Are you all right?"

I didn't look up. I could barely get the words out. "My sister was murdered with an ice pick."

I sensed that Eve Bellamont had sat down again. But I still couldn't look up. I stared at the ticket stub in the Limoges saucer, trying to bring each little word into focus, hoping that if I could hang on to them, I could keep it together.

"Monsieur Owens," she said. "I am sorry but I have to ask you this. How many times was your sister stabbed?"

"Once," I said. "In the chest."

"The heart?"

I nodded.

"Forgive me," she said softly. "Was she raped?"

Again, I could only nod.

"And how did he leave her?"

It all came flooding back. The swaying blue curtains, the big circular ballroom and Mandy's naked body so carefully positioned like a fallen star on the filthy floor.

It broke. Suddenly, it all came out. Everything I had been trying so hard to hold back for two weeks came flooding out. It was almost as if I could feel that autopilot switch tripping off. I hadn't cried at the funeral. But now I put my head down on my arms and started to sob. The ferocity of my grief scared me. But I couldn't stop it. It just kept coming and coming.

I heard her before I felt her. I heard the soft crunch of leather as she came to the table and sat down next to me. I smelled cigarettes and cinnamon, and then I felt her hand on my arm.

It was the only thing that kept me from falling over the edge.

20

In the privacy of Cameron's cramped bathroom, I splashed cold water on my face then sat down on the toilet. Part of me hoped that when I finally got up the guts to go back out there Eve Bellamont would be gone. But when I opened the door, she was sitting on the sofa.

"Are you all right?" she asked.

I nodded.

She rose, slipping her binder into her jacket. "I will be going, then."

"So I'm not a suspect?" I asked.

"No," she said. "I do not believe you attacked Paula Ridley." She hesitated. "Again, I am sorry about your sister."

There was something different in her voice. It wasn't just the usual dry cop condolence.

She held my eyes for a moment, then started for the door.

"I need some air," I said, grabbing a raincoat and Cameron's scarf. "I'll walk you out."

Down on the sidewalk, I paused, patting my coat for my sunglasses. The sun was still unbearably bright. I let out a long breath.

"You are sure you are all right?" she asked.

"Yeah, yeah," I said. I found the sunglasses and put them on before I looked at her. "Look, I'm sorry," I said.

"Sorry? For what?"

"What happened upstairs. For falling apart like that."

"No apologies are necessary, Monsieur Owens," she said. "It is very human to mourn."

I looked away and let out another breath. Every shop around us was shuttered and quiet.

"Listen . . . ," I began.

She was watching me, waiting.

"Would you like to maybe walk awhile?" I asked.

She gave me an odd look, then glanced at her watch.

"Ah," I said. "I'm keeping you from something."

She nodded. "I have to pick up my niece at three. We have a place we must go today." She paused. "Perhaps you would like to come?"

I was dumbstruck. The night Cameron had taken me to the jazz club, he had talked about his fiancée Athena and how he had dated her for a full year before she finally took him home to meet her family. The French, Cameron said, do not allow you in easily. But when they do, they embrace you.

I suspected that Eve Bellamont felt sorry for me and maybe didn't trust me to be alone. And maybe I didn't want to be alone right then.

"I don't want to intrude, if it is some family thing or something," I said.

"It is, but you would not be intruding." She nodded toward the corner. "My car is just over there."

We drove across a bridge near Notre Dame and into a neighborhood that looked a lot like the one where the morgue was located. The streets were empty by Paris standards and I remembered again what Cameron had said about this being a holiday. Eve Bellamont flipped out her cell and made a call as she drove. I understood none of the French, but it was obvious from the softening in her voice that she was talking to her niece.

The car came to a stop in front of a florist's shop. Like the others I had seen, this one was filled with customers. Eve Bellamont honked the horn and a few moments later, a lanky dark-haired teenage girl emerged carrying a pot of yellow chrysanthemums. She stared at me, and I was about to get out and let her have the front seat, but she clambered into the back. I caught a whiff of her youthful evergreen scent but it was quickly overpowered by the flowers. I immediately thought of that D. H. Lawrence story "Odour of Chrysanthemums" and how he had described the flowers as having "a cold deathly smell."

Eve Bellamont said something in French to the girl and she extended her hand to me across the seat. "I'm Juliette."

I took her hand. "*Enchanté.*"

Juliette laughed.

"Is my accent that bad?" I asked.

"No, it is perfect," she said with a smile that was directed more at her aunt than at me. "Do you speak French?"

"That was it."

"Good. We'll speak only English, then. My teachers say I need the practice."

As we drove, Juliette kept up a steady stream of chatter about school, her lacrosse team and a poor boy named Antoine who, from what I could gather, was a mere blip on Juliette's radar. I listened but I was hearing Mandy's voice and thinking of that boy at the funeral who had loved my sister from afar.

Eve Bellamont glanced over at me once or twice but let me stay with my thoughts. I was just grateful for the distraction of human voices.

We parked the car and started walking. Juliette had turned quiet and was trailing behind us.

"Where are we going?" I asked Eve.

"The cemetery," she said.

"What?"

She looked over at me. "Today is All Saints' Day. It is like your holiday, the one where you take flowers to the graves of loved ones."

"Memorial Day," I said. "Except it is for honoring war veterans."

Any aversion I had to being in a cemetery was overcome by my reluctance to make some lame excuse and leave, and I sure didn't want to take the metro anywhere right then. I was trying hard not to think about Paula. So I followed Eve and Juliette.

A small sign on the high wall identified the place as Cimitière du Père-Lachaise. When we walked through the stone gate, I had a sense of being in a world unlike any other, living or dead.

I was used to cemeteries with discreet white headstones on green lawns under magnolia trees. This was a sprawling Gothic necropolis of close-packed mossy mausoleums and ornate age-blackened tombstones. The last russet-colored leaves of autumn clung to the huge trees that arched over the cobblestone walkways.

As we walked deeper into the cemetery, the paths narrowed and the mausoleums grew denser. Some were new, the names clearly visible in the shiny granite. But most were old, their rusted iron doors hanging askew, their small stained glass windows broken, the family names long erased by time and the elements.

There seemed to be quite a few people wandering the

place—old, young, alone, but most with families. Everyone seemed to be carrying pots of mums.

"How big is this place?" I asked.

"Over a hundred acres," Eve said. "Many souls buried here."

"Wait," I said suddenly. "Isn't this where Jim Morrison is buried?"

Eve smiled. "Yes, along with Chopin, Piaf, Balzac, Colette, Isadora Duncan, Oscar Wilde and many, many others who are much more famous than your rock friend."

"So your friend, was he famous?"

Eve glanced at Juliette. "Only memorable," she said.

We turned down yet another winding path, and then Eve and Juliette stopped. They were looking down at a tombstone. It was black granite, fairly new, and very small compared to the others. The engraving said MAURINE BELLAMONT 1974–2000.

"Your sister?" I asked.

Eve nodded.

And Juliette's mother, I thought as I watched the girl kneel beside the tombstone. Juliette pulled out the dead plant at the foot of the grave and tossed it aside. She upended the new yellow mum from its pot and put it in the ground. She carefully tamped down the dirt, then rose, brushing the dirt from her hands.

She and Eve stood there, heads bowed. I didn't know if they were praying or not, so I stood there awkwardly, waiting. A breeze sent a sudden cascade of yellow leaves down around us. Finally, Eve looked up and took a silver flask and three plastic cups from her tote bag.

"Would you hold these?"

I took the cups. She poured some red wine into them,

stashed the flask, took two of the cups back from me and gave one to Juliette.

She and Juliette held up their cups. *"C'est parce que tout doit finir que tout est si beau,"* Eve said.

Eve and Juliette each took a drink, then looked at me.

Juliette seemed to realize I wanted to know what her aunt had said but that I wasn't going to ask. "'It's because everything must end that everything is so beautiful,'" Juliette translated.

Juliette was waiting for me to take a drink, so I took a sip.

Eve collected our glasses and stowed everything away. She went to Juliette and put her arm around the girl's shoulders. She said something softly in French and turned to me.

"Let's walk a little," she said.

"What about—?"

"She likes her time alone with her."

We started down a pathway. There were three old women tending a grave nearby, pulling out weeds and wiping away the wet dead leaves. They were chatting amiably as they worked. A younger couple was standing near another grave, smiling and talking. I heard laughter. Two kids were playing in a pile of leaves.

I had a sudden vision of all those crying girls around Mandy's casket. And of my father sitting in the shadows of his study.

"They seem so happy," I said.

"Who?" Eve asked.

I nodded to the women and the couple with the kids.

Eve's brows knitted. "That surprises you?"

"It's not like that where I come from," I said.

Eve's eyes went to the kids. "It's just the way it is here. That's what All Saints' Day is. It's not a time for sadness. It's a day for honoring the family and remembering good things about those who have passed. It is our way of keeping them alive."

"Your sister was very young when she died," I said.

Eve just nodded and kept walking.

"Can I ask how she died?"

As soon as the words were out, I regretted them. Cameron had warned me that the French were intensely private people, and I barely knew this woman.

"Her boyfriend, Juliette's father, killed her," Eve said. "He was abusive. She was trying to leave him." She paused. "Juliette was only five at the time. She came to live with me. We have only each other."

It was getting colder and I wound Cameron's scarf tighter around my neck and stuffed my hands in my pockets. We walked on, passing more families and couples, who seemed to be enjoying the cemetery as if it were some grand park. Which it was, I realized, the more we walked. Eve Bellamont was quiet, hunched down in her leather jacket, her mass of black curls shimmering in the sun. I found myself glancing at her strong profile and light brown complexion and wondering if she was an immigrant. But from where? Algeria, maybe? I had vague memories from history classes about France colonizing Algeria and the Algerian War, and I felt stupid for not knowing anything about France's ethnic makeup.

"Monsieur Owens, I don't think you should go home tomorrow," Eve said suddenly.

"You said I wasn't a suspect," I said. "Why do you need me to hang around?"

She looked away for a moment, and when her eyes came back to me that mask I had seen so many cops wear had slipped a little.

"Your sister's death," she said. "I am not fully convinced it has anything to do with the woman left in the windmill or any other cases of murdered women here. But I would like to be able to talk to you if I need to."

I was about to say she could just email me when one word she had said suddenly sank in. "You said 'cases.' There are others? Other women, I mean."

She hesitated, then nodded.

"And you have a feeling they are connected but you can't prove it."

Her eyes narrowed. "Yes."

"How many?"

"I don't know. There is so little to go on."

She turned away, as if she was looking for Juliette, but I could tell she was uncomfortable. And I had the sense that this was personal for her in some way. I thought about how Cameron and I had gotten railroaded at the police station and I wondered if Eve Bellamont had hit some walls of her own.

My hand, in my jeans pocket, closed around the necklace.

There was a voice whispering in my head.

Trust her, Bear.

"Inspector?"

Eve Bellamont turned to me.

I held out the necklace.

"Is that Mademoiselle Hoffmann's necklace?" Eve asked.

"It's the one listed on her personal effects report," I said. "But Paula told me she was positive it didn't belong to Casey."

"You should have turned it over to the police when you were at the institute," she said.

"I couldn't be sure I could trust them." I held out the necklace. "Take it, please."

She took the necklace, studying it for a few moments before her eyes flicked back up to me.

Until that moment, I hadn't decided what I was going to do exactly. I had come to Paris on a wave of grief and furious impotency. But I had no plan, no real idea of what I was going to do. I kept thinking of what Mandy had said that night in the bar back in South Beach, that she wasn't brave like me. But I wasn't brave, and the awful truth was, as much as I wanted to find Mandy's killer, I wasn't sure I had the guts to see this through to the end. And I had the strange feeling that Eve Bellamont knew this.

Juliette came up to us. She held out a yellow mum to me.

"For you, Monsieur Owens," she said.

"Why me?"

"Remembrance," Juliette said. "You have someone to remember?"

I took the flower. "Yes, I do."

Eve was still holding the gold necklace. She hesitated then put it in her coat pocket. She looked up at me, as if she were trying to figure out how much more to tell me—or how far to trust me.

"So, you are leaving tomorrow?" she asked finally.

I was suddenly acutely aware of the acrid smell of the chrysanthemum in my hand.

"I want to find the man who murdered my sister," I said. "But I can't do it alone. I need someone to help me. And I think you do, too."

Eve Bellamont just stared at me.

"I'm staying," I said.

21

The next day, I called Delta and canceled my flight back to Miami. My second call was to my boss Darcy to ask for extra time off. I was rechecking my passport—it expired in less than two weeks—when Cameron's doorbell rang. I buzzed it open and left the door ajar. A few minutes later, Eve appeared, holding file folders and what looked like Chinese-takeout containers.

"Could you?" she asked, lifting a knee to keep the containers balanced on the folders. I took them and set them on the table and reached back to help her with her stack of files, but she was already through the door.

"You didn't have to bring lunch," I said.

"It is just some Thai food from the place around the corner," she said.

I looked in one of the boxes. The one thing I had discovered in my short time here was that the French could probably make tree bark taste good.

"Shall we work here on the table?" Eve asked.

I had cleared it, unsure exactly what we were going to be doing. All I knew was that we were going to talk about Mandy, Casey and the woman left in the windmill. That's all Eve had promised me yesterday at the cemetery.

I knew there was no way a foreign investigator was going

to let me in on the details of cases. But I was grateful that Eve was at least willing to listen.

She draped her leather coat over the back of her chair and sat down. She started sorting her colored file folders. There were also several manila envelopes stamped in bright red ink: PHOTOGRAPHIES/NE PAS PLIER.

"How is Paula?" I asked.

"She is holding on," Eve said. "Still not conscious."

"I'd like to go see her."

Eve didn't seem pleased with the idea. "I think we should wait on that."

I didn't argue. Eve opened her top folder and started reviewing a report. Suddenly, she looked up.

"Before we go any further, I want you to know that everything we discuss is confidential," she said. "The press in America has what they call confidential sources, no?"

"All the time."

"And you protect those sources even at the risk of going to jail?"

"Yes."

"Think of me that way," she said. "And protect me as you would any other source. Can you do that?"

I realized in that moment what Eve Bellamont was doing. By working with me, she was crossing a professional line that could get her in trouble with her superiors. And that told me that what I was offering to her—my fragile links between Casey Hoffmann, the woman found in the windmill and Mandy—was important to her.

That made us conspirators in a sense, and I couldn't say I didn't find that intriguing.

"I won't lie to you and I won't keep things from you or betray you in any way, Inspector Bellamont," I said.

"Please call me Eve."

I nodded. "But I'd like to know that you trust me as well."

"I am beginning to," she said. She gave me a cut of her dark eyes and I knew that was all I was going to get for now.

Eve slipped right into business. "Based on what you told me about Mademoiselle Hoffmann's visit to the sewer, I asked our medical examiner to take another look at her case," she said. "What he found is something we would not have noticed unless someone had brought our attention to it."

I waited.

"It is true that she drowned," Eve said, "but the water in her lungs was heavily contaminated with sulfuric and uric acid, chemicals found in the sewers. There were also traces of methane gas in her nostrils."

"You're saying she went underwater in the sewers and then floated out to the river?"

"Exactly," Eve said. "The sewers are designed to overflow into the rivers after heavy rains."

"So it wasn't suicide."

"Some of my associates are saying it could be an accident, but then there is this."

She handed me a photograph of Casey Hoffmann's hand. Despite the puckered skin, I could see a slash on the fleshy part of her palm. It was clear, even to me, that it was a defensive wound, like you might get if you threw an arm up in front of your face to fend off an attacker.

"A knife?" I asked.

Eve shook her head. "It is very thin. Our medical examiner thinks it may have been a wire."

"But she could have gotten it from a fall or a rough journey through the water," I said.

"You sound like my former partner," Eve said, a small smile tipping her lips. "Always playing the devil's side."

"The devil's advocate."

"But I do not believe that either," Eve said. "So, based on what you told me yesterday about the ticket stubs, I traced Mademoiselle Hoffmann's steps the day she disappeared." She opened a folder. "We found her alone on surveillance cameras at the Eiffel Tower and at the entrance to the Musée d'Orsay."

"That's the art museum, right?"

"Yes. We found nothing of her leaving the Musée d'Orsay but we do have this from the sewers," Eve said.

She slid a photograph across the table. The surveillance camera at the sewer entrance had caught Casey Hoffmann and a dark-haired man whose profile was just a blur.

"There's no way he could be identified from this," I said.

"That is true, but it is all we have," Eve said. "And it does show she entered the sewers with someone but never came out, at least not through the exit."

Eve got up and went to the kitchen. When she turned to me she was eating out of the takeout carton with a plastic fork.

"What about the necklace? Do you know anything about it yet?" I asked.

She had a photograph of the necklace. "The engraving says 'Two hearts,'" Eve said. "There are no jeweler's marks, and while it has two pieces and looks as if it would come apart, like a locket, it does not. Our experts feel it is at least twenty years old."

"But we still don't know how Casey got it," I said.

"She was a tourist. They buy things here on impulse, especially from the street vendors."

"But you said it was real gold, and Paula told me Casey was watching her money pretty tight," I said.

Eve considered this, then came back to the table with the takeout carton and sat down. "There was no odd jewelry found with my other victims," she said. "Was there anything found with your sister that was not hers?"

"The only thing that didn't belong to her was that song on her iPod."

"You are sure?"

I reached into my computer bag. "Here's the crime scene photos," I said.

Eve took them, and I used the moment to go to the kitchenette and start into the other carton of Thai food.

"There is much litter," she said. "This is a building site?"

"Yes," I said.

Eve set the photos aside. "Tell me more about the music on the iPod," she said.

I got Mandy's iPod from my duffel. "The police told me they think Mandy's killer dropped it," I said. "But I think he left it intentionally, and I was able to verify that the Rolling Stones song was downloaded during the time Mandy was missing."

Eve's brows arched. "That is very important evidence," she said. "Why do your police not have this now?"

"The iPod was returned to me. I discovered the song after the police barred me from the investigation and I was angry. When I found the article on the Internet about the murder here at the windmill, I thought my job as an investigative reporter qualified me to be an international detective. So, I kept the iPod and hopped a plane here. I was stupid."

"Yes, you were," Eve said.

I didn't say anything.

She nodded to the iPod. "I would like to hear the song."

I handed Eve my earbuds and dialed up the song. If the words disturbed Eve, she didn't let me see it on her face.

"Interesting," she said when the song was over.

"Now do you see how I ended up here?" I asked.

Eve almost smiled. "It is where any good investigator would end up."

It was a small compliment but I was glad to have it.

Eve was fingering the iPod thoughtfully. "Again, I apologize for my bluntness, but we don't have much time today," she said. "Tell me everything you know about your sister's murder."

I spilled it all out, being careful not to leave out any details.

"Do your police have a DNA sample from her rape?" Eve asked.

I nodded. "But her killer . . ." I paused, a creep of heat warming my face. I was embarrassed for Mandy and myself.

"He ejaculated outside of her body?" Eve asked.

"Yes," I said, surprised. "How did you know that?"

As she had done when I first told her about the ice pick, Eve allowed herself a "tell" that let me know things were getting interesting. This time it was a heavy sigh, and I knew there was something definite in Paris that connected to Mandy's murder.

Eve pulled a color photograph from a file and handed it to me. It was a headshot of a young woman with straw-colored hair and high cheekbones. Pretty but rough around the edges.

"That is Tricia Downey," Eve said, "the woman found in the windmill last January. The concierge of her hotel told us that the night she disappeared she asked for directions to

Sainte-Chapelle. It is a church near Notre Dame, a popular tourist attraction, but at night it is open only for concerts."

"Did you find ejaculate with her in the windmill?" I asked.

Eve shook her head. "No, there was nothing."

"But she was stabbed, right?" I asked.

"No, she was garroted with a wire that we did not find. Her neck was nearly severed. She had lost almost all her blood, though there was no blood found in the windmill."

I was discouraged. And confused. Why was Eve giving me information about Tricia Downey when it didn't seem to fit any of the details of Mandy's murder?

"So Tricia Downey was killed with a wire," I said slowly. "Was it like the one that might have made the wound on Casey Hoffmann's hand?"

Eve gave a small nod.

"Isn't it unusual for a serial killer to switch weapons?"

Again, Eve nodded. I got the feeling she was as confused as I was.

"But he left a cassette tape with Tricia Downey," I said. "What was on it?"

"Music," she said. "Most of it was corroded by decomposing body fluids but our techs were able to restore about forty seconds of what sounded like religious music. To me, it sounds like Gregorian chants."

At least I now had my musical connection to Mandy, thin as it was. But what connection could there be between religious chants and the Rolling Stones? And why didn't the other pieces match up?

Eve drew a second photograph from her folder and laid it next to the picture of Tricia Downey. "This is Nicole Duval," she said.

I pulled the photograph closer. This woman had a heart-shaped face, collagen-puffed lips and long hair the color of the sand on Miami Beach.

"She was a high-priced escort from a company called International Beauties," Eve said. "They provide women for men all through Europe but Mademoiselle Duval worked out of Paris. She was not officially working the night she disappeared and wasn't reported missing for days, since she lived a very, shall we say, unconventional lifestyle. It was also her lifestyle that discouraged my department from spending too many resources looking for her killer."

I felt a hard pit forming in my gut. A fourth woman. How many others did Eve have in her files?

Eve went on. "Mademoiselle Duval was stabbed once through the heart with a sharp instrument. She was found nude, with a few drops of semen near her body."

"Like my sister," I said.

Eve nodded. "Nicole's body was found in the Parc des Buttes Chaumont—"

I had to interrupt. "Another park?"

"Yes, in a place called the Temple of Sibyl."

"Is that a church?"

"No. It is a monument. Imagine a very tall gazebo with Roman pillars."

"Was there a musical clue left with her?"

"No."

"Nothing? Maybe it was something no one knew how to interpret. It could be lying with your evidence unexamined."

I realized too late my tone had turned accusatory.

"We have good investigators here," Eve said. "We still have every item we picked up at the scene. I have been looking at it for two years. There is no musical clue in any of it, I promise you."

I felt lousy for questioning the capabilities of her fellow officers. Or her.

"I apologize," I said.

"Accepted."

She opened her last folder and withdrew another headshot of a woman. This one had a creamy complexion, long corn-silk hair worn in a loose braid and the tender blue eyes of a young girl, even though I suspected she was over twenty.

"Hélène Molyneaux," Eve said. "She was a student here at the Sorbonne but was from a city north of here called Beauvais. She disappeared five years ago this month, a few days before she was to go home for her father's sixtieth birthday, a very important event for her since the doctors had told him when he was younger that he would never see fifty."

"Where did you find her body?" I asked.

"We haven't," Eve said. "Hélène Molyneaux was the beginning, *my* beginning. But the case went nowhere and eventually I was told to drop it and move on."

Eve took a moment to pick at her food. I suspected that the act of opening herself up to me, or any stranger, was very difficult for her. Maybe more difficult when it came to her professional life.

Nora had never talked much to me about what it was like to be one of a handful of high-ranking female officers in the violent crimes unit of one of the country's most legendary badass police departments. But as I studied Eve now, I wondered how much misery Nora had kept hidden and how much I had simply not noticed.

"Please go on," I said.

"I know you might be thinking that there is no evidence to connect Hélène to the others," Eve said. "And I know that you are also thinking that all these pieces do not seem to fit. But that does not matter right now. What matters is that I now believe your sister was a victim of the same man I have hunted for five years."

Words had been my life for as long as I could remember. It was the way I made my living, it was the way I made my way in the world. But I couldn't describe the feeling that came over me when I heard Eve say those words and embrace Mandy as one of her own. For the first time in nearly two weeks, I was willing to put my sister in someone else's hands.

"Excuse me for a moment," I said.

I took my laptop to Cameron's bedroom and plugged into his printer. It didn't take me long to find the photo I wanted. I pulled it up on the screen and hit PRINT. The photograph of Mandy printed in vivid color.

I took it back to the table and laid it next to the pictures of Hélène, Nicole and Tricia.

"This is my sister, Amanda Lynn Owens," I said. "She was twenty-one and I loved her very much."

Eve's eyes moved over the pictures, then she picked up the one of Casey Hoffmann and set it next to Mandy's, so the five women were displayed in the order of their deaths.

I had seen a similar exhibit once in a book about Ted Bundy, a display of his victims. They had all been brunettes; the girls in our photographs were all blue-eyed blondes.

I picked up the photo from the surveillance camera, the shot of the unknown man with the blurry face.

"Could we go to the park where this Tower of Sybil is?" I asked.

Eve's dark eyes came up, questioning. "Temple of Sybil," she said, correcting me. "But why? What purpose would it serve? It's been two years."

"I'm a writer," I said. "I look for images that I can put into words and words that I can make into a story. It's just how my mind works. I have to *see* places."

Eve gathered up her pictures, including Mandy's, and put them in the folder. As she stood up, she reached for her jacket.

"If you want to see the temple, we should go now," Eve said. "Juliette is making dinner for me tonight."

I grabbed my jacket and followed Eve to the door.

She stopped suddenly and turned back to me. "Maybe you would like to join us for dinner?"

I hesitated and nodded. Again I was surprised by Eve's willingness to include a stranger in her plans. But then again, maybe I was no longer a stranger.

22

There were, I had discovered, many parks in Paris. They were very important to life in this city, and each was unique, with its own special appearance and mood. Parks, Eve told me, were the "lungs" of Paris, the things that gave Parisians life.

And brought them death, apparently.

The Parc des Buttes Chaumont, where Nicole Duval's body had been found, was on the city's northern edge, in the nineteenth arrondissement.

Like the neighborhood of the morgue, the nineteenth was a working-class Paris that was very different than the tourist brochure version. We passed a market where bright caftans fluttered on plastic hangers and exotic melons and red octopuses were arranged like mosaics. Music blasted from stores advertising cheap CDs, and the air was thick with spices. It seemed to be the home of many immigrants, although I couldn't tell what kind from any of the signs, and I still didn't feel comfortable enough with Eve to ask.

She told me the park was just a short distance from her apartment and that when Juliette was a child they had often gone there on Wednesdays when school was out. Since finding Nicole Duval's body, however, she had avoided the place.

As I walked through the park gates, I thought that there could be a dozen bodies buried here and they would never be found.

With its odd hills, winding paths, drooping willow trees and still green ponds, this park felt like a place of secrets, a place where a man could lure a woman into the dark, where her cries wouldn't be heard, where her body wouldn't be found for weeks or even months.

We walked steadily uphill and when we rounded a bend, I was surprised to see a rocky peak ahead, surrounded by a lake. Through the bare trees, I could just make out a structure of some kind on top.

We climbed higher, crossed a bridge, and I got my first good look at the Temple of Sibyl. It was a tall handsome structure, with Corinthian columns, like a small Roman ruin.

I stopped. I felt the hairs rise on the back of my neck.

"What is it?" Eve asked.

"It's round," I said.

She frowned. "So?"

"The windmill was round," I said. "And the ballroom where Mandy was found, that was round, too."

Eve was looking at the temple now as if she were seeing it for the first time. I mounted the steps and stopped. "She was found here?" I asked, pointing to the center.

"Yes," Eve said, coming to my side.

"Was her body posed, like a star?"

"Yes." She let a moment go by. "Mademoiselle Downey was found in the same kind of position."

"So was Mandy," I said quietly.

I walked a slow circle around the temple with my head down. "You found nothing here with Nicole?"

"Nothing. There was no music, no tape, nothing here with her, Matt."

I heard the frustration in her voice and turned. She was scanning the floor intently, like she was trying hard to remember what it had looked like two years ago. Suddenly, she looked up at me.

"She wasn't killed here," she said.

"But you told me—"

"I know. I wasn't clear. She was killed nearby but then brought up here."

"Where was Nicole killed?"

"Come, I'll show you."

We went back across the bridge and down a different path. I heard rushing water and as we rounded another bend, I was shocked to see an impressive waterfall. Eve motioned for me to follow her, and we crept along a slippery ledge and entered a small cavern.

"We found blood here," Eve said, raising her voice to be heard over the rush of water. "It was Nicole's."

The cavern was littered with bottles, cigarette butts, trash and used condoms. The rock walls were covered with graffiti, most of it in French with a few American profanities and pentagrams thrown in. When my eyes came back to Eve, her expression was grim.

"We bagged up everything we found," she said, as if reading my mind. "We went through everything, Matt, every piece of trash, but there was nothing connected with music."

"But you didn't know then that you were even looking for music," I said.

She nodded slowly. The defensiveness was gone now, every trace of it.

I gestured toward the graffiti. "Maybe he wrote something here."

She came up next to me and scanned the rock. "I do not remember exactly what was there two years ago."

"What does the French say?" I asked, pointing.

"It's just profanities, kids' stuff."

I was trying hard to make out some of the French words, looking for anything that registered. Then my eyes latched onto three words spray-painted in faded red.

CREEPING JESUS HEART

"Was that here two years ago?" I asked, pointing.

Eve stared at it for a moment and nodded. "Yes, I remember it was part of a phrase and we photographed it. I don't remember what the rest of it was."

The three words were an itch in my brain. But I couldn't figure out why. It wasn't just that they were in English. Something about them was weirdly familiar.

If the music on the tape left with Tricia Downey was chants, maybe this was religious, too. I closed my eyes, trying to block out the rush of the waterfall, trying to summon up the hymns from all those Sundays Mom had dragged me to church. Lots of songs about Jesus but . . .

My eyes shot open. "It's a rock song," I said.

"What?"

I spun toward Eve.

The title wasn't coming to me, but I could hear the melody as if it were booming from the speakers in my cottage back home. That vaguely country beat, that nasally voice, that barrage of words and images that had always appealed to the writer in me.

"I know this song," I said. "It's by Elvis Costello."

Then the title came to me like a punch to the stomach. I looked up at Eve. "It's called 'Crimes of Paris.'"

23

We didn't realize it, but we had closed the circle to just the two of us. That was how intense our concentration was as Eve and I sat at her dining room table. My laptop, her case files and all the photographs of the victims—Tricia Downey, Nicole Duval, Hélène Molyneaux, Casey Hoffmann, and Mandy—were spread out before us.

We now had two solid musical clues. But we still didn't know what the songs meant. The Stones song left with Mandy referred back to Tricia Downey in the windmill. Did that mean the others pointed backward as well? Until we could figure out what the "creeping Jesus heart" of the Elvis Costello song meant and decipher what was on the damaged tape left at the windmill, we couldn't be sure what the music was telling us.

We had decided to first tackle the tape, and Eve had gone to the bedroom to find the CD of the music her department techs had made.

Juliette had retreated to the kitchen to finish preparing dessert. Cameron had found a chair in the corner of the small living room where he was nursing a glass of Chablis and thumbing through a magazine.

Maybe it was the smell of strong coffee coming from the

kitchen or the quiet of the living room, but I finally looked up from the crime report I had been reading.

I realized I had been ignoring Cameron all night. I had asked him to join us at Eve's after telling her that he could help us decipher the rock lyric connections. If Eve had any reservations about welcoming a complete stranger to dinner, she was too classy to mention it.

As for Cameron, well, he was taking things with his usual aplomb. All during dinner, while Eve and I had been busy trading theories, he kept Juliette entertained with his stories about covering American rock stars.

I picked up the wine bottle and went over to him.

"Need a refill?" I asked.

"I'm good," he said. He glanced to the kitchen. "But I don't think Juliette is," he added in a low voice.

I looked toward the kitchen, then back at him. "Why?"

He shrugged. "I have the impression she is worried about her aunt."

"She said something to you?"

"No, it's just a feeling."

I went into the kitchen. Juliette was rinsing out a pot. On the counter was a strawberry tart and the little glasses that I knew Juliette would use to serve the Moroccan coffee she had secured from the shop downstairs.

"Your dinner was great," I said.

She turned and gave me a big smile. I realized she looked a lot like Eve. But then again, I had never really seen anything approaching a smile like that from Eve.

"I've never had mushroom soup made from scratch," I said.

"Scratch?" Juliette said.

"My mushroom soup always came from a can."

She smiled again and started cutting the tart into quarters.

"You're a great cook," I said.

"Yes, I know. I could be a professional, but it does not really interest me," she said. "I want to work with computers." She stopped and turned to me. "Monsieur Owens . . ."

"Matt," I said.

She smiled. "Matt." She glanced toward the outer room. "I do not know you, but I feel I have to say this. I love my aunt very much. But I am very worried about her."

I knew Juliette was only sixteen, but suddenly, she seemed much older, like she was the old soul in this home.

"These women who have died," Juliette said. "My aunt, she—" She launched into a quiet flurry of French and then shook her head. "My English fails me sometimes. I am sorry."

"No, it's fine. Go on, please."

She drew in a breath. "My aunt is too . . . worried about the women. It is for her *une idée fixe.*"

"Fixated?" I said.

Juliette nodded. "It has been five years now, ever since Hélène Molyneaux." She shook her head slowly. "You should see her bedroom. It is all there on the walls, the photographs of the women, the reports. It is all there, and she is never able to get away from it."

As hard as it was for Eve to live with this, I realized suddenly it had to be doubly hard for her niece.

"Things were better for a while," Juliette said softly. "I think it was because my aunt believed she had done everything she could. But now, you come here, and I see it all over again. It is bad again."

Bad? Bad for whom? For a moment, all I could think about was Mandy and I felt a flash of resentment toward this girl. But then I found myself staring straight into Juliette's calm brown eyes and I understood.

Une idée fixe. Eve was obsessed. I was obsessed. But to the people who loved us, our obsession meant only pain and loneliness.

"Juliette, I didn't come here to make things hard for you or your aunt," I said. "I'm an investigative reporter. Your aunt is a detective. Both of us are vulnerable to obsession when we find a case that touches our hearts more than others."

"I know," Juliette said softly.

"For people like us," I said, "the truth is the only thing that can relieve that obsession. I want to help your aunt find that. I promise you, I won't make things worse."

Juliette just looked at me, her eyes sad. She hesitated, then picked up a tray. "Would you help me take the dessert to the table?"

"Of course," I said.

When I set the tray on the table, Eve was inserting the CD into a player so we could listen to the music found in the windmill.

"As I said, the tape was very poor quality," Eve said. "But our technicians copied a clean section and looped it."

Cameron brought his tart and coffee to the table and sat down with us. Eve hit the PLAY button.

I had spent countless hours under headphones and had attended a lot of concerts, but this was something I had never heard before. A little like opera or a Catholic liturgical piece, with a solo by an angelic voice that I could not distinguish as male or female.

From the bewildered look on Cameron's face, I doubted he recognized this as anything in his memory banks.

"Well?" I asked.

"I have no clue," Cameron said. "I agree it's very similar to a chant, but there's something vaguely modern about it that I can't put my finger on. Play it again, please."

Eve let the music play again and when it was over, the three of us sat there like our brain batteries had died.

"I think it sounds like the music from that movie about the French Revolution," Juliette said.

We all turned to her. She was sitting at the bar that divided the kitchen and living room, coffee in hand.

"The one with Hilary Swank," Juliette added.

I looked to Cameron. He shook his head. Juliette jumped off the stool and disappeared into her bedroom.

Eve sighed. "She has a thing about the revolution," she said. "She has read every book, seen every play and movie on the subject."

Juliette returned with a laptop. She set it on the bar and clicked on a link for an MP3. The music featured a woman's voice with overlapping chants and a background of delicate bells. It was similar enough to the windmill music to get me on my feet.

"Who sings that?" I asked.

She paged through a few screens and looked up. "The credits say it is Dead Can Dance."

"I've heard of them," Cameron said. "They're a sort of goth-punk group from Australia. They take music from all sorts of cultures and mash it into their own style. Very strange stuff."

"Juliette," I said. "Can you find a list of all their songs?"

She nodded and a few clicks later she had a long list on the screen, some titles in a foreign language, some that sounded like operas, others just plain bizarre.

"It'll print over there," Juliette said, nodding toward a printer in the corner.

I went over and waited for both pages to print, then started back to the table, reading as I walked. I stopped halfway across the room.

"What?" Eve asked.

"They have a song titled 'The Song of the Sibyl,'" I said.

Eve looked to Juliette. Without a word, she started typing, and I knew she was trying to find the piece.

Less than a minute later, her laptop was playing Dead Can Dance's "The Song of the Sibyl." Juliette let it play for its full three and a half minutes, but it didn't take that long for all of us to realize that we were listening to the same music that was on the cassette tape.

"Come sit down, Matt," Eve said.

I dropped into a chair, staring at the cassette player. The song probably had lyrics, but I didn't think we needed them. The clue was right there in the title. The tape that had been found with Tricia Downey in the windmill was a reference to the Temple of Sibyl, where Nicole Duval had been found. And just as the song that had been left on Mandy's iPod referred to a previous crime, so did this one.

I looked up at Eve and Cameron. "The songs are clues to where he left his previous victim."

"So who does the Elvis Costello song refer to?" Cameron asked. "Do you have a victim before Nicole?"

"I have only one other woman, Hélène Molyneaux, but we have never found her body," Eve said.

"Plus she disappeared five years ago," I said. "The time between the other murders is only about a year."

"So if this pattern is true, there are two more victims we have not found," Eve said, her voice tinged with excitement.

I caught Juliette's eye. She was still sitting at the bar watching us. She slowly closed her laptop and went into the kitchen.

"Well, this will tell you where to start looking," Cameron said, holding out a printout of the Elvis Costello song.

I took the printout and spread it on the table so we could all read the lyrics.

"What about the title, 'Crimes of Paris,'?" Cameron asked.

"I don't think it's that simple," I said.

"What about the line 'not a girl from Paris'?" Eve asked. "A reference to another American tourist, perhaps?"

"I doubt it. You would have already found her."

"What about the reference to the Eiffel Tower paperweight?" Cameron asked.

"It would be hard to hide a body there, I would think," Eve said.

"Plus, it's not round," I added.

"Round?" Cameron asked.

"I'll explain later," I said.

My eyes moved over the words a second and third time, then finally stopped on a reference to what I thought was yet another song.

"Cameron, do you know a song called 'Hammersmith Blues'?" I asked.

Cameron froze, and I knew something had registered. "It's not a song," he said. "It's a place, a dance club called the Hammersmith Palais de Danse. The Clash had a song called '(White Man) In Hammersmith Palais.'"

How could I have missed this? I had many of The Clash's albums in my own collection. "Where is this Hammersmith place?" I asked.

"London," Cameron said. "The place closed years ago. I don't know if it's still standing or not."

London.

I glanced at Eve. We both knew a few lines from a song weren't enough.

"I have a friend at Interpol," she said, reaching for her cell. "I will see if he has anything."

I had already pulled my laptop over and was firing up Nexis. I typed in the keywords "Hammersmith London" and "murder." A three-year-old article from the *Times* of London popped onto my screen.

A twenty-five-year-old woman named Allison Stephens had been found dead in the Hammersmith Palais de Danse. I scanned the details, some of which seemed to match our cases, notably that she had been found naked and there had been only a single fatal stab wound to the chest. There was no mention of rape, but I knew from my own experience that when a young woman was found nude, it usually meant sexual assault.

But then a follow-up article came up: A man named Dylan Rumsley had been arrested in the murder. He was Stephens's ex-boyfriend.

Eve had finished her call and was reading over my shoulder. "Was he convicted?" she asked.

I punched a couple keys and another article came up. I looked up at Eve. "Yeah," I said. "Now serving time."

Eve blew out a long breath and sat down. We just stared at each other for a few moments.

Dylan Rumsley's conviction put Eve in a tough spot. If she pursued this, she would be questioning the British police's investigation and their judicial process.

But I was thinking about this faceless man we chased. One murder in America. Four—five if Paula died—in France. And now, maybe one in England. How vast was his hunting ground?

"Do we go or not?" I asked.

Eve was looking at the photograph of Hélène. "Yes," she said. "But we have to make a detour first."

24

The detour was to the town of Beauvais, about fifty miles north of Paris. The reason was to visit the family of Hélène Molyneaux.

I knew without being told that this visit was important to Eve. And as eager as I was to get on to London and the Hammersmith, I had to honor that.

As we rode in a cab from the train station, I could see that Beauvais was a beautiful old city at the foot of some wooded hills on a river. It was the birthplace, Eve told me, of her personal heroine, Jeanne Hachette.

She went on to say that in the fourteen hundreds, Beauvais was attacked by invaders. But when one of them tried to plant a victory flag, a peasant girl named Jeanne picked up an ax, chopped the guy's head off and flung him into a moat. When Jeanne tore down the flag, the village men were inspired to rout the invaders.

As we passed the statue of Jeanne and her hatchet in the square, Eve told me her heroism is still celebrated every October fourteenth. "It is a day when all the men must defer to the women," she said.

"Is this your way of reminding me who's in charge here?" I asked with a smile.

"Take it as you wish," she said.

The cab was stalled in a narrow street, waiting for a truck to unload. The driver rolled down his window and let loose with a tirade in French, but the trucker gave him what I assumed was an obscene gesture and kept calmly unloading his boxes.

Eve used the time to check her phone messages. Her face darkened as she listened, then she hung up.

"Problems?" I asked.

She let out a slow sigh. "The commandant," she said. "He wants to know when I am coming back."

Eve had told me that after she informed her boss about the Hammersmith case, he had given her permission to pursue the new lead. But he had warned her not to ignore her regular caseload, and he hadn't signed off on the trip to London. Eve had cashed in some vacation days and was making the trip on her own dime.

She didn't say more, but I got the feeling she was being kept on a very short leash. I found myself wondering again about what it was like for her at her department.

The trucker was taking his time. Our taxi driver was now reading a newspaper.

"So why'd you become a cop?" I asked.

Eve glanced at me and went back to scrolling through her text messages. "That is a rather personal question," she said.

"Yeah, I know." I paused. "My ex is a cop."

Her eyes shot to me. "Really?"

I nodded. "She's one tough lady."

Eve was quiet for a moment. "Did she talk about her work to you?"

"Sometimes," I said. "But cops are weird about letting civilians inside, you know?"

"Yes, I know," she said softly.

The trucker was almost finished with his work. Our driver laid on the horn for good measure, then went back to his paper.

"Juliette tells me I go inside myself, that I get lost inside myself," Eve said. "It hurts her sometimes, I think, my work."

For a second I thought about telling her about my conversation with Juliette in the kitchen last night but decided against it. "You didn't answer my question," I said instead.

"Why I became a cop?" Eve hesitated. "To prove myself, I think."

"To yourself?" I asked.

She nodded. "And to my father. He was from a little village in Provence, very poor, and went to Algeria when he was only eighteen. Algeria was a French territory and he settled there and started a vineyard."

"Is that where he met your mother?" I asked.

She nodded again. "She was Algerian. After the war for independence, they returned here. It was hard for them."

"Because your mother was Arab?" I asked.

She hesitated. "Yes, and because my father was *un piednoir*."

When she saw my blank expression, she went on. "It means 'black foot.' It is a kind of derogatory term for those who came back after the war."

I wondered what Eve's childhood had been like, whether things were as hard for a biracial kid in France as they could be back in the States. And I found myself thinking of my own father, and how I had always told myself that I didn't need to impress him with anything I had done. Yet he had been the first person I had called when I found out I was a Pulitzer finalist.

"So your father," I said, "how does he feel about your job?"

"He was very proud that I became a *flic*," she said.

"*Flic*?"

"Cop," she said with a smile. "My sister Maurine was very proud of me, too."

"So is your niece," I said.

Eve looked at me but before she could reply, the truck blocking our way chugged off and our taxi lurched down the narrow street.

As we drove, Eve filled me in on the details of Hélène Molyneaux's background. She was twenty when she disappeared five years ago. She was a student at the Sorbonne whose conservative parents had not wanted their only child to leave home for a life in the capital. Hélène, to appease them, took the train home to Beauvais every weekend. She had always, Eve stressed, been a dutiful daughter.

Eve also told me how she came to be involved in Hélène's case. When the young woman failed to come home one weekend and then was not seen in classes, her parents went to the police. The usual missing-person report was filed, the usual investigation done, with fellow students and acquaintances interviewed. There were no boyfriends, no leads, nothing to explain why this lovely, obedient daughter had suddenly vanished. But Hélène's grieving father would not give up. He hounded the Paris police, and eventually, Eve said, she was assigned to "take care" of him.

"I was the lowest-seniority investigator," she said. "And I was the only woman."

I understood. Nora, as a rookie, had always pulled babysitting duty, as she called it. Like not having the Y chromosome automatically made you more compassionate or something.

"Monsieur Molyneaux is a good man," Eve said. She was quiet for a moment. "I perhaps became too close, became too emotionally involved. But it is what it is." She looked at me. "That is the expression, no?"

"That is the expression, yes," I said.

The taxi pulled up to a handsome gray building with a small courtyard. Beyond the iron fence, I could see a bank of tall windows and a carved wood door. Church bells tolled somewhere nearby.

A maid led us to a formal sitting room furnished with chairs and settees too delicate looking to hold my weight. I finally took a chance on a small chair in the corner; Eve stood at the tall windows looking out at the garden. The creak of the old parquet floor made me look to the door.

Gerard Molyneaux was a tall, thin balding man with the slightly faded look of an old priest. His wife was a small bird of a woman who, if she had been blond, could have passed for my mother.

Eve introduced me by name but offered no title. Hélène's parents gave me a gracious nod but their eyes were riveted on Eve as they perched on the edge of the settee.

The conversation was in French, but Eve had told me ahead of time what she intended to tell them. That their daughter's case had been reopened, that it might be related to the deaths of other women, that she was working new leads that might help her find their daughter's murderer.

I wondered if she was telling them what I had come to learn: that Eve would not give up until she found Hélène.

Mrs. Molyneaux was weeping softly. Mr. Molyneaux's face was gray but he was hanging on every word Eve said. Suddenly, one word jumped out of their conversation: Mandy.

And then, all eyes swung to me.

"What?" I asked Eve.

"I told them it was you who did it," Eve said.

"Did what?"

"Found the evidence to reopen their daughter's case. I also told them about your sister." Eve's expression turned contrite. "I should have asked you first."

But before I could say anything, Mrs. Molyneaux rose and came over to me. I stood up. She barely came to my chin. She said something to me in French in a soft voice. I looked to Eve.

"She said she is sorry about your loss," Eve said.

Mrs. Molyneaux hesitated, then embraced me. When she drew back there were tears in her eyes. "Thank you," she said.

I nodded stiffly, overcome. I was saved by her husband, who came forward and put his arm around his wife's shoulders.

"This has been very hard on my wife," he said in English. "She has not been the same since Hélène . . ."

I had an image of my father weeping over Mandy's body at the morgue and standing alone in his study, and I knew Mr. Molyneaux had done his grieving alone.

"I understand," I said.

Mrs. Molyneaux looked up suddenly. "*Souhaitez-vous la voir,* Monsieur Owens?"

Her husband looked stricken and said something softly to his wife, who countered in an insistent tone. He looked back to me.

"My wife wants to show you a photograph of our daughter," he said.

I had already seen Eve's photograph of Hélène. But I knew

Mrs. Molyneaux needed me to see her daughter as she herself saw her.

"Yes, I'd like that," I said with a glance at Eve.

I thought Mrs. Molyneaux was going to offer up a framed picture or something from a purse, but she gestured for us to follow her. The four of us went up a curving staircase and into a bedroom.

It was obviously Hélène's room, and I guessed it hadn't been changed in the last five years. It had stone walls, a graceful arched ceiling and an old leaded window that looked out onto the garden. There was a slightly musty but not unpleasant scent, like you might get in an old cathedral. Beyond that, it could have been the bedroom of any young woman, including my own sister.

A bright blue and green flowered quilt, a bureau with framed photos, a bookcase, an antique dressing table set with perfume bottles and knickknacks. Above the bed was a large poster of a bicyclist from the Tour de France.

Mrs. Molyneaux took my arm and turned me toward a framed portrait on the opposite wall.

The photo I had seen of Hélène had not done her justice. Or maybe this photographer had simply been inspired. Hélène Molyneaux—delicate boned, hair the color of wheat, eyes that made me think of the deepest waters off Miami Beach—had been a rare beauty. The photographer had posed her facing away from the camera but looking back over her bare shoulder. Her long hair was done in a loose braid, like you might see in some Renaissance painting.

I suddenly felt an overwhelming, crushing sadness.

Eve was lingering by the door, watching me. Not trusting my emotions, I looked for something else to focus on. On the top shelf of the bookcase there was a CD player and below that, a row of CD cases.

I couldn't read the titles from where I stood, and there was no way I could gracefully extract myself from the moment to look for musical clues among Hélène's CDs.

Eve was speaking to Mr. and Mrs. Molyneaux, and a moment later Mr. Molyneaux led his wife out. Eve came up to my side at the shelf of CDs.

"What did you say to them?" I asked.

"I saw you looking at the CDs so I asked Mr. Molyneaux if we could have some time to examine the room," Eve said. "Do you see anything?"

I shook my head. "I don't think so. A couple French groups I don't recognize but most of it is classical. Besides, if Hélène was his first victim like you think, he wouldn't have left a clue."

I gave up on the CDs and went to the dressing table. I felt invasive, poking among the girlish things, and remembered a time Mandy had caught me in her room when I suspected she had been secretly smoking cigarettes. Mandy had been furious with me for a couple days but eventually forgave me. She always had.

There was a snapshot in a small frame of Hélène with a brunette girl, their heads together, laughing. "Who's this?" I asked Eve, holding it out.

Eve glanced back at the picture. "Sophie Doussard. She and Hélène were childhood friends. They grew apart some after Hélène went off to the Sorbonne."

"You interviewed her?"

Eve nodded. "Several times. She said Hélène was . . . how do you say it? Of the straight and narrow?"

"There was no boyfriend in the picture?"

"No one special. Boys from Beauvais she dated, yes, but not one special boy. I checked them all out."

"So Hélène led a pretty sheltered life here?" I asked.

Eve nodded again. "Very much so. But Sophie told me Hélène was very excited about being away from home for the first time."

Again, I thought of Mandy, and I wondered if Beauvais was, in its way, like Raleigh. My sister wasn't "brave," she had said. I wondered if Hélène had been.

There was an ornate silver box on the dressing table. Mandy had had a similar one for her jewelry and special keepsakes. I opened the top. Inside was a jumble of jewelry, a few more snapshots of friends, nothing of interest. I was about to close it when a spot of gold caught my eye. I pulled it out.

It was a necklace. Gold chain with a small round medallion.

"Eve," I said.

I held it out and she took the necklace.

"Do you have the necklace that was found with Casey Hoffmann?" I asked.

She shook her head. "It's in evidence. I have a photograph in my briefcase downstairs," she said. "But this one . . ."

"Yeah, I know, it's plain and the other one was engraved. But this looks pretty damn close." I took it from Eve and carefully examined it. It was smaller than the other one and was brass, not real gold. But it seemed to have the same odd structure: two round pieces bound together with the chain running through the gap.

I tried to separate the pieces. To my surprise, they unscrewed easily. The insides were plain metal, the two halves intersected with a straight groove.

"What is this thing?" I said.

Eve shook her head, taking one of the pieces.

I heard a sound and looked up to see Mr. Molyneaux standing at the door. "My wife would like to know if you would like some coffee," he said.

Eve said something in French and went over to him. She handed him the necklace piece. He turned it over in his hand, then came to me.

"Eve said you think this might be important," he said.

"Yes," I said. "Do you know where your daughter got it?"

"When she came home one weekend, she was wearing it. She told me it had been a gift from a friend. I think she said it had something to do with her music."

"Hélène was studying the violin at the Sorbonne," Eve told me.

Mr. Molyneaux looked like he was trying hard to remember something, then he turned and went to the closet. He pulled out a violin case, laid it on the bed and opened it. "I remember she said it had something to do with strings," he said.

"Like a guitar capo?" I asked.

"What is that?" Eve asked.

"It's a clamp guitarists put on the frets to make the pitch higher," I said. I looked back at Mr. Molyneaux.

"I don't know what a capo is," he said. He handed me the necklace piece. "I'm sorry but I am of no help," he said.

"You are a big help, Mr. Molyneaux," I said.

I screwed the two parts of the necklace together. Whoever had given this to Hélène understood its connection to her music. And maybe whoever had given this to Hélène had taken her life.

I turned the necklace over in my hand, noticing again how similar yet different it was from the one found with Casey. One was plain brass; the other was engraved gold. One had been given to Hélène as a gift. And the other one? Was this another signature, like the lyrics he left? But then, why had there been no necklaces left with the others?

Maybe we just hadn't found them. Or maybe the two necklaces meant nothing.

I looked to Mr. Molyneaux, who was still standing at the door.

"May we keep this?" I asked, holding up the necklace.

"Yes," he said. "But we would like to have it back when you are done."

Mr. Molyneaux looked slowly around the bedroom, then he said something about going to help his wife.

As I watched him go, I thought again of my father, and a new realization hit me hard. My father at least had Mandy's body to bury. Hélène's parents had only a ghost to mourn.

25

From the moment we had decided to go to London, I knew that meant we would be going through the Chunnel, the tunnel under the English Channel that connected France with England. I had hoped I could survive the half-hour train trip. But now, just ten minutes into my ride through what looked like an enormous silver gun barrel, I was covered in sweat.

"Are you all right?" Eve asked.

I nodded.

"Are you ill?" she asked.

I shook my head and could manage only one word. "Claustrophobic."

Eve touched my arm. "We're almost there."

I closed my eyes, trying to concentrate on what awaited us in London.

As we were leaving Beauvais, Eve's Interpol contact had called back. He verified the information about Allison Stephens that I had found on Nexis. He had also arranged for Eve to meet someone from "the Met." Eve explained to me that London murder investigations were handled by the Metropolitan Police Service with the help of specialist forces as needed. But apparently, no help had been needed with Allison Stephens's murder. Her ex-boyfriend Dylan Rumsley had been arrested and convicted quickly, and the case was closed.

Eve had told the British police only that she was pursuing a lead on a cold-case homicide in Paris. The lead investigator, Inspector Gregory Harrison, was more than willing to talk to Eve about the possibility that the man he had sent to prison might have also murdered a woman in France.

As for me, I was just along for the ride, posing as a true-crime writer. Eve wasn't comfortable with my charade, but she knew it was the only way I was going to be allowed into the Stephens case. And as she had told Mr. and Mrs. Molyneaux, I had earned the right to be here.

Suddenly the windows in the train went from black to gray as we emerged into the rainy English countryside. I let out a long breath and released my death grip on the armrest.

"Where are we meeting this Harrison guy?" I asked.

"At the club," Eve said. "He wanted to meet in his station but I told him I wanted to see the scene."

"I thought it was closed down."

"He has gotten the keys from the owner," she said. "And by the way, when I spoke with Inspector Harrison, he seemed quite proud of his handling of this case, so let's be very considerate of his work, agreed?"

I knew it was wrong to prejudge, but I was already convinced Harrison had arrested the wrong man. I also knew I had to put those feelings aside once I extended my hand to Inspector Harrison.

The rain and fog nearly obscured the city of London as our cab drove through the congested streets in stop-and-go traffic and—to my occasional pang of terror—there were moments when I thought we were on the wrong side of the street.

We climbed out of the cab into a cold drizzle. Eve popped up her umbrella and we stood on the sidewalk in front of an ugly plain white building with blackened glass doors.

Empty poster frames, once used to advertise concerts, clung to the crumbling façade. Above the doors, ragged concrete and rusty rebar gave the impression that the marquee had simply been ripped off and carted away.

A car pulled up and a lanky, mustached man in a long yellow raincoat and a checkerboard-banded police cap climbed out. Inspector Gregory Harrison carried a worn leather briefcase under his arm.

"Inspector Bellamont and Mr. Owens, I presume?" he said, coming to us. "I'm sorry I'm tardy. I hope your trip was pleasant."

"It was fine," Eve said. "We appreciate you coming here."

Harrison unlocked the doors and we went in. The air was cold, stale and damp. The only light came from dangling bare bulbs.

I knew from my research last night that the Hammersmith Palais de Danse had been London's biggest hot spot for nearly nine decades before it closed in 2007. The Internet was full of pictures of the club in its heyday. Extravagant ballroom galas. Roaring Twenties New Year's parties. And from the sixties up to a few years ago, the stage had been illuminated nightly with a rainbow of lights for bands like the Stones and the Sex Pistols.

But now, the Palais de Danse looked only like some vast industrial ruin. The place had been gutted of fixtures, furniture, the bars and even railings. What must have once been the dance floor was now a big empty space with missing planks that exposed black holes.

The walls were plastered with faded playbills and defaced with graffiti, some of it, strangely enough, in foreign languages. Eve had brought a camera, and I wanted to make sure we got photographs of every word scrawled on these walls.

Harrison began to pepper Eve with questions about her case, but she quickly steered things back to Allison Stephens.

"Inspector," Eve said, "would you be kind enough to summarize your case for us?"

Harrison gave her a smug smile. "Miss Stephens's body was discovered on a Sunday morning by an anonymous caller who said he broke in to vandalize the place," he said. "When we responded, we found Miss Stephens dead there on the stage."

I squinted into the dimness where Harrison was pointing.

"Was she simply lying on the stage or did she look posed?" I asked.

Harrison tipped up his chin. "Come to think of it, she did seem posed in a way."

"Like a star?" I asked.

"A star?"

I hesitated, then stood with my arms and legs outstretched.

"A star," Harrison said. "I suppose one could describe it as such."

Eve tossed me a look that I took as a firm request to stay quiet. "Inspector," she said, "were you able to determine the murder weapon?"

"We didn't find it but it was an instrument similar in size and shape to an ice pick."

"Was she raped?" Eve asked.

Harrison, who was clearly past sixty, blushed. "There was some genital bruising, but we couldn't be sure it wasn't consensual. We found quite a bit of semen inside Miss Stephens and that was what led us to her boyfriend, Mr. Dylan Rumsley. It was an exact DNA match."

"What about outside the body?" I asked.

"Excuse me?" Harrison said.

I ignored Eve's look. "Did you find any semen near her body?"

Harrison's eyes swung to Eve. "Well, yes we did. A very small sample on the stage."

"Did you test it?" Eve asked.

"Well, we assumed . . ."

Eve and I exchanged glances but I kept quiet.

"Were there any other injuries?" Eve asked.

Harrison was starting to look miffed. "She had some bruises on her upper arms."

"What other evidence did you have on Dylan Rumsley?" Eve asked.

"Rumsley and Miss Stephens had been on and off for two years," Harrison said. "Her folks hated the man with a passion but they couldn't seem to break the poor girl's addiction to him. He was older, a ruffian of sorts. Good-looking chap who always had money, though no one knew where it came from."

"Was he abusive?" Eve asked.

"Abusive, possessive *and* jealous," Harrison said. "Miss Stephens filed a non-molestation order that was in effect when she was murdered."

"What can you tell us about the night she was murdered?" Eve asked.

"The two were seen together at a bar not far from here," Harrison said. "Witnesses did not seem to know if they had reconciled. These types of women often go back to their abusers, you know."

I thought about what Eve had told me about her own sister dying at the hands of a violent man. I could see a fleeting shadow of pain in Eve's eyes but I was sure Harrison couldn't.

"Sometime after eleven," Harrison went on, "Miss Stephens left the bar and Rumsley followed her outside, according to witnesses. She was never seen alive again."

"What was Rumsley's story?" I asked.

Harrison hesitated, probably detecting a disparaging edge in my voice.

"Rumsley said he and Miss Stephens argued all the way to the Hammersmith underground when he finally decided he was finished with her. He said he left her at the steps and walked away, intending to drink himself into a stupor."

"Could you verify any of that?" Eve asked.

"According to our cameras, Stephens never descended the stairs at the Hammersmith station or any other," Harrison said. "We had another witness who said he saw Stephens and a man fitting Rumsley's description walking east, away from the bar toward Shepherd's Bush Road, where we are now."

"Could anyone verify where Rumsley was after he left Allison Stephens?" I asked.

"No," Harrison said.

Eve glanced at me and I could almost read her thoughts. The case against Rumsley was good, circumstantial but solid.

I still had Hélène's necklace in my pocket and now I pulled it out and held it up to the light. "Inspector Harrison," I said. "Did you find anything like this with Allison's body?"

Harrison squinted at the necklace. "Nothing like that," he said. "She was found wearing silver skull earrings in her pierced ears. And she had a silver stud in her nose."

"What about in her home?" I asked.

He gave the necklace another look, then shook his head. "I am quite sure she had nothing like this among her possessions."

The doubt must have been clear on my face but Harrison wouldn't let it go. "Mr. Owens, I can assure you I covered everything," he said. "I inventoried everything this girl owned. Besides, Allison Stephens had a very particular style to her dress. This gold necklace would be, I would venture to say, much too demure for her."

I put the necklace back in my pocket. Maybe our killer didn't give a necklace to each victim. But he did leave song lyrics, and I wasn't ready to believe that the Hammersmith clue left in a Paris park was just a coincidence and that Allison Stephens's murder was just a domestic gone bad.

I wandered to an orange playbill lying on the floor and picked it up. It advertised a final performance by The Fall in April of 2007. They had marketed it as the "Last Night at the Palais."

I wondered if this was our lyrics clue, but this whole place was a musical junkyard. It would take us days to examine all the graffiti and litter. And who knew what might have been removed during the last four years?

I also had to remind myself that Allison Stephens's murder was not yet one of ours. It wouldn't be until Eve said it was.

My gaze locked on Harrison's briefcase. Eve had said he was bringing the case file and I had the thought that it might include photographs. He was too proud of his work on this case to resist.

"Inspector," I said, walking back to him, "may we see the case photographs?"

"Of course," Harrison said. He propped the case on his knee, retrieved a thick file of photographs and handed it to Eve. She split the stack in half and handed me the bottom twenty or so.

The first few pictures were taken from where I was standing, on the dance floor facing the stage. I walked to the front of the stage. It was as high as my chest and I circled around the front until I found some steps. I went to the center, stood under the dangling wires of the rusted proscenium and looked down at the edge of the stage.

It was perfectly round.

I sifted through the photos until I found some that showed Allison Stephens's body. The trash around her included the orange playbills, a torn poster for the band Hanoi Rocks, some spotlight gels, empty bottles and other papers too blurred to make out.

I moved on to the close-ups. Allison's feet—small with blue nail polish. Her face—skin too pale, lips dark red. I stopped on a photo of her right arm. I suspected the photographer had focused on the tattoo on her forearm but I saw something else.

A single piece of sheet music—clean and smooth—under the fingers of her right hand. I thought about the placement of the iPod, near Mandy's right hand. And the cassette tape, near Tricia Downey's right hand.

The light was bad and I moved into a slant of gray from a high window, trying to make out the title of the song at the top of the sheet music.

"Dire Wolf." Music by Jerry Garcia, lyrics by Robert Hunter.

A flash drew my eyes to Eve. She was taking snapshots of the graffiti. I wanted to shout at her that I had found our clue, but I didn't want to alert Inspector Harrison.

I considered slipping a couple of the photos into my jacket. But I remembered what I had done to Nora: locking her out of my bedroom while I copied Mandy's photos and taking the iPod halfway around the world.

I went back to Harrison. "May I keep some of these photos?" I asked.

"For your book?" he asked.

I felt like shit conning this man but I still managed a nod.

Harrison smiled. "I anticipated that and I've taken the liberty of preparing a legal release I'd like you to sign."

Harrison dug out a form that restricted my use of the photographs to my "upcoming work of nonfiction." It also forced me to allow Harrison to write the book's foreword. I signed it and handed it back.

I chose ten close-ups of Allison Stephens's body and the area around it. I called out to Eve that I would be waiting outside and left the building before she or Harrison could protest.

Outside, I found an awning to stand under and studied the street, looking for a business that might offer me what I most needed now. My eyes stopped on a chalkboard menu set outside a pub called the Cock and Bottle.

Ploughman's lunch, bangers and mash, shepherd's pie.

And free Wi-Fi.

26

The beer was warm, the pub was cold and we were the only two people in there under fifty.

The bartender was a broad-shouldered guy who talked with a brogue I couldn't place as either English or Irish. He was gone at the moment, trying to hunt me up an electrical adapter for my laptop. My battery had finally died.

Eve had gone to the restroom, so I sat watching a very intense dart game going on in the corner, my hand wrapped around my untouched beer. I was contemplating how to ask for a glass of ice without looking like an ass when the bartender reappeared.

"This should do ya," he said, holding up a black gadget. He picked up my plug and connected everything for me. The screen on my laptop lit up with the desktop of Miami Beach at sunrise.

Eve slid onto the stool next to me. She looked first to the laptop, then to the glass of pink wine sitting on the bar in front of her.

"I asked for a kir," she said.

"The bartender didn't know what it was," I whispered. "So I told him it was like a white wine with a splash of something pink in it."

"Cassis," Eve said. "It is called cassis, and it is purple, not pink."

She took a drink and made a face. "It is something close to a rosé but I don't know what."

Eve noticed the stack of crime scene photos on the bar, the ones I had conned out of Harrison. After sorting through them, she looked up at me with those severe dark eyes.

"Did you steal these?" she asked.

"No, I asked if I could have them."

"For what reason?" she asked.

"I didn't give Harrison a reason."

"What did he *assume*?" she asked.

I sighed, knowing I was busted. "He thinks they'll be in the book." I began to sift through them, looking for the one that showed the "Dire Wolf" sheet music. "I think I found something—"

"No," Eve said, putting a hand on the photographs. "First, I need to ask you something personal."

I sat back, surprised. "Go ahead."

"Your ex-girlfriend," Eve said. "Is she the same police officer working your sister's case?"

I steeled myself for what I was sure was coming—another lecture about my being too emotionally involved in Mandy's case.

"It's not her case but she's sort of assisting," I said.

"I think it's time you made things right with your friend," Eve said.

"Nora," I said. "Her name is Nora."

Eve mumbled something in French and I knew it wasn't good. She took a sip of the pink wine and pushed it away before she turned to me. "I understand your desperation and grief," she said. "But some of your actions in this case have been less than honorable."

I wanted to argue but decided to just keep my mouth shut.

Eve went on. "You have lied to a chief inspector to get photographs. You withheld the necklace from me. And you left your country with a piece of evidence that might very well have helped the Miami police make progress in your sister's case."

I took a drink of the warm beer.

Eve shook her head slowly. "Have you even checked on your sister's case?" she asked.

"No."

She pointed to my laptop. "Please do so now," she said.

I stifled a sigh, and when I loaded in Nexis and saw the headline of the *Miami Times* article, I shut my eyes.

LOCAL MAN ARRESTED IN MURDER OF NC TOURIST

It took me less than a paragraph to discover the local man was the black guy in the Dolphins jersey.

"You knew about this?" I asked.

She nodded. "I just got a call from my contact at Interpol."

It had been almost two weeks since I had last talked to Nora. I had left without telling her anything. I also had not called my parents, leaving them alone with their grief.

"Before we go one step further," Eve said, "I want you to call your friend. I want you to tell her what you've done, tell her about me and my cases, and then ask her if she will speak to me about comparing our DNA samples."

"You want Nora to send you *her* sample?" I asked. "Or the other way around?"

"I am open to either," Eve said. "Your sister's case has not been entered into the Interpol database yet, so I am forced to work directly with Miami. It would help me to have a friendly contact there."

"I'm not sure how friendly she'll be," I said.

"It's time to find out," Eve said.

"It's six A.M. in Miami," I said.

"She will not mind."

I pulled out my cell and tried to fire it up. "I can't get a signal," I said.

"There's a phone right over there."

Since I had no excuse, I rose to my feet, pulled a credit card from my wallet and walked to the phone.

It took three tries to get past Nora's answering machine. When she finally picked up, it took a full minute to calm her down after I told her where I was.

"You picked a helluva time for a vacation," she said.

"This isn't a vacation, Nora."

"You need to be in court in three days to ID the suspect in Mandy's case," she said. "When are you coming home?"

"I don't know. Look, Nora—"

"I can't believe you're doing this, Matt."

"Nora, please, you have to listen to me for a minute. What I am going to tell you concerns Mandy and it's very important."

She let out an angry sigh but was quiet. I gathered my courage and launched into the long story of the iPod, the song "Too Much Blood" and how it had taken me to Paris. I think at that point she threw something across the room.

"You should have given the iPod back to me," she said.

"Would you have believed me?"

Silence.

"Do you even believe me now?"

A few more seconds of silence before she finally answered. "I don't know what to believe, Matt. But that's always been the problem, hasn't it?"

Now I was silent for a moment. There was a burst of laughter from the men playing darts.

"Are you in a bar?" Nora asked.

"A pub."

"Are you drunk?"

She was really pissed off, so I let her have that shot at me. I took a calming breath.

"I think there were other murders here and in France that might be connected to Mandy's," I said.

"Matt," she said. "I know how hard this has been, but—"

"Nora, please. You have to listen to me. Please." As calmly as I could, I told her about the other lyrics and the other dead women. There was silence when I finished.

"I know how all this sounds, Nora," I said finally. "But I'm here with a French inspector. We're working on this together."

"An inspector?"

I glanced over my shoulder. Eve had come up behind me, arms crossed, brow raised.

"Look," I said. "Inspector Bellamont wants to speak with you about our DNA."

"You have DNA evidence?" Nora asked.

"Yes."

"Put him on."

I handed the receiver to Eve. Unsure whether to stay or go, I leaned against the wall in case Eve had questions for me. I heard Eve's end of the conversation as they talked about DNA, the black guy, Mandy's autopsy and the murders in Paris.

As I listened, I felt an odd mixture of comfort and relief. It wasn't just that I had taken some steps to square things with Nora. It was hearing a voice—her voice—and feeling a connection to home that I didn't even realize I had been missing. The relief? I watched Eve's face as it registered excitement over speaking with a fellow cop. Now I had two powerful allies.

Eve finally fell quiet, her eyes cutting to me. She laughed and turned away.

"*Oui*," she said. "Reckless, yes. Crazy, yes." A pause. "He is doing . . . he is coping. Yes. Yes. I shall. Thank you, Detective."

She held out the phone to me and I took it.

"I am still furious with you," Nora said.

But the anger was gone from her voice now. "I don't blame you," I said.

"Things have to be different from now on, you know."

"I know."

"You have to keep me informed on everything you do."

"I know."

"I want to be able to trust you, Matt."

I was quiet for a moment. "And I want you to know you can."

"Okay," Nora said softly.

We said our good-byes and I hung up. When I went back to the bar, Eve was checking her messages. I used the moment to find the "Dire Wolf" lyrics on the Internet. When Eve set her phone down, I handed her the photograph of Allison Stephens's right hand.

"Look," I said, pointing to the sheet music.

"The Grateful Dead," she said.

I turned my laptop so Eve could see the screen. The "Dire

Wolf" lyrics were already displayed, and we took a few moments to read them.

The song began: *In the timbers of Fennario, the wolves are running round.*

I read and reread the verses. The song seemed to be about someone who lived in a frozen village and was being stalked by a wolf that played a game of cards with him.

"It makes no sense," Eve said.

"Yeah, but look at these lines," I said, pointing to the screen.

Don't murder me, I beg of you, don't murder me.

"The only location mentioned in the song seems to be this place called Fennario," I said.

"Any idea where it is?" Eve asked.

I shook my head and switched back to Google to begin a search. "Fennario" appeared on various Grateful Dead fan sites, one of which included an analysis of "Dire Wolf" that concluded Fennario was purely fictional.

"Fennario" also popped up as the title of a song by Joan Baez. Those lyrics varied some from the other song but still offered nothing significant, just phrases like *As we marched down to Fennario, our captain fell in love with a lady like a dove. They call her by the name pretty Peggy-o.*

I glanced at Eve. Her eyes were red with exhaustion, and I realized we had been working at this since leaving Paris at six this morning.

In hopes we would hear something we weren't seeing in the lyrics—and to wake us both up—I downloaded an MP3 of Baez's song. When I hit PLAY, my speakers were on high and Baez's voice broke through the din of male voices like a bullhorn. I fumbled to turn down the sound.

"Leave it on," someone hollered.

I swiveled to see a big man who had been standing in back playing darts. He came toward us, head bobbing to the music.

"Do you know this song?" I asked him.

"To be sure," he said. "That's 'The Bonnie Lass o' Fyvie.'"

Then, to my amazement, he broke into a song that drowned out Baez. His version of the song was twice as fast and so heavily accented that it took all my concentration to understand the words.

But the flower o' them aw lies in Fyvie-o!
O come doon the stairs, pretty Peggy-o,
I'll give you a necklace of amber.
Come doon the stairs, pretty Peggy-o,
Comb back your yellow hair,
Take a last farewell to your daddy-o.

I looked at Eve and knew she had caught the references to blond hair and the necklace.

"What is the name of that song again?" Eve asked.

"'The Bonnie Lass o' Fyvie,'" the bartender said. "It's a common old folk song."

The man who had been singing nodded.

"Five-o is a place?" I asked.

"Not Five-o," the man said. "Just Fyvie. Some say Fennario is just a made-up name for the real place."

I thanked them, bought a beer for the singer and turned back to my laptop. Eve watched as I searched for the words to "The Bonnie Lass o' Fyvie." It was much longer and William the dead soldier had a new name, but there was no doubt it was an older version of the song Baez had recorded and no doubt in my mind that Baez's fictional village of Fennario was, for our purposes, the real town of Fyvie.

"Can anyone tell us where Fyvie is?" Eve asked the group of men.

"It's in Scotland."

"Ya, north of Edinburgh."

"North of Dundee, too."

"And Aberdeen."

I knew about where Edinburgh was on a map and I shivered at the idea of going two towns north of that. I had visions of a dirt-road village and could not imagine our killer at work in such a place.

I looked at Eve and knew she was thinking the same thing. Our whole investigation—with its arcane musical clues and intercontinental connections—was so far-fetched that even I had moments when I wasn't sure we were following the right leads, let alone the right killer.

But I knew we had no choice but to get on the next train to Scotland.

27

We took the train as far north as Aberdeen. It was a trip through rolling yellow pastures that reminded me a little of the foothills of the Smokies in winter. When we disembarked, it was into a biting wind sweeping down from a steel-colored sky. The city of Aberdeen was larger than I thought it would be, with tall Gothic clock towers and streets congested with bumper-car-sized automobiles.

A kind man at the train station directed us toward a "car hire" company, and armed with a map and a GPS system, Eve and I set off for the village of Fyvie. We soon found ourselves in the tall grass of the Scottish countryside, not another car in sight.

Forty-five minutes later, I slowed the car to enter Fyvie. It was a collection of wind-battered fieldstone homes with rock chimneys, a crumbling church and a small school that looked surprisingly like a private academy I had once attended in Raleigh.

Before leaving London, I had run a Nexis search of newspaper articles for murders in this area but had come up empty. Eve's call to her Interpol contact had yielded only a promise to check. We were left to whatever the locals could tell us. So we headed straight for what we knew would be the fount of all news in Fyvie—the town's busiest pub, the Black Bull.

We settled in a wooden booth near the fireplace and within minutes of asking the bartender about a possible murder of a young woman three or four years ago, we got a name—Caitlyn McKenzie. The only other thing he would say is that someone would be over to talk to us.

It was a good hour before a barrel of a man with burnished brown hair came into the pub. He looked our way, took a moment to talk to the bartender, then came over to our table.

He brought with him his pint of beer and an odor of sweet pipe tobacco and soil, as if he spent his days in the fields.

"My name's John Mulligan," he said. "Peter called me and said you're an inspector, ma'am, and you're asking about Caitlyn McKenzie."

Eve nodded and introduced me by name only. "We'd like to ask you some questions. Would you join us, please?"

Mulligan took a second long look at Eve, and I suspected— given her dark skin and gender—he was wondering about her place within the world of French law enforcement.

Eve scooted over, and Mulligan sat down in the booth next to her.

"Why do you want to know about Caitlyn McKenzie?" he asked.

"We're pursuing a possible serial killer," Eve said.

Mulligan's coppery brows shot up. "All the way from France?"

"From France to London to here," Eve said.

"How'd you lock on our Caitlyn?" Mulligan asked. "That

was four, five years ago and she barely made a splash in the papers."

Eve launched into a condensed explanation of why we thought we had an international killer and how we interpreted the musical clues. When she was finished, I laid a printout of the lyrics to "The Bonnie Lass o' Fyvie" on the table.

Mulligan didn't look at the lyrics. He took a slow drink of his beer before he spoke.

"Caitlyn McKenzie was from Westhill, a village south of here," he said. "She disappeared while attending the music festival in Aberdeen four summers ago."

A music festival. But I stayed quiet, my hand encircling my beer glass.

"She was a musician?" Eve asked.

Mulligan nodded. "Fiddle player. She was last seen on the final day of the festival. There was a party that evening. We have witnesses who saw her leave the party and get in a car."

"She wasn't forced?" I asked.

"No, she went willingly, the witnesses said. But there were no leads. Two days later, her body was found up at Slains Castle by a couple of German tourists."

I had seen signs for Fyvie Castle, apparently a big tourist attraction here. But there had been no signs for a Slains Castle.

"Where is this castle?" I asked.

"East of here, on the sea," Mulligan said.

"How far is Slains from Aberdeen?" I asked.

"Forty-plus kilometers."

If our killer had abducted Caitlyn McKenzie at the festival down in Aberdeen, why did he bother to drive nearly thirty miles north when he could have dumped her body in any of the desolate places we had seen on our drive?

"Is this Slains Castle a tourist attraction?" I asked.

"Only for the urban explorers and others who like a taste of the macabre," Mulligan said. "Most ruins here are tended by Historic Scotland but you'd be hard-pressed to call anything about Slains attractive, even on sunny days. It's a place that nature has just been left to get on with. Even haunted, some say."

"How was Caitlyn killed?" Eve asked.

Mulligan's eyes slipped to Eve, then he signaled for a beer refill. No one spoke until he had a foaming pint in front of him.

"I'd like both your words on something first," he said. "Even if your investigation turns out to include Caitlyn McKenzie, I want your assurance that you'll leave her mother and father alone. Not even a visit, mind you. Not one question."

Eve stared at Mulligan, and I knew it nipped at her sense of duty to agree to something like this. In her business, witnesses were crucial, and as difficult as it was, they had to be interviewed.

"You trust me on this, I'll trust you both with what I know," Mulligan said.

"Agreed," Eve said.

Mulligan took a long drink of his beer and wiped the foam with the back of his hand. "She was stabbed once in the chest," he said. "Left naked in the grass, like it was some sacrifice or something."

"Sacrifice?" I asked.

Mulligan nodded. "We thought she might have been kidnapped by some cultists who took her up there to play their sick games. Slains attracts that kind."

"Did you find any evidence to support that theory?" Eve asked.

Mulligan looked uncomfortable. "No, ma'am, nothing to speak of." He took a drink of his beer. "But the cult rumors took hold hard, so we did what we needed to do to calm things down."

"Calm things down? What do you mean?" Eve asked.

"I mean we recorded it as an accidental fall from one of the castle's crumbling stairwells," Mulligan said. "It was done out of consideration for the McKenzies, ma'am. They are deeply religious folk, you see. After Caitlyn was found, they became shut-ins, not seeing anyone but their priest."

"So that's why it was never listed as a homicide in the databases," Eve said.

Mulligan just nodded.

It was an insane way to handle a homicide, but part of me understood. I had worked on a story in my early years involving the rape of a Seminole girl. The tribe closed ranks around the victim's family, rejecting all outside help from the county police. I didn't know what Mulligan was exactly—police chief, mayor, constable—but he obviously had influence over this case. And he had done exactly as much, or as little, as needed to protect the family and this small community.

I was thinking, too, of how I had felt when Jeannie Laughlin asked me for a quote about Mandy, and how I had wanted to keep the world from my mother and father's door.

Eve was trying hard to hide her frustration. "Do you know what kind of weapon was used?" she asked.

Mulligan gave Eve a long look, then shook his head slowly. Clearly, he was embarrassed at how the case had been handled. And from the pained look in his eyes, I was sure he had been at the murder scene.

"Could we take a look at your case file?" Eve asked.

Mulligan drew in a deep breath. "I doubt it would help you much, ma'am. Like I said, we did what we had to do to keep this to ourselves."

Eve sat back in the booth and gave me a pained look. Although Caitlyn McKenzie seemed to fit our other cases, with no solid police investigative records and no access to the family, I knew it was going to be hard for us to connect her with any certainty. We needed something else.

"Mr. Mulligan," I said. "What did Caitlyn look like?"

He blinked a couple times. "She was a pretty thing."

"What color was her hair?"

"The color of brashlagh."

He saw my blank look and gave me a small smile. "It's a wild mustard flower that grows in these parts."

"And her eyes?" I asked.

"As blue as the bluebells."

He held my gaze for a moment, then picked up his pint and slowly drained it. The pub was so quiet I could hear the tick of a windblown twig against the glass. I could feel other eyes on us but didn't look up. I was watching Mulligan, who was staring down at his glass.

When he looked up, first at Eve, then at me, his eyes were clouded with sadness.

"I don't regret what I did," he said. "Not for the McKenzies, anyways. But I do regret that I didn't help to find the man who killed their daughter."

He rose slowly. "Maybe there are things you can see about this that I was too blind to look for at the time. How about we take a drive out to the castle? I think we have enough daylight left."

Mulligan had told us on the drive up that Bram Stoker once stayed at the castle. Other visitors included Samuel Johnson and James Boswell on their tours of the Highlands. As I stared at the ruins perched on the edge of the rugged cliffs, I could imagine it as an inspiration for Dracula's home, but not as someplace any sane person would spend the night.

The arched windows were now only gaping holes in stone walls that stood in defiance of the relentless wind of the North Sea. The noises were haunting—just the crash of waves against rocks and the screech of gulls that were invisible against a dismal gray sky.

Mulligan led us through the ruins of stone corridors, curving staircases and crumbling turrets and into towers that resembled the rooks on a chessboard. Battlement towers, he explained as we walked huddled into the collars of our jackets. The crenellations were so castle defenders could drop rocks or burning oil onto attackers below.

It was in the center of one of these round towers where Mulligan stopped our tour. Above, the clouds swirled like smoke. Below, the ground was dried yellow grass and hard mud.

"The German tourists found Caitlyn here," Mulligan said. "On her back, arms and legs splayed. She'd been stabbed with something thin and long, and she died quickly."

"Was she raped?" Eve asked.

Mulligan nodded tightly.

"I have to ask this," Eve said. "Was the act completed inside her?"

Mulligan seemed surprised at the question but then shook his head.

"Our examiner found no fluids inside her except her own blood," Mulligan said. "That is why we are sure she was raped, because it indicated . . ." His voice trailed off. "The examiner said Caitlyn had been a virgin."

"Did you find any fluids on the ground nearby?" Eve asked.

"Because of the rains, there was no semen or blood to be found on the grounds. We didn't even recover her clothing, and we spent days searching the shore beneath the cliffs."

"What about jewelry?" Eve asked.

"Jewelry? No, she was wearing nothing, not even a ring."

"You said she was at the final day of the festival. Did she take her instrument, a purse or any personal items from her room that night?"

"We found everything she owned back in her room," Mulligan said. "Here, we gathered up some miscellaneous items, bottles, trash, but nothing of significance."

I turned a full circle, scanning the stone walls of the tower.

"Was there anything written on the walls here?" I asked.

"You're looking for your musical clue?" Mulligan asked.

"Yes."

Mulligan was quiet for a moment. "There was something, but we didn't put much by it at the time." His eyes found mine. "But like I said before, maybe we didn't know what to look for."

He walked a few feet away and pointed to the grass. "This

is exactly where she was. We didn't see it until she was turned over when we were taking her out of here. There was something written in ink on her back."

"What did it say?" I asked.

"Just five words—'I had to kill her.'" Mulligan wiped a hand over his face. "We—I—just thought it was something to do with the sacrifice. I told the examiner to clean it off. I never even told her mother and father about it."

My memory started scrolling for matching lyrics, but nothing was coming at the moment.

I looked up at Mulligan. His eyes were watering, but whether it was from the wind or emotion I couldn't tell. Eve began to ask him more questions and I used the moment to step out of the stone tower. The pounding of the sea and harsh winds enveloped me and although I was freezing, for a long time I just stood there and stared at the remnants of this regal castle.

I had no doubt that Caitlyn McKenzie was one of ours.

But why had her killer driven her thirty miles north to leave her in this godforsaken place? How had he known it was even here? Did it mean something to him?

I thought then of the old ballroom, the weathered windmill, the once-elegant dance club. Did each location mean something to the killer? Or were they all symbolic, just a way of forcing others to acknowledge—or perhaps even mourn—the death of things that were once as beautiful as the women he left in their shadows?

I looked up at the battlement tower, then out to the wild sea with its foaming whitecaps. Mandy's killer, I knew in that instant, was no ordinary murderer who killed with single-minded lust. He was more complicated, an educated man with a knowledge and appreciation of the beautiful things in the world, of the historic value of monuments and cultural symbols. And he was a man with a love of music—and not just rock music.

Eve came up to me, her cheeks red from the whip of the wind.

"We need to find out who was at that festival in Aberdeen four years ago," I said. "If I'm right, we'll finally have a name."

"On what could be a very long list," Eve said.

28

It was the off-season, so the Aberdeen festival office was staffed by a lone clerk who explained that the festival attracted thousands of students but few adult guest performers. She found Caitlyn McKenzie in the computer files, but the year Caitlyn attended, she found only three guest artists—all women—and two elderly gentlemen conductors. We considered the idea that our killer might be a member of the festival's staff but dismissed it, given the fact that all his other crimes were committed outside of Scotland.

We had been preparing to head back to the train station when the woman told us we should check with the people who organized the Edinburgh International Festival. It was held during the same time as the youth festival, and it attracted many of the world's greatest performers.

A phone call led us to a man named William Ferguson, who was now retired but in the past had been in charge of booking the guest artists.

We arrived in Edinburgh by early evening. William Ferguson owned a shop on Johnston Terrace called Ferguson and Sons Luthier. As the name announced, the shop specialized in stringed instruments of all kinds. A bell above the door signaled our arrival and a portly man of about seventy with wispy white hair watched us as we approached the counter.

Eve introduced us while I looked around. The tiny shop was filled with stringed instruments of all shapes, sizes, colors and ages—violins, cellos, violas, mandolins, harps and what I thought was called a double bass, a big sucker that a man would have to stand up to play.

"Well, can't say I've met many French inspectors in my day," Ferguson was saying as Eve finished her introductions. "What can I do for you?"

"We are looking for a musician who would have performed at the festival," Eve said. "Most likely during the time period that coincided with the Aberdeen youth festival."

"That would have been the final week of our festival here," Ferguson said. He shook his head slowly. "But the Edinburgh festival is one of the largest in the world. You're talking about thousands of artists. We have all the names on computer at the office, but I couldn't begin to tell you off the top of my head who was here four years ago."

I let out a sigh of frustration. "Could you take us to your office?"

Ferguson looked at me like I was crazy. Then his eyes went to Eve. "May I ask what this is about?"

"We are pursuing a man who we believe murdered five women, including a student at the Aberdeen festival."

Ferguson's face went a shade less ruddy. "Oh dear," he said. For a moment, the only sound was the rain on the windows and the whisper of classical music in the background.

"My memory is not what it used to be," Ferguson said. "I can sometimes recall people by their instruments. Do you know what he played?"

"We think it might be the violin," Eve said. She reached back into her briefcase and withdrew the necklace. "He gave this to a girl who played the violin. One of the other victims also played the violin."

"That is a suppressor," Ferguson said. "But it is not for a violin. It is for a cello. May I see it?"

Eve gave it to him and he picked up a magnifying glass. "This is very old and quite unique. I've never seen one like this."

When I saw he was trying to unscrew the two pieces, I stepped forward.

"They're supposed to come apart, right?" I asked.

He nodded. "Yes, because you put each piece on the string, then tighten it down."

"So these suppressors are something most violinists would have?" I asked.

"Cellists," Ferguson said, correcting me. "Yes, let me show you."

Ferguson produced a flat display case. Some of the suppressors looked much like the ones on the necklaces, but others were just plain narrow tubes made of steel or brass.

"So what do these things do exactly?" I asked, picking up one of the steel tubes.

"It is used to suppress a wolf note," Ferguson said.

"A what?" I asked.

"When a cellist plays a certain note, sometimes a resonating overtone occurs, creating the phenomenon we call the wolf note. It sounds like the howling of an animal. Hence the name."

Eve and I just stared at each other. Ferguson suddenly came out from behind the counter and went to a cello sitting in a stand in the corner.

"Please, allow me to play it for you," he said.

Before we could answer, he pulled up a stool and positioned the cello between his knees. His touch was loving as he placed his fingers high up on the cello's neck and drew the bow across one of the strings. The cello gave a mournful moan. But I had heard a cello before and what I was hearing sounded perfectly normal.

Then, with a slow move of Ferguson's finger down the cello's neck, the cello emitted a hollow, off-key growl, as if the bow had hit a raw nerve deep within the guts of the instrument. It sent a ripple up my spine that I couldn't immediately shake off.

Ferguson stopped. For a long time, none of us said anything.

I was still holding one of the suppressors. "Do all cellists use these things?"

"The wolf is an intrusion in a normal performance," Ferguson said. "But there are some artists who feel the wolf is a natural flaw—a primal response, if you will. They believe if you eliminate the wolf, you lose some of the life, the purity, of the instrument."

Ferguson stroked the neck of the cello. "Some artists spend years trying to find the perfect formula for taming the wolf. But in the end, it's much like any other complex relationship—an eternal power struggle between man and beast."

I stared at the cello resting against Ferguson's chest, thinking about how much its shape resembled the silhouette of a woman kneeling in front of her master. Then I noticed the narrow silver pin that supported the cello's weight.

"Mr. Ferguson, that pin on the bottom, does it come off the cello?" I asked.

"Yes, of course," he said. He laid the cello across his knees and, with a couple turns of his hand, removed the thin steel peg and handed it to me. The tip was knife-sharp and it could be retracted like a telescope.

I looked at Eve. We had found the "ice pick."

She turned to Ferguson. "I am afraid we must have names, Mr. Ferguson. We must know who was playing at your festival four years ago."

He placed the cello carefully back in its stand and looked at us, shaking his head. I was one second from telling him we were going to his office when he held up a finger.

"I just remembered something I have here that could help," he said.

He disappeared behind a velvet curtain and returned a moment later carrying a scrapbook. "These are only my personal keepsakes, but there might be something in here."

He opened the thick book on the counter and flipped through the pages. "Here we are," he said. "This is a mailing for the festival four years ago."

He spread the brochure out like a map on the counter. I scanned it quickly but it was an overwhelming collection of names and faces for everything from opera to dance to theater.

Ferguson ran a finger down the lists of names, then looked up. "We had three orchestras that year and each would have had eight to twelve cellists."

Eve let out a sigh. "Thirty-six suspects."

"We can eliminate the female musicians," I said.

"You said he would have been here the last week of the festival?" Ferguson asked.

"That's right," I said.

"There were no orchestras playing at that point. We had only recitals going on," Ferguson said. He looked down at the list again. "So that narrows it down to the cello soloists—Vanessa Nagano, Sophia Rizzo, Thomas Baker and Laurent Demarais."

"Do you recall where the men were from?" I asked.

"Mr. Baker was from California, and Mr. Demarais was from France. Paris, I believe."

Eve and I exchanged a quick glance.

"What do you know about Demarais?" I asked.

Ferguson hesitated. "I remember that he was a bit unpleasant. He had very little patience with the staff and volunteers."

Eve had moved away. She had her cell out and was punching the buttons.

"Is Demarais famous?" I asked Ferguson.

"Not on any grand scale," he said, "though he has managed to attract some acclaim in certain critical circles. His performances are somewhat, shall we say, uneven."

"Then why did you book him?" I asked.

"The younger crowd seemed to find him appealing, and we are always watching our audience demographics," Ferguson said. "He's a good-looking chap in that moody way the young seem to fancy. My word, you don't think that he—?"

I heard a tinkle of a bell and looked up. Eve had left the shop. Through the window, I could see her standing under the awning, gesturing as she talked on the cell. I knew we still needed to check every cellist who had been at the festival so I asked Ferguson if I could have the brochure. When he gave it to me, I thanked him for his help and hurried outside.

I huddled next to Eve in the cold rain, listening to her call. There was an urgency in her voice and although she was speaking French, I understood this much: Laurent Demarais. Home residence. Search, question and detain.

When I heard her say British Airways I knew we were bypassing the train and flying home. I didn't blame her one bit. I was anxious to get back to Paris now, too.

Had I been able to get to my laptop, I would have been searching for a photo of Laurent Demarais. I was burning to know what he looked like. But most of all, I wanted to be in the same room with him, to stand next to him and look into the eyes of the man my sister saw as she took her last breath on that filthy ballroom floor.

I moved away from Eve, out from under the awning, and let the cold rain run into my face.

It was the first time in my life, I acknowledged without reservation or regret, that I had felt the urge to kill.

29

Sweat streamed down his face. He blinked it away and kept going. Closing his eyes, he let his body sway as if it were part of the instrument clasped between his thighs.

No orchestra behind him now, but he didn't need it. No sheet music, but he didn't need that either. He knew the Dutilleux concerto by heart, even though he had not played it for five years, not since Hélène. He hadn't even wanted to attempt it because he had always been afraid of what he would feel when he did.

It was called *Tout un Monde Lointain.*

All the world, distant.

That is how he felt now—cut off from everyone and everything. Alone, invisible, every question still unanswered, every cry unheard.

He had reached the pizzicato now, and he plucked at the strings violently. But he didn't feel it. He didn't feel anything until—

A fierce sting on his face. He jerked back, dropping the bow. He felt his cheek. It was bleeding.

It took him a moment to realize the D string had snapped.

He set the cello on the floor and went to the bathroom. The gash on his left cheekbone was bleeding heavily. He grabbed a towel, pressed it to his face and returned to the salon.

His eyes went to the cello on the floor. He picked it up and carefully laid it on the settee. Gingerly, he took the towel off his cheek. The bleeding had slowed, at least. He set about removing the string but when he saw fresh blood droplets on the cello, he had to stop.

Pressing the towel back to his face, he went to the table by the window. He sat down and opened the laptop. The screen glowed blue, the only light in the apartment.

He hated the machine, but this afternoon he had lowered himself to the role of a common researcher and slogged through the vain little worlds that the stupid and lonely had created out there on the Internet.

It had not taken him long to find what he needed.

The girl he had killed in Miami was named Amanda Owens. The prime suspect was a young black man. The lead investigator was a Hispanic woman. The man he had seen with Paula Ridley was the dead girl's older brother, Matt Owens, newspaper reporter.

The American man had ruined everything.

But now Laurent had a name. And he was sure he knew the reason Owens had sought out the Ridley woman. He had perhaps even figured out how important the necklace was. Why else would he force the Ridley woman to give it to him?

And there was no doubt in Laurent's mind. Matt Owens had his necklace.

A pounding on the door broke his thoughts. He ignored it. He had too much to think about right now.

What were his options? He would simply have to steal it back, probably killing the American in the process. But where and when? He did not know where the man was staying. And maybe he had turned the necklace over to the police. Laurent did not know how far their investigation had progressed. He had read nothing in the newspapers about a serial killer, just a small article on the "mugging" of the Ridley woman in the metro.

Again, that incessant pounding.

He set the towel down and went to the door. He paused to turn on a lamp, blinking in the light, before he jerked the door open.

"Why haven't you answered your phone?"

Maud, his agent. Brown curls coiled from the rain, bracelets clinking like wind chimes, her coat musky with the filthy drizzle of the streets. And as always, toting a sagging briefcase.

"Why haven't you answered my calls?" Maud asked again.

"I've been busy."

She gave him a long hard look, then pushed her way into the apartment, going to the table by the window and snapping on a light.

"I have some contracts for you to sign," she said, opening her briefcase.

He came up behind her and closed the laptop before she had a chance to see it. She turned to give him a hard stare.

"What happened to your face?" she asked.

"Nothing."

She reached up to cup his chin, but he slapped her hand away and retreated to the shadows. She drew back, rubbing her wrist.

"Laurent, what is wrong with you?" Maud asked. "You look like hell. When's the last time you shaved? Or bathed?"

Bathed? Shaved? He couldn't remember doing either lately. How long had it been? Three days? Five? Had he not washed since Halloween night?

He looked down at his hands, at the blackened half-moons of his nails. Was that dirt or blood? Was it his or someone else's?

What was *wrong* with him?

"Laurent?"

He looked back at Maud.

"The school in Spain needs a signed contract," she said, holding out a paper. "I have you on a morning flight to Madrid the day after tomorrow. You can pick up your ticket at the airport."

"I'm not going."

Her mouth dropped open. "What?"

"I said I am not going."

"It would be very easy for them to replace you."

"Let them. I have some urgent business to attend to here. I cannot leave on Monday."

"You'll have to give back the advance," Maud said.

"I don't need the money."

"I know you don't. But you need to—"

"*Tais-toi!*" he yelled.

Maud was stunned into silence. Then her eyes narrowed. "How dare you tell me to shut up? How can you speak to me like that? I work hard for you . . ."

As he stared at her, she seemed to grow smaller and smaller, as if he were watching her fall down a deep dark tunnel. He saw her mouth moving but didn't hear anything coming out. She had been useful to him once. But now? He didn't need her anymore, didn't need anyone telling him what to do.

His gaze slipped to the cello on the settee. He went over and picked up the broken string. He could easily loop it around Maud's neck before she even realized what was happening.

Had he actually thought that? Could he actually see himself squeezing the life out of this stupid woman simply because she was repulsive? He turned his back to her, blocking the drone of her voice, still not sure that killing her wasn't exactly what he wanted to do on this miserable night.

He palmed the string.

"Laurent, look at me."

He didn't. He could only stare at his hands and think of *her* and wonder if she would be disappointed in him. Would she see him as the failure he was or would she still love him?

"Laurent, are you signing the contract or not?"

"No."

"Then fine," she said.

"Leave me," he said.

Leave, you mouthy pig. Leave and I let you live.

He turned his back to Maud, staring at the cello as he waited for the sound of the door closing. He heard the tinkle of her bracelets.

"Laurent, look at me," she said softly.

He refused.

"You've had these moods before," she said. "You know it will pass. We've been together for such a long time now, been through so much. I've always been there for you."

"For your twenty percent," he said.

"Why are you hurting me?" she asked softly.

He didn't answer.

He heard the bracelets again and, out of the corner of his eye, saw her put the contract on the table. The next thing he heard was the click of her heels on the parquet and then the closing of the door.

Alone. Again. The whole world, distant.

Tonight, it was probably best if he were left alone. It would have been too great an effort to kill Maud. He had been forced to do that with the Ridley woman, but he hadn't enjoyed it at all. It wasn't like the women he chose. There was no release in it, no sense of purpose. It was just getting rid of something that was in the way, as one might squash an insect.

Laurent moved back to the window and wiped the condensation from the glass. Black umbrellas scuttled like beetles along the quay below. Buildings shimmered like shards of tin. Car headlights knifed through the mist. The wavy old glass of the leaded windows refracted everything into pieces, like the world outside was a vast gray Cubist painting.

Streaks of blue now in the gray. What was this?

The streaks seemed to pulsate as they grew larger.

Or was it all in his head now?

Then he heard the sirens. The streaks of blue had stopped moving. They were right outside his window now, directly below.

Police. They were looking up at the building. Looking for him.

He jumped back from the window, his heart hammering, his mind racing. How had they found him? What was happening? Why were they here? No time to think about that now. He had to get out of here.

He grabbed his trench coat from the chair and started for the door. *No, that is how they would come.* He would go out the servants' stairs in the back. He started toward the kitchen but then stopped.

His eyes went to the cello on the settee.

It would slow him down. He had to leave it.

He went through the kitchen and down the narrow dark stairs, down three flights, past the garbage bins and the barking dog, until he emerged into the courtyard and a misty rain. Out on the street, he paused to pull in a deep breath. His car was parked in front of the apartment, so he couldn't chance going to it. He would have to find another way.

But where would he go?

He shut his eyes, concentrating. It was difficult now, but if he tried hard, he could summon it, pull the one thing from his memory that kept him from feeling as if he were splintering into pieces.

Yes . . . there it was. He had it, he could see it now, see the old stone house. It was still there, that one memory always the strongest and yet most fleeting, the memory of her in the golden light of the bedroom. He could see her, feel her arms around him, hear her voice.

La musique est l'amour à la recherche d'un mot. Music is love in search of a word.

There was only one person he wanted to be with, if only in his mind. If, indeed, he still *had* a mind.

And there was only one place he wanted to be.

Home. He needed to go home.

30

As I stood at the open door of Laurent Demarais's apartment, one emotion churned through me—rage.

Rage that a soul so twisted and black could dwell in a world of such beauty.

Demarais's home took the entire top floor of what Eve told me was once the town house of a seventeenth-century financier. From my vantage point at the entrance, I could see only a large circular foyer and beyond that, through a high archway, a big room bathed in the light of a chandelier. Between the comings and goings of the cops, I got glimpses of heavy silk draperies, antiques mixed with sleek modern furnishings and thick Oriental carpets over a herringbone parquet floor.

There was a large crystal vase of white roses on the table in the foyer. I watched a petal fall to the table, then another. I closed my eyes, turning away.

I was exhausted, hungry and dirty after the trip back from Scotland. Eve and I had spent the last six hours either at an airport or in the air, and I still had not found time to boot up the laptop to find Laurent Demarais or the title to the lyrics I believed had been left for us on Caitlyn McKenzie's back—*I had to kill her.*

I felt someone touch my arm and opened my eyes. Eve was standing there. Her hair was a wild mess and she had mascara shadows under her eyes.

"It looks like he left in a hurry," she said. "They found his appointment book. It lists his touring schedule for the last several years. His recital dates seem to correspond to the times the victims disappeared."

"Including Mandy?" I asked.

Eve nodded. "There is another thing. They found his laptop. It was still running and there was an article on the screen from your newspaper back in Miami."

"What?"

"It was about your sister's murder. He must have been trying to find out more about her—or you."

I didn't even want to think about the implications of that right then. But at least we now had proof that we were on the trail of the right man.

"Did you find anything, belongings from the victims?" I asked. "Is there anything from Mandy?"

"Matt, you are exhausted," Eve said. "Please go home and I will call you later."

I shook my head. "I can't. We're so close to catching him."

"We have no idea where he is. Also, there is an itinerary here for a trip to Spain and Italy."

"Have you checked the air—"

"Of course," she said crisply. Then she let out a tired sigh. "You cannot stay here. Please, go home and get some rest."

I looked over her shoulder at the apartment. A man wearing a badge and latex gloves was bringing out a cello, tagged with an orange ticket. The end pin was still in the cello. He also had a clear plastic bag with what looked like a string in it. He put the cello on a settee in the foyer.

"Have they found other end pins?" I asked.

"Yes," Eve said quietly. "We are taking them all but so far there is no visible blood on them. We did find some blood drops on the floor and in the bathroom."

As much as I wanted to stay so I wouldn't miss anything, I suddenly felt an urge to be out of here, away from this place and anything he had touched. But I stood there, staring at the cello, as if I thought it might tell me something that would ease the pain in my chest.

"Eve!"

I saw a burly man in a raincoat standing under the archway. Eve said something to him in French, then turned back to me.

"Go, please," Eve said, gently pushing me out the door. "I promise I will telephone later, no matter what time it is."

Eve went back to join the man I assumed was her boss, a commandant who had scowled at me an hour ago when we came up the elevator. There had been dozens of officers and inspectors here then, but now only a handful remained. I knew Eve would be here for a long time and I knew I would receive no phone call tonight telling me Laurent Demarais was in custody. He was "in the wind," as I had once heard Nora refer to a fleeing suspect. I got in the elevator. When I checked my watch I was surprised to see it was only midnight. Eve and I had been on the move for days and although my mind was reeling with ideas, I could feel my body giving out.

Down in the lobby, I slumped to a bench and dialed Cameron. He bolted awake when I told him I needed him to do a search for new lyrics. We were both quiet while he booted up his computer.

"You ready?" I said quietly, knowing my voice carried well across the marbled lobby.

"Go."

"'I had to kill her.'"

Cameron started to type, then stopped. "Wait, I think that's from Guns N' Roses, 'Used to Love Her.' You know the song: 'I used to love her but I had to kill her . . . and I can still hear her complain.'"

There was something familiar about it, but with my brain fading fast, I needed Cameron to quote the whole song to me. I scribbled the lyrics on the envelope that had held my train ticket, nothing registering until Cameron got to the line *She's buried in my backyard*.

I looked around the lobby, then at the stairway that led up to Demarais's apartment. We were on an island in the middle of the Seine called Île Saint-Louis. It was a dense neighborhood of narrow streets, shops and apartments. No open ground anywhere that I had seen. Did Demarais have another home? Or did he mean "backyard" only symbolically?

I thanked Cameron and told him I'd be home soon. It was only after I hung up that I realized I hadn't told Cameron we finally had a name for our killer.

Funny, I thought as I stared at the envelope. Demarais wasn't just Eve's suspect anymore. He had morphed into "our killer"—hers, mine, Cameron's, Nora's and, in a small way, Juliette's. Maybe that was why I was pissed about being thrown out of the apartment upstairs. I had come to think of Eve as a partner and now, suddenly, she was a cop again and I was a reporter shoved back behind the yellow tape.

I tucked the envelope in my pocket and had just stood up when I felt a rush of cold air. A woman scuttled in the front door, her umbrella trailing water, her leather briefcase spotted with rain.

She was immediately stopped by the concierge and started a tirade in what sounded to me like really bad French. The concierge was clearly having trouble understanding her, or was refusing to. I started to leave but then heard a name that stopped me.

Laurent Demarais.

There was urgency in the woman's voice that I read as concern for Demarais. Was this a girlfriend?

I walked over. "May I help you?" I asked.

The woman spun to me. "Good God, someone who speaks English," she said in a heavy British accent. "Are you with the police? Someone called me to come here—"

"The police called you?" I asked.

"They said there was a situation. Now I ask you, what in bloody hell is 'a situation'? Is Laurent injured? Has he tried to harm himself?"

"Who are you?"

"I'm his agent, Maud Wilkinson, and I want to know immediately what is going on upstairs."

Maud Wilkinson's eyes kept darting toward the elevator. It was just a matter of time before some cop came down, and I wanted a shot at her first.

I led her to the bench and sat her down, trying to establish a sense of authority. I hoped she was too distraught to figure out I wasn't a cop.

"My name is Matt Owens," I said. "I'm working with Inspector Bellamont on—"

I stopped myself, knowing I was about to cross a line that would make Eve and her boss very unhappy.

"Is Laurent all right?" she asked.

A uniformed policeman came in the front doors and crossed the lobby to the stairwell. I didn't flag him down. I knew I had just made a second bad decision I'd have to explain to Eve.

"Do you know where he is?" I asked.

Maud looked confused. "I saw him a couple hours ago. I don't know—" She pushed her wet hair back from her face. "Please tell me what's going on here."

"There's a schedule up in his apartment for engagements in Spain and Italy. Could he be on his way—"

"No, no," Maud said. "He told me he wasn't going, that he wanted to cancel. He was upset and ill-tempered. He had cut himself and wouldn't even tend to it properly. He was . . . please, is he all right?"

I thought about the *Miami Times* article on Demarais's laptop. "Did he ever say anything to you about a woman in the States? A woman named—"

"Woman?" Maud's eyes were back on the elevator. "No, no, he never said anything about a woman. He'd just come back from the States a few weeks ago. He had a good performance in Atlanta and another in Miami. Things were going so well."

I pulled out my notebook and started taking notes. "How long have you known him?" I asked.

"Ten years, he has been with me about ten years." She seemed close to tears. "Has Laurent killed himself?"

I looked up quickly. "As far as we know, he's fine."

Maud let out a wine-scented sigh. "Please, you must tell

me why the police called me. Has he harmed someone?" she asked.

I held her eyes and knew I could never be a very good detective. I could not lie to this woman. "We think he may have harmed many women."

"God," Maud whispered.

As the color drained from her face, I tried to evaluate her reaction. She obviously cared for Demarais, yet she had been the one to suggest he might have harmed someone.

"I need you to tell me more about Demarais," I said.

"What do you want to know?" she asked.

"Start when you met him," I said.

Maud began her story quietly, telling me she had gone to a concert in a church on the Left Bank, where Demarais was playing with a second-rate quartet. She said she had seen something more in him—"a passion unlike anything I had seen before"—and took him on as a client. Within three years, he was performing with major orchestras and eventually in solo bookings. But no matter how good his reviews were, she said, he never felt he was quite good enough.

I asked her if he had any family, thinking Demarais might seek refuge with a sibling or someone. But she said he never mentioned family or friends. There were no graves to visit on All Saints' Day, not one personal photograph anywhere in the apartment.

Women? Lovers?

Maud hesitated just long enough to make me wonder if she had ever been in Laurent's bed or perhaps had wanted to be.

"I had the feeling there was a woman once," Maud said. "He sometimes told me he had to go see someone, but he never mentioned anyone by name. For six months, he seemed happy, and onstage, he was magical. I have a tape from that time, and I play it whenever I question whether he's worth the trouble he causes me."

"So what happened?"

Maud shrugged. "He told me he wanted to go on a long tour. It was quite sudden. For six months he had refused to go anywhere and then he wanted to go as far away from Paris as I could book him."

"Did he seem different?"

She nodded. "It was as if a light had died inside him," she said. "He did a lot of touring after that. I got the feeling he was running away from something here."

The elevator door opened and two men stepped out. I recognized one as Eve's boss, the commandant. He spotted Maud and headed our way. The commandant said a few words to me in French that did not sound nice and, with a firm hand, took Maud's arm and escorted her away.

I knew the commandant would tell Eve that I had interfered. I had two choices. I could leave now and escape Eve's wrath or stay and face her.

I stayed, and five minutes later the elevator doors opened and Eve stepped off.

"You cannot keep doing this to me," she said. "I told you to go home and instead you ask questions of one of my witnesses that you have no right to ask."

"I didn't find out anything important."

"That is not the point!" Eve said. "I have already had to explain your presence to my superiors, explain why I have involved an American in this investigation, explain why he accompanied me to London and—"

"I'm sorry, Eve," I said. "I never meant to cause you trouble, but you knew exactly what I wanted the first time we talked—to find my sister's killer. And you agreed to work with me."

"And you with me," she hissed.

"And I have," I said. "By the way, those words that were found on Caitlyn McKenzie's body? They're from a song called 'Used to Love Her' by Guns N' Roses." I thrust the envelope at her. "Here's the lyrics."

She grabbed the envelope.

"It's about a woman buried in a backyard, something that you and I can both see is not here," I said.

She fell quiet as she read the words. The last of my energy was draining away and I leaned my head back against the cold marble and shut my burning eyes.

We were both exhausted and short-tempered. And while I owed Eve a lot, she owed me some support right now. I was part of this investigation and I wasn't going to be pushed aside.

I felt something touch my arm and opened my eyes. It was a large manila envelope.

"I thought you might want to see this," she said.

I took the envelope and slid out a photograph. It was an eight-by-ten color glossy publicity photo of a man.

Laurent Demarais.

Black flowing hair. Long-lashed dark eyes under heavy black brows. A hint of a smile on his full lips—confident, insolent.

For more than two weeks I had chased a killer who seemed more phantom than man. And now here I was, looking at the face of the man who had killed my sister.

"Go home," Eve said. "Get some rest. I need you to be able to think straight."

She left me alone. For a long time, I sat in the empty lobby, unable to take my eyes off the photograph of Demarais. My body was shutting down and my brain was fuzzy with thoughts I knew were irrational.

I desperately needed sleep, but I knew it would not come tonight. Not with the face of this monster in my dreams.

31

He took the RER heading toward the suburb of Dourdan-la-Forêt. At the station, he rented a car and drove south through the countryside, his eyes trained on the rearview mirror. But no one was following him.

Even when he entered the village of Saint-Aubin he didn't let up on the accelerator. No matter. The narrow streets were deserted, the yellow lights from the windows the only color in the gray mist. There was no one out tonight, there was no one to see him.

He felt calmer here, away from Paris. He felt safe again. He was invisible.

Had he always been this way? Or was this new, just a manifestation of this feeling of losing himself? Was he disappearing? That was how it felt now, like he was being sucked downward into some dark place by an irresistible force.

Through the slow sweep of the wipers, he could see he was back out in the countryside again. But where was the turnoff? It had been so long since he had been here—fifteen, twenty years? He could vaguely remember the letter that came years ago from the lawyer telling him the estate was his. But he had never felt the need to return—until now.

There! Something familiar—the huge gnarled oak. And yes, the road was just beyond it. He swung the wheel left.

The road turned rutted and narrow. He entered a tunnel of bare black trees. Overgrown bushes scraped the sides of the car, and he was forced to slow to a crawl.

A sharp turn and there, suddenly, was a high iron gate. He slammed on the brakes.

Was this even the right place? Where were the lilacs? Where were the two stone lions that used to guard the entrance?

Why couldn't he remember?

He got out of the car. He paused at one of the pillars anchoring the gate, then began pulling at the dead ivy. His fingers tore at the thick tendrils. Finally, the old blue and white ceramic sign appeared.

VILLA EUTERPE.

He stepped back, panting, laughing.

He wasn't crazy. This place was real. It wasn't some fragment from his dreams. It was *real*.

The gate was unlocked. He pushed it open, got back in the car and proceeded down the narrow road. His heart was hammering as he peered out the windshield. Then, suddenly, the house took shape in the mist. He stopped the car and stared at it.

Three stories, gray stone nearly hidden by dead ivy, two thrusting chimneys, mansard roof, black shutters—*hadn't they been blue?*—blocking the windows. Nothing looked like he remembered.

And yet . . .

He turned off the car and got out. He walked quickly around the side of the house, moving beyond the overgrown shrubs and trees, until . . .

Yes. Oh God, yes, it's there!

His eyes were drawn to the tower on the east side of the house. Round, with a peaked roof and small high windows.

Whispers.

He stared into the shadows. He was sure he heard someone whispering. Was it her? He looked up at the swaying cypresses. Just the wind in the trees.

A cracking sound. He spun to the left. Eyes, staring at him from the trees, someone hiding in the woods. Was it him? No, it couldn't be. He was dead, his bones buried in Highgate Cemetery, his black soul banished to hell for what he had done.

A deer suddenly broke out into the open. It stared at him for a moment, then leapt back into the trees.

Laurent let out a breath and looked back to the tower.

He had to get inside.

But every door was locked, every window was shuttered. The lawyer had sent him a key. Why hadn't he remembered to bring it?

He stood in the middle of the gravel drive, staring at the house. His head was throbbing, as if there was a storm of memories inside him trying to get out.

He closed his eyes, trying to bring up an image of the house as it had been during his boyhood. There had been a secret door once . . .

Laurent! Laurent! Où ês-tu?

He could hear his father yelling for him, looking for him. And suddenly, he could see himself, running down the back stairs, through the kitchen and down into the cellar. And then . . .

Laurent's eyes shot open. He hurried to the back of the house, his eyes raking the darkness for the opening. He spotted it, the old door in the ground, almost hidden by the over-grown bushes. The coal chute.

It had been his secret way of getting out of the house when things got bad. But he had been eight then, and so much smaller.

There was no choice. He had to try. Besides, he had been in smaller tunnels than this before.

He flung open the door and with a quick look into the darkness slithered down the hole. He emerged sweating and dirty in the pitch-black cellar. He felt his way along the cold stone walls and up the stairs. With the creak of a door, he was in the kitchen.

He didn't linger. The dining room was just beyond, he remembered. From there, he could make his way. The old parquet floor groaned under his feet. With the windows shut-tered, it was nearly dark, and he cursed himself for not bring-ing a flashlight. He stopped in the middle of the dining room.

Beyond, through the French doors, he could see the dark sweep of a staircase curving up into pitch-blackness.

He looked around the dining room, his eyes zeroing in on a credenza and silver candlesticks. He grabbed one and lit the stub of the candle.

The room shivered to life. The ghostly white shapes of the covered furniture. The glint of a chandelier. The blank space on the blue wallpaper where a stern-faced old woman in a lace cap used to stare down at him during dinner.

He went into the entrance hall and slowly climbed the staircase. At the top he paused. To the left, the hallway branched off to the bedrooms. There, the first door on the left, that is where his room had been. And beyond?

He stared into the darkness. His father's bedroom.

He started down the hall toward it. The door was ajar and he pushed it open. The candle flickered in the cold draft. More white shapes, a smell of must and tobacco. He felt a knot in his stomach and moved quickly through the room to the adjoining one.

Here, he stopped.

Her room. Smaller than he remembered. A large white square that he was sure was the bed. And over there, in the corner, was that—?

He pulled off the sheet, sending the dust motes dancing in the candlelight.

Her dressing table. Empty of its perfumes and powders, but yes, it was the same one. The memories came bubbling up. The smell of talcum, the gold lamplight, the glint of silver earrings. He could see her sitting there, see himself cross-legged on the floor, looking up at her as she braided her long blond hair.

Music. He heard music. He spun to the window.

No, just the wind.

He went to the large white shape by the window and pulled off the sheet. It was the chaise longue where she read her novels and where she sat when he played for her.

I can't do it, Maman.

Yes, you can, mon petit.

It's too hard and Papa will—

Just play it for me, Laurent. Like we are the only two people in the world.

And it was all there, in his head, in his heart, as if he were eight years old again, his fingers burning as he tried to play *Tout un Monde Lointain.*

It was there too, the softness of her hands as his mother slipped the necklace around his neck, whispering that it, like the music, was something special between just the two of them.

Deux coeurs.

He felt something tear deep in his chest and a sob escaped from his lips.

Don't cry, mon petit, I will be back. Please, don't cry.

He set the candle down and went to the window. He un- latched it and pushed open the heavy shutters. The cold air rushed in. There was nothing to see in the darkness below, but in his mind he could see his mother standing at the black car, see her pale face looking up at him, see Father guiding her into the backseat, see the car disappearing in the trees.

See her . . . disappearing.

He turned away from the window, wiping his face.

He picked up the candle with a shaking hand and left the bedroom.

Outside, he stopped. His eyes went to the right, down the other hallway. He peered into the darkest place where the light fell away.

There was no choice. He had to go into the tower.

The hallway led to the east wing of the old manor house, to the servants' quarters, storage rooms and a vast beamed attic where once, as a boy, he had thought the rustling of pigeons were the murmurings of ghosts.

It was there at the end of the long narrow hall that he found the spiral staircase. He hesitated at the bottom, then started up.

Again the music came. More wind? No, now he was sure it was real. It grew louder, drawing him upward.

The door. The music was pounding in his head now. He pushed on the heavy wood and went in.

The music stopped suddenly. Just quiet. And cold. So cold here that he could see his breath in the shimmer of the candlelight. But he was sweating so hard his shirt was wet beneath his coat.

He walked to the center of the room and set the candlestick on the stone floor. Slowly, he turned in a circle, his eyes taking in every detail. Of course it looked different now, empty of all furnishings and anything of comfort. The gilt mirror, the draperies, the Aubusson carpet, all gone. The damask chair where he had sat down to play was gone. And the bed where she—

Gone. Everything gone now. Except the memories.

They were all there in his brain. If he had ever thought they had been a dream—or a nightmare—he knew now that they were real. And if he had thought that coming here might somehow bring him peace, he knew now that it wasn't possible.

He was thirteen now. Here in this room. The music was back, drifting in his head and mingling with the memories.

Play for me, Laurent.

I don't feel like it.

Play it. Play it, like you did for your mother.

No. I don't want to.

Yes, you do. You know you do.

I don't want to do this anymore.

You can't stop yourself, Laurent, you know you can't.

The vibration of the cello between his legs. The touch of her hands on his chest. The press of her warm lips on his neck. The purr of her voice as she read the poem, over and over and over.

Tout un monde lointain, absent, presque défunt
Le poison qui découle de tes yeux, de tes yeux verts.
A whole world distant, absent, all but dead.
The poison that flows from your eyes, from your green eyes.

The words were beautiful, but from her lips they sounded ugly and profane. And always, the sight of her naked white body, green eyes blazing, black hair spread like snakes, as she writhed on the bed.

The sigh of the cello. Her screams of pleasure. The whole world distant, absent, all but dead.

He dropped to his knees on the cold stone floor, his hands pressed to his face. He was trembling. Not with sadness. Not even with grief anymore. It was rage.

He had to find her. He had to kill her.

32

Eve's phone call woke me at six thirty A.M. She was so agitated that for a second she didn't even realize she was speaking French. When I calmed her down, she hit me with the news.

A body had been found in a manor house outside Paris. The estate, which had been vacant for years, was in the name of Laurent Demarais.

Dawn was still an hour away as we drove south from the city amid a blur of headlights. Eve stayed quiet until we hit a thick darkness dotted with occasional window lights and a rare passing car.

"The son of a bitch did not call me," she said.

"Who?"

"Commandant Boutin. This morning—at five A.M.—they discovered a manor house in Saint-Aubin that used to be owned by Laurent Demarais's mother. He inherited it from her."

Eve lit a cigarette. Her fingers shook as she drew in the smoke and exhaled.

"So how'd you find this out?" I asked.

"A friend at the station called me. I would not have heard that they found a woman's body there. I would not have heard any of it."

I didn't think she wanted to talk about why she had been

left out of the loop, so I steered her to the case. "Is this an old body or a new one?" I asked.

"She was killed last night."

This didn't make sense. The lyrics left in Slains Castle mentioned leaving a body in "my backyard." But until now, all the lyrics had referred to previous victims, not a victim yet to come. The lyrics left on Caitlyn McKenzie's body should have pointed backward to Hélène. But now, I wasn't sure what to think.

I peered into the darkness ahead of us, the questions multiplying with every mile. Who was the new victim? Had he left us new lyrics? Had the cops caught Demarais there? I also wondered why Eve was suddenly being sidelined. But I decided to let all of them go for now, figuring Eve was too pissed to talk.

We passed through a village, then we were out into the countryside again. In the spare light of dawn, I could make out a stand of white wind turbines, their giant blades piercing the gray sky.

Finally, we arrived at the estate. I caught a glimpse of high stone walls and a wrought iron gate. The clot of police cars and vans prevented us from going very far, so Eve was forced to park a good ways from the house.

As we got out of the car, Eve looked at me over the roof. "I am sorry," she said. "As angry as I am at all of them, you still have to remain here. I promise you after I find out what is going on inside, I will be back for you." Then she turned and walked into the mist.

I looked at the old house sitting in the gray curl of early morning fog. My eye went immediately to the tower. It was built of gray stone like the rest of the house, with a dark red cone-shaped roof and small arched windows of leaded glass.

That's where this new body was, I suddenly knew, in that tower.

I started to get back inside and out of the cold when I spotted the yellow rain poncho and police cap Eve had left in the backseat. With a glance at the officers, I retrieved the poncho and cap and put them on. Head down, I walked toward the manor house.

The open doors did little to negate the musty smell. The place was all shadows, marble and high ceilings, and what few pieces of furniture remained were covered with drop cloths. In the hallway, I passed an elegant grandfather clock with hands frozen at three forty-five.

In what I assumed was a living room, I saw two uniformed officers, framed by a dark marble fireplace that had to be six feet tall. One of the cops gave me a nod and said something to me in French. When he gestured toward a curved staircase, I gave him a nod and went upstairs.

I followed the voices to the second floor and down a hall to the right. No one paid me any attention; everyone was focused on the open door at the end of the hallway.

I inched up to the heavy wooden door. The round room was maybe twenty feet in diameter. A portable light had been set up, and in its glare I saw the naked body of a woman propped against the stone wall like a rag doll, head down, hands crossed over her stomach.

Her black hair fell like tangled wires to her shoulders, hiding her face. She had been stabbed so many times that her breasts looked riddled by machine-gun fire. Lines of blood streaked her skin like red threads, some ending in the folds of her belly, most of it dripping into the thatch of black pubic hair.

I didn't want to look any more but I couldn't stop.

Her hands . . .

They weren't just crossed over her stomach. They had been deliberately positioned with her fingers forced inside her vagina.

I saw Eve coming toward me and did a quick scan of the tower's details. But I could see nothing—no graffiti, no sheet music. Just the woman's body and the blood.

"You need to leave now," Eve said in a low firm voice as she took my arm.

It wasn't until we were back outside that I pulled in a deep breath. Eve's expression was livid as she looked first to the manor house and then back at me.

"Eve, I'm sorry," I said. "I had to see it for myself. If I caused you—"

"It was not you," she said. "They did not notice you were there. It happened before you arrived. I was told I am being removed as lead investigator in the case."

I was quiet, remembering a time when Nora had come home with the same problem. One of her first homicide cases had taken an unexpected turn toward a well-heeled Miami businessman and the case was taken from her and handed off to a crony of the DA.

It was early in our relationship and I had little respect for her ambition or needs or anything else. I had taken her to dinner and after one too many margaritas tried to tell her that she knew it was a boys' club when she took the detective's exam.

As I studied Eve's face now, I understood just how cruel my response had been.

"I'm sorry," I said.

She turned away, arms crossed.

"There are other things we can work on, Eve," I said.

She spun back to me. "I do not want to be relegated to a desk and a computer, Matt. I have worked so hard on this, and now I am, I am . . ."

She wiped roughly at her face. "I am sorry. Police officers are not supposed to be so . . . emotional."

She reached into her coat and pulled out her cigarettes. The pack was empty and she crumpled it and tossed it to the gravel.

"Come on, I will take you back to Paris," she said.

"Then what?" I asked.

"Then I will come back here. The commandant is calling in the cadaver dogs and diggers. He is convinced that the Guns N' Roses lyrics left with Caitlyn McKenzie mean that we should be looking here for other victims."

"I thought you said he took you off the case as lead?"

Eve's eyes were on the uniformed police. "I do not care. I need to be here when they find Hélène."

"I don't think she's here," I said.

Eve looked back at me. "But the lyrics said, 'She's buried in my backyard.'"

"I know that, but the rest doesn't fit. This woman is brunette. She doesn't fit the physical profile of the other victims. And did you find any musical clues up there, any lyrics?"

She shook her head slowly as she stared at the uniformed officers.

"Hélène isn't here, Eve," I said softly.

"How can you be so sure?" she asked without looking at me.

"Because he didn't bury any of the others," I said. "He didn't hide them. This murder is different, and when we find out why, maybe we find him."

In the distance, I could hear sirens. I looked to the gate and saw another police car pulling in. I guessed the search teams would arrive soon.

Eve's deep sigh pulled my attention back to her.

"You are right," she said. "He has broken his pattern. There is something happening with him now, something he can no longer control. Have you ever heard the term 'devolving'?"

"Yes," I said. "It refers to a serial killer who is losing control, spiraling downward."

She nodded slowly. "And he knows we are looking for him. That will make him even more desperate."

"Think about this for a second," I said. "Tricia Downey's body was almost drained of her blood. There wasn't one drop found in that windmill. She was killed somewhere else. It wasn't here. And it sure as hell wasn't in that beautiful apartment back in Paris."

Eve was looking at me now.

"We need to find his backyard," I said.

33

The sun was coming up. He had to hurry. But he had to be careful, too. He knew that they were looking for him now, but he doubted they would be looking for him in this part of Paris. Still, he couldn't take any chances, so he left the locked rental car in a crowded parking garage. He started away but stopped cold.

Red smears on the door.

He slowly brought up his hands. Blood. He looked down at his clothes. He was covered in blood.

How had he not noticed this on the drive back to Paris?

He used his sleeve to wipe the blood off the car and left the garage. Out on the street, he walked fast, head lowered, passing the shuttered shops. As he approached the boulangerie at the corner, he saw lights on inside and crossed to the other side of the street.

The feeling of invisibility was gone now. Everything had changed. Now he felt exposed and vulnerable, like an animal without its shell.

He turned onto rue Myrha and sprinted the rest of the way to number forty-four. He was out of breath by the time he got to the top of the stairs. A fumbling of the key and he was inside. He locked the door and leaned back against it, closing his eyes.

Screaming. He heard someone screaming.

He went to the table and switched on the lamp.

The screaming stopped.

There was no one here. He was imagining things.

He looked down at his bloody hands.

No, this was real. This was her blood, and it was her screams he had heard still echoing in his head.

He went to the futon and dropped down onto it, trying to clear his mind, trying to remember where he had been, what he had done. Why was it so hard? What was happening to him? He could not remember the last time he had slept.

He shut his eyes.

Lights on the screen of his eyelids. Sparks of blue, like he could almost see the synapses firing in his brain.

Things were coming back.

The apartment on Île Saint-Louis. He could remember suddenly the flash of blue lights on his window and looking down and seeing the police cars below. He could remember running and a long ride in the night and the manor house in the mist.

He could remember watching the dark-haired woman as she left the café in the village, following her, pulling her into the car and hitting her to make her stay quiet, dragging her up to the tower and . . .

Screaming. It was her screams he had heard, the screams of this faceless woman he did not know. And now he could remember it clearly, even remember what he was thinking as he stabbed her.

I know you are not her. But you will do.

In the cold, his clothes had stiffened with her blood. He felt a jumping in his arms, like insects scurrying inside his veins.

He needed something to calm him. He needed his GHB. But all his drugs were at the other apartment and there was no way he could risk going back there now that they were looking for him.

There was no choice. He would have to go down to the streets and buy something. He would have to buy other things, too. Some clothes, and something to eat.

But first, he had to get rid of the blood.

He staggered to the bathroom, peeled off his sticky clothes and turned on the tap. The water was cold, as it always was in this place, and he drew in a sharp breath as it stung his face and bare chest.

The stink of his body repulsed him. He longed for the warmth of his bath on Île Saint-Louis. For clean sheets and hot coffee, for the smell of flowers and the sound of a Brahms sonata. But that was gone now. All of that life was gone. Everything of comfort, pleasure and beauty was gone forever now.

The water ran red between his fingers.

Blood . . . too much blood.

There had been so much of it. Not the faceless woman's blood. Hélène's blood.

His eyes drifted to the bathtub.

He had buried it, he thought, buried all the memories. But now they were back, as clear as the night it happened.

It had begun at Le Coupe-Chou, near the Sorbonne. He picked Hélène up after her classes and took her to his favorite restaurant. There, watching her face in the glow of the fire-place, he asked her to marry him.

She had said nothing, then . . .

I don't think this can work, Laurent.

I love you, Hélène.

I need time. Please don't press me. You know I hate that.

Will you stay with me tonight?

But it hasn't worked before, Laurent.

Please, Hélène. Just for tonight.

Why had he brought her to this ugly place instead of the Île Saint-Louis apartment? Was it because he knew what he was going to do? He saw her repulsion when he opened the door. He felt her stiffening as he led her to the futon. He heard her protests as he started to unbutton her blouse. It was like all the other times he had tried to make love to her and failed. Except . . .

This time when he looked down at her white skin, this time when he wound her long braid between his fingers, this time when he couldn't get hard, couldn't do anything, this time something deep inside him broke.

He hit her. She screamed.

He hit her harder to make her stop. She clawed at his face, drawing blood.

Who would have thought a small girl would have so much blood in her?

Even now, he couldn't remember stabbing her. He could only remember waking up, like emerging from a trance, and seeing the blood. And Hélène's body curled on the floor.

He had cried.

And now, standing at the mirror, he cried again. Cried as

he remembered what he did next. How he picked up her body and put it in the bathtub. Found the knife and began cutting off her arms. Hours later, when the knife broke, he stopped and fell into an exhausted sleep. The next morning, he went to the Arab store on rue de Suez and bought a saw and two large pots. By sunset, he had finished.

He carefully wrapped her bleached bones in a blanket and carried them out in a duffel bag. He put her in a dark place, close by so he could visit her whenever he wanted.

He had loved her, after all.

The sound of running water drew him back. He shut it off.

What's done cannot be undone. What's done cannot be. What's done cannot. What's done. What's done . . . what?

It was like a slap to his face.

He had forgotten about it until this very moment.

Where had he put it?

He hurried from the bathroom and returned to the other room. He stood, naked, his eyes searching the shadows as he struggled to remember. Five years had passed, and his mind was not clear right now.

Then his eyes went to the far corner. He walked slowly to the metal shelf lined with compact discs. He reached into the alcove behind the rack and pulled out the Goffriller Rosette cello.

He set it tenderly on the floor. He knelt and stretched his arm deep into the shadows of the alcove, pulled out the rectangular box and laid it next to the cello. With trembling fingers he wiped the dust from the ebony surface before opening it.

His eyes filled with tears as he stared at what lay inside. He wanted to touch it but he was afraid if he did he would leave a trace of the blood that he was sure still clung to his hands.

Instead, he rose slowly, retrieved a chair and placed it in front of the open box.

He sat down and picked up the cello and bow. The burnished maple of the Rosette, touched by the hands of the greats for hundreds of years, glowed in the dim light.

He began to play, for himself and for her.

34

Once again, we set up operations around Eve's kitchen table. Cameron and I were on our laptops, trolling Nexis for anything we could find on Laurent Demarais—which was limited to reviews of his cello performances.

Why was there so little on this man's personal background?

The answer came when Eve accessed her database at work and discovered that Demarais had legally changed his name in 1996. His birth name was Lawrence David Gilchrist.

From there, she got his birth certificate and his parents' names: Camille Demarais and Charles Gilchrist. Eve found a death certificate for Camille, who had died in 1985. Charles Gilchrist had died in 2004, when Lawrence was twenty-nine.

The small apartment grew quiet except for the tapping of computer keys, the occasional chirp of cell phones and our murmured exchanges. At some point, my nose was pricked with the smell of strong coffee.

Someone set a cup by my elbow. I looked up into Juliette's face, still flushed from the cold outside. I hadn't even heard her come in from school.

"I got a hit," Cameron said.

He swung his laptop toward me. I was looking at an article from a 1983 issue of French *Vogue*.

"It says they—Gilchrist, wife and son, Lawrence—divide their time between a London town house and a restored French manor house named Villa Euterpe that has been in Camille Demarais's family for four generations," Cameron translated for me with a smile. "Euterpe was the muse of music."

I couldn't read the article but the pictures said it all. It was a home design spread, photographed at the Saint-Aubin manor house, clearly in better days. Gardens in full bloom, the rooms filled with gilt antiques. There was a photograph of "*le chef d'orchestre éminent*" Charles Gilchrist. He was tall and thin with a high forehead, a receding dark hairline and a sour expression on a long face. He was standing over someone sitting in a chair. For a second, the other person didn't register. Then I realized I was looking at Lawrence, at age seven or eight. He was a scrawny kid, with serious dark eyes, his small hands holding a cello.

I scrolled through more photos of rooms. Then I stopped cold.

A woman in a blue gown sitting in a chair holding a violin. Heart-shaped face, blue eyes and a long braid that draped over her shoulder. The caption identified her as Camille Demarais but I could have been staring at an older version of Hélène Molyneaux.

"Eve!"

She came over to the table. Cameron was already staring at the screen over my shoulder. Finally, Eve let out a sigh and moved away.

I looked over to see her heading out onto the tiny balcony and Juliette watching her. Eve closed the door behind her and lit up a cigarette. I watched her, thinking that I should go out there, take her a coat or try to talk to her. But Cameron's voice pulled me back.

"I think I just found Lawrence's first review," he said. "It's from the *London Times*. It's dated 1987. Lawrence would have been . . . ?"

"Twelve," I said as I moved my chair next to Cameron's and started reading.

By Nigel Adams
Arts Critic

We are all amazed when we witness a child prodigy. But when is the line between encouragement and child abuse crossed? Yes, prodigy Arthur Rubinstein performed almost to age 90. But for every Rubinstein, there is a Ruth Slenczynska, who made her debut as a pianist at age 6 and was driven so furiously that she suffered a breakdown at 15 that ended her career.

This is what was running through my mind as I watched Lawrence Gilchrist make his debut at the Wigmore Hall Tuesday evening. I will say little of the performance itself. I prefer to speak of the young man as a sad example of exploitation. Why are we enthralled with these organ-grinder-monkey displays? I posit that we attend to hear how well the child can pretend to be an adult. Or worse, as in the case of Gilchrist's father, Maestro Charles Gilchrist, we might be looking for some sad miniature ideal of ourselves.

I have seen many poised prodigies. But I fear that some are permanently damaged by the ambitions of those pulling the strings. Lawrence Gilchrist may mature into an artist, but at what price?

"That's cold, man," Cameron said.

Eve came back, bringing with her the smell of smoke. She went to the stove and poured herself some coffee. She and Juliette spoke softly in French. Eve seemed to be trying to reassure Juliette about something.

"I found some dirt in the *London Sun*," Cameron said.

Eve came over to stand next to me. Juliette perched on the barstool, watching us as she sipped her coffee.

"'Are those notes of discord we're hearing from the Continent?'" Cameron read. "'French sources tell us Lon-Phil baton boy Charles Gilchrist's marriage may finally be over. Wife Camille has suddenly decamped from Villa Euterpe and is nowhere to be found. And who was that lovely brunette on Gilchrist's arm at The Ivy last month? The family au pair Simone Renard, bien sûr.'"

"Aw, gee, the poor kid," I said. "First a bad review and then his dad starts boffing the help. It's enough to drive you to—"

I caught Juliette's eye and knew I had gone too far with the sarcasm. But a part of me didn't care. I didn't want to know how tough Lawrence or Laurent had it as a kid. I just wanted to find the fucker who had killed my sister.

"Maybe we should concentrate on Britain," I said. "He knew about the Palais de Danse and the festivals there. He lived in London. Maybe that's where he's gone."

"He can't. He'd need to show his passport," Cameron said.

I rubbed my stiff neck. I noticed the sun had painted the wall deep yellow and glanced at my watch. Somewhere, I could hear a church bell tolling. I got up to get a coffee refill but decided instead to uncork the bottle of red wine sitting on the counter.

I had just sat back down in front of my laptop when Eve snapped her cell shut.

"I found out something about his time in England," she said. "He has a juvenile record. In France, these records are sealed, but a friend gave me some information I am not supposed to have. So this goes nowhere else, understood?"

We nodded, but I wondered who she thought Cameron or I would tell.

"Charles Gilchrist and his son, Lawrence, moved from the manor house and relocated to London when Lawrence was fifteen," Eve said.

"What about his mother?"

"There is nothing about her anywhere."

"And Simone?"

"She moved to Lyon, took a position at a girls' school and as far as anyone could tell, never had contact with Charles again."

"Sounds like someone was kicked to the curb," Cameron said.

"So what about this criminal record?" I said.

"Lawrence began running with punks and doing the club scene. His juvenile record in Britain is for possession of a false ID, possession of cocaine and ecstasy, along with several arrests for receiving stolen property."

"Maybe that's how he knew about the old Hammersmith," Cameron said.

"Maybe it was also his way of rebelling against his father pushing him to be a cellist," I said.

Eve gave me a long look before she went on, reading from her notes. "When he was seventeen, he was arrested for stabbing his father."

"Jesus," Cameron said.

"He could have been tried for attempted murder, but it seems Charles Gilchrist had second thoughts about his only son going to prison. He used his influence to convince the magistrate that his son should receive psychiatric treatment instead."

"And the court agreed."

"Yes," Eve said. "We are lucky in that his father sent him back to France, to L'Hôpital Esquirol, right here in Paris."

"Please tell me that you don't have confidentiality laws for hospital records," I said.

"We do, but not for mandatory psychiatric incarcerations," Eve said. "Since he was a prisoner of the state, he has no right to privacy."

"Who do we talk to?" I said.

Eve looked down at her notes. "Dr. Agnès Faucheux. She still works at the hospital."

I was halfway out of the chair when Eve put up her hand. "Matt, sit down," she said. "My friend has a phone call in to her asking her to meet us later."

I sank into my chair. Eve was right; I needed to slow down. We had been moving nonstop ever since we left Paris for the Hammersmith club. I needed some scotch in my veins and some warm food in my belly.

Eve had moved to the kitchen and was getting out some bread and cheese. I was considering going out to buy a bottle of scotch when Cameron spoke up.

"I found her," he said.

"Who?" I asked.

He turned his laptop toward me and I found myself staring at a photo of a woman with wavy black hair. I was immediately struck with the sense that I knew her, or at least had seen her somewhere before.

Then I saw the date on the edge of the photo—1993—and realized I hadn't seen *this* woman but one who only resembled her. I had seen her this morning in the tower room of the Saint-Aubin manor house, propped up against the wall like a bloody rag doll.

"Who is this?" I asked.

"Charles's mistress, Simone Renard," Cameron said.

35

Dr. Agnès Faucheux was sitting in a banquette in the back of the café where she had agreed to meet us. Her salt-and-pepper hair was cut in a short pixie style and a splashy yellow scarf set off her plain gray suit.

She had been on the staff of the adolescent psychiatry unit of the nearby L'Hôpital Esquirol for more than twenty years, and I guessed that the neutral expression she wore as she watched us approach had been honed by two decades of dealing with disturbed teenage offenders.

The doctor was drinking one of those pink things Eve liked, and as we slid into the banquette I struggled to remember its name so I could order her one. But Eve beat me to it, ordering a kir for herself and a scotch for me.

After Eve made the introductions, the doctor's eyes, magnified behind the heavy lenses of her big glasses, cut from Eve to me and back to Eve. She seemed mildly uncomfortable with a reporter at the table and I was about to assure her of my role when Eve did it for me.

"We think Lawrence Gilchrist may have committed a very serious crime," Eve said quietly. "Monsieur Owens has been working with me only to help find him. He will not be writing about it. Everything you say to us will be treated as evidence and used only at trial, should there be one. I promise you."

Dr. Faucheux stared at her for a long time, not looking away until the waiter set down our drinks. I got the feeling she was not shocked that her former patient was in trouble, but I was a little surprised that she asked no questions. She simply launched into a narrative of her experiences with him.

Her voice had the husky edge of a lifelong smoker. "I didn't meet Lawrence Gilchrist until he was seventeen," she said. "But the one thing I remember is that right from the first moment he walked into my office, I thought him an unlikable boy. Some of the other patients described him as *un drôle d'oiseau.*"

Eve translated for me. "A weird guy."

"We understand that he was sent to a hospital for stabbing his father," I said. "Can you tell us more about that?"

She took a long slow drink of her kir before she spoke. "Lawrence hated his father," she said. "To understand why, you have to go back to when Lawrence was just a boy. Charles Gilchrist was almost forty when Lawrence was born and he was a rather cold man. He was a renowned conductor."

"He guided his son's musical studies," Eve said.

"Guided?" The doctor shook her head slowly. "He was obsessed with the idea of Lawrence being a world-class cellist, and he pushed him very hard. Lawrence told me once that his father made him practice the same piece over and over for hours on end. It was a difficult piece for a boy. It was called *Tout un Monde Lointain.*"

Eve translated again: "The whole world, distant."

"Lawrence was sometimes beaten if he did not do it to his father's satisfaction," the doctor said.

I felt a prickle of anger. I didn't want to hear anything that humanized this monster. "So Demarais stabbed his father just because he pushed him too hard in music?" I said.

"No, that wasn't all," Dr. Faucheux said. "The boy was quite lonely growing up and was perhaps overly attached to his mother. I believe that Lawrence's hatred for his father was ignited when his mother was removed from his life."

"What do you mean, 'removed'?" I asked.

"She was institutionalized," she said. "Lawrence was only eight at the time."

I thought of the London newspaper article that said Camille had "decamped" from the manor house. Powerful people like Gilchrist always found ways to keep things like this private. I had a fleeting memory of a time when my father had conspired to keep a colleague's alcohol rehab stay out of the papers.

"Was she mentally ill?" Eve asked.

"On one of the few occasions that Mr. Gilchrist met with me to discuss his son, he told me his wife suffered from early-onset dementia," she said.

"Was Lawrence ever allowed to see her?" Eve asked.

"No, she died in the institution when Lawrence was ten." She took a drink of her kir. "Lawrence never got over her death. By the time he came to me, it was obvious he had overly idealized her—or rather her memory."

"What about Simone Renard?" I asked.

Dr. Faucheux seemed surprised I knew the name.

"The newspapers claimed she was Gilchrist's mistress," I added. "How did Demarais feel about her?"

Dr. Faucheux hesitated before she answered. "His relationship with Simone was complicated," she said.

I thought it was an odd choice of words. Plus, there was that sadness again in her voice and I wondered just how dispassionate the doctor had been about her young patient. I was about to ask the doctor more about Renard when Eve interrupted.

"How long was he under your care?"

"Just under a year. When he turned eighteen, he was legally allowed to check himself out."

"Did you have any contact with Lawrence after he was released?" Eve asked.

The doctor shook her head. "He had a trust fund from his mother's estate to live on. We had no contact, none at all. But then twelve years later—Lawrence was by then thirty—he suddenly appeared at my office."

"Why?" Eve asked.

"He asked if he could resume our therapy."

Eve and I exchanged looks. "This was five years ago, right?" I asked.

"Yes. I was very surprised to see him. He told me he had changed his name legally to Laurent Demarais and that he was playing his cello again, even performing professionally. He looked very good, almost happy. I was pleased because in many ways, despite what his father had done to him, I always felt that music was the only thing he had any feeling for, other than his mother."

"Can you tell us why he wanted to see you?" Eve asked.

Dr. Faucheux hesitated and I realized that we were no longer dealing with an incarcerated juvenile whose records were public. We now had a traditional doctor-patient confidentiality problem.

"Before I do that, I need to know more about what you think Lawrence Gilchrist has done," Dr. Faucheux said.

Eve leaned over the table, her voice soft so as to not attract the attention of the other customers. "We believe he has murdered five or more women."

That practiced, neutral façade suddenly cracked. Dr. Faucheaux couldn't hide her horror. She drained her kir and when she set the glass down, her hand shook.

She murmured something in French and Eve answered curtly but didn't bother to translate. The doctor asked if she could have another kir. Eve motioned to the waiter.

"These murders," Dr. Faucheux said finally, "they began about five years ago?"

"As far as we know," Eve said. She launched into a quick recap of our case, detailing the murder methods, the musical clues and the fact that all the victims were young, blond and beautiful. She showed the doctor their photographs, ending with Hélène Molyneaux. Then she pulled out a photograph of Camille Demarais.

Dr. Faucheux stared at the ones of Hélène and Camille. "They could be twins," she said quietly.

"May I ask a question, Doctor?"

Faucheux looked to me. "Please."

"Serial killers symbolically kill someone they know and hate. That's a common pathology, right?"

She nodded.

"If he loved his mother so much, why is he killing women who look like her?"

"I don't think it is his mother," Dr. Faucheux said as she pulled the photo of Hélène Molyneaux closer. "I think it is this woman."

I saw Eve blanch slightly. "Explain, please," she said.

"Five years ago, when Lawrence came back to see me, he told me he was in love," Dr. Faucheux said. "He wanted reassurance that he could be . . . in a normal relationship. He wanted to know that he could project love onto another human being the way other people did. He even confessed to one day wanting children."

"Did he tell you the woman's name?" Eve asked.

Dr. Faucheux nodded. "He said that her name was Hélène." She pushed the photograph away. "Had I known she was so much like his mother, I would not have encouraged him."

"But something went wrong, didn't it?" I said.

The doctor looked up at me. "I don't know. I only saw him twice. Then he disappeared again, as suddenly as he had come."

"He killed this woman," I said, pointing at Hélène's photograph. "How could you not see something was wrong, Doctor?"

"Matt—" Eve said.

The waiter brought the fresh kir, giving the doctor a moment to compose herself. I tried to do the same, tried to calm my anger. It seemed obvious to me what had happened. Demarais had wanted assurance he could be normal. And normal to any adult man meant being sexual in a loving way. I suddenly felt like I knew exactly what had happened with Hélène, because he had the same problem with every woman. He tried to make love to her and he couldn't.

Dr. Faucheux had not touched her new drink. "There is something I did not tell you about Lawrence," she said. "It concerns Simone Renard."

"Go on, please," Eve prodded.

"One summer, when he was thirteen, Lawrence played a performance for his father and some friends at the manor house in Saint-Aubin. He played *Tout un Monde Lointain*. Simone by then had become Charles Gilchrist's mistress and hostess. She had developed a fondness for the piece and asked Lawrence to play it for her whenever they were alone in the house, which was often, since Charles was usually in London."

I knew what was coming but I stayed silent. So did Eve. The doctor went on, her voice so low we both leaned forward to hear it.

"These private recitals turned into sexual sessions," the doctor said.

"She seduced Lawrence?" Eve asked.

Dr. Faucheux shook her head. "Not exactly. She would pleasure herself while he played the piece for her."

"How long did this go on?" I asked.

"He told me it went on from the time he was thirteen until he was fifteen," Dr. Faucheux said. "It never went beyond his watching. He was never allowed to touch her or please himself." She took a drink. "God, he hated that woman."

I thought about Charles Gilchrist's sudden relocation to London.

"Gilchrist caught them together," I said.

"Yes," Dr. Faucheux said. "He sent Simone away and took his son back to England. One would think he would blame Simone, but he blamed Lawrence for everything."

"But when Lawrence tried to kill him, Gilchrist didn't send him to prison," I said.

Dr. Faucheux nodded. "I thought at the time he was saving his son's life. Now you tell me he has become a murderer. I do not know what to think. I only wish . . ."

Dr. Faucheux shook her head slowly. Eve pulled a final photograph from her briefcase. It was the crime scene photo of the brunette woman in the tower room. She had been identified as a Saint-Aubin woman, abducted as she was walking home from her job in a café in the village.

"This was his last victim," Eve said.

Dr. Faucheux studied the photo, clearly unbothered by its graphic nature. "You described the other victims as intricately arranged. This scene looks uncontrolled. This may signal a psychotic break."

"If that's true, then what's he likely to do next?" I asked.

She shook her head slowly.

I pressed her. "Where would he go? Does he have any other family?"

"His father died about six years ago. There is no other family. Lawrence is completely alone." She paused. "You said he has disappeared?"

Eve nodded.

"I am not surprised. Lawrence grew up in isolation. It is what he knows, what he is comfortable with. I would not be surprised if he eventually kills himself. If he does, you will never find his body."

The café was filling up with the after-work crowd. I watched a group of young people come in, laughing and joking.

We had learned more than we could have hoped for, but we were no closer to finding Demarais than we had been this morning at the manor house.

"Doctor," I said, "do you have any idea where he might be?"

She shook her head slowly. "I'm sorry I cannot be of more help." I heard the doctor saying something about having to get back to the hospital. But my brain was still locked on Laurent, or Lawrence, or—

"Doctor," I said.

She was standing, putting on her coat, and looked down at me.

"You said he changed his name," I said. "Could he possibly be using a different name now?"

Dr. Faucheux blinked, like she was suddenly remembering something.

"When he first came to the hospital, he had completely drawn into himself," she said. "For weeks, he would not even talk to me. His personality was so fractured, you see. He wanted to be neither British nor French. He asked me to call him Larry."

"Larry?"

She paused. "Larry Marsh," she said.

"'Demarais' translates to 'from the marsh,'" Eve said.

She picked up her cell and punched in a number. I guessed she was telling someone to do a records search for Larry Marsh.

I felt the doctor's eyes on me and looked at her.

"Larry Marsh," she said softly. "He said it was a nothing name for a nothing boy."

I paid the check and the three of us left the café. The doctor politely declined Eve's offer of a ride back to the hospital, saying she wished to walk for a while. Her expression told me the doctor was going to need some time to come to terms with everything we had told her.

As I watched Agnès Faucheux walk away, Eve's cell rang.

She listened, said a few curt words, then snapped the cell closed.

"He has a second apartment in the name of Larry Marsh," she said.

"Where?"

"La Goutte d'Or." She grabbed my arm. "Backups are on their way there. Let's go."

36

The white wedding-cake dome of Sacré-Coeur loomed in the dusk ahead. As Eve steered the car down a hill, the church vanished from view, leaving me with the odd thought that a week ago, I wouldn't have been able to name Sacré-Coeur—or been able to find it.

But I knew now exactly where I was. We were heading toward the eighteenth arrondissement, on the far northern edge of the city, to a neighborhood called La Goutte d'Or.

Eve laid on the horn and let loose a tirade of angry French. I glanced over at her, wondering how much she had slept in the last two days. I was worried about her, worried that her obsession with finding Hélène—and her anger about being sidelined in the investigation—might cloud her judgment.

But even as I thought about that, I was dealing with my own sense of urgency. We both had the feeling that the net was closing, and we were hoping that Demarais hadn't figured out that it was closing around this second home.

I was thinking about what Dr. Faucheux had told us about Laurent or Larry or whatever the hell he called himself and wasn't paying close attention to what was outside the car's windows. But as we turned onto a narrow, dark street called rue Myrha, I stared.

We were only a mile or so from Eve's place, but in contrast to her neighborhood, this one looked run-down, almost abandoned. Nearly every storefront was shuttered or reinforced with heavy gates. There were peeling signs in Arabic and walls scarred with graffiti.

"Number forty-four. There it is," Eve said.

We parked the car in an abandoned lot. The men lingering outside a cafeteria eyed us as we got out of our car. The building we faced had a shuttered Laundromat on the ground floor and few lights on above. Some of the windows were boarded up.

A police officer stood outside. Eve said something to him in French and he shook his head. She stared up at the building, then went back and popped open the trunk. She came back holding a crowbar.

"He says there has been no sign of Demarais, but either way, we're going in," she said.

"Just us and him?" I asked.

"You can stay here."

"I'm going with you."

We entered a dark vestibule that smelled of cat urine. I followed Eve and the other cop up a narrow staircase, feeling my way through the darkness, counting five flights.

At the top, Eve slapped a switch on the wall and a bare bulb lit up the narrow hall's peeling blue paint. A radio was blaring somewhere but Eve didn't hesitate as she wedged the crowbar in the door with the number 5 painted on it.

The cop and I lent our weight to the effort. Finally, the door frame gave way with a loud crack.

It was dark inside. Eve reached inside her leather jacket and pulled out a gun. She motioned for me to stay behind. I didn't argue.

She and the officer slipped inside the apartment. The hallway light went off. I stood in the dark, heart hammering, counting off nine seconds before they returned.

"He's not here," she said. She gave the officer some directions and he headed down the stairs. "He'll keep watch," Eve said, "until the others arrive."

I followed Eve inside the apartment. When Eve turned on a lamp, I blinked the room into focus.

Dark walls, two windows covered with an African-print cloth, bare pipes against the low ceiling, a stained futon, a battered table and chairs, a metal rack holding CDs and a cheap portable player. A kitchenette, and a door standing ajar to reveal the edge of a toilet. The place smelled like rotten meat.

Eve handed me a pair of latex gloves and I put them on. She started systematically going through drawers. My eyes were drawn to the rack of CDs. With a chill, I realized it was like looking at my own collection. Lots of American and British classic rock from the sixties, seventies and eighties, with a few foreign groups I didn't recognize. I pulled out the Rolling Stones CD *Undercover* and turned it over. It was the sixth cut—"Too Much Blood."

As I was putting the CD back, something caught my eye. It was a tattered book. The spine read THE WILD BOYS. I pulled it out.

The cover showed a bare-chested teenage boy pointing a rifle. The subtitle was *A Book of the Dead*. The author was William S. Burroughs, the drug-addled icon of the Beat Generation writers. A lost memory floated back. I had left my copy of *Naked Lunch* on a train somewhere along my trek through Indonesia and was secretly glad to be rid of the burden of finishing it.

I thumbed through the book, noting that many passages had been underlined, some signposted with emphatic exclamation points and French phrases. I wondered if this was Demarais's handwriting.

There was an old yellowed paper stuck in the middle. I unfolded it. It looked to be a map of some kind. It was hand-drawn and all in French, but I figured one abbreviation—*bu du MONTPARN*—might be the boulevard du Montparnasse, the street near Cameron's apartment where the café Le Select was located.

I stuck the map back in the book, deciding I needed to show it to Eve later. I was slipping it into my coat when she emerged from the bathroom. She looked pale.

"What's wrong?" I asked.

She shook her head. "The bathtub," she said. "I can't be sure, but I think there are old bloodstains. And I found this."

She was holding a cello end pin by its tip. Even from where I was I could tell it looked like it was coated with dried blood.

Eve shook out a plastic bag from her pocket and dropped the pin into it. "Look for others," she said, heading to the kitchen.

I saw an alcove behind the shelf of CDs and, figuring it was a closet, went to it.

At first, I couldn't make out what I was looking at. But then the spare light picked up the gleam of burnished wood. I reached in, grabbed the cello by the neck and pulled it out.

"Eve," I called out.

She came to my side. "I don't think he would leave without this," she said.

I took the cello to the futon and laid it down. The only reference points for what I was looking at were the instruments I had seen in that music shop in Edinburgh. But even to my eyes, this was old and valuable. I had a vision of Laurent Demarais's hands caressing this beautiful thing, bringing it to life. And a second image of his hands violating Mandy, bringing her to her death.

I felt my stomach turn. The smell of this place, the vibrations of evil here, it was all making me sick.

I heard a strange cry, like the mew of a cat. It took me a second to realize it was Eve. I looked to the kitchen. Her back was to me and she was bent over something on the counter. I went quickly to her.

"Eve? What's—?"

She slapped something closed and then spun away from me, her hand covering her mouth. I watched her stumble into the other room, then I turned to the counter.

It was a long ebony box, like the kind pool players use to store cue pieces. It looked like the cello bow boxes I had seen at the music store in Edinburgh. I opened it.

"Oh God," I whispered.

The color was faded, the luster long gone. But there was no doubt about what I was looking at. Hélène Molyneaux's braid.

I closed the box and turned. Eve was standing at the window, looking down at the street. I went to her.

"Eve," I said, touching her arm.

Suddenly she doubled over, clutching her stomach. I wrapped her in my arms and held her as she cried.

37

After Eve pulled herself together, she called the station. Her plan was to leave two officers in the shadows of the street and another one in the apartment for a stakeout, in the hopes that Demarais would return to what he thought was his only safe haven.

But she was overruled by her commandant. She told me that Boutin saw no purpose in staking out Demarais's apartment and told her to arrange a thorough search of the apartment immediately.

Eve tried to hide her disappointment from me, but I could see the constant dismissals were taking their toll. After she got off her phone, she snapped at the uniformed officer to canvass neighbors for leads on Demarais. Then she told me I should go wait in the hall.

Two investigators showed up first, followed by the forensic team. After the techs swabbed the futon, they vanished into the bathroom with their kits and brushes. Another man soon followed with a screwdriver and a wrench.

They were taking apart the drain in the bathtub.

My eyes drifted back to the ebony box with the braid inside.

At least Eve now had confirmation that Hélène had been killed by Demarais. She probably had been killed right in this apartment. But where had he put her body? Where was his "backyard?"

I heard a flurry of French. It was a tech standing at the kitchen sink holding tweezers. Even from here I could guess what was probably in them—dried human tissue.

Then I heard a clanging sound and saw another tech pulling two pots from a cupboard. They were big, like the kind used to boil lobsters.

I turned away, trying to find a spot to focus on. I looked up at a bulb and stared at it until my vision had halos floating in it. What I was thinking was almost too grotesque to contemplate.

Demarais had cut up Hélène and boiled away her flesh.

I moved to the stairs and sat down in the corner to avoid the policemen taking bags of evidence down the five flights. I forced my mind to other things.

I thought about the copy of *The Wild Boys* in my jacket pocket and the map tucked inside of it. I was anxious to analyze the map and the book to see if either provided any hint as to where Demarais might go. But I couldn't risk having it confiscated before I showed it to Eve.

My phone chirped with a text message from Juliette wanting to know how we were doing. I called her and assured her that Eve was fine. I was about to hang up when she told me the hospital had called. At first I was confused, then Juliette mentioned Paula Ridley.

"Oh God, did she die?" I whispered.

"No," Juliette said. "Actually, the nurse who called said Mademoiselle Ridley might be up to speaking with someone tomorrow. Would you please share that with my aunt?"

"I will," I said.

"I made some soup. I will have some ready for you when you get here," Juliette said. "If you want to sleep on the sofa, I can prepare it."

"I might do that," I said. "Thank you."

As I was hanging up, I saw a man trudge up the stairs carrying a kit and something the size of a bleach bottle. The label read CHEMILUMINESCENCE. They were going to luminol the room.

I went back to the door. Most of the techs were packing up. Boxes and bags were being hauled out by the armfuls. The luminol man was bent on one knee, mixing a solution. He said something and people started huddling near me at the door. Eve took a place a few feet ahead of me and we watched as the man sprayed the room.

Someone closed the door behind me. Then the lights went off and the blue-black glow of the lamp came on.

The futon was covered in a bluish-green glow. Low-light cameras starting clicking. The luminol man sprayed the wall above it. It lit up like the backdrop in a house of horrors.

Eve had told me Tricia Downey's neck had almost been severed. This spray of blood across the wall—was this the result?

The door bumped open behind me and I heard a deep voice speaking French. I recognized it as the commandant's and took the opportunity to slip out of the apartment. I made it to the street without anyone questioning me.

The night was cold and crisp. As tired as I was, I wanted to wait for Eve, so I withdrew *The Wild Boys* from my coat, moved into a slant of fluorescent light coming from the cafeteria and started to read chapter one.

I heard the commandant's voice and turned to see him and Eve in the foyer of the apartment building. I didn't need to understand a word of French to know he was furious with her.

As Eve came out, the wind blew open her leather coat. She seemed oblivious to the cold, and to me.

"Eve!"

She had started down the street and she spun back and waited for me.

"I've been taken off this case," she said. "I am to have no more involvement in anything to do with Hélène Molyneaux or any of the others."

"What?"

She was silent.

"God, Eve, I'm so sorry."

She looked back toward the apartment building. Her car keys were in her hand and I gently took them from her so I could drive her home—to Juliette, a good glass of wine and a warm bed. Anything else, like my pilfering of the book, could wait until tomorrow.

38

It was past midnight by the time we got back to Eve's place. Juliette came out from the kitchen as we entered. Her eyes went from Eve's haggard face to mine and back to her aunt's. Eve didn't say a word, just tossed her leather jacket toward a chair and went to her bedroom, closing the door.

The jacket had landed on the floor. Juliette picked it up and hung it on a hook by the door. Then she turned to me.

"What happened?" she asked.

I let out a tired sigh and went to the sofa. It was made up with sheets and a pillow. I perched on the edge, arms resting on my knees, and looked up at Juliette.

"We found a second apartment owned by Demarais," I said. "It was where he killed . . ."

My voice trailed off. Not because I was trying to spare Juliette. Five years of watching her aunt hunt this monster had earned her the right to know everything. I didn't finish my thought because I didn't know who had died in that hellhole. No one knew for sure, at least not until DNA matching came back. And I suspected someone would soon be calling Beauvais to talk to Hélène Molyneaux's parents about that.

Juliette was still waiting for my answer.

"We found some . . . evidence that might show he took Hélène Molyneaux there," I said.

Thank God Juliette let it go at that. I didn't want to tell her about the braid. She was looking at the closed bedroom door.

"Is she okay?" she asked.

"She's very tired, she—"

Screw this. Juliette had a right to know about Eve, too.

"She got taken off the case tonight," I said.

Juliette murmured something in French. It sounded angry, hurt and deeply protective all at the same time.

She looked again toward the bedroom, then back at me. "There's some soup," she said. "I will get—"

"I can help myself," I said. "You go help your aunt."

She whispered a quick "*merci*" and was gone. I sat for a moment, then forced myself to get up and go to the kitchen. I ladled out a big bowl of what looked like vegetable stew and took it to the table and sat down. My eyes went to the bottle of wine on the counter but I was too damn tired to get up again, so I just ate the soup in greedy gulps.

After rinsing the bowl and pouring a glass of red wine, I went back to the sofa. I pulled off my shoes, sank back into the cushions and closed my eyes. The apartment was quiet, but I could hear voices and laughter drifting up from the Moroccan coffee shop downstairs. I was too tired to take off my clothes so I slumped down and started to pull the blanket up over me. But something was jabbing me in the hip.

I reached into my jeans pocket and pulled out *The Wild Boys*.

The copyright page said it was published by Calder Press, 1972. I flipped it over and read the back copy. It was about a tribe of renegade teenage boys who reject society and women and create a secret world underground where they indulge in violence and homoerotic sex.

I was certain it was no accident that this was the only book in Demarais's apartment; it had to have meaning for him. But as I leafed through the yellowed pages, my brain was too fuzzy to make sense of the passages that had been underlined or the French handwritten notes in the margins. I came to the paper that had been stuck inside and unfolded it.

I stared at the crudely drawn map for a long time, again focusing in on "bu du MONTPARN." Then I noticed a second street, one that before tonight I would not have recognized.

"MYRHA." That was the name of the street where Demarais's apartment was located.

I was far from an expert on Paris geography but even to my eye—except for Myrha and Montparnasse—none of the other markings on the map seemed to be streets. They had strange names like Petite Niche, Le Bunker Allemand, Bar des Rats and La Crypte. I knew I wasn't looking at a map of Paris. So what the hell was I looking at?

I heard a sound and looked up. Juliette had come out of the bedroom. She looked over at me.

"You're still awake?"

I nodded. "Thanks for the soup."

She gave me a small smile and pushed back her curly hair, a gesture that exactly mirrored Eve's.

"How's Eve?" I asked.

"Asleep," Juliette said.

She poured herself a glass of wine and sat down. The lamplight brought her pretty face into high relief. She looked so very young and so very old, all at the same time.

"I know this sounds selfish," she said, "but a part of me is glad she is not on the case anymore."

I nodded in sympathy, but something that had been gnawing at the back of my brain was pushing to the front now. It was the realization that with Eve now off the case, my conduit to this investigation was gone. Even if Demarais was found, I would not be a part of it. And if Dr. Faucheux's notion that he might kill himself turned out to be true, then I would never have the satisfaction of seeing Mandy's murderer brought to justice. I felt a sudden and crushing depression.

I glanced at my watch. Almost two. I began to fold up the map.

"What is that?" Juliette asked.

"I wish I knew," I said. I held it out to her. "Want to take a look?"

She took the map, studied it for a moment, then looked up at me. "Where did you get this?" she asked.

I showed her the Burroughs paperback. "Stuffed inside this book in Demarais's apartment. It has his street written on it—rue Myrha—but even I can tell it's not a map of Paris."

"It is Paris, but not any Paris you can see."

I just stared at her dumbly.

"It is underground Paris," she said.

"Underground?"

She held the map out to me. "It is a map of the catacombs."

"The what?" I looked down at the map, then back up at her. "What kind of catacombs?"

"Paris was once a big limestone mining place," she said. "It was shut down centuries ago, but all the old tunnels and catacombs are still there. It is all closed off now."

"How big?"

"Hundreds of kilometers. They run under almost the whole city. No one really knows how far."

I glanced at the map, at the intricate web of intersecting arteries and all the strange names. "Do you know what these names are?" I asked, holding out the map.

She didn't take it. "Places down there," she said softly.

"What kind of places?"

She rose abruptly, picked up her wineglass and went to the kitchen. She poured out her wine and began rinsing glasses. I followed her.

"Juliette, this might be important. What do you know about this?"

She shut off the faucet and turned to me. "Kids go down there to explore, to have parties. Sometimes they stay there for days, camping out."

"I thought you said it was closed off."

"There are secret ways to get in," she said.

The Burroughs book was about a bunch of violent teenagers who live underground. It was no coincidence that Demarais had this map.

"Have you been down there?" I asked.

She nodded. "I only went down once and I did not go very far. I was terrified. I will never go back there." Her eyes held mine. "Please don't tell my aunt. She would kill me if she knew."

"Juliette, you've got to show me these catacombs," I said.

"No, no," she said quickly.

"Please, Juliette," I said. "This could be where Demarais is hiding. You have to help me with this."

Juliette was quiet, head bowed.

"Juliette," I said softly. "This isn't like you just stayed out late or something. You need to step up and tell Eve what you know."

"She has always trusted me," Juliette said.

I nodded. "I understand that you don't want to disappoint her, but if you have a good relationship with someone, like you do with Eve, you should be honest with them."

She bit her lip. I resisted the urge to press her harder.

"All right," she said finally. "I know someone who goes down there. He is *un kata*."

"A what?"

"*Un kata*," she said. "A cataphile. An urban explorer. I will call him tomorrow."

"Thanks." I hesitated, then gave her a hug. She stiffened slightly in surprise but when she pulled back, she gave me a small smile.

"I will tell my aunt in the morning," she said. "Good night, Matt."

I said good night and Juliette went to bed. I went back to the sofa and collapsed into the cushions. The apartment was quiet. Even the coffee shop below was finally quiet. I had visions of Demarais holing up in some cave, crawling around in a tunnel somewhere below my feet, laughing at me. I had to get a grip.

The apartment was getting cold. I turned off the light, lay back and pulled the blanket up over my chest.

I was just drifting off when I heard a chirping noise. It took me a couple seconds to realize it was my cell. I jumped up and hurried to my jacket draped across the back of a chair. I pulled out the cell and flipped it open.

"Yeah?"

"Matt?"

"Who's this?"

"Nora."

"Nora? What—?"

"Oh God, I just realized . . . what time is it there?"

"I don't know, around two A.M."

Some fumbling sounds four thousand miles away. And then came the telltale soft beep in the background, the warning that my cell was losing its charge.

"Nora? Are you there?"

"Yeah, I can hear you. Matt, I'm sorry to call you so late. It's early here, and I didn't—"

"No, no, it's okay." I went back to the sofa and sat down. Nora's voice was like a balm.

"I have some news," she said.

"Good, I hope."

"They did a rush on that semen sample your inspector sent. I just got the results. It's a match, Matt."

I was quiet. It was almost like I could feel my heart slowing in my chest, like it was taking a rest after a long hard run. We didn't know where Laurent Demarais was, we didn't know if we would ever find him. But at least now I knew—beyond all doubt—that my journey hadn't been in vain.

Another warning beep from the cell. Nora said something, but I caught only a couple words. Something about thanking me for handing her the name of their suspect, that Darius had been released and that Detective Molina would be moving forward with the case.

I suddenly felt like I was a million miles from home, and this tiny thing pressed to my ear was my only lifeline. I was thinking about what I had told Juliette, that if someone cared enough about you, you could be honest with them, even when you had screwed up. Especially when you had screwed up.

"Nora?"

"I'm here."

"I'm sorry."

A beat or two passed before she spoke. "For what?"

"For screwing things up. For not being straight with you. For . . . hell, I don't know. I'm just sorry."

There was silence on Nora's end. For a second, I thought she had hung up or the cell had died, but then she said, "Matt? Are you still there?"

"Yeah, I'm here."

The cell beeped again.

"So, when are you coming home?"

"Soon," I said.

The cell beeped again. Then once more. I was seconds away from losing her.

"You think you could pick me up at the airport?" I asked.

The cell went dead.

I closed it and lay there in the dark, holding it against my chest, watching the shadows moving across the ceiling.

The light in the second-floor window suddenly went out. Laurent stepped out of the alleyway. He had been standing down here watching the apartment for nearly two hours.

It had turned bitterly cold during the night, but his rage burned so hot now he barely felt anything else. It had started hours ago, at dusk, when he left his apartment on rue Myrha to gather food, clothes and, most important, the drugs he needed. But he had never bought drugs on the street before, not even as a kid in London, so it had taken him longer than he anticipated. Then, supplies in hand, he turned onto rue Myrha and saw the jam of police cars outside his building.

How had they found his secret place? And what was happening up there?

He had retreated to a vacant building slated for demolition. There, he peered between two boards, watching the cops coming down carrying bags. Then a man emerged from the doorway with his Rosette cello. He was carrying it by its neck, like it was a dead animal.

If it hadn't been for the Valium he had taken he would have ripped the man's throat open with his bare hands.

But Laurent had stayed where he was, watching, waiting. It was late when the man and the woman emerged. As they passed, he realized with a start it was the American man who had been with the Ridley woman. Matt Owens, the brother of the girl in Miami. The dark-haired woman? He saw a flash of gold in the streetlight. A badge. She was a cop. When they drove off, he followed them.

Followed them here.

He stared up at the dark windows. Was this her home? Were they lovers? His mind spun with questions. But he knew this much: The American was staying here.

Laurent stuffed his raw hands in his armpits. The clothes he had bought at the African bazaar smelled of stale cigarettes but they provided him with more than warmth. They helped him blend in. And that was what he needed to do, because now there was nowhere for him to hide.

He ran a shaking hand under his nose. The drugs were starting to wear off. His body felt empty, like everything inside him was slowly liquefying, and he had a sudden and horrible feeling that it was all going to end soon, that *he* would end soon.

He reached in his coat and his fingers closed over the plastic bag of pills. No, he couldn't take another one. He needed to save them. He still had things to do.

First, rest. He would go to the one place on earth where they would never think to look for him.

He would go to Hélène. He would rest with her.

And then he would come back for his necklace.

39

The bar was near the Sorbonne; the lettering on the faded red awning read EL MELOCOTÓN. It was supposedly a cataphile hangout. As I left behind the bright afternoon sun to go inside, my eyes struggled to adjust to the cavelike interior.

It was a hole-in-the-wall student dive, advertising a glass of wine for two euros and even cheaper beer. The music was a mix of classic and new rock. I found a table in the back and sat down to wait for someone named Trevor.

I had woken up that morning on Eve's sofa, half-drugged by the first good sleep I had had in days. No one else was up yet, so I slipped out and made my way back to Cameron's place. Juliette called me a couple hours later, saying her friend had found a cataphile who might talk to me. She didn't offer anything about her talk with Eve, and I didn't ask.

As soon as we hung up, I called Eve's cell. I caught her just as she was arriving at the station. She told me investigators were still digging up the Saint-Aubin manor house grounds and that Demarais's apartment on rue Myrha was still being processed. She had been relegated to routine duty. When I told her I was going to talk to someone about the catacombs, she wasn't happy. But after a long pause, she added that she couldn't tell me what to do. Before she hung up, she invited me to dinner and said she would pick me up at eight.

I knew Eve's pride was badly wounded and that she wanted to find Demarais as much as I did. But now that she was on the outside of the case, our investigative options were very limited. I had nothing at stake here; she had her career on the line.

A waiter finally came to my table. It was around noon, so I ordered a beer and tapas.

This morning, when I had asked Cameron about the catacombs, he told me a small portion had been turned into a museum, the entrance just blocks from his apartment. I found an old Michelin guide on his shelf.

I opened it now as I waited for my food. It didn't take me long to figure out the guide's listing for the catacombs covered only the "official ossuary," with no mention of the vast secret labyrinth Juliette had described.

It talked about how the limestone mining that had started with the Romans had turned Paris's underground into a honeycomb of tunnels. When the ground began to cave in, the mines were closed. Then a second problem arose: The city's cemeteries were too full, so they kept building walls around them to stack the bodies. Finally, with thirty generations of the dead piled ten feet high, the walls gave way, spilling decaying corpses and disease into the streets. So in mass processions, led by black-veiled priests, the remains of *"les innocents"* were transferred down into the catacombs. For two years it went on, until they gave up the pretense of ceremony and just started shoveling the bones into wells and holes. Six million souls ended up underground before the catacombs were sealed off for good.

But the curious living still found their way in. Visiting royalty looking for thrills, noblemen out to impress their mistresses, even Napoleon, who thought visits to the dead would strengthen his son's spine. And on one memorable night in April 1897, a hundred society guests got a secret invitation to the catacombs to hear a full orchestra play Chopin's "Funeral March" and Beethoven's *Eroica*.

The bar was filling up fast with students, most male.

I watched them, wondering if any of them realized that the explorations they thought so modern and dangerous were once a lark for ladies in silk dresses.

I went back to scanning the crowd for someone who looked like a Trevor. Forty minutes later, the food and beer were long gone.

"Screw this," I muttered, and started to get up.

At that moment, a short wiry man came through the crowd to my table. He was maybe fifty, stoop shouldered, with a hawkish face. He stood there, his dark birdlike eyes fixed on me.

"You the one asking about *les katas*?"

"Are you Trevor?" I asked.

"No."

"Where's Trevor? I'm supposed to—"

"Trevor won't talk to *flics*."

"I'm not a cop."

"Your friend is."

The guy gave me a hard stare, then pulled out a chair and sat down. He was wearing an old white dress shirt with sleeves rolled to reveal sinewy brown arms. He wore an odd black braided bracelet and a thin silver chain around his neck, and gave off an odor of strong tobacco.

A waiter set a small carafe and two glasses down between us. The older guy said something in French and the kid disappeared.

"Would you take a drink with me?" the man asked, picking up the carafe.

"Sure."

He poured out two glasses of the mahogany liquid and pushed one toward me. I took a drink, expecting wine but getting instead a syrupy liqueur tasting of berries and black licorice.

The man's eyes were fixed on me. "Do you like it?"

"It's different."

"I am Basque. It is *Le Patxaran,* the drink of my people."

I took another drink. "So if you're not Trevor, who are you?"

"Pierre. I own this bar."

For some reason, I didn't believe that was his real name but decided to let it go. In the background, Jim Morrison was singing "People Are Strange."

"I need to know about the catacombs," I said.

"Go to the museum."

"Look," I said, leaning over the table. "Maybe you've heard, but the police are looking for a man who has been murdering women here. We—I think the catacombs are important to him somehow."

Pierre just stared at me.

I reached in my coat and pulled out my cell. I found Mandy's picture and held it out. "This is my sister. He killed her."

Still, no change in his expression. I snapped the cell shut. I was about to get up and leave when I remembered the map. I got the paperback out of my coat and pulled out the map. As I unfolded it, I watched Pierre's face for a reaction and I saw a twitch of an eyebrow.

He pulled it across the table and looked at it. "Where did you get this?" he asked.

"First you tell me exactly what I am looking at here."

"This is a map of the catacombs."

"I know that. What do these names mean?" I asked, pointing to several of the notations.

Pierre shrugged. "Places that *les katas* find. If you find a new place, you have the honor of naming it. Like Magellan or Columbus."

He pointed to a spot called La Plage. "This means 'the Beach.' It is a big cavern filled with sand. This one, Salle des Partouzes, means 'the Orgy Room.' And this, where it says Carrefour des Morts, that is 'the Crossroads of the Dead.'"

He fell silent, examining the map again. "I must ask you again," he said, "where did you get this?"

When I pulled the map back to my side of the table, Pierre let go reluctantly. I had the sudden feeling that he knew the person who had drawn this map.

"Do you know a man named Laurent Demarais?" I asked.

"No."

"Lawrence Gilchrist?"

He shook his head as he took a drink.

"What about Larry Marsh?"

His black eyes met mine. He set his glass down.

"I knew him," he said.

"How?"

"We were friends."

That didn't jibe with the Larry or Laurent that I had put together in my mind. Social misfit, loner, psychopath, murderer. Monsters didn't have friends.

"I need to know everything you can tell me about him," I said.

Pierre glanced around, then leaned back in his chair, studying me for a moment before he spoke. "I knew him when he was nineteen or twenty," he said. "He was part of a group of kids who hung out together. They called themselves Les Sauvages."

I paused, then reached back in my coat pocket. I tossed the Burroughs paperback on the table.

Pierre looked down at it and nodded. "Yes, *The Wild Boys*. I remember this. He used to read passages to the others." He picked up the book, thumbed through it and set it down. "I was older than the others, sort of an outsider. I don't think they trusted me."

"What did the group do?"

"Mostly got drunk, did drugs, listened to music, sometimes played music. But the main reason behind it was exploring."

"Exploring? In the catacombs?"

He nodded. "And many other places. Abandoned buildings, hospitals, the sewers, the closed parts of the metro. When we exhausted all the possibilities here, I helped them organize trips. Larry seemed to always have money, so it was easy. We went wherever there was a ruin to break into. An old château outside Brussels, a porcelain factory in Berlin, an asylum near San Sebastián in Spain."

"Slains Castle in Scotland?" I asked.

Pierre stared at me for a moment, then nodded.

"Larry was fascinated with ruins," he said. "The more beautiful it once was, the more he loved it."

Images clicked through my head. The Palais de Danse, the windmill, the temple, the ballroom.

"Your sister," Pierre said. "You believe he murdered her?"

"Yes," I said.

Pierre reached for the carafe and started to pour himself a fresh glass but then set the carafe down.

"He had this old guitar," Pierre said. "He and the others would go down below and he would play songs. He knew the words to every song. The others, they were impressed with him. Girls were impressed with him. He was very good with that guitar, like a real musician."

I saw no point in telling him Demarais was a professional cellist.

Pierre went on. "There was one song—he said he wrote it—that I cannot forget. It went something like, 'After ten years in the home, he dug her up and made a cage of her bones.'"

I recognized it immediately. It was from an old Warren Zevon song.

Pierre was shaking his head. "Once, when he was high, he told me he killed a girl and hid her body in the catacombs."

"When was this?" I asked.

"A long time ago, maybe fifteen years."

None of our victims went back that far. But I knew that with serial killers, the first victim was always significant.

"Did he tell you her name?" I asked.

Pierre shook his head. "I didn't believe him. I didn't listen to him. He was a liar. He said he was American and that he was very rich. He said he once played in a rock band in London. He said he had killed his father." He paused. "Maybe I should have listened harder."

I stabbed the map with my finger. "He drew this, right?"

He looked around the room, at the young men hunched over the bar and huddling at the tables. "It was different then," he said. "There were only a few of us who went down there, and we did it with respect. Now there are so many, so many *touristes*; they come from everywhere looking for the big adventure." He gestured toward a nearby table. "Those boys there, they call themselves the Cave Clan. They came from Australia. Paris—and the catacombs—it is their Mecca. They communicate with each other on the Internet. It is their jungle drums, heard around the world."

"Did Larry Marsh make this map?" I pressed.

His eyes came back to me. "Yes, he drew this. It is better than anything they make now, even with their fancy computers. He knew every corner, every cavern down there, every twist and turn. He would go where no others had the courage to go. It was his own special world."

"You said explorers would name the places they found," I said. "Did Larry have a special place?"

Pierre thought for a moment, then shook his head. "Not that he ever told me."

Again I looked at the map. There had to be a hundred, two hundred names, all in French, and none of them that hinted at something special to Demarais.

"How long could a person survive in the tunnels?" I asked.

"It is not just tunnels. There are hundreds of alcoves, culs de sac, rooms and passages, some no larger than a coffin," Pierre said. "There is no light, only blackness."

"But if you knew—"

"People get lost. People have died." Pierre reached in his shirt and pulled out the silver chain. "Do you see this?"

There was a small skeleton key on the chain.

"This is in remembrance of Philibert Aspairt. He was a porter at the Val-de-Grâce hospital. In 1793, he went down into the catacombs in search of the monks' wine caves. His skeleton was found eleven years later just meters from the exit. His ring of keys was found with his bones." He put the chain back in his shirt. "The old *katas*, we wear the key to remind us of our mortality."

I leaned across the table. "But if someone knew the catacombs, how long could he survive?"

"With the right supplies, as long as he wished."

Pierre picked up the carafe and poured himself a fresh drink. He hesitated, then gestured toward my glass. I shook my head, staring at the map.

"You are thinking of going down there?" he asked.

I looked up. I planned on asking Eve tonight if her department would search the catacombs. But with the manhunt for Demarais now spread all over Europe, I doubted anyone would take such a request seriously.

"You think you can go wandering down there with your little flashlights and find him?" Pierre said. "You do not want to go there, believe me."

"Will you take me?"

My question surprised Pierre. Hell, it surprised me. I had no intention of going underground.

He shook his head. "I was almost buried in a cave-in. That was the last time. No, I will never go down there again."

"What about someone else?"

Pierre glanced around the bar. "They won't help you. It is all a big game for them now, a big game between them and the *kataflics*. They trust no one." He picked up the glass and downed the liquor.

I glanced at my watch. It was almost three. I wanted to get to the hospital and see Paula. I started to fold the map.

Pierre's hand on the map stopped me.

"I can tell you this much," he said. He jabbed at the paper with his index finger. "This is an old map, and no one has one like it now. Many of the passages and places on this map no longer exist."

"What do you mean they no longer exist?"

"Not officially. They have been long blocked off by the police or have been lost to cave-ins. No one knows about this world now."

I folded the map and put it in my jacket and rose.

"I can tell you one more thing with certainty," Pierre said, looking up at me. "If that is where he has gone, you will never find him."

40

When I got out of the taxi the sun was blindingly bright. The weather—and my experiences in Paris—had been so bleak during the last few weeks, it literally gave me a physical lift to walk in warmth for half a block to the American Hospital in Neuilly.

After leaving the cataphile bar, I had called the hospital to get Paula's okay for a visitor. I wasn't sure if she harbored any ill feelings toward me for leaving her in Châtelet station, but the nurse told me Paula would see me. I stopped at a street vendor outside the hospital and bought her a bouquet of violets.

Paula was sitting up in her bed, one of three patients in a large room. Her kinky brown hair was tied loosely with a pink band. Her skin still lacked color, as if all her blood had not yet been replenished. But her eyes brightened when she saw me, and I knew she would be okay. And I knew she didn't hate me for abandoning her.

An older man stood near her bed. He had the same frizzy brown hair as Paula, and his eyes reflected his exhaustion after what was probably a long and disorienting flight. I assumed it was Mr. Ridley.

Paula confirmed that with an introduction. He gave me a weary handshake and excused himself, mumbling something about a phone call to Paula's mother.

Paula looked to me and I held out the violets.

"Purple is your color, right?" I said.

She smiled and gestured toward a vase on the nightstand. "Could you put them in there?" she said. "I would do it myself but I can't sit up any further."

"No problem."

As I worked the stems into the vase, I noticed the bulge of bandages under Paula's hospital gown. More bandages covered parts of her neck. Scars crisscrossed her arms and hands like streaks of red ink.

"I look terrible, don't I?" Paula asked.

"Not to me," I said. "Your heart is beating. That's all that counts."

Her eyes welled with tears. I wanted to hug her but I was afraid I would hurt her. I handed her a Kleenex and waited until she wiped her eyes.

"I feel so stupid I got taken in by him," she said. "He was so sweet to me."

"That's how he is, Paula," I said. "He knows how to win people's trust. Please don't feel bad. There are at least five other women who didn't make it away from him alive."

Paula lay back against the pillow and drew a breath that looked like it hurt.

"Paula, could I show you a picture of the man we think did this and ask you if it's him?"

"I already did that for the police," Paula said.

"If you don't mind, could you do it again for me?" I asked. "I'm not in tight communication with the police."

"Okay."

I slipped the publicity photograph of Laurent Demarais from my coat pocket and showed it to her. A flitter of horror crossed her eyes, then she nodded. "That's him. I've forgotten his name already. Demolay? Demay?"

"Demarais," I said.

"Have the police caught him?" she asked.

"No, but the whole city is looking for him," I said. When doubt darkened her face, I added, "They'll find him, I promise."

"So I'm not in any danger?"

"Since we know who Demarais is, he has no reason to worry about you identifying him. Plus there's a guard right outside your door."

"I guess he must've figured out I don't have his stupid necklace."

"Excuse me?" I asked. "The necklace?"

"Yeah, the one I told you didn't belong to Casey," Paula said. "When he was attacking me, the whole time he was screaming that he wanted his necklace. He seemed to know it should've been in the bag I got from the institute."

I was quiet. We didn't know how Casey had gotten the necklace, but it was clear now that Demarais had wanted it back so badly that he had tried to kill Paula to get it. The guy in the music shop said it wasn't an ordinary suppressor. So what the hell did it mean to him?

"Matt," Paula said, "do you think he'll come after you?"

"Me? Why would he come after me?" I asked.

"Maybe he thinks you have the necklace," Paula said.

"Did you tell him you gave it to me?"

She frowned, as if she was trying hard to remember. "No," she said. "But he asked me . . ."

"What?"

Her eyes came up to mine. "He asked if I gave it to the man I was with."

"How did he know about me?" I asked.

"He had to have followed us from the institute," Paula said. "He came up to me just minutes after you walked away. He had to have seen us together."

It had never occurred to me that Laurent Demarais had seen me with Paula. But if Demarais believed I might have his precious necklace, why hadn't he already come after me? I forced a reassuring smile for Paula.

"The police have the necklace," I said. "I'm sure Demarais must realize that, so I'll be fine. But thanks for worrying about me."

We fell silent. The sounds from the corridor filtered in but I wasn't listening. I was thinking about that *Miami Times* article about Mandy that was on Demarais's computer.

"I'm afraid."

Paula had spoken in a bare whisper. I looked back at her.

"Paula," I said gently, "he won't come—"

"No, it's not that," she said. "I'm afraid to go home. I don't know how I'll be able to go back to work or do anything anymore. I feel like I don't know me anymore. I jump at the smallest noise, and the things in my dreams . . ."

I took her hand. Her eyes welled and she looked away at the window.

"Paula, listen to me," I said. "Right after my sister was killed, I was afraid. I didn't know how to act or what I was supposed to say to people. I was afraid of being alone, but I didn't want to be around anyone else. I was afraid to go to sleep because I thought I would dream about her, and I was afraid to wake up because it hurt too much."

She turned back to me. "But you weren't afraid to come here by yourself and look for him," she said.

There was an edge of dejection in her voice and I knew she was somehow comparing her trip to France with mine. Though we had come to Europe for two completely different reasons and would be going home with two different experiences, we shared one thing: Our time in Paris had forever changed our lives.

I dug in my pockets for a business card and wrote my personal email address on the back. I handed it to her.

"I have to get going," I said. "But I want you to email me when you get home, so I know you're okay. Promise me you'll do that?"

She nodded.

I hesitated, then leaned in and kissed her gently on the forehead. I started toward the door.

"Hey."

I turned back.

"Thank you," Paula said softly.

"For what?" I asked.

"For coming here to see me." She smiled. "You're a good man, Matt."

41

As I was leaving the hospital, I called Cameron and asked him to meet me at the catacomb museum. I wanted to see the place before my dinner with Eve tonight so I could get a sense of what we might be up against in hunting Demarais. I asked Cameron to come along because after my experience in the sewers, I didn't want to go underground alone.

He was waiting for me outside the entrance, a small grim metal house that looked a lot like one of those decrepit mausoleums in the cemetery I had visited with Eve on All Saints' Day.

It was an hour before closing time and the ticket agent warned us we would have to hurry. We were the only ones going in. We descended a tight spiral staircase, hurried past the rooms with the museum exhibits and walked through a series of stone tunnels lit by the kind of lights you'd see in a mine.

Cameron told me he knew little about the forbidden part of the catacombs, just that the police waged a constant war against the kids breaking in illegally. And that a couple years ago, someone had fallen in a well and drowned.

The air grew colder and drier, and I fell silent. I felt a tightening in my chest and fought back my claustrophobia, trying not to think about the fact we were nearly a hundred feet underground. The only sound was the crunch of our shoes on the wet gravel.

But it wasn't as bad as the sewers, and I was beginning to think the catacombs were some huge joke foisted on tourists when we came to a stone portal. The carving above it read ARRÊTE! C'EST ICI L'EMPIRE DE LA MORT.

Even I could figure out this one: *Stop! Here is the empire of death.*

We entered a small dim room. At first, I thought I was looking at walls built of stones. Then it registered with a jolt—the walls were constructed entirely of human bones. Tibias and femurs by the thousands were neatly stacked, their knobby ends interspersed with row upon row of skulls, like a macabre mosaic.

The stacks rose over five feet and stretched horizontally as far as I could see. The bones ranged in color from gray to ocher. Some of the skulls wore coatings of green moss.

I stood transfixed. The black eye sockets of the skulls stared back at me.

Once I got over the shock, I began to appreciate the efficiency of the stacks. I remembered a fact from the guidebook: Six million bodies had been brought here from the cemeteries. There were no complete skeletons. The purpose had been to stack the remains with maximum compactness, so all the large leg bones were laid together, as were the arm bones. I wondered what had happened to all the smaller bones—the ribs, the spines, the fingers.

"Good lord," Cameron whispered. "I had no idea."

I turned toward him. He was shaking his head.

"We haven't got much time," I said. "We'd better get moving."

We entered another room like the last. More stacks, and a stone plaque denoting the cemetery where the bones came from. A third room held yet more bones, though the stacks weren't as neat. We ducked and entered a room reinforced with concrete blocks.

I stopped cold. No neat stacks here. Just huge piles of bones heaped on the dirt floor. There was an old wheelbarrow and a pitchfork. Cameron translated the plaque for me, telling me this was a re-creation of how the catacombs looked in the seventeen hundreds when the bones were first brought here.

We moved on to the next room. It was like the last, more piles of bones. I felt something cold and wet touch my neck and jumped. I looked up. Water was seeping from the rough limestone ceiling. It had formed small stalactites and was dripping down, glazing the bones piled below. They glowed in the milky light.

My heart was starting to kick up again so I took several deep slow breaths.

"You okay?" Cameron asked.

"Yeah, I'm fine."

We increased our pace, intent on finding the exit now. We passed through more bone rooms with cemetery plaques and navigated dark narrow tunnels reinforced with stone buttresses.

Finally, we came to another crypt. There were more bones here but it was a gate in a dark corner that made me stop. I went slowly to it.

It was heavy iron, like you'd see in some medieval castle. There was a large padlock on it. I grasped the iron bars and stared into the tunnel beyond. I couldn't see much, just more rough limestone walls and a low ceiling. Then the thin light fell away into blackness.

I heard Cameron come up behind me but I didn't turn.

"How far do you think we've come?" I asked.

"The sign at the entrance says the museum runs about two kilometers. I'd guess we've covered about a mile."

I was staring into the blackness beyond the gate. "These tunnels go on for hundreds of miles under the city," I said.

Cameron was quiet.

"He's in there somewhere," I said.

I could feel a rush of cold air on my face, like something was breathing on me. I let go of the iron bars and stared at my hands. They were coated in red rust and they were shaking.

I felt Cameron's touch on my shoulder. "Come on," he said. "I'm getting you out of here."

42

He could feel the eyes of the Moroccan men on him as he sipped his coffee at the table near the window.

He hadn't bathed in three days. His whiskered face was streaked with dirt and his dark hair was slick with oil. His shabby clothes and his shoes were caked with mud. The men knew he wasn't one of them. But to anyone else who might look his way he could have been mistaken for just another sullen worker finding solace in his coffee after a long day at the Peugeot factory.

He used his sleeve to wipe the condensation off the window glass and looked at the building across the street. He had been watching it all day.

A light was on but he was almost certain the apartment on the second floor was empty. He had seen the American leave that morning. And the woman cop had left soon after.

A strange calm had come over him in these last hours. Everything had been readied, everything was in place. He drank his coffee, listening to the clucking of the Moroccans' speech and the loud rumble outside of metal gates being pulled down over storefronts. When the darkness fell, he rose, tossing some coins on the saucer. He slipped on the old coat, pulled up the collar and stepped out into the cold.

There was no concierge, no keypad for the building; he had

made sure of that earlier. He had also examined the locks and determined he needed only the short crowbar from the rental car to break in. He didn't bother to hit the light timer in the vestibule, just climbed the two flights quietly in the darkness.

At the top of the narrow stairs, he found the door for the apartment that faced the street and paused. There was a strong smell of cooking here and—

Was that music coming from the apartment?

Had he somehow missed seeing the woman cop's return? Had he been wrong about the American? No, no . . . he was positive neither of them had returned. Laurent dropped back against the wall, the crowbar in his hand. He knocked, just to be safe.

The music was loud. He knocked harder. The music was softer now. Then from behind the door: *"Qui est là?"*

He felt in his coat pocket, and his fingers closed around the telescoping end pin. No matter. This person would not stop him. Whoever it was would surely open the door if he said he was delivering something from the police.

"J'ai une livraison de la police," he said.

The click of the lock, then the door opened, held by a chain. A flash of white blouse and glimpse of a face. For a moment he thought it was the woman cop, then realized it was a girl.

A girl whose eyes suddenly darkened with fear.

He didn't hesitate. He threw the full weight of his body against the door. When she tried to slam it, he thrust the crowbar between the door and the jamb and gave a hard jerk. She screamed and disappeared. Two more jerks of the crowbar and the chain broke.

He threw open the door. It banged back against the wall, rebounding to hit him in the chest. He thrust it away, slammed it and staggered into the room.

His mind clicked, his senses registering everything in an instant. An empty room. Something cooking. Rock music coming from the speakers.

The girl. Where was she?

There, in the kitchen, crouching behind the bar. He threw the crowbar to the floor and started toward her. Her back was to him and he reached in his pocket for the end pin.

She spun.

A glint of metal and a flash-burn on his face as the kitchen knife slashed him. He screamed and backhanded her, catching the side of her head.

He saw the knife skitter on the tile and disappear under a table. The girl staggered and slid to the floor.

Blood was pouring from the gash on his chin. His skin was on fire. His mind was on fire.

She was crawling away. He moved backward, barring her path to the door. She scrambled to her feet and ran to the rear of the apartment. He heard a door slam.

He struggled to get past the pain, get his mind clear.

Kill the girl. Find the necklace. Then go.

He went down the narrow hallway and looked in the first open door. A small empty bathroom. The second door was also open. He peered inside. A blue bedroom.

His eyes went to the closed door at the end of the hallway. He tried the knob. The door was locked.

He braced his back against the wall and kicked at the door. The jamb splintered and he pushed the door open.

She was standing on a desk, struggling to get out of a small window. He lunged, grabbing her ankle and pulling her down onto the desk. She screamed, clinging to the windowsill.

He picked her up and threw her into the corner. She hit the edge of the desk, upending a lamp, then bounced to the floor.

She was moaning. He reached into his coat pocket and pulled out the end pin.

He froze.

There, on the wall.

He took two steps toward it. He stared at the photograph. *Hélène?*

He couldn't see clearly! He spun, looking for the overturned lamp. He grabbed it off the floor and set it on the desk.

In the bare-bulb glare of light, he saw her. Hélène. Then, slowly, he became aware of the others.

They were all here, all the girls. And . . .

He heard a moan and looked at the dark-haired girl curled in the corner. She wasn't moving. He turned back to the large bulletin board above the desk. A publicity still of him with his cello. Photographs of the windmill, the temple, the Palais de Danse, Slains Castle, the ballroom in Miami.

His gaze went now to a poster board that listed all the names of the girls, dates, where he had left them and—

All the lyrics and song titles.

He stared at it all, feeling a small swell of wonder, even pride.

A color photograph caught his eye. At first he couldn't figure out why it was here, then it registered.

It was a picture of the girl in Miami with a man. They were laughing and it looked like it was taken in the dance club. The top of the man's head was cut off. But he knew it was the American.

His lips curled up in a small smile.

For years, he had fooled them. He had created the game, carefully chosen each girl, laid down the clues, planned out each step. But no one had figured it out, not the police in England, Scotland, Miami or here. An American—not a cop, but a reporter—he had been the only one to see.

Again his eyes swept over the photographs, fascinated by the montage of music, ruins and lovely faces. He had never seen the girls all together before, and until now he had never really appreciated how beautiful a puzzle he had created.

His gaze dropped to the papers on the desk. He saw a file with his name written on it and flipped it open.

More photographs. Of Villa Euterpe, and of the tower, and the bloodied body of the brunette. He tossed them on the floor.

Another stack of photographs. This time of his apartments on Île Saint-Louis and in La Goutte d'Or. Close-ups of his bedroom, his laptop, the bathtub on rue Myrha. And a photograph of his Rosette cello—*what were those ugly black smudges on its body?*

He stared at the cello photograph, a choking anger rising up in his throat. How dare they touch his things?

He ripped the photograph in two and tossed it aside, going back to the file. What else did they have of his? What else had they violated?

Newspaper articles . . . with names highlighted in yellow. Charles Gilchrist. Simone Renard. A review from his London debut. A London police report detailing his juvenile record. A grainy copy of a photograph of him with his mother that made his chest feel as if it were splitting in two.

He picked up a paper. It was a report from Dr. Faucheux. He read it quickly, his anger and embarrassment burning hot.

He threw the file across the room. He looked up at the bulletin board, then with a cry began tearing at the photographs. He ripped them to pieces, then, with a sweep of an arm, scattered the papers and files on the desk to the floor.

Finally, he stopped. He leaned on the desk, eyes closed, pulling in deep calming breaths.

He opened his eyes. Blood droplets. His face was still bleeding, the drops falling onto . . .

He picked up the photograph, his breath quickening. It was the necklace.

A moan.

His eyes shot to the bed. The girl was still lying on the floor but she was stirring.

He went to her and held the photograph in front of her face. "Where is this?"

Her eyes fluttered but didn't open. He grabbed her hair and yanked her head back, thrusting the photograph in her face.

"My necklace. Where is it?"

Her eyes focused, then she shook her head.

He let go of her hair. She cowered against the wall, whimpering. He sat back on his haunches, trying to think. It had to be in this room. He rose and began searching through every drawer, emptying every box, tearing through the closet.

"Stop!"

He spun to the girl. She was pulling herself up from the floor.

"It isn't here," she said. "It's at the police station."

"You are lying."

She shook her head slowly. "Why would I lie? It is evidence. Where else would it be?"

His mind was spinning. Of course, she was right. How could he be so stupid? But now what? What could he do, what would—

Something on the floor by his feet. He bent to pick it up. It was a small framed photograph of two dark-haired women.

He looked to the girl. Yes, it was her. And the other one?

When he thrust the frame in front of her face, she recoiled in fear.

"Is this your mother?" he asked.

She looked at it, then closed her eyes.

"I think it is," he said.

He tossed it aside. "She is a cop. She can get the necklace."

The girl glared at him. "She will never give it to you," she said.

He allowed himself a small smile. It was clear in his head now what was going to happen. The game was ending and he had to control it. He scanned the room, looking for what he needed. Pen? Paper?

He touched his face and looked at his fingers. It might be a nice touch, he thought, to leave this in his own blood. But he wasn't willing to sacrifice that much.

There was a tube of lipstick on the floor and he picked it up.

He went to the wall over the desk and wrote in bold letters.

DEUX COEURS POUR LE SIEN

He tossed the lipstick aside and looked back at the girl.

"It's time for us to go," he said.

43

It was almost eight thirty by the time Eve picked me up outside Cameron's building.

"Watch the box," she said as I opened the passenger door.

I picked up the pink box and held it in my lap as she pulled out into traffic. It was warm on my legs and smelled of apples. I hadn't eaten all day and was looking forward to one of Juliette's dinners.

It was Friday and the traffic was heavy. As we crept along, I filled Eve in on my visit with Paula and told her I believed Demarais had attacked her to get the Deux Coeurs necklace. I also told her about my meeting with Pierre. I decided not to mention my trip to the catacomb museum. Maybe it was stupid male pride, but I didn't want to explain that the whole time I was down there all I could think about was getting out.

"So you believe that is where he is hiding?" Eve asked.

"Where else could he be?"

She chewed on her lip, her eyes trained on the steady stream of red taillights ahead. "We can get search teams down there. I will talk to someone in the IGC."

"What's that?"

"L'Inspection Générale des Carrières. They are in charge of the catacombs."

"The *kataflics*."

She glanced over at me and nodded. Eve was quiet for the rest of the ride to her apartment. I knew she was still trying to come to grips with being pulled off the case. I didn't push her. I told myself we could both use a couple hours of downtime tonight, away from the damn case, talking about something else.

Eve unlocked the apartment and I followed her in, carrying the patisserie box. Eve stopped and I bumped smack into her.

I heard a sharp intake of breath.

The room was in shambles. Everything had been upended or opened. Books and CDs on the floor. Tables overturned. Dishes broken. Newspapers, papers and—

"Juliette!"

Eve disappeared down a hallway but came right back, her face ashen.

"She's gone!" Eve said.

She yanked her cell from her belt and a few seconds later came a tirade of French. I heard Juliette's name, then Demarais's, but nothing else registered. I looked around, hoping to see something, anything, that would help.

I went to the kitchen. It was trashed like the rest of the apartment. Then I saw it. A smear of blood on the white tile. And the edge of a knife sticking out from under a table.

Suddenly, Eve snapped the cell closed. She looked up at me. "He's got her," she said, her voice cracking.

"Eve—"

She was pacing in a tight circle. Her cell rang. More frenetic French, ending in Eve shouting into the phone before she hung up.

She turned to me, covered her face and burst into tears.

I folded her into my arms.

*   *   *

The first policemen were there in minutes. They tried to push me outside, but I refused and took charge of getting Eve to calm down. While the cops went to work securing the apartment and the building, I sat with Eve on the sofa, holding her hand so she wouldn't get up and do anything to contaminate the crime scene.

Commandant Boutin arrived with three inspectors. He said something briefly in French to Eve that sounded sympathetic, then dispatched the inspectors throughout the apartment. He eyed me with suspicion but must have decided there was no way he was going to be rid of me, so he switched to English.

"I was told you believe Demarais has kidnapped your niece," he said to Eve. His eyes traveled around the trashed room. "What makes you sure she was even here when this happened?"

"She was expecting us for dinner," Eve said.

"There's blood on the kitchen floor," I said.

Boutin's eyes swung to me, then away to the inspector in the kitchen who was bagging up the knife. Down in the hallway, I could see the flashes of a camera.

Boutin went on to ask Eve a series of questions about neighbors, Juliette's boyfriends and other cases Eve had been working. At first I couldn't figure out what he was trying to get at, then I realized he had to eliminate all the more mundane possibilities.

"It is him," Eve said. "It is Demarais. He took Juliette."

Boutin looked around the living room. "Do you have any idea what he was looking for?"

"His necklace," I said.

"What necklace?" Boutin asked.

I told Boutin as simply as I could what Paula Ridley had told me.

Boutin turned to Eve. "This necklace is in evidence, yes?"

"Of course."

"Then that is probably why he broke in," Boutin said. "He knows you are a police officer and he might have believed you had it. Juliette may have been—and I apologize for my bluntness—but she may have simply been in his way."

"Then he would have killed her and left her here," I said. "But he didn't. He took her, and there has to be a reason why."

"You have to find him," Eve said.

"We will," Boutin said. "We have doubled our presence at all train stations, airports and borders."

"He won't leave France," I said. "He'll go underground."

Boutin turned to me.

"The catacombs," I said. "He's a cataphile and he has a special place somewhere."

Boutin looked at Eve. "Do you believe this could be true?"

"Yes," Eve said. "I believe the catacombs should be searched."

Boutin let out a sigh. "Inspector Bellamont, we are processing two apartments, and fifty men are searching the grounds of the Saint-Aubin house. We are working at full capacity. You know how extensive the catacombs are. I cannot justify such an undertaking right now."

I glanced at Eve and saw she was close to tears.

At that moment, a technician came up to Boutin's side. He said something in French and handed Boutin a digital camera. Boutin stared at the screen for a moment, then held it out to Eve.

"We found lyrics," he said.

"What?" I said.

Boutin ignored me and held the camera out to Eve. "They were left on the wall in the back bedroom."

Eve took the camera and stared at the screen for a long time. When she looked up at me, her eyes were steady. So were her hands when she handed the camera not to me but back to Boutin. I started to demand to see the camera but Eve's touch on my arm kept me silent.

"I know the procedure," Eve said to Boutin. "I will have to vacate my apartment so it can be processed."

Boutin nodded. "And I am afraid you will also have to go on administrative leave."

Eve turned to me. "Will you help me pack some things?"

I didn't know what the hell was going on but the look Eve shot me said to just keep quiet. I followed her down the hall to the bedroom.

The technician glanced at us and went on with his work. Eve took my arm and pulled me toward a desk. That's when I saw it, scrawled in lipstick on the wall.

DEUX COEURS POUR LE SIEN

"It says 'Two hearts for hers,'" Eve whispered.

"It's a ransom note," I said.

Eve nodded.

He wanted a trade. The bastard wanted a trade—Juliette for his fucking necklace. I looked in Eve's eyes and knew she felt what I did: a surge of hope that if we were right, then Juliette was still alive and would remain alive until Demarais made contact with us to arrange a trade.

But how would he find us?

Then it hit me.

Demarais was a man who thought he was superior to everyone else. He liked the spotlight, the attention, the satisfaction that came from leaving riddles only he understood. He would never sink to the behavior of a common kidnapper. There would be no phone calls, secret drop sites or complicated directions. There was only the game, to be played by his rules.

I took a deep breath. He would not come to us. We would have to go to him.

44

It took Eve less than ten minutes to sign the necklace out of evidence at her station.

"Do you want me to keep it?" I asked as she got in the car.

She stuck the plastic bag in the pocket of her leather jacket. "No," she said. "I stole it. I will pay the consequences."

She was silent on the ride back across the river. We both knew there wasn't time to treat this like an ordinary kidnapping. That's why we didn't tell Boutin what "deux coeurs" meant. Even if we could convince him it was not lyrics, he would still want to follow proper procedures. Call in other divisions. Set up phone taps. Wait for hours to be contacted. By then, Juliette would be dead.

When I asked Eve where we were going, she told me only that we were meeting someone who might help us.

I was surprised when she led me to the shuttered entrance of the catacomb museum. It was very cold. I stuck my hands in the pockets of my coat and looked around. The Place Denfert-Rochereau spun with blue neon, red taillights and life. Taxi horns, laughter from a nearby café, music pumping from a passing car.

I tried not to think about Juliette, somewhere far below in the darkest of places. I shivered, reliving the dank breath I had felt standing at that iron gate in the catacombs.

I took out my cell phone and scrolled down to Nora's number, suddenly wanting to hear her voice. But before I could punch in the number, Eve was at my side.

"He is here."

I snapped the cell closed. Eve linked her arm through mine and steered me toward a stone building with a French flag over the door. The man stood in the shadows, the streetlight silhouetting his square inspector's cap.

As Eve and I approached, he took one last drag on his cigarette and tossed it to the ground. But he didn't move into the light to meet us. We had to step into the darkness with him.

"Maurice, this is my friend Matt Owens, from Miami," Eve said. "Matt, Inspector Fournier is the head of the catacomb team. The cataphiles call him Tonton."

He nodded to me but didn't extend a hand. I looked to Eve, knowing she needed to take the lead here. This was her friend, a fellow cop, a cop who knew the underground as well as beat cops knew their streets. I guessed that Eve was hoping to convince him to organize a search of the catacombs. But the fact that he had asked to meet her outside his office told me that probably wasn't going to happen.

"I did not want to tell you everything over the phone," Eve said. "I think that Demarais took Juliette into the catacombs."

"You've told Boutin this?" Fournier said.

"Yes, but he believes Demarais has already killed Juliette and left the country."

I wondered why Eve did not tell Fournier about the ransom note and the necklace, but then I realized she couldn't trust him with the knowledge she had stolen evidence. If Fournier took the necklace, we had nothing to bargain with.

"What do you want from me?" Fournier asked.

"Boutin refuses to search the catacombs," Eve said.

Fournier shook his head slowly. "Eve, I do not have the authority to intercede in a homicide investigation."

Eve grabbed his sleeve. "Maurice, he has Juliette," she said. "You know her, you have sat at my dinner table and dined with her. You cannot let her die because of one man's stubbornness and a book of rules."

"Eve, Boutin is probably right," Fournier said. "No one except an insane man would take a victim into the catacombs and expect to survive for any length of time. It is dangerous enough for the young men who know what they are doing."

I thrust the old map at Fournier. "Demarais knows what he's doing," I said. "He drew his own map."

Fournier withdrew a penlight from his pocket and took the map. After he had studied it, he looked at me. "If this is your guide, then you might as well go down there blind."

"We know the map is outdated but the layout hasn't changed, has it?" I asked. "They're not building new passageways, are they? What can be different?"

"Many areas have been completely blocked off," Fournier said. "Some have caved in. There are even new areas that *les katas* have discovered and that may not be shown on your map."

"Please," Eve said, "if you do not want to put your team at risk, then take us yourself. If we find nothing, I will tell no one you helped us. If we are caught, I will take all responsibility."

Fournier held the map out to me but he was looking at Eve. "*Je suis désolé*, Eve," he said.

He went on in French, his hand on Eve's arm. I thought about intervening, saying something to help pressure him, but changed my mind. He was Eve's friend and a fellow cop.

If she could not convince him to break the rules, then neither could I.

Eve started away down the sidewalk. She walked fast, with an obvious fury.

"Eve, stop," I said.

She leaned on the car, head down. I didn't know if she had any clear ideas or a plan. I didn't even know if she was crying. I only knew I had to offer her something.

"Let's go see Pierre," I said.

El Melocotón was packed by the time Eve and I got there around ten thirty. Eve had lapsed into a hard silence on the way over. I knew exactly what she was feeling—a rage born of impotency. It had seethed inside me in those first hours after Mandy vanished.

We pushed through the throng of bodies, trying to find an open table. A couple vacated a corner and I fought off two guys to claim the spot. Eve dropped down into the chair and I went off in search of Pierre.

I didn't know the guy's last name and I doubted his claim that he owned the place. When I asked the bartender, he mumbled something in French and turned away.

When I went back to Eve, she looked up at me with anxious eyes. "Where is he?"

"I don't know."

Eve leaned back in the chair and closed her eyes.

I sat down across from her. From a speaker over our heads came the pounding of The Call's "The Walls Came Down." I ran a hand across my eyes. When I looked up, Pierre was standing there.

He stared at Eve for a moment, then looked at me. "What do you want?" he asked.

"We need to know where Larry Marsh went," I shouted above the music.

His eyes were still on Eve. "You are the cop," he said.

"Yes."

Pierre looked back at me and shook his head.

"Look," I said. "He's got her niece. We need to know where he is, damn it."

Pierre's eyes went back to Eve. "Your niece?"

"Yes," Eve said.

Pierre shouted something to the bartender, then turned back to me. "Come with me," he said.

We followed him past a curtain and down a spiral staircase. Pierre unlocked a door and led us into a small room packed with beer and wine cases and lit by a single bare bulb. A desk was wedged in the corner next to a file cabinet. He pulled out a chair for Eve and motioned for me to pull up a crate.

"I cannot help you," Pierre said. "I wish I could, but I don't know where he would be."

I reached in my coat and pulled out the catacombs map. I spread it open on the desk. "He's in there somewhere," I said. "You said he had a special place. Help us find it, please."

Pierre hesitated, then came forward. He braced himself by his hands on the desk and peered at the map.

After a moment, he looked up at me. "Monsieur, there are too many names on this map, some not even readable anymore."

"Try," I said.

He said something in French to Eve in a tender voice.

"Try, damn it!"

Pierre's eyes shot to me.

"Matt—" Eve said.

Then, suddenly, it came to me. That sliver from the song left with Caitlyn McKenzie in Scotland—*She's buried right in my backyard.*

It had to be a reference to that shithole apartment on rue Myrha in the eighteenth arrondissement.

"Does this map cover the eighteenth arrondissement?" I asked.

He hesitated, then pointed at the map. "Most of the catacombs are down here, on the Left Bank. This is where the limestone was mined, where everyone goes now and where the museum is. But up here . . ." He pointed to the top of the map, north of the river, where the lines and names grew faint and far between. "This area is different; this is the gypsum mines. It is unexplored and untouched, and very dangerous. Many cave-ins there. The kids today, I do not think they even know it is there."

"Did Larry Marsh know about it?" I asked.

Pierre nodded. "I remember that he was living in an old apartment in La Goutte d'Or. He told me he had discovered a place nearby that led down into the mines. One night, we went down there together. That is where I got caught in the cave-in. He dug me out. I never went back."

I began to scour the names on the map, but the French and the faded handwriting defeated me.

"Eve," I said, pointing. "Does anything stand out to you?"

She leaned into the light and peered at the map. Then, with a straightening of her spine, she pointed to a spot on the map. The writing was so faded that it took me a couple seconds to see it—*Deux Coeurs.*

I looked up at Pierre.

"Can you take us there?" I asked.

He shook his head, muttering in French.

I looked to Eve. She was just staring at him.

"Look," I said, "we need your help here."

"You don't understand," Pierre said. "These mines, this whole area, it has been closed off for decades. I was there a very long time ago. For all I know, these passages do not even exist now. And this place you want to go, it is very far in." He held up his hands. "No, no, absolutely not."

I pushed up from my chair. Thoughts rushed through my brain like a wildfire. None of them made any sense, but none of them stopped my words.

"Then we'll go down alone," I said.

I looked at Eve. It took her a moment to completely grasp what I had said, then she moved away from Pierre toward the door. I snatched the map from the table.

"Wait!" Pierre said. "You do not even know how to get in."

"You said it was near his apartment," I said. "We'll find it."

"Stop," Pierre said. "Please."

Eve and I both turned to look back at him. In the harsh light of the bulb, Pierre's face was etched with deep lines.

"All right," he said. "I will show you the entrance and take you down. After that, you are on your own."

It was past midnight. We were standing on a deserted corner in front of a shuttered *bar-tabac* with no name. The only other place nearby was a vacant storefront that had once housed a grocery. But it was the view across the street that had us staring.

High iron fences surrounded huge gaping holes in the ground. Only the glint of a streetlight told us what was below—the tracks of the railroad lines that ran along Paris's western perimeter down to Gare du Nord. This was where Pierre had said he would meet us.

I looked to Eve, but all I could see clearly was the glow of her cigarette as she inhaled.

I heard a sound and spun. I saw a yellow hard hat and took the man to be a worker coming off a shift. But then I recognized the stooped gait.

Pierre gave Eve and me a hard stare as he approached.

"I told you to come prepared," he said.

I was wearing my jeans, an old army fatigue jacket and a pair of Cameron's hiking boots. Eve had resorted to what was in her car—an old red parka and work boots.

We were clutching flashlights, mine a cheap plastic thing I found in Cameron's kitchen and Eve's a heavy foot-long monstrosity that I was sure doubled as a duty weapon.

Pierre, in contrast, looked like photographs I had seen of Pennsylvania coal miners. A jumpsuit with a utility belt hung with a coil of rope, pickax and small shovel. A compact backpack. Knee-high rubber boots. His hard hat was mounted with a halogen lamp.

"Let's go," Pierre said.

We followed him down the dark street. Then, suddenly, he slipped from view. When we caught up, he was standing in an empty lot between two abandoned buildings. He held back a piece of chain-link fencing and motioned for us to go through.

We clicked on our flashlights to cross the trash-strewn lot, struggling to keep up with the darting Pierre. Suddenly, we were at the top of a narrow crumbling staircase that clung to the side of a two-story retaining wall. I stared down into the dark abyss of the railroad yard. Pierre was already halfway down the stairs and not looking back. We quickly followed.

After about a hundred yards, Pierre stopped, waiting for us to catch up.

"This is it," he said.

I trained the flashlight beam on the spot in the wall where Pierre was pointing. All I saw was old brick defaced with graffiti—and behind some dead ivy, a rusted door, like you'd see on a large kiln.

Pierre slipped the pickax from his belt and jammed it into a crevice. With a loud groan, the door opened.

Pierre took a step back. "It has been opened recently," he said.

"That means he's in there," I said.

"Or some kids discovered it," Pierre said.

Eve stepped forward and shined her flashlight into the opening. The light was strong but fell away into nothing after maybe thirty feet.

"Are you sure you want to do this?"

We both turned to Pierre.

"Yes," Eve said.

Pierre turned on his headlamp. "Stay close behind me."

We entered the hole, Eve following Pierre and me trailing.

I knew immediately that my flashlight was inadequate. We were in pitch-blackness and if it hadn't been for the bouncing play of lights ahead of me, I would have had no sense of my surroundings. We were in a narrow tunnel, maybe four feet wide and six feet high. There was a damp smell and the ground was spongy under my boots.

I took two deep breaths of cold air to calm my heart. I tried not to think of the fact that we were less than two stories under street level right now and how much farther down we had yet to go.

Eve had stopped. Pierre was kneeling. Then suddenly he disappeared. With a kick to my gut I realized he had gone down a hole.

I came up to Eve's side and stared down. In the blue halogen glow, I watched Pierre climb down what looked like an old sewer.

Eve gave me a glance, stuck her flashlight into her belt and lowered herself in. I didn't give myself a moment to think. Cramming the flashlight into my pocket, I grabbed the cold metal rungs and followed.

I counted twenty-five rungs before my feet hit solid ground. I whipped out the flashlight. The beam caught Eve and Pierre before revealing the smooth gray walls of a low-ceilinged cavern about ten feet across. Unlike the passage above, it was cool and dry with an odd chalky smell.

"Are we in the gypsum mines?" I asked.

"Not yet," Pierre said. "We have a long way to go." He was looking around, and in the beam of his headlamp I saw three openings.

"Give me the map," Pierre said.

I pulled it out of my jacket and handed it to him. He folded it to reveal only the top quarter, stared at it for a moment, then looked toward one of the openings.

"I will stay with you awhile longer," he said, tucking the map inside his jumpsuit. "We go this way."

We entered a dark passage just wide enough so I could touch each side. I was following Eve and didn't realize she had stooped down. I banged my forehead on the ceiling.

"Fuck!"

Flashlight beams swung in my face. I squinted, holding my head.

"You are bleeding," Eve said.

"What?" My hand was red.

Beyond Eve, Pierre was staring at me. He was so short he could stand upright. He said nothing, just turned and went on.

As we hurried to catch up, I stayed in a slight crouch, my left hand braced against the cold wall to keep my balance.

I don't know how long we walked, thirty, maybe forty minutes. The passage twisted and turned in so many directions I felt as if we had lost our way and had doubled back. But I kept my eyes on Eve's back, silhouetted in the glow of Pierre's light far ahead.

By the time we stopped, my legs were shaking from the effort of walking in a half crouch and I was sweating despite the cold. We were in a chamber about the size of a walk-in closet. Pierre was studying the map. Eve was drinking from her canteen. I was staring at the openings off the chamber.

I counted five. The largest was maybe five feet, the smallest about two feet. Pierre didn't seem interested in any of the openings. He was staring at a pile of white-gray rocks in one corner.

"What's wrong?" Eve asked.

Pierre looked up at her. "It is blocked," he said.

"What is?" I asked.

"That is the way into the gypsum mines," he said, nodding at the rocks.

"Maybe it's one of those passages," I said, pointing.

"No. It is this one. And it is blocked."

Eve and I went to his side and looked at the map. I couldn't tell where the hell we were but Eve said something in French and Pierre pointed to a spot on the map. Eve said something else and Pierre responded sharply, stabbing at the map.

Eve looked at me. "He insists this is the way in."

"It can't be," I said. "How'd Demarais get in if it is?"

Pierre shook his head and folded the map. "We go back," he said.

Eve said something to him that I didn't understand but the tone was unmistakable—pleading. Pierre shook his head harder.

"Listen to me, both of you!" he said suddenly. He pointed to the rocks. "That is a cave-in. There is nothing in there."

"Juliette is in there," Eve said.

He looked at Eve. "*Je suis désolé*, mademoiselle," he said more softly.

I grabbed Pierre's jumpsuit. "You have to help us."

Pierre threw off my hands with surprising strength, pushing me backward.

"I am going back," he said. "Are you coming?"

I held out my hand. "Give me the map," I said.

He hesitated, then thrust it at me.

"And your shovel," I said.

"You cannot—"

"Give me the damn shovel!"

With a look at Eve, Pierre pulled the shovel from his belt. He paused, then unhooked the coil of rope and tossed both to my feet.

"One more thing," I said. "If we don't show up at your bar tomorrow, I want you to go to the police. Ask for Commandant Boutin. Tell them where we are."

Pierre just stared at me. Then he reached into his jumpsuit and pulled out the chain with the tiny key. He held it out. I took the chain.

"May God be with you," he said, and turned.

I watched the glow of his headlamp until it disappeared.

I put the chain in my jeans pocket and I picked up the shovel. My hands were shaking as I started to dig.

46

It took less than ten minutes to dislodge the larger rocks at the top of the pile. Eve was holding the flashlight from below and when I looked back at her I knew she was thinking the same thing I was—that this looked less like a cave-in than a carefully constructed barrier.

When I trained the flashlight on the hole I had dug, I was encouraged to see the passage beyond was cut with a higher ceiling. But like all the others, it turned and twisted into blackness.

I squirmed through first, landing with a hard thud on the other side. I helped Eve climb through.

We continued on, Eve in the lead holding the big flash-light.

It was dry and cool, maybe fifty degrees. The only sound was the crunch of our boots. The passage widened and nar-rowed but always in a disorienting twisting pattern. I was managing to stay calm but couldn't stop thinking that we were at the mercy of a map drawn by a madman.

We seemed to be going steadily downhill. The walls were close, straight and smooth, the ceiling maybe six inches above my head. I was imagining what it must have been like for the gypsum miners down here hundreds of years ago. And then I was remembering what it felt like to be buried alive.

"Matt?"

Eve had stopped and was looking back at me.

"You are breathing very hard. I can hear you," she said. "Are you all right?"

I nodded tightly.

Eve looked at me skeptically. "Why don't you go ahead?" she said.

I nodded and took her heavy flashlight, grateful to have something to focus on besides my childhood memories of that emerald mine. We moved on.

The passage was narrowing quickly. The walls were now rough and gouged, like huge hands had clawed at them trying to get out.

I stepped on something and heard a dull snap. I swung the beam to my feet. At first I thought I had stumbled into a woodpile. Then it registered.

The knobbed ends of a femur.

Then others. Bones. A carpet of them ahead of me, brown-gray with a fine coating of white gypsum dust.

I couldn't move. Couldn't step back and couldn't go forward.

I jumped when Eve touched my shoulder.

"Matt," she said softly.

I couldn't take my eyes off the bones.

"You knew they were down here," she said.

Her voice was barely registering. I was seeing horse carts and black-robed men shoveling bodies into wells.

I felt her cold hand on mine as she gently moved the flashlight, directing the beam upward, away from the bones.

"Matt. We have to keep moving."

I began to walk, forcing myself to ignore the crunching under my feet.

Finally, the sound stopped, and I was left with only the steady beat of my heart echoing in my head.

The flashlight beam hit a wall ahead. As we approached, my heart sank. We were in a small alcove. It looked like a dead end. Eve came up behind me and held the map under the light.

"Did we miss a turn somewhere back there?" she asked.

"If we did, I didn't see it."

Eve swung her light behind us but there was nothing but the bounce of the beam off the gray walls. We were silent, neither wanting to give voice to the idea that we had to go back and begin again. We had been down here more than two hours already. We were tired, cold and scared.

I took the map and studied it. "This has to be the right way," I said.

Eve was turning in a slow circle, scanning the walls with her light.

"Matt, look."

I followed her flashlight beam upward. There, about five feet up and tucked near the ceiling, was a hole. It was no more than three feet in diameter.

"That can't be the way," I said.

"There's nothing else," Eve said.

I hesitated, then stuck my flashlight in my jacket. "I'm going through."

She grabbed my arm. "You can't fit in there."

"He did," I said.

Her grip on me tightened. "Let me try first. I'm smaller."

"Eve—"

"Don't **argue**. Give me a boost."

She put her heel in my palms and I pushed her upward. She grabbed the edge of the hole and wiggled halfway through.

"What **do** you see?"

Her voice was muted. "It looks like a drop about four meters to the ground. I'm going down."

"Eve, be careful, you—"

She disappeared and I heard a sharp cry from the other side.

"Eve!"

No sound from the other side.

"Eve!"

I grabbed the edge and pulled myself up, wedging my shoulders into the hole. I got through, freed an arm and shined the light down.

The beam caught something red far below. Eve's parka.

The red moved and I let out a hard breath.

"Eve!"

"I'm—"

"Stay there, I'm coming in."

"No! Don't move!"

"What?"

"I hit a ledge or something and fell off it. It is several meters more after that to the ground."

She moaned.

"Are you hurt?"

"I . . . my leg. Or my ankle. I cannot tell. I lost the flashlight. It is here but I cannot reach it."

"Don't move."

"Matt, do not try to come in here."

"Shut up. And don't move."

"Okay, okay . . . but try to get to the ledge. It is to the right, about three meters down."

There was no way I could do this holding the flashlight. I hesitated, then tossed the light down, aiming it away from the red spot of Eve's parka. A thud and it went out. I could make out the dim glow of Eve's flashlight somewhere down there.

Slowly, painfully, I eased my body forward into the darkness. There was a rush of cold air on my face. I was hanging now, braced on my thighs, my hands trying to get a hold on the walls but grasping only smooth rock.

There was nothing left to do but let go.

I gave a final push and tried to curl to cushion the blow.

I hit the ledge with a violent thud that pushed the air from my lungs. I grabbed at the darkness, my fingers finding rock, my legs dangling. I lay there for a long time, trying to get my breath. Then I carefully turned onto my belly and looked down.

Eve was propped against a wall. I could see the flashlight maybe six feet away. It gave me just enough light so I could see that I had maybe a five-foot drop to the floor.

I eased off the ledge and landed with a jolt. I crawled to the flashlight and swung it to Eve.

She threw up a hand against the light but not before I saw her face, white with pain. She was holding her ankle.

"How bad is it?" I asked, going to her.

"I do not know," she said. "Help me take off my boot."

I knelt and unlaced her boot. Her hand came out to my shoulder and I could feel her breath, warm and fast against my cheek.

"It hurts," she whispered.

I gently removed her boot, lowered her sock and shined the light on her ankle. Even with my limited medical training, I could see the ankle was badly sprained, maybe even broken. Already the tendons and muscles were swollen.

It was over, I knew. We had already been walking two hours and there was no way Eve could go on. I would have to leave her here and return to the surface for help. My eyes swung back up to the hole we had crawled through.

"No," Eve said. "You must go on."

I looked back at her quickly. "I can't leave you here," I said. "I have to go back and get you some help."

"No, it is only a sprain," she said.

The air around me felt suddenly thick and close. I knew exactly what Eve was telling me. I would be going on alone.

She pulled something from her parka. It was the evidence bag with the necklace inside. I put it in my pocket. Then she shifted and pulled something from her hip. She took my hand and pressed her gun into it.

I hesitated, then took it from her. I had fired rifles and shotguns growing up. I had hit the clay pigeons, targets and once a jackrabbit bolting through the brush. But I had never fired a handgun. And I had never aimed anything at a human being.

"How many rounds do I have?" I asked.

"Fourteen," Eve said.

The gun was heavy in my hand. From the moment we had decided to come down here, we knew we had to have a plan. The most important thing was to rescue Juliette. But Eve also wanted to bring Demarais out alive. The map told us there was no other way out of Two Hearts, so we had been confident we could do this. But now everything had changed.

Eve touched my arm. "We cannot do what we planned now," she said.

I was quiet.

"Matt, do you hear me?"

I did hear her but I wasn't listening. I was thinking of Mandy and the man who had taken her from me. I was thinking of what I would feel if I saw him and what it would feel like to kill him.

"Matt."

I looked into Eve's eyes. "Just make the trade," she said.

"Eve, I want—"

Her hand tightened on my arm. "Don't," she said.

She let go. I rose slowly and stuck the automatic in an inside pocket of the fatigue jacket. I pulled out the map and tried to estimate how long it would take me to reach Two Hearts. I guessed I was about thirty minutes away.

I looked down at Eve. She looked as comfortable as she could be, foot propped up, her back against the wall. I had many things going through my mind but one pushed forward, strengthened by my fear of this place and the man we chased.

"Do you have any other weapons with you?"

Eve stared at me as if she didn't understand.

"If he circles back somehow and finds you."

"I have a knife," Eve said.

I nodded tightly and turned from her, stepping carefully over the rocks that littered the ground. Eve's voice came from behind me, gentle with concern.

"*Dieu soit avec vous.*"

I stopped and looked back at her.

"God be with you," she said.

I moved on, stooping slightly to enter the passageway. Within a few feet, I was completely surrounded by craggy gray walls and dusty air stirred up by the shuffle of my feet. The silence that had been with us for hours suddenly felt thicker and I realized it was because I was missing the rhythm of Eve's breath in sync with my own.

As I followed the twisting passage, I alternated between walking and crawling, and the constant shifting of the gun against my chest became my companion.

I had walked for maybe fifteen minutes when I smelled what I could only imagine was dirty water.

A glimmer in my flashlight beam ahead. I stopped. A pool of water lay in front of me, as wide as the tunnel and seven or eight feet long, its surface as smooth as green glass.

Beyond, it looked as if the tunnel went on as before, a narrow gray corridor of rock.

I looked around for a stick to put in the water to gauge its depth but saw nothing but rock. Then something caught my eye, a long bone, covered in dust.

Dear God, forgive me, I thought as I picked it up.

I lowered the bone into the water, grateful that it hit bottom before it was totally submerged. I could only hope that the pool was the same depth all the way across.

I started forward. The water rose to my calves, sloshing over my boots, then rising to my thighs. Halfway across, I lost my footing. I fell forward, gasping as the cold water hit my chest. I thrashed around, dropping the flashlight. The darkness closed in and I felt a panic rising in my chest. Then I saw a faint glow in the water, reached in and came up with the huge police flashlight.

By the time I crawled out the other side, I was shaking. I

dropped down onto the dusty floor to gather my wits. A quick check revealed that Eve's gun seemed fairly dry.

Shivering, I got up and moved on. I was dismayed to see the passageway starting to narrow again. The path was angling uphill, too, and before long, I was forced to my knees. Still, the passageway continued to shrink until I found myself flat on my belly, looking into a rectangle-shaped hole about the size of a large heating vent.

I wiggled forward and twisted my body so I could shine the light into the hole.

Bones. As far as I could see.

A brown, jagged carpet of them in a passageway no larger than a coffin.

I closed my eyes, fighting back the nausea. I couldn't do it. I couldn't do it.

Then out of silence came the whisper.

Be brave, Bear.

I pulled in a deep breath and slithered forward into the hole. My eyes closed, I started a soldier's crawl across the bones. I could feel the sharp edges rip at the sleeves of my jacket. I could hear the dry crunch, like beetles being crushed, as they broke under the weight of my body.

Finally, when the space widened into a small corridor, I pulled myself up and sat back against the wall. My entire body was shaking. Tears burned and I closed my eyes.

When I opened them, I saw a glimmer in the distance. I thought my mind was playing tricks on me. But no, something was definitely down there.

Far down in the tunnel a light glowed.

I pushed to my feet and started toward it.

47

I stopped and held my breath, the shuffling of my boots leaving a soft echo in my ears. A cold dampness saturated my toes and blood soaked my sleeves where I had rubbed my elbows raw from crawling over rocks and bones. I was shaking—from the exertion, but also from fear.

The light seemed to come and go, like a firefly on a warm summer night.

Was I hallucinating?

If it was Demarais, I couldn't risk him seeing my flashlight beam. I took a deep breath and switched it off.

The darkness engulfed me. For several long seconds, I was so paralyzed I couldn't breathe. The light reappeared. It was shimmering, like candlelight.

I stuck the flashlight in my jacket and moved toward it. Then I realized that even as the light was becoming stronger, the walls were narrowing around me again.

I felt a sickening wave in my gut as I was forced to my knees by the cocooning of the passage. Only the image of Juliette's face kept me going.

I felt the scrape of rock on my head, then a slow trickle of blood down my forehead. I wiped it away and kept crawling toward the light. Then, suddenly, I was at the mouth of the funnel, an opening maybe three feet wide. I ducked and slithered through.

Even before I lifted my head, I knew I was in a place much larger than any of the passageways I had come through.

I stood on burning legs and pulled in a chestful of air. I was in a cavern maybe thirty feet high, twenty feet across.

I drew the gun and did a quick scan of the candlelit room, holding my breath. It was only after seeing no sign of Demarais that I allowed myself a moment to take in the details of the space around me.

In the flickering candlelight, the crudely carved walls glowed gold, glinting with gypsum crystals. I looked up at the soaring ceiling, where the rock walls leaned inward, seemingly held up only by old timber braces.

I was in Two Hearts.

My ears alert for any sounds, I focused on other details—the rocks that formed makeshift shelves and tables, the plastic grocery bags, empty water bottles, coils of rope, a shovel and pickax. There was a foul smell, like something long-buried but recently unearthed.

He was in here somewhere. And so was Juliette.

Gripping the gun tighter, I walked slowly around the cavern, peering behind every rock and into every recess. I thought about yelling out Juliette's name, but I didn't want to alert Demarais. And I was hoping against all hope that maybe he wasn't even here, that he had somehow gone back to the surface and I would be able to find Juliette and get out of here before he returned.

But then I remembered the map showed no other entrance or exit from Two Hearts.

That's when I saw the glimmer of light between two stalagmite-type rocks. Was there another room beyond this one?

A crazy thought ricocheted through my brain. A heart had four chambers. Did this space have four as well?

I realized the light coming from between the rocks was different than it was here. It glowed red. I went toward it, wedging my body between the fang-like rocks.

The second chamber was much smaller. The red glow, I saw now, was coming from small votives. They were clustered around a large niche carved in the far wall.

As I moved closer, my breath caught in my throat.

Inside the niche was a skull, propped on a pillow of candle wax. It was so white, so clean, it looked as if it were made of ivory.

A piece of dark blue cloth spilled from the niche like a small waterfall. The rest of the bones lay in neat rows on the blue cloth. The smallest bones, fingers and toes, lay on the top shelf. The ribs and vertebrae were laid out in the middle. And the larger long bones were arranged in increasing size down to the floor, where the thigh bones lay crossed over the heart-shaped pelvic bone.

This was Hélène Molyneaux.

I closed my eyes. My only thought was for Eve. I was grateful she wasn't here to see this grotesque shrine.

I heard a whisper and spun, thrusting out the gun. But there was no one, just the flicker of shadows.

And . . .

I felt my gut churn.

. . . the feel of cold breath on my face.

Just wind, it's just wind.

There was no one in this second room. I frantically scanned the rock for openings but could see nothing. Then my eyes picked up the barest glint of gold light. It was coming from a slit fifteen feet above, evidence of a third chamber. But where was the damn opening?

Another breath of wind brushed by me. Where was this air coming from if there were no other openings to Two Hearts? I saw something move in the far shadows. Gun outstretched, I went toward it.

The movement I had seen was the flutter of a tattered cloth. As I moved closer, I saw it covered the opening to another chamber. I could just make out more light, faint behind it. Gypsum dust wafted into the air as I moved the cloth and stepped into the next room.

The light came from a single candle, offering me little more than deep shadows.

Then my eye caught a flash of white in a corner. As I neared, the form took shape.

Juliette.

Her arms were over her head, her wrists bound by ropes looped over a rock above. She heard my footsteps and raised her head. Her eyes, dull with pain and exhaustion, widened as she recognized me.

I started toward her.

Suddenly, he stepped out from the shadows behind her.

I froze, my gun aimed at Demarais's chest.

For a second, there was only silence. Then, slowly, Demarais started clapping his hands.

"Bravo, bravo," he said.

I couldn't move. I couldn't believe what I was seeing. The man who had been nothing but a ghost to me for three weeks was now standing before me. I couldn't believe what I was hearing. He was laughing at me.

My finger pressed against the trigger. Then Eve's voice came to me.

Don't.

Demarais stopped clapping. The sound echoed for a moment then died.

"You've found the girl," he said. "Orpheus has come for his Eurydice."

Demarais burst into laughter.

"Shut up, you sick fuck! Shut up!"

The move was lightning quick. The tip of the end pin was at Juliette's throat before I could focus. She began to whimper. My brain raced with the idea that I might be able to put a bullet into his brain faster than he could jam the end pin into Juliette, but I knew I couldn't chance it.

My eyes jumped between Demarais and Juliette. Except for the bruises on her face and blood on her blouse, it didn't look as if he had hurt her. That gave me hope Demarais would take his ransom and let us walk away.

I pulled the necklace from my jacket. "Here's your damn necklace," I said.

"Take it from the plastic," Demarais said.

I tore the bag away and held the necklace out. "It's yours," I said. "Now let her go."

Demarais's eyes locked on the necklace. For a moment, he was silent, then his gaze drifted back to me.

"I release her, you will shoot me," Demarais said.

Suddenly, Mandy was there in my head, the way she looked on the table in the morgue, her pale-marble skin, her cold lips. And my father was there, too, crying. Then my mother, telling me it was not my fault.

I brought up my other hand to steady the gun.

Don't. Don't!

"I won't shoot you," I said.

Demarais smiled. He lowered the end pin just enough for Juliette to take a full breath. He held out his other hand.

"Toss it to me," he said. "Carefully."

I threw the necklace at him. He caught it against his chest.

"Send her to me!" I shouted.

Demarais untied the ropes from Juliette's hands. She slumped, caught herself, then stumbled away from him. She was sobbing as she fell against me. Demarais was playing with the chain of the necklace.

I pushed Juliette behind me and leveled the gun again at Demarais. I knew she was safe. We could walk away. But still, I couldn't move.

Juliette grabbed my arm. "Please, Matt, let's go."

"The girl is right," he said. "Be off, with your tail between your legs."

Juliette jerked at my arm but I pushed her hand aside.

"Why do you linger?" Demarais asked. "You are already the hero of your story. There is nothing else for you to do. *Partez!*"

"Matt, please," Juliette whispered.

Demarais took a step toward me. "I just realized what you want," he said. "You want to know about her."

For a second, I didn't understand. Then it hit me. The bastard was talking about Mandy.

"You want to know what happened," Demarais said.

"Don't you talk about her!"

"You want to know how this could have happened. One moment she was there and then you looked away and she was gone."

"Shut the fuck up!"

Demarais moved closer to the candle and the steel tip of the end pin glinted like a large needle.

Don't. Don't. Don't.

Demarais's voice was soft, almost singsong, when he spoke again. "I have always loved my baby sister . . ."

My grip on the gun tightened. The bastard was reciting lyrics.

"And I was often cruel," Demarais continued.

"Shut the fuck up!" I screamed.

Juliette was pulling at my arm but I pushed her away.

"You know that song, don't you?" Demarais asked. "You lived that song, didn't you?"

I straightened my arms, thrusting the gun closer to Demarais. My vision tunneled, the corners edged in black. All I could see was his face, half-gold, half-black, eyes glimmering like wet stone.

"I really must be going," Demarais said. "There are other little sisters waiting for their next dance."

With a flick of his wrist, Demarais collapsed the end pin and put it in a backpack. He slung the backpack over his shoulder and turned away from me.

Suddenly, I saw the opening behind him. There, behind the cage of rocks, another passageway, leading away from Two Hearts.

I pulled the trigger.

Explosions of sound. Flashes of white light.

The dying echo of the gunfire, a stinging in my hands. Then, finally, a silence so thick it felt as if my ears were bleeding.

"Matt!"

I stared into the blackness before me. I could see nothing. What had I done?

"Matt!"

I pushed Juliette's hand off my arm and moved forward into the dark passage. My foot hit something and I stopped, knelt and put out my hand.

I felt his arm first, then followed the rough fabric of the coat to the center of his back. My hand grew warm and sticky with his blood.

"Matt?"

"I'm here," I said. "Stay where you are."

I found Demarais's neck and pressed my finger to his skin. Not just one place but many, holding my breath as I felt for a pulse anywhere a human being might have one. Nothing. Nothing. Nothing.

I pushed to my feet and, drawing a hard breath, I turned away and walked back to Juliette. Her hand was extended and I grabbed it. Even as we started to walk out of the chamber, she didn't seem to want to let go. Neither did I.

48

The sky was still dark gray but there was a pale bleed of pink above the roofs. From my position in the backseat of the police car, I could not see anything except the chain-link fence through which Pierre had led us six hours ago. The narrow street was clogged with police cars and ambulances. The cold November air smelled of oil and baking bread.

I had been sitting here since before dawn, and even though I had endured incomprehensible things since Mandy's disappearance weeks ago, this last hour had felt like the longest of my life.

Eve had still not been brought out of the tunnels. Juliette and I had retraced my route back to her, but Eve had insisted that we leave her and get Juliette out first.

The moment Juliette and I emerged from underground, I had used Eve's cell to call the police. As we waited for them, I realized the map was no longer in my jacket. I had lost it somewhere in the tunnels, probably in the water. And now the searchers had nothing but my memories of the tunnels to guide them to Eve.

A spray of flashlights suddenly swept over the vacant lot.

I heard an eruption of voices and saw uniformed officers running in the direction of the recessed railroad tracks beyond.

My breath came out in a painful exhale.

Eve was strapped to a board, carried by paramedics. A tall man took off his cap and I recognized him as Maurice Fournier, the head of the *cataflics*. I watched as he leaned down to Eve and took her hand.

A flash of white caught my eye and I saw Juliette throw off a blanket and run across the street, pushing her way to Eve.

Immediately, an officer pulled her away. Even half a block away, I could hear her sobbing. It was heartbreaking, but I had followed enough investigations to know the cops would keep us apart. They interrogated us separately to make sure our stories were in sync and to catch those details that didn't match.

I sat back down on the cruiser seat and put my head in my hands.

Our stories.

The walk away from Two Hearts had been long and quiet. Juliette asked only about Eve. I told her that Eve was fine, left behind only because of a sprained ankle, but I don't think Juliette comprehended a word I said. It was not until she fell into Eve's arms that she even seemed to understand she was safe, that they were both safe.

And it was not until then that I felt the heaviness of Eve's gun in my jacket. I removed it and held it out to her.

What happened, Matt?

I shot him. Three times.

She weighed the gun in her hand, popped the magazine and checked the number of cartridges left.

You emptied the gun, Matt.

I had shot a man fourteen times.

In the back.

I had no knowledge of the French judicial system or homicide laws, but I knew that I had committed murder. I knew that you couldn't shoot even a monster in the back.

It was Eve who first gave voice to the idea that we could somehow hide this. That we could crawl out, dispose of her gun in case anyone ever found Demarais and never say a word to anyone.

That meant Eve's career would survive, but she and the police would have to continue the charade of looking for a man who was already dead.

It meant that Juliette would be criminally complicit in covering up a murder and be forced to keep the secret for the rest of her life.

And it meant that I would be able to go home a free man. I would be able to walk away again, untouched, from a pile of wreckage I had helped create.

Eve was the one who suggested we lie.

I was the one who said we had to tell the truth.

And we had. I had given my statement to a detective and was sure Juliette had done the same. Commandant Boutin would talk to Eve, then he would come to me.

Again I waited. The sun appeared above the building, a white glow behind frosted glass clouds. The air grew warmer but still I felt chilled. I closed my eyes.

"Monsieur Owens."

I must have dozed off because I jumped at the sound of the commandant's voice. He stood next to the open car door, peering in at me. Fournier came up behind him.

I pulled myself to my feet and stood next to the cruiser. I was taller than Boutin and had to look down to meet his eyes.

"You should never have come here," Boutin said.

For a moment, I thought he meant the tunnels. Then I realized he meant Paris.

"You have interfered in an investigation," Boutin said. "You have caused an innocent American woman to be attacked. And because of you, Inspector Bellamont's career is over."

I thought of telling him what was in my head, the only thing that had been in my head from the moment I watched Demarais disappear into the passage—that I couldn't let him kill anyone else. But I knew what was coming once this story broke. And I knew that this petty man would do anything he could to protect his rank and reputation. I had made him look foolish and he had the power to make me, and Eve, pay.

"It would be best if you would just leave," Boutin said.

My God, is he going to let me go?

"But that cannot happen," Boutin said. "You have confessed to a murder."

Boutin looked toward Fournier, who was giving directions to a group of men who were obviously equipped to go down into the tunnels.

"When they find Laurent Demarais," Boutin said, "you will be charged with murder."

Boutin turned, snapped out some French to a nearby officer and walked away. The officer came over to me, drawing his handcuffs from his belt. He spoke French but I understood what he wanted. I turned and put my arms behind my back.

He put me inside the car. I sank back in the seat and leaned my head against the glass. Across the street I saw Juliette and Eve staring at me.

I was exhausted, but I was seeing two things clearly. Juliette was alive, and my life was over.

The first night I didn't sleep. I lay in the dark of my cell listening to the din of French. Despair and rage sounded the same in any language.

Finally, on the second night, exhaustion claimed me. I fell into a black hole of dreamless sleep and awoke with a start.

The light from the small window was bright, hinting at morning. But what morning? How long had I slept?

I had talked to more detectives whose names I did not remember, always telling the same story. They offered me no information in return. I called Cameron, and I remembered asking for a lawyer. Since then, the cops had left me alone.

I could remember little else. I was wearing a blue jumpsuit but I couldn't remember changing clothes. I couldn't remember eating.

It was as if my mind was shutting down, and that's what scared me most. Not the phone call to my father that I still had not made. Not the murder trial that could put me away for the rest of my life. I was scared that I didn't know who I would be after this was over. The man who had crawled across those bones was gone. I had no idea who was still left inside me.

Sleep saved me again. I was drifting off when a noise jarred me awake. I looked toward the bars.

Cameron.

"Hey, Matt."

I rose and went to him. "How'd you get back here?"

"You can pay me back later."

I smiled and leaned my head on the bars. I caught a whiff of Cameron's foul cigarettes. It smelled like perfume.

"How you holding up?" Cameron asked.

I shook my head slowly. "They haven't charged me yet. Nobody's telling me anything. I don't know what the fuck is going on."

"Eve's getting you a lawyer," Cameron said.

I looked up at him. "How is she doing?"

Cameron held out a newspaper. "See for yourself."

I took the copy of the *Herald Tribune* and opened it up. The story was stripped across the top in a bold headline.

SERIAL MURDERER KILLED IN CATACOMBS

Cameron had written the story himself. He quoted unnamed police sources. I was sure the information came from Eve.

I read it quickly, digesting the main points. The story detailed our pursuit of "an international serial killer" and his fatal shooting by American journalist Matthew Owens. It also credited Inspector Eve Bellamont's dogged five-year investigation for solving cold-case murders in France and Great Britain. There was a quote from Hélène Molyneaux's father about finally being able to bring his daughter home. There was a quote from Inspector Gregory Harrison about reopening Dylan Rumsley's case and another from John Mulligan in Fyvie about reopening his investigation into Caitlyn McKenzie's death. There was a quote from the Miami Beach

PD lauding the French police's cooperation in their investigation.

I scanned the rest of the story quickly. Cameron had described Juliette's abduction and our journey to Two Hearts. It also said that I was in custody, awaiting formal murder charges.

I lowered the paper and looked at Cameron. He held up a stack of other newspapers.

"They're all trying to follow up with it this morning," he said. "And it's on CNN."

I shook my head, knowing I had to call North Carolina. And Nora. "Cam," I said, "how could you do this to me?"

"Do what?"

I waved the newspaper wearily.

Cameron was quiet for a moment. "Don't you see, you poor bastard?" he said softly. "This is what's going to save your ass."

I looked down at the newspaper in my hand. Somewhere in my fogged head, it began to come together. The story was irresistible; it already had a life of its own. Eve would be lionized as a savior of not just her own niece but the memories of five other women. Demarais would be vilified as the monster he was. And me?

I looked up at Cameron. "I still murdered a man," I said.

A loud clang echoed in the corridor. I leaned forward against the bars to see who else might be coming to see me.

It was a guard, the heavy keys on his belt clinking as he walked. He stopped next to Cameron and said something in French. Cameron stepped back against the wall. The guard stuck a key into the lock on my cell door. A buzzer rang and the door slid open.

"*Vous êtes libre de partir,*" the guard said.

My eyes shot to Cameron. His mouth hung open.

"He says you can go," Cameron said.

The guard said something else.

"He says there are no charges," Cameron said. "He wants you to follow him."

The guard started away. I had heard the words but I couldn't move. Cameron pulled on my arm.

"Go, go," he said.

I stepped into the corridor and followed the guard into another room, where my clothes and personal items were stacked next to my muddy boots. My passport lay on top.

A different guard was waiting with a clipboard. He filled out a form while I hurriedly threw off the jumpsuit and pulled on my clothes.

The guard thrust the clipboard into my hands. "Sign here, here and here," he said, stabbing his pen at various lines on the form.

I hesitated, afraid I was somehow being conned into signing a confession that would put me back in jail. The guard cleared his throat.

"It is a standard release form," he said. "You are just certifying you have received your belongings and that you are leaving our facility in good health."

I was going to ask permission to go find Cameron so he could read the form when the guard stepped close to me.

"Inspector Bellamont is waiting for you outside," he said, indicating a red door at the end of a long hallway. "Sign the form. It is not a trick."

I scribbled my name and within seconds pushed out the door into the sunshine. I was in a cobblestone walled courtyard packed with cruisers. My clothes were stiff and gray with gypsum dust. I was still holding my passport. I opened it, staring at my photograph. It was so old I still had my beard.

Eve was coming toward me, moving gingerly on crutches over the cobblestones.

I went quickly to her. I knew she might find a hug awkward but I couldn't resist. I was sure she was responsible for getting me out of that cell. I embraced her, crutches and all.

"How are you doing?" she asked when I drew back.

"I'm fine," I said. "How about you?"

She glanced at her bandaged ankle. "It is just a bad sprain. I will heal."

"And Juliette?"

"She is in the car," Eve said. "She is well."

I started over to the car, but Eve caught my arm. "Wait. I must speak with you first."

I turned back to her, and as I stood in the warmth of the morning sun, my joy at being free began to erode. Something was wrong.

"Inspector Fournier's team found Two Hearts late yesterday," she said.

I said nothing, more confused than I had been a few minutes ago. Eve went on.

"They did not find Demarais's body."

A few seconds passed while my brain tried to process this information.

"Then they had to be in the wrong place," I said.

"No, it was Two Hearts," Eve said. "They found everything else you described. Hélène's bones, the red candles and the end pin. No Demarais."

"That's fucking impossible."

Eve was silent. Her eyes were steady on mine, dark with suspicion.

"You don't believe me?" I asked.

"I don't know what to believe."

"Then ask Juliette," I said. "She saw me shoot the bastard."

"Juliette saw you fire the gun," Eve said.

"Eve," I said. "He's not some ghost! I checked. He was dead. He was there."

"He was not there, Matt. He was not anywhere nearby. They searched every tunnel down there."

I spun away from her, walking a tight circle. As crazy as it was, as impossible as it was, the fact that they found no body was the reason I had been set free. No body. No crime.

I looked back at Eve. "The cartridges," I said. "They had to have found the cartridges."

"Not a one," Eve said.

"Bullets," I said. "There had to be holes in the walls." Eve shook her head and looked up at me. She had the same question in her eyes now that had been there two weeks ago in the cemetery. *Can I trust you?*

I thought I had answered it.

"Matt."

Eve's voice drew me back. "I owe you so much," she said.

"But you don't believe me."

She hesitated. "It does not matter."

"It does to me, Eve."

We were quiet for a moment. Eve's eyes went to the passport in my hand. "You are going home?"

I exhaled. "No choice. It expires in two days."

She gave me a small nod. "I will make sure Juliette sees you before you leave."

"What about you?" I asked. "What will you do now?"

"I will go on looking for him."

For a moment I didn't know what she meant. Then it hit me like a jab to the chest. Demarais. She would go on just like before, except now she would be hunting a ghost.

And there was no way I could stop her.

50

My flight was scheduled to leave at noon. The one-way next-day ticket to Miami had set me back almost three grand. It was a small price to pay.

The ticket was safe in the breast pocket of my blue blazer, along with my passport. I was cramming the rest of my stuff into my duffel when Cameron came to the door of the bedroom.

"Was it something I said, dear?"

I turned and gave him a smile. "You could come visit me in Miami, you know."

"Been there, done that, bought the guayabera."

I picked up the fake Burberry scarf I had been wearing for the last three weeks and held it out to Cameron.

"Keep it," he said. "Something to remember me by."

"I won't need a wool scarf in Miami and I sure as hell won't need anything to remember you by," I said, folding the scarf and laying it on the bed. I looked around the room to see if I had forgotten anything. My jeans were crumpled in the corner, where I had left them last night. They were caked with the dust and mud of the tunnels. For a second, I thought about leaving them, but then I picked them up and gave them a good shake.

Something fell to the floor. I picked it up.

It was the silver chain Pierre had given me back in the tunnel before he left. I had forgotten about it. As angry as I was at him for leaving Eve and me on our own in the tunnel, it was only right that I return this.

"We better get going," Cameron said.

"Yeah," I said. I stuffed the jeans in the duffel and zipped it. "But we need to make a quick stop first."

Maybe I should have been surprised to see that El Melocotón was crowded on a Sunday morning, but I wasn't. The place was packed with young men, just as it had been on both my other visits. But as I walked in, I sensed something had changed.

Faces turned toward me, talking ceased. As I made my way through the bar to the beat of Duke Ellington's "Caravan," the wall of bodies gave way.

Pierre was sitting at his table in the back. His dark eyes were expressionless when he looked up at me.

"Would you take a drink with me?" he asked.

Cameron was waiting in the car; I had only minutes to spare, and I was still pissed at Pierre for leaving us in the tunnels. I sat down across from him and he poured out two glasses of his Basque liqueur. When I didn't take a drink, Pierre set his glass down.

I pulled the silver chain from my pocket and set it on the table. "I thought you'd want this back," I said.

Pierre looked at the chain but didn't pick it up. Then he reached into his pants pocket and set something on the table next to it.

It was the Deux Coeurs necklace.

I stared at it in shock. Then it clicked, and I looked up at Pierre.

"It was you," I said.

Pierre didn't blink. I could feel the weight of the young men's eyes on me. I leaned back in the chair and shook my head slowly.

"How did you do it?" I asked.

"Do what?" Pierre said.

"He was there. I killed him. And then he wasn't there. You're the only person who knew about Two Hearts, knew he was down there."

"That is true," he said.

"There was another way in?"

"There are always other ways."

"And you got there before the cops?"

"We always do."

"You took the cartridges?"

Pierre nodded. "We were on our way, coming back to help you, and heard the echoing of the shots. We arrived in Deux Coeurs just after you left. We took the cartridges and the bullets we found in the walls."

I just sat there, stunned. "And you left the end pin," I said. "Why?"

"It needed to be found."

I shook my head slowly. "But why?" I asked. "Why did you do this for me?"

Pierre picked up the silver chain and fingered the small key. "I gave this to you for luck, but also because I no longer deserved it. I needed a reason to wear it again. So it was not just for you, Monsieur Owens."

Pierre slipped the chain over his head and tucked the key into his shirt. He picked up his glass.

"Will you take a drink with me now?" he asked.

The music had stopped. I turned around and looked at the young men. They raised their glasses subtly in my direction, then turned away.

I picked up my glass and took a drink.

There was only one question left.

"Where is he?" I asked.

"You have nothing to worry about," Pierre said.

I leaned forward. "But I need to know—"

"He is in the darkest place. That is all anyone needs to know."

I looked at my watch. If I didn't leave right now, I would have no time left to say good-bye to Eve and Juliette at the airport. I rose, putting the Two Hearts necklace in my pocket.

"*Dieu soit avec vous*, Monsieur Owens," Pierre said.

We shared drinks together at the airport. Cameron had a beer, Juliette a Coke, and Eve ordered one of those pink drinks. Kirs, they were called, a mix of dry white wine and black-currant-flavored liqueur called crème de cassis. I didn't know if Nora was familiar with the drink, but I planned on introducing it to her.

I wasn't sure why. Maybe I just wanted to share with Nora a memory of Paris. Maybe I sincerely believed she would like them. That alone was enough to make me want to try.

My eyes drifted to the departure board, then around the cocktail table. All the small talk about jobs, family and inept airport security had been exhausted.

I knew our jobs were safe. My editor Darcy had asked me last night on the phone if I would write of my adventures in France, maybe even consider a book she could edit. I had told her no.

There *were* things I wanted to write about that I had never considered before. I just wasn't sure yet exactly what they were. But I did know they didn't concern Mandy or Laurent Demarais. And I knew it had nothing to do with that stillborn novel in my drawer.

Eve's job was saved by Cameron's now internationally syndicated stories. Commandant Boutin couldn't fire a legend. He hadn't even admitted publicly that the body of the "international serial killer" had mysteriously disappeared. That would be admitting that Demarais still might be out there stalking the streets of Paris and beyond, and there was no way the police were going to admit that.

During our few minutes at the airport café, I opened up and told Eve, Juliette and Cameron a little about Mandy and my parents. Juliette was fascinated by the Civil War and asked me questions I couldn't answer. Overall, I must have painted her a pretty nice picture of my home, because she asked me if she could visit me one day in North Carolina and eat grits. I told her my folks, especially my mother, would like that very much.

By eleven, it was time for me to head through security, and there was only one thing left to say. And one person to say it to.

I asked Cameron and Juliette to excuse us and I took Eve a short ways down the concourse.

We stopped at a window that overlooked the runway. I took Eve's crutches and helped her down onto a bench. The smell of baking bread and strong coffee drifted from somewhere. A soothing babble of French floated around us. They were smells and sounds I would always have in me now.

When I sat down next to Eve, her eyes were expectant. I took her hand and turned it palm up. Then I reached into my pocket and withdrew the Two Hearts necklace. I laid it in her hand.

"I didn't lie to you," I said. "I killed him and I left him lying there on the floor. Pierre led a group down there after we got out. I don't know what they did with the body. He wouldn't tell me."

The stunned expression on Eve's face almost made me wish I had not dropped this on her now. But she had to know the truth, and it occurred to me in that moment exactly why.

"I couldn't leave here letting you think he was still out there, Eve, letting you go on looking for him," I said. "I couldn't do that to Juliette."

"Juliette?" Eve said.

"She really needs you to let him go," I said.

Eve's eyes teared.

"We both need to let it go," I said.

She hesitated, then nodded. I heard an announcement in French for a Delta flight, then it was repeated in English.

"That's my flight," I said.

We went back to the café and gathered my duffel and computer bag. Cameron, Juliette and Eve walked me to the security barrier. I held back tears as each of them embraced me, but they flowed when I felt Eve's arms around me.

"Be happy, Matt," she whispered.

"I will," I said.

I didn't trust myself to look back as I went through security and down the corridor to my gate. I was in my seat on the plane before I even allowed myself to think about the things and people I was leaving behind in Paris.

But there were things I needed to do at home. I had looked away for just a moment and my mother and father were gone. I had looked away for just a moment and Nora was gone. I had looked away for too many years, and in that long, long moment, I had lost everything that mattered.

The stewardess was coming down the aisle telling people to turn off their electronic devices.

There was still time.

I flipped open my cell and punched in Nora's number. As I listened to the ringing go on, I realized it was only six in the morning in Miami. I let it ring anyway.

Finally, I heard her voice, hoarse with sleep.

"Nora, it's Matt."

A long pause. But at least it wasn't "Matt who?"

"Where are you?" she said finally.

"On the plane. I'm coming home."

Another long pause. The stewardess was hovering over me, insisting I turn off the phone.

"Nora, are you there?"

"Yes, I'm here."

"Will you pick me up at the airport?"

The pause was so long this time I closed my eyes.

But then, when she finally spoke, it was as if she were right next to me.

"I'll be there for you," she said.

Turn the page for a look at P. J. Parrish's
riveting suspense novel,

THE LITTLE DEATH

featuring Detective Louis Kincaid

available now from Pocket Books

The top was down on the Mustang, and the road ahead was empty. Louis Kincaid was not sure exactly where he was going.

He had never driven this road before. On all of his trips over to the east coast, he had taken Alligator Alley, which cut a straight, expedient slash across the Everglades from Naples to Fort Lauderdale. Always in the past, he had arrived quickly, done his job, and headed straight back home.

But this time, an impulse he did not understand had led him to the back roads.

The map told him he had to stay on US-80, but the highway had changed names several times already, narrowing to meander through cattle pastures and tomato farms, offering up a red-planked barbecue joint, a sunburnt nursery, or a psychic's bungalow. Three times, the speed limit dropped, and US-80 became Main Street, passing Alva's white-steepled church, La Belle's old courthouse, and Clewiston's strip malls. From there, the towns fell away, leaving only the vast flat expanse of the sugarcane fields, broken by a row of high power lines, marching like giant alien soldiers to the horizon.

The wind was hot on Louis's face and the scenery was a blur of color—the high green curtain of the cane and the denim of the December sky. The sun was behind him, and he had a strong urge to turn the car around and head back home. But he had made a promise and had to see this thing through.

Soon he reached the sprawling suburbs of West Palm Beach. The fast-food joints and gas stations grew denser the farther east the car went, ending in the pastel warren of old downtown West Palm Beach.

At the Intracoastal, Louis steered the Mustang onto a low-slung bridge that connected the mainland to the barrier island. He had the thought that the bridge looked nothing like the one that led from Fort Myers over to his island home on the Gulf. The Sanibel–Captiva causeway was a plain concrete expanse that leapfrogged across rocky beaches dotted with kids and wading fishermen.

This one looked like the drawbridge to a Mediterranean castle, complete with two ornamental guard towers.

The bridge emptied onto a broad boulevard lined with majestic royal palms and fortresslike buildings that looked like banks. There was no welcome sign, no signs anywhere. He guessed he was in Palm Beach now.

"Mel, wake up," he said.

No sound or movement from the passenger seat.

Louis reached over and jabbed the lump. "Mel! Wake up!"

"What?"

"We're here. Where do I go?"

Mel Landeta sat up with a grunt, adjusted his sunglasses, and looked around.

"Take a right on South County Road," he said.

"Where? There's no street signs."

"I don't know. I haven't been here in a long time. The island's only fourteen miles long and a mile wide. If you hit the ocean, you've gone too far."

Louis spotted the street name painted on the curb and hung a right. The financial citadels of the boulevard gave way to boutiques and restaurants.

"Where we meeting this guy?" Louis asked.

"Some place called Ta-boo. Two more blocks and hang a right onto Worth Avenue. You can't miss it, believe me."

In the three years Louis had been in Florida—despite the fact his PI cases had taken him from Tallahassee to Miami—he had never made it over to Palm Beach. But he knew what Worth Avenue was: the Rodeo Drive of the South, minus the movie stars. He slowed the Mustang to a crawl, looking for a parking spot. Some of the store names he recognized—Armani, Gucci, Dior, Cartier—but most didn't register. What did register was the almost creepy cleanliness of the street. From the blinding white of the pavement to the gleaming metal of the Jaguars and Bentleys at curbside, Worth Avenue had the antiseptic look of an operating room.

He pulled the Mustang in behind a black and gold Corniche. Mel sniffed the air like a dog. "Ah, the sweet smell of money."

The only thing Louis could smell was perfume. It took him a moment to realize it was wafting out on an arctic stream of air-conditioning from the open door of the Chanel boutique. A security guard, dressed in blue suit and tie, was stationed just inside the door.

Mel got out and stretched. He pulled his black sports coat from the backseat and slipped it on, then looked at Louis.

"Did you bring a jacket?" he asked.

Louis stared at him.

"A sports coat," Mel said. "I told you to pack one."

"It's eighty degrees," Louis said.

"Get it," Mel said.

Stifling a sigh, Louis popped the trunk and shook out his blue blazer. The Chanel guard had come out to stand just outside the door and was watching him.

"Hey, buddy," Mel called out. "Which way is Ta-boo?"

The guard's eyes swung to Mel, giving him the once-over before he spoke. "Two blocks back," he said.

They headed east down the wide sidewalk, pausing at a corner for a Mercedes to turn. Louis's gaze traveled up the imposing coral stone façade of the Tiffany & Co. building to the statue of Atlas balancing a clock. It was one-forty. They were late.

"You still haven't told me how you know this guy," Louis said as they started across the street.

"I knew him when I was with Miami PD," Mel said. "I helped him out once when he got in a jam."

This was certainly more than a jam, Louis thought. Reggie Kent was the prime suspect in a murder. A murder gruesome enough to have made the papers over in Fort Myers. A decapitated body had been found in the fields on the westernmost fringe of Palm Beach County. The head had not been found, but the mutilated corpse was identified as a Palm Beach man named Mark Durand.

The sheriff's department had connected the dots, and they had led sixty miles east and across the bridge, right to Reggie Kent's island doorstep.

That was all he knew, Mel had said. Other than Reggie Kent was scared shitless. And that he was innocent, of course.

"This must be the place," Mel said.

The restaurant's large open window framed two blond women sitting at a table sipping drinks. Inside, it was as cool and dark as a tomb, the long, narrow room dominated by a sleek bar. Beyond, through a latticed entrance, Louis could see a main dining room.

Louis knew that Mel probably couldn't see well. His retinitis pigmentosa allowed him to see blurred images if the light was bright, but at night or in the dimness of a bar, he needed help. Not that Mel would ask.

"What's this Reggie guy look like?" Louis asked.

"I haven't seen him in ten years. Blond, stocky. Nice-looking guy, I guess."

The bar was packed, mainly with more blondes, who had given them a quick, dismissive once-over. There was a man sitting at the far end, waving a hand. Louis led Mel through a sea of silk and tanned legs.

The guy who had signaled them slid off his zebra-print bar stool. "Mel," he said, "My God, you haven't changed a bit."

"Neither have you, Reggie," Mel said, sticking out his hand.

Louis knew Mel couldn't see the guy well, but the lie brought a smile to Reggie Kent's face as he shook Mel's hand. In the blue reflected light of the saltwater aquarium behind the bar, Louis could see Reggie's face clearly. He was probably about fifty, but his round, pale face had an oddly juvenile look. His skin was pink and shiny, almost like the slick skin of a burn victim. Wisps of blond hair hung over wide blue eyes. He wore a pink oxford shirt beneath a light blue linen blazer and white slacks.

As Reggie Kent hefted himself back onto the bar stool he revealed a glimpse of bare pink ankle above soft navy loafers. The whole effect made Louis think of a giant Kewpie doll.

"You've saved my life," Reggie Kent said.

"Let's not get ahead of ourselves," Mel said.

"Yes, yes, of course." Reggie ran a hand over his brow. The bar was frigid, but Louis could see a sheen of sweat on the man's face.

"This is Louis Kincaid, the guy I told you about," Mel said, nodding.

Reggie focused on Louis. "You're the private investigator." His voice had dropped to a whisper, and his blue eyes honed in on Louis with intense curiosity before darting away. "You need a drink. How rude of me. Yuba!"

The bartender appeared, a tall woman with long, sleek black hair and almond-colored skin, wearing a white shirt and a black vest.

"You need a refill?" she said in a softly accented voice.

"Yes, another Rodnik gimlet. And whatever my friends are having. Just put it on my tab."

The woman hesitated.

"What?" Reggie asked.

"Don says I can't run a tab for you anymore," she said quietly. "I'm sorry, Reggie."

Even in the dim light, Louis could see the red creep into Reggie's face. Louis pulled out his wallet and tossed a twenty onto the bar. "Bring us two Heinekens and the gimlet," he said.

The bartender nodded and left.

Reggie was staring at something beyond Louis's shoulder. Louis turned and saw two women looking at Reggie and whispering.

The bartender brought the drinks and eyed the twenty. "That's fifty-six dollars, sir."

"What?" Louis said.

Mel laughed.

Louis dug out two more twenties. "Keep the change."

The woman took the bills and left.

"Nice tip," Mel said.

"It's all I had," Louis said.

Mel took a drink of beer. "All right, Reggie, why don't you tell us exactly what is going on?"

Reggie took a big drink of the gimlet. "Well, it's like I told you on the phone. Four days ago, they found Mark's body out in the fields, and then they just showed up at my door and told me I had to come into the police station to answer some questions." He paused, shutting his eyes. "I had to go to that place and identify him. He . . . had no head. But he had this birthmark on his chest and—"

Mel interrupted him. "This Mark guy was a friend of yours?"

Reggie managed a nod.

"A good friend?" Mel asked.

Reggie picked up his glass and drained it. "Not really. I only knew him for a year, I guess."

"So why were the police so interested in talking to you?" Louis asked.

Reggie took a moment to meet Louis's eyes. "We were kind of in business together."

"What kind of business?"

Reggie looked to Mel.

"You have to tell to us, Reggie," Mel said.

Reggie blew out a long stream of cigarette smoke. "I'm a walker."

"What, like a dog walker?" Louis asked.

"Dog? Oh, good Lord, no," Reggie said. "A walker is . . . well, an escort of sorts." Reggie saw the look on Louis's face and held up a hand. "Not what you are thinking, I assure you. It's rather hard to explain."

Louis and Mel exchanged looks.

"Suppose you try," Mel said. "You know, like we're in fifth grade?"

Reggie looked to the dining room. "See that woman sitting by the fireplace? That blonde in the chartreuse Chanel suit?"

Louis and Mel swiveled to look. Louis focused on a woman in green with cotton-candy hair. Her face had the same taut look as Reggie's, and had the lighting been kinder, she might have been mistaken for being in her fifties. But her neck and hands betrayed her as somewhere past seventy.

"That's Rusty Newsome," Reggie said. "I was supposed to escort her to the Heart Ball on Saturday. Her husband, Chick, never goes to anything, so I always take her." He met Louis's eyes. "That's what I do. I take women to dinner or charity balls or the club. I pay attention to them if their husbands are too bored . . . or too dead."

"You make a living at this?" Louis asked.

Reggie gave him a small smile. "There's a lot of clubs in this town and a lot of widows in each club."

"They pay you?" Louis asked.

Reggie tilted his chin up. "Sometimes they give me a little cash. Sometimes they give me little gifts. It's not just about the money, you see. It's about having a door into a life I could not really afford on my own."

Mel took a long drink from his beer. "I always thought you were a hustler, Reggie."

Reggie looked wounded. "Some might see it that way. But there are good hustlers, and there are bad hustlers. A bad hustler is always trying to get something out of someone. I am always trying to give these women something. I am the first to admit I have no real talents or ambition. But I am a wonderful listener, I know about wine and food, and I am very good at bridge. I know how to make a lonely woman feel happy."

"Is sex part of this walker deal?" Louis asked.

Reggie's eyes shot to him. "Never. The women I know are not interested in sex."

Louis shook his head slowly. "Mr. Kent, I do a lot of work for wives whose husbands are cheating on them. Every time I find a guy's been charging escorts to his Visa, he claims he just did it for the pleasure of the lady's company."

"This is different," Reggie said, reddening. "What a walker offers is friendship. And sometimes a friendship is more intimate than a marriage. But it never, ever involves sex. We are not gigolos."

He picked up his glass and downed the last of the gimlet. Louis was hoping he wouldn't order another one.

"Your friend—what's his name again?" Louis asked.

"Mark," Reggie said softly. "Mark Durand."

"You said he was a walker, too?" Louis asked.

Reggie nodded slowly. "He was just starting out as one, and I was sort of introducing him around, helping him get connected. He would have been a great walker."

"But he turned up headless in a cow pasture," Mel said.

Reggie nodded and looked at his empty glass with longing. Louis wondered if Mel had a credit card.

"How many times have the cops questioned you?" Louis asked.

"Three times," Reggie said with a sigh. "It was in the *Shiny Sheet*. They even used my picture. Awful, just awful."

"Why?" Louis asked.

"Why what?"

"Cops don't question someone three times without good reason. Why do you think they're after you?"

Reggie was silent.

"Talk to us, Reggie," Mel said.

"I was with Mark the night before his body was found," Reggie said. "We had a dinner at Testa's and . . ." Another big sigh. "We had a fight. Everyone saw it."

"About what?" Mel asked.

"What does it matter now?"

"It matters," Mel said.

"Mark had been staying at my place, and he told me he wanted to get his own apartment," Reggie said. "I told him he should stay with me for a while longer."

"That's it?"

Reggie nodded.

"You two weren't—?"

Reggie stared at Mel. "Together? Oh no, no. Mark was quite a bit younger than me. No, there was nothing between us. We were just friends."

Mel drained his beer, set the glass down, and leaned back in his chair, crossing his arms. "Don't lie to us, Reggie."

"I'm not. Like I said, it was just a business arrangement. I was trying to help him. But Mark insisted he was ready to go out on his own and I knew he wasn't ready. This town will eat you alive, and I didn't want that to happen to him."

Mel was silent. Louis waited, watching the two men, wondering what the history was between them. Mel hadn't told him much about Reggie Kent, just that he had known him back in Miami. He wondered how the hell Mel had ever hooked up with a piss-elegant guy like this.

Reggie leaned forward. "You've got to help me, Mel. Please. I don't have anyone else to turn to."

Louis was afraid the guy was going to cry.

"They've hung me out to dry," Reggie said. "Even the police are against me."

"They're cops, Reggie, they're supposed to be," Mel said.

Reggie shook his head vigorously. "No, you don't understand. The police are here to protect us. When that horrible detective from West Palm Beach came here to question me, Lieutenant Swann came with him. They are my friends."

He picked up the pack of Gauloises, but when he pulled out a cigarette, his hand was shaking so badly he dropped it. Mel caught it before it rolled off the table. Mel looked at Louis, then back at Reggie. "So what do you want us to do?"

"Find out who killed Mark," Reggie said.

"Just like that?" Mel said.

"I told you, Mel, I have money. I can pay you. And your friend of course."

Louis was quiet. There was something about this guy he didn't like. His desperation was genuine enough, but something was slightly off. He was sure the guy was lying about something. Or, at the very least, leaving something out of the story.

"Please, Mel," Reggie said.

Mel held out the cigarette to Reggie. "Look, let us go have a little chat with your Lieutenant Swann and we'll get back to you."

Reggie looked to Louis, who nodded.

Reggie took the cigarette and grasped Mel's hand. "Thank you, thank you."

"Easy," Mel said.

Reggie nodded and sat back in the chair, running a hand across his sweaty face. His wide eyes were darting over the crowded room now. He waved at someone and tried a smile but it faded quickly and he dropped his hand.

"I think I better go home," he said softly. "There's a nicely chilled bottle of Veuve Clicquot in my fridge. I think I shall go home and get shit-faced drunk."

He picked up his cigarettes, rose, and held out his hand. Mel shook it. Reggie turned to Louis. "Forgive my manners. I've forgotten your name."

"Louis Kincaid."

Reggie smiled. "Thank you, Mr. Kincaid."

Louis gave him a nod. Reggie took one last long look around the dining room and walked unsteadily back through the bar and was gone.

Louis turned to Mel, who smiled.

"Welcome to Bizarro World," Mel said.